Returning

Can One Ever Go Back?

By

George D. Schultz

authorHOUSE™

1663 LIBERTY DRIVE, SUITE 200
BLOOMINGTON, INDIANA 47403
(800) 839-8640
WWW.AUTHORHOUSE.COM

© 2005 George D. Schultz. All Rights Reserved.

No part of this book may be reproduced, stored in a retrieval system, or transmitted by any means without the written permission of the author.

First published by AuthorHouse 04/13/05

ISBN: 1-4208-1606-3 (sc)

Printed in the United States of America
Bloomington, Indiana

This book is printed on acid-free paper.

Returning

ONE

The biting chill of the November evening knifed through his light jacket, as he climbed the creaky, in-need-of-a-coat-of-paint, circular, metal staircase – to the porch of his second-floor apartment, in southwest Houston.

"Damn," he muttered to himself. "My Yankee blood must really be thinning out. Well," he laughed mirthlessly, "who wants fat blood?"

He trudged to the top of the stairs.

"God! It's cold! I can just imagine how the natives must feel."

He coughed.

"Or," he muttered, "maybe I don't."

He stopped short of the door to his apartment. His eyes narrowed – focusing on the two large floor-to-ceiling windows. Looking into his living room, he was surprised to see that the old, chipped-plaster, black-and-red, lamp was lit. The lamp atop the warped, garish, TV table – the faded, tin table which sat next to his ragged couch.

He was certain that he'd not left the light on.

He peered inside.

His stare locked onto the figure of an elderly man! The interloper was decked out in a bright-blue suit. The silver/white-haired intruder was seated – most uncomfortably – on the seedy chair. The one which matched his equally-run-down couch.

Ah, 1979! It was certainly a year for surprises! There had been times when he'd wondered if he'd ever see 1980! So near, yet so far – as some cornball sage had once said. A stranger – one making himself at home in his apartment – certainly wasn't helping. That qualified as a surprise. A helluva surprise.

He was positive that he'd made no noise as he'd come up the steps. Well, of course, there was the obvious creakiness of the stairs themselves.

He decided that his best plan of action would be to sneak back down to the parking lot – as stealthily as possible! Get down there – and call the police!

As he turned – to creep back down to the ground level – he was stopped by a soft, yet penetrating, voice! It came from inside his apartment. The voice – the most-compelling voice – bade him enter!

There was a strangely soothing quality in the tone – which, somehow, made our hero a little less apprehensive. He was at a loss to explain why.

He approached the door – and began to insert his key.

"It's open," advised the interloper.

Pushing his way into the apartment, he did his best to appear indignant. It didn't work.

"I don't know who the hell you think you are," he blustered. "But, you're in my apartment."

"I'm perfectly aware of that," replied the man, with an indulgent smile. "I didn't take anything."

"Hmmmmph. Not much here to take. My stereo, maybe. Such as it is. Maybe my records … if you're in to schmaltzie music. That's about it."

"Aren't you curious as to who I am? What I'm doing here?"

"It seems to me that I already told you that I haven't the foggiest idea who you are. I … I should be upset! But, I'm not. And I can't figure out why I'm not." He laughed – in spite of himself. "The fact that I'm not upset," he continued, "that's what upsets me … if that makes any sense."

The elderly one smiled once more.

"Yes, Jim, it does. It makes perfect sense. Tell me. Of whom do I remind you?"

"How … how do you know my name?"

Returning

"Oh, I know a lot about you. But, go ahead and answer my question, Jim. Of whom do I remind you?"

"I ... I don't believe this! I just flat-assed don't believe it! You break into my place ... and now we're gonna play *Twenty Questions*? What's even more stupid ... dumber still ... is the fact that I haven't thrown your butt out of here!"

"Do you feel threatened by me?"

"Well ... no."

"That's why you haven't thrown me out. Now, for heaven's sake, Jim. Relax ... and tell me of whom I remind you."

"I ... I can't believe I'm doing this! This is un-be-damn-lievable!"

Jim sighed deeply – and seemed to simply deflate. He had no indignation left. Not a trace. He tugged against his left earlobe. He'd not done that in months.

"I don't know," he muttered. "It must be the hair or something ... maybe the suit ... but, well, you kind of look like a character out of an old musical. An old movie. This guy was ... well, he was kind of a go-between. Between heaven and Rita Hayworth."

"Excellent! Wonderful! Very good, Jim. Do you remember the name of the movie?"

"Yeah," sighed Jim. "It was called *Down To Earth*. Rita Hayworth played Terpsichore ... the goddess of the dance. She decides to come down to earth ... and star in some live musical production that some guy was doing about her. She thought it was all wrong ... what he was doing. The guy was the fella who did *The Jolson Story*."

"Larry Parks?"

"Yeah. Larry Parks. It wasn't really all that great of a movie. But, there was a song from the flick that I'd always liked." He laughed. "Like most of the stuff that appeals to me," he went on, "the stupid song never got anywhere."

"I know," laughed the intruder. "The song was <u>They Can't Convince Me</u>. I also know that you happened to have come by an old seventy-eight recording of it. Just a couple weeks ago. Got it at the flea market. Record was by Elliot Lawrence. By his band. Am I right?"

Jim was completely dumbfounded.

"How ... how could you know that?" he asked. "How could you possibly know? Nobody ... absolutely nobody ... ever heard of that record. Ever heard of that song."

"As I told you, I know a lot about you, Jim. So much about you ... that it'd probably frighten you. But, getting back to the movie, you believe that I look like the go-between? The man who was the ... well, the buffer ... for Rita Hayworth?"

"Yeah."

"Do you know the character's name?"

"I should. Yeah. It was ... uh ... it was ... "

"Mister Jordan?"

"Yeah. Mister Jordan. You look just like him ... the guy who played Mister Jordan."

The older man smiled. That disarmingly infectious smile! It didn't "take"!

"Look," exclaimed Jim. "Listen, I don't understand what's happening. What's the deal, here? You must've had some reason for busting in to the apartment. It's not to steal any of the crap I've got here. And it damn sure isn't to play guessing games."

"Ah, but you're wrong about that, Jim. You're wrong about the guessing games."

"And that's another thing! How do you know my name?"

The visitor held up a hand.

"All in good time," he responded. "All in good time. I was certain you'd remember the motion picture ... and remember the role of Mister Jordan. That's why I took this form. I was ... "

"Took this form? What the hell are you talking about? What do you mean 'took this form'?"

"You might show me the courtesy of not interrupting me, Jim. Now, I happen to know that you get upset ... very upset ... when someone interrupts you."

"I'm ... well, I'm sorry. But ... well, it's very unsettling. Damn unsettling. How do you know so much about me?"

"I was about to explain. Now, please! Sit down! You're making me very nervous."

Jim sighed heavily, once again, and pulled at his earlobe – also, once again.

Then, he plopped his 225-pound, 6-foot, frame onto the scruffy old sofa. The couch wheezed in protest.

"I should be pissed off," he muttered.

"But, you're not. And … if you'll just bear with me … I'll tell you why you're not. I know that you're Jim Sidorwitz. I know that you were born in Detroit … in nineteen thirty-two. I also know that you spent four years in the Navy. Do you want to know the dates?"

"No, dammit. You seem to have all the damn answers."

"You were married eighteen years … to the former Kathleen Vargo. You and she have been separated for about seven years. She was from Brownsville … southern-most tip of Texas. During your marriage, you lived most of your lives up in Detroit."

"So?"

"Just trying to prove to you that I've studied you. Studied you pretty closely. Now, please. Don't interrupt. Kathleen is back in Brownsville. With your three youngest children … the ones you call 'The Dirty Rats'. They're sixteen, fifteen and thirteen."

"Look. This is all very … "

Once again, the interloper held up a hand.

Your 'Number-Three Son' … Danny … is also down there. Runs a pizza restaurant. Your other three kids are up here, in Houston."

The flood of information – every particle of it correct – was overwhelming!

The elderly one continued: "Your 'Number-One Son' … Dave … and his wife live in the next block. 'Number-Two Son' … Doug … and his wife are about two miles away. Little white bungalow … just off Hillcroft. Your oldest daughter … Cynthia … she and her husband live about three blocks away. You're intensely proud of all seven of your children. Each and every one of them."

"Hell. Everybody knows that."

"Even strangers, Jim? Strangers … who break into your place?"

Jim laughed once more. As before, in spite of himself.

"Well," he allowed, "just about everyone."

"You've also been in the rent-a-car business for most of your life."

"Yeah? So?" Jim had been at a loss to think of anything else to say in response – unable to come up with some kind of pithy reply.

The visitor smiled once more. Why did he have to be so damn disarming?

"I know," the elderly one said. "These are things that anyone could've found out … if they'd done a little research."

"That's just it. Why, on earth, would anyone bother? Who the hell would want to research me? Why would anyone even bother?"

"I'm getting to that, Jim. One of the reasons … the main reason, actually … is that you're exceptionally sentimental. Very sensitive. And about as nostalgic as they come. You're a complete nut … freak, I guess they say nowadays … when it comes to music. Especially what you refer to as 'square music'. 'Schmaltzie music'."

"Well, like I said before, everybody knows that."

"You're also probably one of the most naïve people alive."

"Oh, I don't know. I don't think I'm all that naïve. I am forty-seven, y'know."

"Doesn't matter. You are, you know. One of the most naïve people alive. Far more than you think. Believe me. You're more trusting than most people these days. You'll believe almost anything anyone'll tell you."

"Till I find out that they're lying to me," groused Jim. "Then, I don't believe anything they tell me. It's an either-or thing, I guess. I don't really think that I'm perceptive enough to be able to really tell who's lying and who isn't. So, till I know that you're lying to me … well, I'll just go ahead and believe you."

"And you got to where you didn't believe anything … not one thing … that Alice would say."

That was a real jolt! It literally knocked Jim backward! The intruder had plainly scored a resounding TKO!

"How … how do you know about Alice?" His voice was reduced to a hoarse rasp. "Dear Lord! What do you know … what could you know … about Alice?"

"Well, I know that you dated her for years in Detroit. I know that you used to call her your 'Veteran Fiancée'. I know that she never

Returning

took anything at face value. Never believed anything anybody had to say. Always found some hidden meaning. In everything. You got to where you couldn't handle that. Simply couldn't cope with it."

Once again, Jim let go a humongous sigh. All the wind had, by then, seeped out of his sails!

"I got to where I felt like I shouldn't have to," he said. "Hell, it was after one of our more spectacular arguments ... Alice and me ... when Kathleen decided that she was gonna move back down to Texas. Back down to Brownsville. I guess the kids wanted to go, too. And, with the job situation in Detroit being what it was ... and with Alice and me on the outs ... I just figured it'd make sense for me to move on down to Texas too. Get my fanny out of there. Wanted to have a shot at a much better job market. Be close to the kids, too. Make a clean break ... finally ... with Alice."

"It wasn't that clean, though, was it?"

"Naw. Hell. We still write every now and again. She spent a week down here with me ... about six months after I moved out from up there." He sighed once more. "What can you do?"

"What, indeed?" responded the interloper. "What, indeed?"

Again, that infectious smile.

"You know, Jim," the visitor said, "that you're an incurable romantic. In some ways, though, Alice was too. You may find this difficult to believe, but, she was ... in her way ... almost as big a romantic as you are. Trouble is ... she's a cynical incurable romantic."

"I didn't know they made such an animal."

"Oh, we manufacture all kinds," the elderly one replied – with that patented smile, once again.

"Dammit!" Jim was back to being indignant. "Here we go again! Now, what the hell does that mean? Who the hell are you, anyway? I know that you look like Mister Jordan, but ... "

"Actually, I'm Mister Horne. My first name is Gabriel. Now, with your sense of hoke ... of out and out schmaltz ... that has to mean something to you, Jim. Simply has to."

"Oh, please! Look. I may be naïve and trusting and all that. But, I'm not a complete idiot. Now, I really don't know what it is you're selling ... but, I really don't have any more time to sit here and chit-chat. It's really starting to get far out."

"If you'll just hear me out, Jim, I think you'll find it'll get even further out. But, I'm non-violent. I won't take up any more of your valuable time than necessary. You wouldn't give the bum's rush ... not give the bum's rush ... to someone who looks like he may have cavorted with Rita Hayworth. Would you?"

"All right, Mister Jordan," sighed Jim. "You win."

"Mister Horne."

Jim clenched his fists – and scrunched his eyes shut!

"All right," he muttered. "Okay, you win Mister <u>Horne</u>. Make your pitch. Then, get the hell on out of here ... and let me fix something to eat."

"Fine," responded Mr. Horne – smiling even more broadly. "But, Jim? Do me a favor. For the next few minutes ... just for the sake of argument ... allow yourself that I just might be exactly who I say I am. As far-fetched as it may seem, just imagine that I could possibly ... just possibly ... be from heaven. From heaven, Jim. Even if it's a one-in-ten-trillion shot. Let the incurable romantic in you allow that there could just be that outside chance. Allow ... just for the heck of it, just for a few minutes ... that I'm who I tell you I am. Suspend disbelief, I believe, is the term."

"I dunno. I mean, this is terribly ... uh ... well, it's awfully damn screwy."

"It is that, all right" acknowledged Mr. Horne nodding in affirmation. "But, Jim, try and accept what I'm saying, at face value ... no matter how big a stretch it might seem. Be just like you've always wished Alice had been. Like you always wished she would be. Okay?"

Jim tried not to smile. It was a losing battle.

"All right," he answered. "All right. I'll try. I'll ... I'll do my best. But, so far, it's awfully cockamamie."

"Yes. Quite right. And I dare say it'll get even more cockamamie. But, just give it a chance. I'm not really hurting you ... or, really, even bothering you ... am I?"

"No." Another industrial-strength sigh. "No, I guess not."

"Good. Now, let me tell you, first off, that my rank ... or what-have-you ... up there is approximately what you've been taught an archangel is. It's just that things are quite ... well, quite different up there. Different than what you've been led to believe. Much more informal, for one thing. Very relaxed. I think the expression they use today is laid-back. Let me let you in on something: Some of the boys ... we'll call 'em 'boys' for want of a better term ... and I have a little bet going."

"A bet? In heaven, they bet? They ... they gamble?"

"Well, more or less. Sometimes it gets a little boring ... even for us. Even up there. So ... from time to time ... we make little bets amongst ourselves. We happen to know that ... as nostalgic as you are ... we know that you're exceptionally prone to fantasize about the past. True?"

"True," Jim conceded, with a worried nod.

"We've seen you get all dewy-eyed at some of the memorabilia from the thirties and forties. Every time you hit the old flea market. We know that you've got dozens of records and cassettes of all those old radio shows ... even the obscure ones like *That Brewster Boy* and *The Whistler*. We also know that you dream ... dream constantly ... about that house in which you lived, on Grandmont Street. Up in Detroit. The one in which you lived ... when you were five, six and seven."

"How ... how could you know that? How could you possibly know that?"

"Please, Jim. Just do what I suggested. Just imagine ... imagine for the next few minutes ... that I actually am who I purport to be. Please. Try and do that. Now, I also happen to know that you dream about your father's old thirty-seven Ford. The black club coupe. Does that shake you up?"

"You know it does."

"Now for the *piece de resistance*! I'm further aware that, lately, you've been half-wishing you could ... somehow ... be sent back in time. Sent back to the thirties or the forties. Sent back there ... knowing what you know now. Nineteen thirty-nine, in particular. True?"

What little color had remained in Jim's face became a thing of the past.

"No one," he rasped, "absolutely no one could know that! I've never mentioned it to anyone. Not even the kids. I've told a few people ... mostly the kids ... about the house on Grandmont. Even Pop's old Ford. But ... but, I've never told a soul about wanting to go back in time. Ever. Afraid that they'd think I'd ... that I'd ... well, totally flipped!"

"I know," replied Mr. Horne, with that smile.

"I ... I don't understand. Who ... who are you?"

"I've been trying to tell you, Jim. I've been trying to tell you who I am. It's just fortunate that patience happens to be one of my virtues. Contrary to what you learned at *Saint Mary's of Redford*, we're not all possessed with each and every one ... with each and every virtue ... y'know. Not in abundance, anyway. I realize that Sister James Mary taught you differently."

"Sister James Mary? Good God! That was almost forty years ago! Thirty-five, anyway."

Mr. Horne nodded – impatiently.

"To get back to my story, Jim," he resumed, "all of us ... there are four of us who pretty much pal around together up there ... we have a number of theories as to what would happen to you, if you were, all of a sudden, plopped smack-dab back into ... say ... nineteen thirty-nine. How you'd react back there. What you'd do back there. Our theories are many and varied. That's what all the bets are about."

"You really do then? You really do bet up there? You ... you really do?"

"Yes. Yes, we do. Of course, the currency is a little different. But, the idea's the same. Anyway, we all have our pet theories about what would happen ... how you'd behave, what your life would be like ... back there. If you were coming from this era."

"Well, if you're such a big-deal archangel, I'd have to think that you'd already know that. Know all those things. Have all the answers. Especially if we're talking history, here."

"Wrong! We can't look into the future ... even though the future, in this case, would be the past. There's no way we could know

... actually know ... what you'd do. Not until you actually do it. We can make some very educated ... I hope ... guesses. We think they're educated, anyway. But, we can't really know anything. Not unless ... and until ... it actually happens."

"Really?"

"Trust me. Would an archangel lie to you?"

"I ... I don't know," Jim replied – sighing heavily, again. "I don't know anything anymore."

"Well, we might," advised Mr. Horne, with a soft laugh. "We might tell you a little fib here and there. But, I'm really and truly leveling with you. I'm telling you the honest-to-God truth."

"Look. My head is so numb now, Mister Horne, that I don't even know whether I can separate reality from fantasy anymore. Hell, I could be having a pipe dream. Are you telling me that you've got the power to send me back in time? To a year ... a year like, maybe, nineteen thirty-nine?" He snapped his fingers. "Just like that?"

"Well, not just like that, Jim. It's a little more complicated. It'd take some doing. But, yes! We are geared up to do that. Are you interested?"

"I'm sure I must be slipping a cog here, somewhere. But, yeah. Yeah, I guess I would be. I guess I am. Interested, that is. It's been something that I've always ... "

"Don't be too hasty now, Jim. There are a number of possible disadvantages. You really ought to take them into consideration."

"Disadvantages? Like what? What disadvantages?"

"Well, suppose you died tomorrow."

"Oh, thanks a lot! That's a comforting thought."

"As I told you, we have no way of knowing. If you were to die tomorrow, it would be on a day in thirty-nine. You'd have simply disappeared from here ... from Houston. No one ... not your kids, not Kathleen, not anyone ... would ever really know what happened to you. You see, Jim, you'll have to live forty years ... just to get back here! To get back here ... to where you are now. To get back to nineteen seventy-nine."

"You ... you mean I'd continue to age?"

"Of course! Certainly! Of course you'd continue to age!"

"Oh, wow! Then, by the time seventy-nine rolled around again ... for me ... I'd be eighty-seven? I wouldn't be forty-seven anymore? I'd ...why, I'd have aged forty years! Overnight! Forty damn years! In one night! Is that what you're telling me?"

"Yes. I'm afraid that's what I'm telling you, Jim."

"God! My ... my chances of making it back ... they'd be practically zilch! I'd ... I'd ... why, I'd never see my kids again!"

"That's probably correct. I have ... we have ... no way of knowing whether you'd make it back or not. The odds, though, would seem stacked against it. That's why I brought it up. Why I mentioned drawbacks, in the first place. Jim, I know how much you love your kids. I personally admire your relationship with 'em. With all of your kids. All of us 'boys' do. We all admire what you've got. We all think it's neat."

"Yeah," Jim muttered, absently, pulling at his earlobe. "I don't ... I don't know, Mister Horne. Never seeing my kids again ... that'd be ... "

"Actually, there might not be as much disadvantage as you might imagine, Jim. For instance, if you were to live another sixteen years ... which isn't all that off-the-wall, as they say, nowadays ... that would bring you to nineteen fifty-five. You'd be able to see Dave ... your first-born. A year later, Doug'd come along. You wouldn't be that far away from Danny ... in fifty-eight ... or Cynthia, in fifty-nine. Presumably, you'd be well enough fixed ... financially ... that you could kind of observe 'em. Maybe even be able to see the kids that followed. Your 'Dirty Rats'. See 'em all again ... but, you know, from afar."

"From ... from afar?"

"Yes. Naturally, you wouldn't be able to tell them who you really are. You can't tell <u>anyone</u> where you're from. That you're from the future. But, you could become a sort of ... a sort of ... sort of a friend of the family. In the sixteen years, you'll be sixty-three ... if my mathematics are correct. You certainly ought to look a good deal different than you did the first time you were in fifty-five. You were only twenty-three then. Of course, you'd have to stay somewhat aloof. You certainly couldn't enjoy them as sons and daughters. Couldn't truly relate to them ... not as your children, at any rate."

"Yeah," agreed Jim, with a wistful sigh. "I sure couldn't."

"The other side of that coin, though, is that you'd also be free from all the pressures that go with being a young parent. Trying to keep afloat financially ... while doing your best to raise so many kids. Seven kids, you know ... that's a lot of kids."

"Tell me about it."

"This way, maybe you could see your kids come into the world ... from once or twice removed, of course. Watch 'em grow. You'd be in a much more relaxed atmosphere. You already know how well they turned out. It may be that you could enjoy them in a ... well, in a different way. It could be a totally new dimension of enjoyment for you. Not having to work three and four jobs to support them ... as you did, when they were all in school. Could be a much more enjoyable situation for you. Quite possibly."

"Kind of ... kind of like, maybe, having my cake and eating it too."

"Well, more or less. Jim, you've worked hard ... awfully hard ... all these years. This could be a sort of second chance for you ... if you worked it right."

"How about Kathleen? She's worked as hard as I have, through the years. Harder, probably. Maybe she'd like a fresh start too. Maybe she'd like a chance ... just like this one."

Mr. Horne smiled – indulgently.

"Well, we're getting a little afield, Jim. Actually, the bet is about you ... not about Kathleen. She's never really been all that nostalgic. I really don't think the thirties ... or the forties ... would hold all that much allure for her."

"Yeah," Jim nodded. "Yeah, you're probably right. Our tastes always were pretty different."

He worried his earlobe once more. He must be more agitated than he thought!

"It's ... it's certainly something to think about," he mused. "Going back in time. It's not ... it's not as if I'd be entirely without the kids. All I'd have to do would be to live ... to survive ... past nineteen fifty-five?"

"Precisely. It's not as though you see them every day, anyway. How often do you see the four in Brownsville? Every six weeks? Every eight weeks?"

Letting go another industrial-strength sigh, Jim arose and walked to the huge windows. He stared out across the pool, past the other side of the complex – and into infinity.

"Yeah," he allowed at length. "I try, you know, to make the trip more often. I talk about going once a month. But, it's a seven-hundred mile round trip, and I … "

"Exactly. Even the ones up here. How often do you actually see them? Of course, I'm aware that they all have Sunday breakfast over here, with you, every week … unless you're in Brownsville. But, during the week, how often do you actually see them?"

"I see what you're saying, Mister Horne. Still … "

He tugged again at his earlobe – and turned to face his mysterious visitor.

"Look," he said, "even if I do make it back to here … back to the present … I'd be eighty-seven. How on earth would I ever explain the fact that I've aged forty years? Aged forty years … and all while the kids were asleep for one night. How'd I ever explain something like that?"

Mr. Horne nodded – and turned loose that enigmatic smile of his once more.

"I know," he replied. "I know. It'd be kind of a hairy situation. Almost a *Brigadoon* in reverse. Well, maybe some of the 'boys' and I … maybe we could help you along those lines. I don't know the exact answer. No one could. In forty years, not only would your looks have changed … changed dramatically … but, your whole entire situation could be vastly different. Probably would be vastly different. Maybe you'd have married someone. Started another family. Raised a whole bunch of different kids. Who can tell?"

The statement – to the effect of starting another family – caught Jim completely off guard. He'd not thought of that. Another family? A whole bunch of different kids?

The prospects were frightening – at first flush! Still, they did hold an inexplicable element of excitement. A dimension of delicious mystery.

"Look, Jim," soothed Mr. Horne. "We'd have forty years to think of something. We've got some pretty inventive minds up there. If you'll keep the rules, I'm sure that we can work something out."

"Rules? There'd be rules?"

"Of course rules. You can't just go back to the thirties or forties … and write hit songs that weren't composed till the fifties. You can't invent things … things that no one ever thought of till the sixties. You certainly can't hunt down Lee Harvey Oswald … and do him in! Shoot him or something … before November twenty-second, when nineteen sixty-three rolls around. In short, Jim, you can't do anything to alter the course of history."

"Alter the course of history? Wouldn't anything I do … wouldn't that alter the course of history? Look, Mister Horne. Listen. I'm really afraid that I'm getting into something … something where I'd be biting off more than I could chew. And that's even allowing that you can do what you say … that you can really send me back to thirty-nine, in the first damn place. And … even if you could … I don't know that … "

The elderly one held up a hand.

"I'm speaking of major events, Jim," he assured. "Earth-shaking events … like President Kennedy's assassination, you know."

"Yes, but … "

"Obviously, with your knowledge of the future … well, you're bound to have an effect on minor stuff. Day to day things, Jim. Things like the price of a stock or two. Maybe a few property values, here and there. What I'm saying is that you can't … well, you couldn't try, for instance, to fix things so that Harold Stassen actually gets the Republican nomination in forty-eight. Couldn't do anything like that."

"I … I never really thought of anything like that. I mean … God … hunting down Oswald and … "

"I know, Jim. But, eventually you would have. As I said, inconsequential things … minor stuff … well, that's not going to bother us. It won't make a heck of a lot of difference … in the big picture. But, Jim! The great events of history … well, they're not going to change! If you were to try and alter them … well, I'm afraid that you'd be bowled over! Bowled over … by the weight of history. The overwhelming weight of history ... if you know what I mean."

Once again, Jim worried his earlobe. His head was back to swimming!

"I've never been much good at knowing what anyone meant, Mister Horne," he said. "That was my problem with Alice. She'd say one thing ... and I was supposed to know that she really meant something else. Meant just the opposite. Hell ... then, she'd get all bent out of shape, when I couldn't tell the difference. So, you have to be kind of blunt with me. Really blunt with me. Have to hit me right in the puss ... if you want to get through to me. Are you telling me that, if I tried to alter the course of history, that you ... you and the 'boys' ... would do me in?"

Mr. Horne smiled once more. However, most of the previously-overwhelming warmth was missing.

"You're more perceptive than you give yourself credit for, Jim," he responded. "But ... to answer your question ... that's about the size of it. That may sound rather un-angelish. Forgive me, Sister James Mary ... but, that's exactly what I meant. I kind of shudder at the phrase 'do you in' ... but, that's precisely what I was getting at."

"You're right on that," replied Jim, turning back – to gaze out the window once more. "It does sound damn un-angelish."

"Another thing, Jim. As I mentioned before, you'd be forbidden, of course ... forbidden ... to tell anyone that you're from the future! Forbidden to tell anyone! Anyone at all! No matter who he or she is. Who he or she may be. Absolutely verboten!"

"Oh, this is stupid!" spouted the younger man – wheeling around, once again, to face his guest. "Stupid, stupid, stupid! I can't believe this! I can't believe that I'm standing here talking ... talking like some kind of idiot ... talking to something that's probably a figment of my imagination!"

Mr. Horne arose – and placed his arm around Jim's shoulder.

"I'll tell you what," the visitor offered. "You decide what you want to do. You'll need some time. Heaven knows, it's not your ordinary, common, garden-variety, decision."

"You can say that again," muttered Jim.

Returning

He yanked at his earlobe once more – as the older man made his way to the center of the room.

"Unfortunately, though," Mr. Horne advised, "I can't give you as much time as I probably should. Look, Jim … it's just a little before seven o'clock now. In five hours … five hours and a few minutes … it'll be midnight. I'll come back then. Midnight. I'll come back at that time. I'll have to know your decision then. Either way, I'll respect what you decide. No more sales pitches. You can count on no more sales pitches. Whatever you decide … well, that's what we'll fly with. At this point, it's up to you. I won't try and persuade you … one way or another. All up to you, from this point on."

Jim's knees were beginning to sag. He walked back over to the seedy couch – and plopped himself down, once again.

"Look,' advised his visitor, "if you do decide to go back, let me assure you that we'll have an identity all set up for you. Plus, you'll be in Detroit. Your natural habitat. I'm sure that you'd be much more comfortable up there.

"I guess," replied Jim, absently – worrying his earlobe. "I suppose."

"Put on your pot of coffee … as you always do … and think on it, Jim. I'll be back at midnight. You're a good man. Make your own decision. Do whatever it is that you want to do."

With that, Mr. Horne disappeared! Simply vanished! One second, he'd been standing in the middle of the room! The next second, he was gone! No movie-type "fade out"! No puff of smoke! He simply was no longer there! Amazing! Incredible!

It took Jim fully three or four minutes to rise from the tattered old couch, make his way – slowly – to the kitchen, and begin to build a pot of coffee.

Periodically, he'd mutter to himself: "You really don't have a full set of dishes, Jim." Or, "You're flying with your flaps down." Or, "You don't have both oars in the water." Big help.

From the time he was a child, Jim had been aware of the fact that he'd spent an inordinate amount of time in what amounted to a fantasy world. He knew that. He'd never considered it much of a problem.

He thought back to when he was a schoolboy, in Detroit:

From the seventh grade on, he'd skipped school. Each and every year. Spring was not spring – without Jim not showing up for 25 or 30 days in a row. He knew that the truant officer would inevitably come for him. And still he would skip.

He'd always intended to go back to the classroom, of course. Tomorrow! But, he never did. Eventually, of course, he'd wind up facing the truant guy – who was more and more upset with him every year!

After three consecutive years of his playing hooky, Jim's parents were beside themselves.

They'd enrolled him in a public agency, called *The Children's Center*, on Woodward Avenue, close by the Art Centre. Each week, he would speak with his counselor, Miss Wilks – for 10 or 15 minutes. That little confab usually followed a brisk two- or three-minute go at the ping pong table. (During that first spirited little contest, Jim had whacked a ball – with all his might – and hit his beautiful counselor on her ample left breast. He'd never been so embarrassed in his life.)

"Helluva start," the 47-year-old Jim mused – as he stared at the pot on the stove.

It was beginning to perk.

Another sigh – as he thought back to his very-attractive counselor. After their little talk, Miss Wilks would "stash" young Jim in the game room. With all the other "disturbed" children – all known as, and referred to as – "friends". Nothing else! No other term! ("This is our new friend, Jim," was the way he was invariably introduced to all the other new "friends".)

While young Jim matched wits with the "friends" in such fascinating endeavors as *Sorry*, Miss Wilks always held a conference with Dolly, his mother. In another room.

After working with high school-Jim – and Dolly – for almost two years (during which time he'd skipped another three weeks – twice) the professionals at the *Center* had come to the conclusion that they could do nothing for the young, habitual, truant.

"He just hates school," Miss Wilks had advised his mother.

"Thanks a lot," Dolly Sidorwitz had grumped. "That, we already knew."

An upshot of the exposure to the people at the *Center* was the advising of Dolly, by Miss Wilks, that her son tended to fantasize an abnormal amount of time. His day dreams were – in the counselor's opinion – excessive! Extreme! Exceptionally overdone – in length, in depth and in frequency! And in overwhelming detail!

"It's probably relatively harmless," Miss Wilks had opined. "But, it should be a cause of some concern. He may reach a point … sometime down the road … where he, maybe, won't be able to distinguish reality. Won't be able to distinguish it from fantasy."

It wasn't until Jim was in his early-twenties that Dolly had told him of Miss Wilks' analysis. During the eighteen months between the time Jim had been discharged from the Navy – in the spring of 1953 – and the time he'd married Kathleen – the fall of 1954 – he had lived with Dolly and his sister, Dee.

Dolly had hammered – almost without pause – on Miss Wilks' fantasy-trip theme, during Navy veteran-Jim's stay with her. Dee had confided to her brother – on more than one occasion – that Dolly was certain that her now-adult son was, even then, spending far too much time in his own little dream world.

Dolly was terribly worried about him. She was sure that his tenuous grasp on reality was affecting his vision of marriage. His upcoming marriage! Upcoming too fast!

Her fear was that Jim was fantasizing a dream-world of wedded bliss – like something out of all those hokey **MGM** musicals that he'd always adored. He was Gene Kelly, she was sure! And Kathleen – his intended – would be Judy Garland. Good luck!

Jim, in his clerking job, was not making nearly enough money, his mother was certain. Not nearly enough to allow him to even consider marriage! Especially when he'd constantly spoken of having a large family. As things stood, he was having trouble enough just simply meeting the $42.00 monthly payment on his prized 1949 DeSoto.

Jim had disregarded Dolly's warnings! Her sermons! Eventually, her constant preaching! It had begun to really upset him! The two of them wound up having many fallings out – especially as the wedding date drew nearer. Things became grim enough, as the weeks to the nuptials had dwindled. So disturbing that the groom-to-be had – on more than one occasion—told his mother to "butt out"! Something he never could've envisioned himself doing. Words that he'd have sworn he'd never have said to Dolly. Ever!

Jim was of the opinion that, at that point, he'd outgrown his penchant for spending too much time in the land of make believe. But, when all was said and done, who knew? Who actually knew?

In 1953, after all, he was 21-years-of-age. He was certain, though, that Dolly had continued to worry about his "affliction" through the ensuing years. Through the ensuing decades.

Now, in 1979, as he stared at his percolator, images of being confined to "The Funny Farm" had begun to dart into and out of his mind. He had "gone over the edge"! He was certain of it!

Mr. Horne was, obviously, an invention of his overripe – out of control – imagination. His fantasy world must have – as Dolly had feared – taken total and complete control of what had laughingly been referred to as his sense of reality. There could be no other answer!

A person simply cannot be transported back through time! Well, or forward, either! It was a physical impossibility! Was it not?

The fragrance of the brewing coffee filled the kitchen. Jim sighed once more. It was an evening of sighs. He'd refined it, by then, to an art.

Up to that point in his life, he'd believed that he'd always been able to distinguish between his mind-wandering hopes and dreams – and the stark, unforgiving, "real world". There were times, to be sure, when he didn't <u>want</u> to make such a distinction.

Fantasy, from time to time, made an excellent hiding place. Especially when the seven children were all in school – and Jim was working 20 hours a day. Seven days a week. When he'd gone the better part of three years – without a day off.

However, he had never before so totally mistaken one for the other.

Still, Mr. Horne had seemed so real! Apparently, hallucinations always did! Jim had never smoked marijuana – had never taken any form of drug! Would he be able to tell whether he was actually hallucinating, or not? Was he on the verge of losing his sanity?

It was a frightening prospect!

The coffee had ceased its noisy percolating. That quickly? He poured himself a cup of the hot, steaming, "joe" – laced it with too much cream and way too much sugar – then, seated himself at his cheap Formica-and-wrought-iron dinette table.

Sitting there – staring at the far wall – he tried every imaginable avenue to escape the onrushing tide of disjointed images! Visions which gushed – like some kind of overwhelming avalanche – over, around and through his troubled, befuddled, mind!

Maybe he should fix himself something to eat. He'd been ravenous – when he'd left the office. His appetite, of course, had long since vanished. His appetite – along with his sanity! Another room-flooding sigh.

His arm had never felt so heavy – as he picked up the phone and dialed.

After four rings, a young, feminine voice answered. "Hello?"

"Hi, Hogan. How are you, Baby?"

"Oh hi, Dad," replied his eldest daughter, Cynthia. "What's up?"

"I ... well, I don't know, Honey. I just wanted to talk to you. Just needed to talk to you. I've ... I've got a bit of a problem."

"Problem? What kind of problem?"

"Well, I've got ... I think I've got ... got this chance. To ... to make a trip."

"Hey! That's great, Dad! What kind of trip?"

"Well ...that's just it, Baby. I can't ... I really can't tell you."

"Ooooooh," his daughter enthused. "Top secret, huh?"

"Yeah. I guess you could say that, Darlin'. You know that we've been ... well, we've been really close. Always been able to tell one another virtually anything ... no matter how personal or private."

"Yes?"

"Well ... well, it just upsets me. Upsets me that I can't tell you about this one. But," another sigh, "I can't. I just can't."

"Gee, Dad. Look ... I don't mind you not telling me. But, I hate to see you wrestling with ... wrestling with something or another ...

whatever it might be. That's what you're doing now. I can tell. If you can't tell me about this big, mysterious, trip ... well then, you can't. That's okay. I know you would if you could."

Once more Jim sighed.

"I really don't know what to do," he confided. "Especially since my job has really started to go so well. Now that the new guy, Charlie, has taken over ... well, things have been going my way. I got my raise, by the way! A healthy ... a really healthy ... one! Biggest raise I've ever gotten ... in my whole life! Nothing else even close! For the first time in my life, I'm starting to make some really serious money! I mean really serious money! It's wonderful! As a matter of fact, I really don't see how they can afford to pay me that much!"

"Don't question it, Dad," answered Cynthia, laughing warmly.

"Okay. I won't. Ya talked me into not questioning it ... smooth talker that you are. I won't question it. It's wonderful!"

"That's so neat, Dad. I'm so glad that things are finally starting to break for you. It's about time."

"Well, I don't know if it's about time ... but, it is great! I was gonna buy some new furniture this payday. Now ... this thing has come up. And I ... I ... I just ... "

"Dad! I've never heard you like this! Is everything okay? Are you okay? Are you all right? Do you need some money? I've got maybe sixty-five or seventy dollars over here. I can let you have that till payday. Do you want me to bring it over?"

"No, Honey. I'm fine. Honest. But, thank you for caring. You're truly my saint. Makes me just a tad upset, though, that I can't tell you the whole thing ... and find out what you think. Hell, ever since you've been thirteen or fourteen, I've been able to bounce things off you. More so ... in some ways ... than your brothers."

"Well, if you can't tell me, you can't. That's okay. I just feel kind of helpless. Are you sure you don't need me to come over? Mike's working late ... and I can be there in a couple minutes."

"That's nice of you, Baby. But, no. I'm fine. I really am. I feel a lot better, though ... just to be able to talk to you. I still don't know what the hell I'm gonna do ... but, I feel better."

"Dad, all I can tell you is to do what you think is right. Whatever's best for you. You know that we'll understand. We all will. We love you. All of us."

"That makes me feel even better. That's nice of you, Baby."

"All part of the soivice. Whatever you decide, Dad ... that's good enough for me. And I'm sure it'll be fine with the rest of us. We all want what's the best for you."

"I'm a lucky dad."

"Nah. We're all lucky. It's great that we're all so close."

"Well, Hogan, thanks for lifting muh spirits. I luff you. I luff you very much."

"I luff you too, Dad. We all do. Let me know what you decide."

"I'll try, Baby. G'night."

"G'night, Dad."

Jim hung up the phone. It was a major effort to pull himself out of his chair – and to drag himself to the kitchen. He refilled his cup. He'd never felt so old in his life. Or so tired.

Reseating himself, he again stared – blankly – at the far wall. It was as though he'd just discovered that it was adorned by literally hundreds of eight-by-ten photographs. They were mostly enlargements of snapshots he'd taken – with his "hokey little one-ten camera" – over the years. Virtually all of the photographs were of his children.

There were ten or twelve pictures, though, of Alice – his "Veteran Fiancée". No one could see them, though. They loomed behind a few of the pictures of the kids. He'd been unable to bring himself to throw them out. So, he'd "hidden" them.

He took a long, deep, drag on his coffee – emptying the cup. Once again, he plodded back to the kitchen – and poured another. The acrid liquid seemed to be taking on a terribly gamey aroma.

"God! There's so much to consider," he mumbled aloud – as he dropped back into his chair, at the table. "So damn much to consider! If this thing is for real ... what do I do?"

The muttering turned into full-fledged conversational tone.

"What in the hell do I do? I'd love to go back. I'd really love that."

He took another swig of coffee. It was cold! Already! God! Already?

"Dear Lord! Here I am! Sitting here like some kind of jerk …talking to myself. Literally talking to myself."

There were too many complications. His head was aching. How long had that been going on? Maybe forever. Maybe he was just beginning to notice.

If it really happened that he could go back in time – actually did go back in time – and survived the forty years, what would he tell his children? How could he ever explain having aged forty years? Literally overnight?

If – as seemed much more likely – he failed to make it back over the four decades, he would simply have disappeared. Disappeared off the face of the earth! How would his family – his wonderful kids – how would they ever handle that? Dear God!

"It'd be awfully damn heavy for 'em," he heard himself say. "Awfully damn heavy."

Neither Mr. Horne – nor the "boys" – would have to worry about coming up with some plausible explanation for Jim's having aged forty years in one night. It most assuredly had been a pretty safe promise – an exceptionally safe promise – for the archangel to make. If, of course, he <u>was</u> an archangel. If he wasn't a figment of Jim's imagination.

<u>Here we go again</u>!

If there was a Mr. Horne – and he was an archangel – he'd undoubtedly never have to deliver on this promise.

What could Cynthia – his "little Hogan" – be thinking at that moment?

His cup was empty! Again! He refilled it and sat back down.

"What the hell am I doing? This whole thing's all in my mind! Or whatever in hell is left of it! Gotta be! It figures," he mused, glumly. "I get a helluva raise … the old mind goes south! I guess the gods are bound, bent and determined that old Jim just isn't supposed to make a decent frigging buck! Ever! Ever in his whole damn life! Ol' Jim has got to say poor as hell! Like … never to have a pot to piss in! Or a damn window to throw it out of! Ever!"

He took another pull on his coffee. It was cold again. Amazing!

"I wonder if I can afford a shrink ... with my new pay raise. God knows, I sure need one. I'm ... hell ... I'm even talking to myself."

He stared at the pictures on the wall again. The silence was deafening. An old cliché – but, apt. Apt as could be.

It occurred to him – with a shock – that he'd not put on any music! Unheard of! He'd been home – for who-knew-how-long? And he'd not put on one of his schmaltzie tapes? Unheard of!

Dragging himself to his feet once more, he padded over to the small, inexpensive, stereo – on the other ratty TV table. This one was beneath all those 8 X 10s. He dropped in one of the many cassette tapes, lying on the clouded plastic cover.

He stood – and waited for the music to begin. Once the strains of *All The Things You Are* – by Mantovani's Orchestra – filled the room, he felt better. The Jerome Kern evergreen had always been his all-time favorite. The first song on the tape!

An omen? A positive omen? He sincerely hoped so!

Swept up by the music, Jim attempted, once more, to grapple with his decision!

His decision! Assuming, of course, that Mr. Horne even existed. Existed – other than in Jim's troubled mind. His warped mind? His demented mind? His totally nuts mind?

His cup was empty again! Incredible! So was the coffee pot! Even more incredible! He put his cup in the sink, spritzed some liquid dish detergent into it – then, put it to soak.

"Dammit," he rasped – as he watched the steaming stream of hot tap water fill the cup, "what am I gonna do? What the hell am I gonna do?"

"Yes Jim! What <u>are</u> you going to do?"

The resonant voice of Mr. Horne filled the tiny apartment!

Jim hurried into the living room! There – seated in the ragged old chair – was Mr. Horne. The same chair, in which he'd been sitting five hours before! Five hours? Impossible! Five whole, entire, long, 60-minute, hours?

The time had simply gone too quickly! Maybe that was part of the hallucination!

He was certain that he could not possibly have spent the whole five hours – drinking coffee and staring at the stupid wall! Especially with no schmaltzie music playing!

Impossible! Could never happen!

"Jim. Jim, I've got to know. I have to have your answer. I realize that it's a monumental decision. But, I have to know. Have to have your answer … at this time."

"How'd … how would it work?" he asked weakly. "I mean … are you just gonna wave your arm, or something? And, all of a sudden, I'm back in nineteen thirty-nine."

That patented warm smile. It seemed to set the entire apartment aglow. A warm, soft, rosy glow!

"No, Jim," he responded. "No. You'll just simply go to bed. Go to sleep. And … when you wake up … you'll be in nineteen and thirty-nine. Simple as that. For you … easy. For me … diff-ee-cult, as Senior Wences would say."

"I'm … I'm not going to wake up here … here in Houston … am I? I mean, this place was way out in the boonies forty years ago. I'd have snakes crawling all over me!"

He shuddered! He was scared to death of snakes! Hated them! Abhorred them!

"No, Jim. Nothing like that. You'll wake up in Detroit. In nineteen thirty-nine! Trust me."

"Uh … Mister Horne. I usually sleep in the nude. Would that be a problem? I mean … I … well, I could sleep in my shorts, if need be. Fully clothed … if need be."

Mr. Horne's smile broadened to a grin. A grin that was just as warm.

"Don't worry," he assured. "Don't give it a thought, Jim. Sleep in the nude, if you wish. It's absolutely no problem."

Jim clenched his fists! He scrunched his eyes shut!

Then, he blurted: "Okay! Okay, Mister Horne! I feel like I'm not wrapped too tight! But, if you do exist …and if this isn't some kind of spooky pipe dream or something … and if you do have the power to send me back to nineteen thirty-nine ... then, then yes! Yes! I want to go! I want to go back!"

"Fine, Jim. Splendid. Now, all you have to do is to go to bed ... as you normally do. Do your normal thing. This is about your bedtime anyway. Just go to sleep ... and leave the rest to me. To me ... and the 'boys'!"

"Don't talk to me about normal. Whatever is happening tonight ... well, it sure as hell is anything but normal!"

Mr. Horne laughed.

"Well," he said, "don't worry about it. Just get ready for bed ... and crawl in. It's that simple. Goodnight, Jim. Goodnight ... and goodbye! And good luck!"

Once again, Mr. Horne vanished!

"Good luck," mumbled Jim. "Good luck he says. I'll need good luck. Every damn ounce of good luck. Where I'll probably wake up is ... it'll probably be in the damn loony bin! Malfunction Junction!"

Heaving one more massive sigh, Jim walked into his tiny, ill-furnished, bedroom.

He was amazed at how heavy his arms and legs had become! He was exhausted!

He decided to forego his nightly shower. Removing his shirt and trousers, he hung them up – and was in the process of pulling down his undershorts.

"Maybe I'd better not."

Climbing into bed, Jim fairly melted into the sheets.

He was troubled! Greatly troubled! Troubled – by the fact that he'd kept his shorts on.

The words "Oh ye of little faith" began to flash on and off in his fast-numbing mind! Like some out-of-control neon sign!

It was a gargantuan struggle – but, he managed to reach under the covers, with both hands, and skitter himself out of his blue-and-white briefs.

He was asleep – before they hit the floor!

TWO

CLANG! CLANG! CLANG! The bell fought its way to the surface of Jim's being – from the subterranean depths of a troubled, tormented, sleep.

CLANG! CLANG! CLANG! It was getting louder!

Jim rolled fitfully – from one side of the creaking bed to the other.

Wait a minute! Creaking? Bed? What creaking bed? The one piece of furniture in his apartment which did not creak was – his bed!

It had been a terribly restless night – topped off by the damndest, weirdest, dream!

A dream – in which he was supposed to have been sent back to 1939! Imagine!

CLANG! Where was that stupid bell coming from?

He dared not open his eyes!

Could it be that it was <u>not</u> a dream? The bed, actually, felt rather funny, beneath him. Felt sort of – well, sort of strange!

CLANG! And there was that damn bell again!

Could it be? Could it possibly be?

Bright sunlight had been assaulting his clenched eyelids! The dazzling brilliance was at once reassuring and frightening! A typical November day in Houston would be cloudy – and, most likely, rainy! Chilly, too! Cold! It had been damn cold when he'd gone to bed! The warmth – and the mind-boggling brightness – sure didn't feel much like a Houston winter.

CLANG! CLANG! CLANG! That goofy bell again.

Tentatively – ever so slightly, ever so slowly – he cracked open one eye!

Through the narrow slit, he recognized <u>nothing</u>! Not a blessed <u>thing</u>!

Both eyes shot wide open!

He had not the slightest idea where he was!

The unfamiliar bed creaked in protest – as he sat up!

He was completely dumbfounded! Totally bemused! He was in a room – one which he'd never seen before! In his entire life!

It couldn't <u>be</u>! It <u>had</u> to be a dream!

He was in a corner room – heaven knew where! It put heaven one-up on him!

Two large windows were situated to the right of the brown headboard! The headboard of the old metal bed. Another pair of even-larger windows took up most of the wall – ten or maybe twelve feet from the right side of the bed. All were open. A fresh, brisk, breeze played at the gauze curtains – sending them flapping merrily.

Across the room – on the wall opposite the foot of the bed – stood a ponderous, well-worn, walnut dresser. Amazing!

His head was swimming! As overwhelmingly as it had spun the night before!

The night before! In Houston! In 1979! Good heavens!

Next to the old dresser, he noted – as he began to take inventory – was a door with something Jim hadn't seen in years! In years and years and years! It was a transom! An honest-to-God transom! Incredible!

Against the rear wall – to the left of the bed – stood a newer, blond-ish, chest of drawers. A door was situated on either side of the chest – presumably, leading to a bathroom and a closet. At least, he <u>hoped</u> that one of them was a john.

It had taken Jim's eyes fully a minute to acclimate themselves to the overwhelming brightness. The glare – the overpowering brilliance – was flooding the room. That was also incredible – considering the fact that the sun was not shining directly into his new abode.

His new abode! How about that?

Equally stunning was the freshness – the out-and-out sweetness – of the breeze, as it wafted in, through the open windows.

Jim could stand it no longer!

Bounding out of bed – in the nude – he rushed to the pair of windows to his right – as his ears welcomed one more CLANG! The bell seemed much more remote.

He peered out – to see one of the huge, old, yellow streetcars, as it disappeared into the distance. Heading away. To the "burbs"! It had come from downtown.

He recognized the thoroughfare! Recognized it immediately!

Grand River Avenue!

He was! He was in Detroit! In 1939! It had to be 1939!

Flowing slowly – but steadily – up and down Grand River was a plethora of Packards, DeSotos, Nashes, Studebakers, Hudsons, Grahams, LaSalles – and a whole gang of Model A Fords!

Jim knew exactly where he was!

The room was located on the second floor – of a two-story building – at the corner of Grand River and Mansfield. Directly across Mansfield, stood the majestic – the heart-warming – sight of *St. Mary's of Redford* Catholic Church!

As a child, Jim had attended the red-brick school behind the mammoth, constructed-of-stone, church. He had loved that church! And the school! One from which he'd never skipped! It hadn't been till the year after he'd been taken out of *St. Mary's* – and sent to *Cadillac Elementary School* on Schoolcraft – that he'd begun playing hooky! Skipping school for three and four weeks at a crack!

Two nuns, dressed in their blue habits and black veils – The Sisters of The Sacred Heart – were strolling along the narrow, semi-circular, drive, which traversed the front of the church. Jim wondered if one of them could possibly be Sister James Mary!

His knees began to wobble! Shooting pains were exploding inside his chest! His head was beginning to get caught up in some sort of cyclone! He was fast becoming terrifyingly dizzy!

It was all too much! Just too much! Too damn much!

He teetered backward!

It was at that point that it occurred to him: He was stark naked!

Heaving himself – helter-skelter – toward the bed, he began to laugh! Laugh convulsively! Laugh uncontrollably – as he landed crossways! His feet dangled off the side of the rather lumpy mattress! His arms stretched down toward the floor on the other side!

After a minute or so, the wooziness began to subside! The laughter did not!

He was beginning, he was certain, to laugh himself out – when he was startled by a rather-insistent knocking on the door! The one beneath that amazing transom!

"Mister Hayworth? Mister Hayworth?" It was a woman's voice. "Are you all right, in there, Mister Hayworth?"

Looking – frantically – around the room for something – anything – with which to cover himself, Jim saw nothing!

He sprang from the bed – and dashed toward one of the two doors which book-ended the blond chest! He fervently hoped it would be a closet! Nope! A bathroom!

Well, actually, he was glad to see that!

Frenzied, he tried the other door! It <u>was</u> a closet! Thank heaven!

Heaven? Thank heaven? Once more, he began to giggle!

"Beg your pardon, Mister Hayworth?" It was that same voice – from the other side of the door with the transom!

Jim cleared his throat. Weak from the unending gales of laughter, among other things, he did his best to shout, "I'll be right there! I'll be with you in … in just a … in just a minute!"

There appeared to be a generous amount of clothing in the closet. That was a relief! He'd not thought to have inquired of Mr. Horne, the previous night, whether he'd have clothes to wear in his new venue. The sly, fun-loving, archangel could very well have "faked him out" – and sent him into his new life <u>naked</u>! Jim shuddered!

Spotting a pair of dark-blue slacks – dangling from an "elephant" hook, on the inside of the door – he quickly donned them! Then, he made his mad dash for the door under the transom!

Opening it a crack, Jim beheld a rather-graying, forty-ish woman – dressed in what was, at that time, referred to as a housedress. She was further clad in a huge apron – which practically covered the dress. Uniform of the day for a housewife – in 1939!

The lady smiled – as Jim opened the door.

"I'm Helen Shaddon," she announced. "Your landlady." Her voice was surprisingly rich. The tone was out and out melodic. "Pleased to meet you," she added.

Jim was taken with the unmistakable, beneath-the-surface, non-cosmetic, beauty of his new landlady. A wholesomeness. A genuineness. Qualities, our hero had lamented, which seemed to be totally <u>missing</u> from the culture of the seventies.

"We've ... we've never met?" he asked, scratching his head.

"No. Of course not. How could we meet? Didn't you just get into town last night? In the middle of the night?"

"Yes. Yes, of course. Ah ... I just ... I just meant that you looked ... looked familiar. Thought I might've known you from somewhere."

"No. I've lived here all my life. Here in Detroit. Guess I'll probably die here. Where'd Mister Horne say you come from? Houston? That's in Texas, someplace ... isn't it?"

"Uh, yes," replied Jim with a smile. "In Texas someplace. But, I used to live up here ... years ago. Years and years ago. So, I'm not entirely a stranger in these parts. Uh, Mister Horne ... he was the one who set all this up?"

"If you're askin' if he was the one who rented the room, of course he did. Of course he did. He gave me the rest of this month's rent money yesterday. What did you think?"

"Confident sonofagun," muttered Jim – to himself.

"What? What was that, Mister Hayworth?"

"Huh? Oh, nothing. I just wasn't sure whether it was ol' Gabe, or maybe one of the other guys ... one of the other ... uh ... 'boys' ... who'd set up these diggings."

"These what?"

Jim laughed, nervously. Obviously "diggings" was not a 1939 word! He'd most certainly have to watch that sort of thing.

"Uh ... diggings," he answered. "Texas word. Means living quarters."

"Oh," Helen replied, with a confused nod. "Gosh. They must certainly talk funny down there ... or wherever Texas is."

"Yeah. They're a million laughs."

"You sure do talk funny, Mister Hayworth. Almost like a foreign language or somethin'."

"Or something."

"Anyway, Mister Horne said that you'd be in late last night. Must've been awful late. I have the room across the hall ... and I'm a light sleeper. Especially the last eighteen months or so. That's when my husband ... my Walter ... when he died. And then ... just after that ... my son, Jeff, he went and joined the Navy. Poor boy. His father dyin' like that ... it hit him hard. And I ... well, I ... I just couldn't stay in that big old lonely house. So, I sold it ... and bought this building. And I ... oh Lord! Look at me. Goin' on like this. I didn't mean to bore you, Mister Hayworth. I just get to talkin' and ... "

"No! No, really! Go on! It's very interesting. Really. I'm sorry ... about your husband, I mean. It must be awfully tough being a widow ... in this day and age."

She looked at him quizzically.

"No tougher," she replied, "than any other day and age, I don't imagine."

Jim smiled. Mrs. Shaddon, of course, couldn't know of the many and varied government programs which would be implemented in the future – to help others such as herself.

Such as herself? That wasn't nice. She seemed pretty independent. Very self-sufficient. He didn't believe she'd need the government to take care of her!

His smile broadened.

She scowled.

"What's so funny?" she asked.

"Nothing, Mrs. Shaddon. Absolutely nothing."

"Say ... you are a funny duck, aren't you."

"So I've been told. But, you were saying? You sold your house? Sold it ... and bought this place?"

"Oh. Yes. There wasn't much insurance money, y'know. My Walter was in construction. Fell off a scaffold, one day! Him and two other men. Walter and Tom Hack ... they both died. The other fella ... the third one ... he pulled through. Thank the Lord. It was quite a shock to us ... to Jeff and me ... I'll tell the world."

"Yes. I'm sure it was."

"Poor Walter. He just went to work one day … one morning … and he never came back. Never came home. The company … they paid for the funeral and all. Send me a small pension every month. I had enough money saved up … and with the little bit of insurance money I got … I was able to pay off the mortgage on my house. Jeff … that's my son … "

"I know. You mentioned that."

" … he upped and joined the Navy. I just couldn't stay in that big old house. Not all alone. Oh, it was a nice place and all that. Over on Forrer… down near Schoolcraft. Anyway, I went and I bought this place. This building. Has five rooms up here … and, of course, the grocery store and the cleaners downstairs. Land sakes! Listen to me! I been talkin' here … like I didn't have anything else to do. I don't usually talk that much with any of my tenants. Especially when they're new. Especially when they're men."

"Am I the only man here?"

"No. No, there's a man named George Roberts. He's in number four … next door. He's a nice man. Good bit older than you are, I'd wager. I've got room one, there. Lady with a long Polish name … she's in number two. Nice lady. Widow … like me. Older, though. Spends a lots of time in Ohio or someplace … with a couple of her children. Not here … not all that often. Room three is still vacant. Mister Roberts has room four … like I said. And you've got number five, now. I swore I wasn't gonna take in any more men. Mister Roberts is a nice man … but, I sometimes wonder about him. The way he looks at me, sometimes. And I think he maybe sneaks a woman in up here ever' now and again … if you'll excuse the reference."

Once again, Jim found himself smiling broadly.

"I sure don't see what's so funny, Mister Hayworth."

"It's nothing," he replied. "Nothing funny at all. You're just one of the most charming ladies I've ever met, is all. One of the most enchanting ladies I've ever met."

Helen Shaddon blushed.

Jim hadn't seen anyone – male or female – blush! Not in years! He'd almost forgotten what it looked like. In the seventies, no one

– but, no one – blushed! Ever! It was almost a sign of disgrace – or, at the very least, an indication of some kind of terrible weakness – to be found with a flushed face!

"I'm sorry, Mrs. Shaddon," he soothed. "I don't mean to embarrass you. Another trait I guess I must've picked up in Texas. When we see something ... we go ahead and mention it. I'm intrigued by you. I'd invite you in ... except I know it's not proper. And I certainly wouldn't want you to get the wrong idea."

Her complexion became even more scarlet!

"I ... I don't know what to say," she stammered.

"You don't have to say anything, Mrs. Shaddon. You're a very charming lady. I call 'em as I see 'em."

"What's that mean?"

Oops! Another phrase out of the future!

He smiled once more – and did his best to explain:

"It's something a baseball umpire once said. It simply means that, when a person is enchanted by another person ... as I'm enchanted by you ... it behooves that person to say so."

"You sure do talk funny."

"So they say. Mister Horne did pay the rent, did he?"

"Yup. Oh! Excuse me."

"Excuse you? Excuse you? For what?"

"Well, we both know a lady shouldn't say 'yup'."

"In your case, Mrs. Shaddon, I find it delightful."

Once again, the woman blushed.

"Anyway," she muttered, "Mister Horne paid it up for you for the rest of the month ... the rent, I mean."

"What's ... ? Jim caught himself before he'd blurted out his question.

He was going to ask her the day and the month. And – maybe even – the year!

"What was it you were gonna ask me, Mister Hayworth?"

It was not until that moment that the name had hit home! She'd been calling him "Mister Hayworth"!

His new identity! Hayworth! After Rita, no doubt?

It was almost as though his landlady wasn't standing there!

"Mister Horne," he muttered. "You're a piece of work."

"What was that, Mister Hayworth? Mister Hayworth? Are you sure you're all right? I mean ... well, you're actin' kinda strange. Are you sure that ... well, that there's nothin' wrong with you? Somethin' that maybe I should be knowin' about?"

"Uh ... no. No. I'm fine. I ... what I was going to ask you, though, was ... was ... was how much is the rent here?"

"You don't know? You move into a place? And you don't know? Don't know how much the rent is? That sure don't sound right."

"Well ... ah ... you see? This whole thing just came up sort of suddenly ... and I had to ... I had to fly in here ... all of a sudden ... last night, so ... "

"You flew in? You mean ... on a air-o-plane?"

"Yes," Jim nodded. "Yes. Mister Horne said that he ... or maybe one of his associates ... they'd set the whole thing up. It all happened so fast that ... that I didn't have a ... have a chance to find out a whole bunch of things that I need to know."

"Well, the rent's twelve dollars a month. That's not too much, now, is it? I mean, 'cause if it is, I can ... "

"No," he smiled. "No ... twelve dollars is fine. I can handle that."

"Handle that? Boy. They sure do talk funny out in Texas. As I was sayin', I wasn't gonna take in any more men boarders. But, this room's been vacant for a good while now, and ... truth to tell ... I can use the money. So, when Mister Horne came and he ... "

"Uh ... Mrs. Shaddon? When ... exactly ... when did Mister Horne get here? It was yesterday? What time was it?"

"Time? Oh, lessee. I guess it musta been ... oh ... three-thirty. Yesterday afternoon. There or thereabout. Maybe a-quarter-to-four."

Gabriel Horne was nothing – if not confident. On the other hand, "yesterday" was in 1979! Wasn't it? Jim's head began to spin once more.

"Mister Hayworth? Say ... maybe you better go back and lay down a spell. I was ... I was just kinda worried. I heard all that laughin' and such in there. I didn't know what to think."

"I'm all right, Mrs. Shaddon. I'm fine. Really. You know how ... sometimes you'll remember something funny? Hits you out of a clear blue sky? And you know how you'll get to laughing? And you can't stop? And the more you try ... the worse it gets?"

She nodded. Even that was charming.

"When Walter was alive," she said, "I'd sometimes get like that."

"Well, that's what happened to me. It was a tough trip back here, and I just ... "

"Back here?"

"Yes. I mentioned that I lived here once before."

"Oh, that's right. I guess you did."

"And now that I'm back, I ... I guess it's a way of letting off steam."

"Boy. The way you talk, Mister Hayworth. Texas must be a whole different place."

"Very different. You'd never believe how different. Anyway, I'm here now ... and I'm fine. And I'm tickled pink to meet you."

"Never had no one tell me nothin' like that before."

"More Texas talk, I guess. What I mean is ... that it's really a pleasure to meet you. I know that we'll get along famously."

"We will ... if you pay your rent on time. And keep to yourself. No wild parties. And no women up here. None!"

Jim laughed.

"No problems," he assured his new landlady. "I'll be the best li'l ol' roomer ... in the whole state of Michigan."

George D. Schultz

THREE

As enchanted as Jim had been with Helen Shaddon, he was just as content to terminate the conversation. He'd become more and more antsy – yearning to set about taking inventory.

There would be lots, he imagined, to look over!

There had been a fleeting glimpse of a wallet lying on the older dresser. As soon as he'd closed the door, he'd hurried to snatch up the billfold! He fumbled, clumsily, as he opened it.

Three hundred dollars in cash! And – in the old-fashioned coin compartment –ninety-three cents in change. As near as he could figure, in 1939 terms, he was almost wealthy! Not filthy-rich, of course – but, he didn't seem to be hurting either. It was seldom that he'd ever had $300 in his clutches at one time – even in inflated seventies dollars. Not after he'd sat down and written checks for all his bills, for heaven's sakes.

"For heaven's sakes," he mumbled to himself – and began to laugh once again! It took a massive effort to nip another boisterous outburst!

At least, he'd never had three-hundred 1979 dollars left over – until the new owners had taken charge of the company for which he'd worked, in Houston. By coming back in time, of course, he'd turned his back on what seemed about to become a very lucrative position. First one in his entire life. Ah, so.

In the window compartment of his newly-acquired wallet, a Michigan driver's license stared back at him. Well, it didn't exactly stare. This was well before anyone thought of putting a person's photograph on licenses. This was a "backwards" copy of some kind of Photostat. White typewritten data on a black background. Complete with his signature – Parks Hayworth – also in white. His signature? The name? His new moniker? It was <u>Parks Hayworth</u>!

A little celestial humor, no doubt. Obviously, it was not sufficient that Jim be given Rita Hayworth's last name. He'd wound up with a first name derived from Larry Parks – Miss Hayworth's costar in a movie that wouldn't be made for six or seven years.

The flick, of course, was *Down To Earth* – the picture from which Mr. Horne had "borrowed" the character of Mr. Jordan. More or less.

Once again, dizziness seemed about to overtake the newly-minted Parks Hayworth. Could he not look at anything? Not gaze on a single thing? Could he not <u>do</u> anything? Did <u>everything</u> have to cause his head to whirl? Was light-headedness to be his natural state, in this new life of his? If so, it was going to present a massive problem!

To further complicate matters, the giggles began to overtake him once more – although, thankfully, not to the extent of a few minutes before.

He lay back down, on the creaky old bed – totally bemused. The entire situation was simply mind-boggling! Would he ever be able to accept it? To cope with it? To contend with the irreversible "new life" he'd consented to undertake. Irreversible! God!

Slowly a gradual numbing – the realization of the finality of his state – began to set in! For better or for worse, he was – irreversibly – living in, as Garry Moore would say (some years later on TV), *That Wonderful Year*! *That Wonderful Year – 1939!*

Our hero's head began to wheel – even more rapidly! He began to shiver! He felt as though he would be sick at his stomach!

The stark realization was setting in! It would be sixteen long years! Sixteen whole, entire, 12-month, years! That's how long it would be – before his first son, Dave, would be born! The prospect left him aghast!

Suddenly, it had become a withering – an overwhelmingly-withering – outlook!

His kids! They were beyond his reach! He was cut off from them! Dear God! What had he done? Even Kathleen – the mother of his children – would be a mere four-years-old! What would he do? What <u>could</u> he do?

Already he missed his children! Missed them desperately! Never had he felt so lonely! So abandoned! He didn't even have any photographs of his kids! Compare <u>that</u> to a whole wall-full of eight-by-ten glossies! Pictures of kids, kids and more kids!

He was becoming more and more melancholy! Immersed in a terribly bleak morass!

"God! What a mistake! What a horrible damn mistake!" Had he said that aloud?

Probably. Was it loud enough for Mrs. Shaddon to have heard him? Possibly. If she was lurking outside his door. What must she be thinking?

All through his life, when he'd been blue, he'd always looked to his music – his schmaltzie music – to pull him out of his doldrums. Looking around the room – which, somehow, seemed so much more unfamiliar than when he'd first opened his eyes – he searched for a radio or a record-player. He found none!

Not only was the room terribly alien – it appeared downright hostile! Phonographs, he knew, were quite rare in 1939. But radios? The "wireless" was a thriving industry. Was it not?

"First priority," he mumbled, with a massive sigh, "get a damn radio. Maybe a phonograph too."

There, of course, would be no FM radios available. Well, maybe there were. He thought back to the huge, floor-model *Freid-Eisman* AM/FM radio/phonograph that his parents had bought in 1940 or 1941. Frequency Modulation had been a new-fangled toy!

There had been two FM stations in Detroit – W45D and W49D. Within a year or two, the *Fried-Eisman* would need a special adapter to pick up the even-newer-fangled FM signals. An adapter that Dolly and Bernard Sidorwitz had never bought. They'd paid over $500 – an outrageous price, in the early-forties – for the set. And all they could pick up was the AM signal! The same, identical, stations – which a person could pick up on any ten- or twelve-dollar radio.

There were boodles of radios available for less than twenty bucks. Were there not?

Well, the big, blond-wood appliance had been a beautiful piece of furniture.

The record player, now! That was high-tech stuff! It had an actual changer – built right in! Hoo! You could actually put a stack of fifteen, 10-inch, 78-RPM records on that remarkable changer! Of course, that first record – dropping onto the metal turntable – hit with a loud CLACK! A couple times, he remembered, the record involved had wound up actually broken!

All at once, that $300 that Mr. Horne had bequeathed him didn't look all that overwhelming!

It would be another seven or eight years – before the launch of commercial television. That was okay with Jim/Parks. He'd reached a point, in the seventies, where he seldom "watched the tube".

Maybe, in his new life, he'd be ready – ready once more – for the likes of *Kukla, Fran & Ollie* and maybe even *Uncle Miltie*, when those shows would become available. Much more desirable than the pap the networks purveyed in the seventies. If our boy had been turned-off by the fare available in 1979, he'd have just about gagged at what TV network primetime had devolved to, as the 21st century had arrived. It is doubtful that our hero could ever have envisioned what "Four-Letter-Word TV" would "progress" to – in 2004 or 2005.

Slowly, his blue funk began to lift. Ever so slowly. It was not as though it was a certainty that he would never see his children again. Mr. Horne had, after all, advised him that he might be able to observe them from, hopefully, a more relaxed – less-pressurized – position. "From afar", as the archangel had suggested. Certainly that was not a bona fide impossibility. In the meantime, he would have to do what he could – to enjoy his new life. There was absolutely no way that he would be able to change it, anyway.

He was well beyond turning back! Eons beyond!

As his depression faded, the dizziness began to subside!

What a roller coaster he was on! An out-of-control ride! Unless he could keep a tighter rein on his emotions, he realized, it would be very difficult for him to adjust to – or even survive in – his new era.

Under the best of circumstances, the adjustment was bound to be a monumental task! Much more tremulous than he could ever have imagined.

The human psyche, he was certain, was not devised to withstand such a staggering change! Something he'd have done well to have been aware of in 1979.

In the sixties and the seventies, the *National Aeronautics and Space Administration* had conducted exhaustive tests to determine the effects of weightlessness on the human body. No such studies could've been undertaken to determine how a man – or a woman – would (or could) cope with time travel. And this voyage had been "only" 40 years. Not as though he'd been transferred back to Christopher Columbus' time. Or to the age of The Crusades. Or to the Civil War. What would that – any of those – have done to him?

Maybe – in addition to being the subject of a celestial wager – he might, very well, be some sort of guinea pig. Possibly, depending on how he fared, others maybe would be transferred back – or launched forward – in time. Maybe this was all a big-time experiment!

On the other hand, maybe others had already been thus transported! Had fared much better than Jim/Parks had! Mr. Horne, after all, had not assured him that he would be the first to embark on such a journey. The subject had never come up!

He shook his head – violently – from side-to-side!

The possibilities were endless!

"Might as well enjoy it ... or at least try to," he murmured.

He heaved himself up from the crotchety old bed – and made his way to the window, once more.

It was then that he realized the reason that the sun was so bright: The air was without the dense, pervasive, eye-watering, breath-challenging, pollution – which would cause so many problems three or four decades down the road.

He became completely absorbed, once again, in the many cars – moving up and down Grand River.

In the sixties and seventies, he'd attended every old-car exposition in the Houston area. He'd even traveled to shows in Dallas and San Antonio.

Returning

In Houston, there had been two companies which specialized in restoring old cars – mostly those of the forties and fifties. Jim – now Parks – had always seemed to be at one or the other. A number of times, he'd persuaded Cynthia – Hogan – to snap a few photographs of her father standing in front of, or along side, some of those "classics"! Those beauties for which he'd always had "a soft spot in my head".

Now, looking down at the busy street, he saw literally hundreds of those "classics"! His cup runneth over! And just think: In the forties, there would be thousands upon thousands more of those wonderful cars! He stood there – totally transfixed! Enraptured at the sight of the old – well, no longer old – automobiles!

As when he'd first gazed out at the bustling street, he was amazed at the number of Model-A Fords still in existence! Incredible!

Finally, he walked back to his closet. He'd intended to inventory all his worldly possessions – as soon as he'd bade Helen Shaddon goodbye.

"Can't seem to concentrate on anything," he mused aloud. "Not a damn thing!"

In the closet, he spotted two herringbone suits – and another of exceptional-quality tweed. Along side those suits, hung three lightweight sport coats. In addition, a half-dozen pairs of slacks – as well as six heavily-starched white dress shirts, six pastel-colored shirts and six summer tee shirts – completed a more-than-generous wardrobe. All brand new! Never before had our boy been so well-fixed – from a sartorial standpoint. Never! Most often, he'd looked rather seedy! Financial restraints and all that! Hard to become a fashion plate under those conditions.

Three pairs of shoes were lined up on the floor – including a pair of brown-and-white oxfords. (They would be called "saddles", in the forties – when virtually every high school girl would wear them. "Saddles" and bobby socks! And – in the fifties – "poodle" skirts and somewhat-tight sweaters would join them, as the uniform of the day.)

In the chest of drawers, Parks found belts, ties, underwear, socks, a sleeveless black sweater, a yellow woolen pull-over and a dark-brown cardigan. A small jewelry box contained three sets of cufflinks, two collar clasps and three tiepins.

Much more generous than he could've imagined. Much more charitable than he'd ever expected. Well – truth to tell – he hadn't known *what* to expect. But, the bequest was far more lavish than anything to which he'd felt entitled.

It wasn't until that point that he awakened to the fact that something had been rattling around in the pocket of his slacks! The dark-blue slacks that he'd snatched off the "elephant" hook – and had thrown on to answer the door. The door under that cool transom.

He reached in – and fished out a brown-leather key case. Inside were three keys – one of which, presumably, was to the door to his room.

The other two were car keys! Ford keys! Dare he hope? Could it possibly be?

Was it possible that Mr. Horne would have blessed him with a 1937 Ford club coupe? A black one? Just like the one his father had owned? Just like the one he'd dreamed of? Dreamed of so many times?

Maybe! Just maybe!

How would he find out? He dare not ask Mrs. Shaddon! She was wary enough of him as things stood. All it would take would be for him to ask his landlady what kind of car he owned – and where it might be parked. He might as well have gone ahead and actually asked her what day and month – and, hell, even what year – it was.

Quickly removing his slacks, he donned underwear and socks. He selected a pale-blue sport shirt from the closet. Then, he put on his pants once more.

Seated upon the bed – tying his shoes – it occurred to him that he would do well to make the bed. He was on shaky enough ground with Helen Shaddon, as it was. She'd probably place a great deal of importance upon the tidiness of his room. Or lack of same.

He threw the bed together – straightening as many of the more flagrant wrinkles as his fast-evaporating patience would allow! Then, he bolted out the door! The one under the transom.

In the hallway, he noted that all five rooms opened off an inverted-U-shaped area – which featured a stairway in the center.

The stairs, of course, would lead down to Grand River. Fighting an overwhelming impulse to trundle down the stairs – two and three at a time – he took each step in deliberate sequence. What an effort that took!

No cars were parked on Grand River. There, of course, didn't figure to be.

He hurried around the corner, onto Mansfield – past the small grocery – and to the rear of the building.

In the cinder-covered lot, sat four cars! A 1934 Packard, a 1936 Studebaker and a 1936 Hudson. The fourth was a 1937 Ford! A black club coupe! Just like his father's.

His knees began to wobble – as he made his way to the gorgeous auto. To the '37 Ford! It was unlocked!

He climbed inside! The first thing that caught his eye was the odometer! The car had seven miles on it! Seven miles! Brand new! How did Mr. Horne – and/or the "boys" – manage that? A brand new 1937 Ford! In 1939! Well, presumably 1939!

Was he really in 1939? Maybe he'd been sent back to 1937! Maybe Mr. Horne – and/or the "boys" – had made a typographical error! That didn't seem likely. Mr. Horne had gone to too much trouble – setting up a whole new I.D. and providing him with all those clothes! And getting him that room across from Mrs. Shaddon! There had been simply too much preparation – for Parks Hayworth to be the subject of some "typo"!

Still, it was terribly disconcerting!

Nothing, of course – neither the money, the clothes, the room or the car – had been negotiated the night before. The night before – the one that was 40 years in the future. Everything had been the largess of the archangel's generosity!

He looked up and uttered a silent thanks to Mr. Horne – and to the "boys".

Taking stock of his prized '37 Ford, he realized that he'd forgotten that the ignition key fitted into a lock-device, which protruded from the steering column – down close by the dashboard. The assembly operated upon the same principle as would those found on all cars built after 1969. Once the ignition was turned off, the steering wheel locked – after a quarter-turn in either direction.

Another similarity to the cars of the seventies: The Ford had no window vents in either of the doors. They were called "no drafts" in those days. People who drove Buicks, back then – like his Grandfather Swenson – flaunted them! You had to buy a much more expensive automobile – to have the privilege and pleasure of actually owning a car with the wondrous "no drafts"! And Grandpa had certainly been proud of his Buick! A pale-green 1938 four-door model. Two years newer than the 1936 Dodge that Jim Sidorwitz's father had been driving at the time.

Slipping the key into the lock on the steering column proved to be highly traumatic! Suppose it didn't work? Suppose the key didn't turn the tumblers? Maybe his heart-felt thank you to Mr. Horne – and, of course, to the "boys" – had been premature! What then?

What if this wasn't his car? What if the actual owner should walk up – at the moment he was attempting to start the vehicle? He was certain that Helen Shaddon would hear about it – even if Parks should be able to talk his way out of having to grapple with the Detroit Police Department! With their Grand Theft Unit.

Maybe it was even Helen's car! Who knew?

He turned the key! Success! Thank God! And thank Mr. Horne! And thank the "boys"!

He pressed the starter button on the dash – to the left of the steering wheel! The car started immediately! Funny – it was running much more loudly than he'd remembered Pop's car doing.

There were so many little things about the car to thrill him: He'd forgotten, for instance, that the Ford had no temperature gauge. Not as such. There was a small thermometer – filled with red liquid. It was located in the same round display which housed all the other gauges – to the left of the speedometer. The driver could ascertain how hot or cold the car was running – simply by observing the level of the red solution! Down-right amazing!

Opening the glove compartment, Parks found himself staring at an official-looking document. It was the title to the Ford! Unencumbered! In the name of Parks Hayworth! At the Grand River address. The registration certificate was neatly paper-clipped to the back of the title!

It was <u>his</u> car! His! The property of Parks Hayworth! He was astounded at how quickly he'd come to refer to himself by his newly-assigned moniker!

"Thanks again, Mister Horne. Thank you! You and the 'boys'! Thank you! Thank you! I'm … I'm most grateful!"

The car even had a radio! He'd forgotten that the dial was in the form of the old Ford V-8 emblem. The base of the "V" pointed to the frequency that the set was receiving. The speaker was mounted just above the two-piece windshield. Hidden beneath the headliner fabric. There was a good bit of distance between the top of the windshield and the roof of the car – more than enough to accommodate the small speakers of that era.

Parks flicked on the radio – and pointed the base of the "V" at 760 – station WJR, "high atop the Fisher Building".

An old soap opera – *Bess Johnson, Hilltop House* – was signing off. He listened – grinning broadly – as Frank Gallop intoned, "Tune in tomorrow … same time, same station … when <u>Lifebouy</u> presents another heart-warming chapter of 'Bess Johnson, Hilltop House'". Was that great or what?

Parks basked in a warm, satisfying, glow. The program – centered around an orphanage – had been one of his Grandmother Swenson's favorites. One of many soaps to which she so faithfully listened. Each and every day!

Ah, his grandmother! His best buddy! Parks – as little Jimmy – had gotten caught up in a whole bunch of his grandmother's soap operas. He had positively lived to spend as much time as possible in her dinky "Dog House" – a tiny three-room bungalow, which sat at the back of a long narrow lot on Burnette Street.

The newly-minted Parks Hayworth pushed the floor shift up into reverse gear, cut the wheel to the left – and backed to the point where the car was aimed toward the exit. Toward Mansfield. It was one of the strangest sensations he'd ever experienced: The automobile – even in such short distance – handled in a completely different manner than any car he'd ever driven. Completely foreign.

Rolling out of the parking lot, he turned left – and coasted the few dozen feet to Grand River.

Once traffic had cleared, he made the left turn onto the busy thoroughfare. Fortunately, he'd allowed himself more room than he'd thought necessary to enter the traffic flow! The car would take some getting used to. He had expected it to be slow and extremely stodgy – spoiled as he'd been by the high-powered machines of the fifties, sixties and seventies. However, he had never dreamed that any car would drive out as sluggishly as his prized "Dream Car"! Amazing! He still loved it, though.

He drove the half-mile to Greenfield Road, amazed at the number – and the vastness – of all the open fields along the way. One day, of course, the real estate would be occupied. Completely built-up. By many and varied – and, in most cases, huge – stores.

Turning right onto Greenfield, he drove south – past Schoolcraft Road, across Fullerton Road and past Plymouth Road – to West Chicago Boulevard.

As he slowed to make another turn, it occurred to Parks that he had intended to buy a newspaper – to determine the exact date. The exact date of the beginning of his new life. Presumably in 1939.

That had gotten lost in the excitement over his car! Or had it? Maybe, subconsciously, he was saving the deliciousness of knowing the exact day and date for last! Just as he'd used to save the frosting on his cupcakes for last, when he was a boy. Cupcakes! It had years since he'd had a genuine bakery cupcake. Those "jobbies" put out by **Hostess** were good. But – pre-packaged as they were – they didn't qualify as bona fide cupcakes. Those you got only from your neighborhood bakery. Every neighborhood had a bakery. Not any more. Not in the seventies. Definitely a vanishing breed. Parks wasn't even sure that they made cupcakes in the seventies.

He reached for the turn signal – to indicate his right turn, onto West Chicago – and found himself grappling on the left of the steering column for a device which would not be introduced for two or three years. His grandfather's 1941 Buick would have them – turn signals, for heaven's sakes – and little Jimmy would be amazed that such a high-tech accessory could be manufactured.

What would they think of next?

Negotiating the turn onto West Chicago, Parks passed one of the old Ford buses.

From the final few months of 1938, West Chicago – and, to a point, Schoolcraft – seemed to have been the last of the bus routes (on the West Side, anyway) which still featured the tiny vehicles. Other, busier, routes had begun to run the newer, much larger, coaches – units which actually featured doors at the front and in the rear. Amazing! The engines of the newer models were – wonder of wonders – <u>inside</u> the bus. Can you <u>imagine</u>? An engine – inside!

Little Jimmy had, of course, been astounded at such highly sophisticated stuff.

On West Chicago, in 1939, the old Fords still plodded along.

After playing tag with the bus – a distance of about a half-mile – Parks peeled off onto Grandmont Street. His old neighborhood! Few houses stood in the block, nearest West Chicago, in 1939.

One of them, though, was the house in which he'd lived when he was five, six and seven! His "Dream House"!

How he had loved that home. Always! He'd hated the thought of moving from the place – despite the fact that he'd been only seven at the time. Consequently, the smaller house on Penrod Street – to which the Sidorwitz family had moved in late 1939 – had always paled by comparison. Little Jimmy, in fact, had never given it a chance. The new place could never compare with his wondrous "Dream House". Nothing could.

The house on Grandmont was – literally – a "Dream House". One of little Jimmy's recurring dreams was the one in which he had crawled up into the attic – through the amazing squared-hole in the ceiling of the linen closet. The hole – in the dream – had been barely big enough to accommodate him.

Once through that magical threshold – in this special, oft-repeated, dream – he had literally discovered a heaven! In his very own attic! Really! A bona fide heaven! The dream had been repeated – in one form or another – over the forty-some ensuing years.

Jim Sidorwitz – in Houston, in the seventies – had continued to dream about that house. He'd sometimes wondered what Miss Wilks, of *The Children's Center* – would have made of that. Or his mother. His more recent dreams of the place were not so much about the heaven in the attic. Not all the time, in any case. The themes and visions were many and varied. He had always awakened, terrifically saddened to find that it – once again – had only been a dream. The house was not really his! A God-awful come-down!

Well, for a while, anyway – too short a while – the house had been his again. Even if only in a dream.

Parks eased his beloved Ford to the curb, in front of an open field – two lots away from the enchanted home. He killed the motor – and sat in tranquil silence.

The place still had a mystique about it! He could almost visualize a sort-of spiritual mist encompassing it!

He wondered if the Sidorwitz family still lived there. Since he had no idea as to the exact date, he really could not be sure whether Dolly and Bernie might have carted little Jimmy off to Penrod as yet. The heart-breaking move had occurred sometime in 1939. Late in the year, it seemed to him.

Five unblinking minutes later, Parks was startled to see the gleaming-white front door open!

A young woman emerged out onto the porch! Parks felt himself becoming the slightest bit dizzy once again. The woman was his mother's sister – his Aunt Juanita!

Because Dolly worked, his aunt had taken care of little Jimmy – during those early years.

Parks remembered her as having been very pretty. But, she was much more beautiful than the picture he'd stored in his memory. She was absolutely gorgeous!

Then, the most mind-boggling sight of all: Parks saw himself! Little Jimmy Sidorwitz! Age Seven! The child had walked out onto the porch!

It was an incredible sensation! His head continued to swirl!

Obviously, school was out for the summer. Otherwise, little Jimmy would've been one block north – at *Calvin Coolidge Elementary School*. Unless it was Saturday or Sunday. It certainly didn't feel like it should be the weekend. *Hilltop House*, for one thing, would not have been on the radio. The next edition had been promised for tomorrow. So, it wasn't even Friday.

School had to have been out for the summer – a situation which had always made little Jimmy ecstatic! Even at that tender age.

Playing hooky was in the far-flung future for the boy. But, the seed was germinating!

Parks fought to focus his eyes on the porch. His aunt had disappeared back inside the house. She returned a moment later – with Jimmy's tricycle! That brand new red-and-yellow one that he'd gotten from Santa Claus the Christmas before. Aunt Juanita carried the trike down off the porch. Little Jimmy climbed aboard.

The boy headed down the sidewalk – pedaling past where Parks continued to stare in wonderment. He was headed toward little Marilyn Faffenberger's house.

Leaning across the front seat, Parks managed to roll down the window in the passenger's door – that he might hear himself, as a seven-year-old, call from outside the little girl's house:

"Mari-lynnnnnnn!"

Parks – never having felt quite so old in his life (another recurring emotion) – climbed out of his Ford. He wobbled down four lots. Standing in front of the Faffenberger house, he watched himself call out once more:

"Mari-lynnnnnnnn!"

At that point, little Jimmy turned! He saw 47-year-old Parks staring at him.

His little face looked up – and broke into a big, infectious smile!

"Hi", said the lad. Had little Jimmy's voice actually sounded like <u>that</u>?

Tears welled up in Parks' eyes.

Looking down at the innocent youngster, he struggled to get out a hoarse, "Hi".

It was too much!

Parks could barely see – as he groped his way back to his cherished Ford. Once inside, he stared, blankly, at the dash! A whole entire series of even-more-brain-numbing questions ricocheted, pell-mell, through his mind.

Parks tried – frantically – to remember if, as a child, he'd taken notice of some old geezer! An old geezer who'd said, "Hi" to him, in front of Marilyn's house – and then had broken down. Apparently, as Jimmy, he'd not paid much attention.

Of course, if Jim Sidorwitz had not agreed to Mr. Horne's plan, the old geezer would never have been standing in front of the Faffenberger place! So, go figure!

It was – truly – a mind-warper! Parks' journey into the past was most certainly starting off much differently than he'd visualized.

He'd had no conception of the many tortures to which he seemed to be constantly subjecting himself. He wondered if Mr. Horne had known. Not likely. Mr. Horne and the "boys" had sent him – according to the archangel – on that incredible voyage so as to witness his reactions. Much coin of the realm (whatever that currency might be), he imagined, must've already changed hands up there.

Well, he knew not what was going on "up there". But, he was certainly reacting much differently than he ever would've expected "down here". Reacting to everything! Reacting much differently! Not a predictable emotion in the carload!

Twisting around in his seat – and peering out through the two tiny back windows – Parks watched Jimmy and Marilyn ride their tricycles down her driveway and out onto the sidewalk. The little couple pedaled back up toward the "Dream House" – "driving" past the Ford.

Marilyn would be six-years-old – to the best of Parks' recollection.

Watching the two children riding their trikes up and down the sidewalk, brought back an avalanche of happy, heart-warming, precious, memories.

"Kind of like the Ghost of Christmas Past," he rasped aloud.

For fully a half-hour, he sat, transfixed – and, tearfully, observed the little boy and little girl, as they rode up and back on the sidewalk, past his car. They seemed oblivious of him – wrapped up, as they were, in their own little world. They were probably playing "Bus Drivers" – their favorite tricycle game.

Finally, Parks started his beloved Ford once more. It had taken a few minutes – his head resting against the back of the seat and his eyes scrunched closed – to semi-rid himself of the cursed light-headedness, which seemed his constant companion.

He eased the car up Grandmont, toward Plymouth Road – three blocks away.

Slowing, as he passed *Calvin Coolidge Elementary*, he looked at the vacant building. Stared intently at it. He had attended the school in kindergarten – as well as in the first grade.

He remembered his teacher from the initial semester of the first grade. Miss Brock always seemed to be spanking him. But, then, Miss Brock always seemed to be spanking somebody. Times were sure different back then, he reflected.

Then, it occurred to him: He was in "back then"! That's where he was – at that very moment!

His favorite teacher had always been "Pretty Miss Mahon". He'd gotten her in the last semester of the first grade. He'd always referred to her as "Pretty Miss Mahon". As a six-year-old, he'd been madly in love with her. She was the most beautiful woman in the world. Well, next to Dolly Sidorwitz, of course.

Rolling to a stop at Plymouth Road, Parks turned right – and drove back past Greenfield, across Schaeffer Highway, Meyers Road and Wyoming Road, to where Plymouth Road ended. The artery flowed – at a 45-degree angle – into Grand River, one block from Oakman Boulevard.

The Oakman/Grand River intersection was one of the larger shopping areas, on Detroit's northwest side – in those pre-shopping mall days.

He continued past the **Liggett's** drug store, past **Miller's Optical** past **S.S. Kresge's** and **Sears**. Across the railroad tracks, sat the **White Tower** hamburger joint! He'd always remembered the restaurant with such fondness. Many a delicious hamburger had been consumed there. A goodly number of them by James Sidorwitz.

Parks peeled off a left turn – into "**The Tower's**" parking lot.

Walking back to Grand River – then across the tracks – he zeroed in on two racks of newspapers, in front of the **Sears** store. He noticed the store's hours: Open 9:30 AM to 5:30 PM – Monday through Wednesday. On Thursday s, Fridays and Saturday s – voila! – they were open all the way till 9:00 PM! All stores were closed Sunday!

Somehow, reflected Parks, people managed to get all their shopping done – even with such "restrictive" store hours.

He thought of Kathleen. In the mid-seventies, the huge department store, for which she worked, had forced her – and a bountiful number of other employees – to report for duty each and every Sunday. Or face dismissal!

Progress! You can't beat it!

He looked down at the two metal news racks. The red one contained copies of The Detroit News. The orange one was filled with a copious number of the current edition of The Detroit Times. The third daily – The Detroit Free Press (to be known from the mid-seventies forward as "The Freep") – used much smaller boxes. Virtually all of them were mounted on telephone poles – at the busier bus stops throughout town.

Parks was thrilled to see The Times – a Hearst publication which had gone under in 1960.

He dropped his on-your-honor three-cents into the coin slot – at the top of the orange rack – and removed one paper. He could, of course, have removed all eight or ten of them – and never put one penny into the tiny coin box. He could've pilfered the News box as well. But, of course, he did not. No one did back then. Well hardly anyone.

He thought of the large, locked, almost-armor-plated, boxes which had come into existence in the early-sixties. No newspaper could afford to allow its product to be displayed in anything other than the secure, thief-resistant, boxes. It would've been suicidal. A withering testimony to how times had changed. Progress! Ya can't beat it!

It took a concentrated effort – required a monumental strain – for Parks to force his eyes to focus on the date, under the masthead of the newspaper.

August 4, 1939!!!

August fourth! Nineteen thirty-nine! What a beautifully glorious – what a wonderful – day! What a nifty era! Obviously, the emotional roller coaster was ascending!

Tucking The Times under his arm, he made his way back across the tracks – to the **White Tower**. One of many stores belonging to his favorite hamburger joint chain.

Their ten-cent hamburgers smelled every bit as delicious as he'd remembered. Maybe more so. Probably more so. Parks inhaled deeply – savoring the aroma. That wonderful essence! That glorious fragrance! And there were no patties on the grill!

He recalled that this particular **White Tower** had been closed in the late-sixties or early-seventies. The last time he'd driven past the place, it had become a soul food joint.

Dolly had written to Jim – a month or so before Mr. Horne's visit – and had advised him that they were going to demolish the **Sears** store! Parks looked out the window, across the tracks, at the hallowed building. It was beautiful! So beautiful! So bright! So new! Almost glowing! How could anyone ever dream of ever tearing it down? Ever?

He heaved a massive sigh. Progress! You simply can't beat it!

Spreading his treasured newspaper on the counter, he ordered two hamburgers and a cup of coffee. He was the only patron in the place.

The first order of business, in his perusal of The Times? It would have to be, of course, the comics – referred to, in 1939, as "the funnies".

He'd remembered *Thimble Theater* – starring *Popeye*, of course. He drank in *Little Annie Rooney, The Lone Ranger, The Phantom, King of The Royal Mounted* and *Bringing Up Father* – which featured Jiggs and Maggie.

There were other strips, though, that he'd completely forgotten: *Toots & Casper, Tillie The Toiler* and *Tim Tyler's Luck*, for three.

Blondie – which had switched to The News, when that paper had absorbed The Times, in 1960 – was much the same as the 1979 version, with two notable exceptions:

Alexander had been a pre-schooler – called "Baby Dumpling" – and Cookie was not yet a gleam in Dagwood's eye. Blondie and Dagwood, though, looked pretty much the same – as did their dog, Daisy. The pups, of course, had not yet been born. Their house – and thirties-era stove and ice box – were almost exactly the same.

So were the Woodleys next door. So was Mr. Dithers, Dagwood's boss. So was their mailman – who was forever being run over by Dagwood, in the latter's haste to get to work on time.

Of all the strips, Parks mused, *The Phantom* had changed the most – yet had stayed the same. The story lines weren't much different. But, the drawings had, as time had gone by, become sharper – much more sophisticated. The cartoons in front of our hero seemed – well – primitive.

So immersed was Parks, that he was not aware that the short order cook had placed his hamburgers and coffee in front of him. She'd had to "Harrumph!" three times before grabbing his attention.

The dowdy woman advised him that he owed her the munificent sum of 26 cents: Two hamburgers at ten-cents, a nickel for a cup of coffee – and a penny tax.

The prices – which he knew he would continue to encounter, were, of course, far removed from those to which he'd been subjected in the seventies. The same meal, in 1979, probably would, he fancied, cost almost four bucks! And taste like bubble wrap!

It made Parks appreciate, once more, the $300 that Mr. Horne – and the "boys" – had bestowed upon him.

He bit into one of the hamburgers. Never had he tasted a steak which was more delicious – more succulent! In the sixties and the seventies he'd bemoaned the fact that – practically without exception – all the fast-food-joint hamburgers had come to taste like cardboard. "No <u>real</u> hamburger joints" around, he'd lamented.

He surprised himself – with the speed with which he'd devoured the two sandwiches. As Jim, he'd been one of the slowest eaters in the Western Hemisphere. The lady, who was the short order cook, looked at him – as though he'd not eaten in years.

If she only knew!

"Could I have two more, please?" he asked her. "Just exactly the same way you fixed these. They were delicious. My compliments to the chef."

As the woman, impassively, slapped two more pre-shaped patties onto the grill, Parks began an attempt to evaluate his financial situation. Throughout his life, finances had never been far-removed from his consciousness. He'd always been so broke! Broke!

Always! Every damn day! Every damn year! Never, it seemed, were there two stupid nickels to rub together! Ever!

After working two and three and four – and, at one point, five – jobs at one time, in a what-seemed-futile effort to support Kathleen and their seven children, Jim Sidorwitz had always been painfully aware of his financial situation. Under the best of circumstances, the family finances had always been precarious. And that was on good days!

He decided that, with Mr. Horne's $300 – and a car with a clear title – he was probably as well-off as he'd ever been, in his entire life! Definitely as well-off.

True, he'd just received a magnificent raise from his new boss in Houston – a more generous boost than he could ever have hoped for. Especially from a brand new employer. The man had only taken over the car-rental company two weeks before.

Consequently, the huge increase had not had a chance to really take effect!

"Story of my life," he muttered. "The minute I get some bucks coming in … I'm off onto something else. Some wild and crazy thing! Tilting at damn windmills or something."

He'd spoken too loudly. The lady behind the counter gave him a quizzical look. He had never seen anyone raise an eyebrow – quite like the cook had arched hers.

Parks smiled weakly – and resumed his mental calculating: Three hundred dollars, of course, would not last forever. He would have to get a job! Obviously!

Most certainly, procuring employment was not going to be easy!

The country was in the depths of a back-breaking depression! He'd not actually considered the depressed economic situation – when he'd pondered, so fondly, his trip back through time.

He turned to the classified section of his priceless paper. The precious-and-few jobs available were listed in categories labeled "Help Wanted – Female" and "Help Wanted – Male". Such "offensive" – such "sexist" – classifications were verboten where Parks had come from. Progress! Is progress great – or what?

The smattering of jobs advertised in The Times called for mastery of a skilled trade – in virtually every case. A bitter pill! Parks was not at all mechanically inclined.

Alice – his "Veteran Fiancée – had referred to him, on numerous occasions, as a "total putz", whenever he'd attempted even the simplest of household repairs. Why, replacing the furnace filter had always been a major undertaking. It took him four times longer to install a new plug on the end of a wire than would've been the case with any other person – regardless of age, race, creed, or color.

The withering realization that he was now far-removed from the then-booming Houston 1979 job market began to overtake him. He'd been on this same damn roller coaster all day! What was one more massive dive downward? He should be getting used to it – despite the fact that he'd never experienced such a day in his entire life! Not even close!

What would he do? What could he do?

White-collar jobs were almost non-existent for a male, without a degree – or document able years of management experience. What would Parks be able to document?

What indeed?

"Well," he rasped. "I'm going to have to come up with something."

"What? Whazzat?" The cook was placing his third and fourth hamburgers in front of him.

"Uh ... I'd ... I'd like another cup of coffee."

The woman plopped the second cup of "joe" on the counter – and picked up another 26 cents.

Parks' mood began to improve. The old roller coaster was ascending once again.

He felt certain that Mr. Horne had provided him with a goodly amount of money – by Parks' standards, anyway – because the archangel was aware of the fact that the subject of his celestial wagering would have a problem finding employment. Yet, he didn't bestow so much filthy lucre that his minion would not soon have to find a means to support himself.

Very astute! Very astute, indeed! He guessed that angels were gifted that way.

Returning

Another surprise – one of many: He couldn't believe the gusto with which he'd become accustomed to his new identity and name. After 47 years of thinking of himself as Jim, it was startling to realize the ease with which he'd begun to consider himself as Parks Hayworth.

He'd become Parks! Just like that! Amazing!

FOUR

Parks – fresh from his triumphant reappearance at the **White Tower** – tooled his cherished Ford down Grand River, once more.

Still savoring the four hamburgers – more food than he'd consumed in a long time – he turned onto Burnette Street, heading down toward West Chicago. As Burnette crossed West Chicago, the street made a sharp jog to the left. Otherwise, traffic would clatter into the front window of **Freddie's Bar** – a neighborhood tavern where Jim Sidorwitz's maternal grandparents had been known to tip a glass or two.

Parks made the left – and then the immediate right – and continued along Burnette Street. Halfway down the block – between West Chicago and Westfield – sat his grandparents' "Dog House".

The tiny three-room home had been built, for some obscure reason, at the very back of the exceptionally long, rather narrow, lot. His widowed grandmother had sold the house in 1952 – while Jim was serving in the Navy. Jim had never known who the buyer had been. After Grandma had moved out, the house had held no allure for him.

However, in 1939, the place would be alive – vibrant in the wondrous presence of his loving grandparents. Both of them!

While the residence had no bathtub or shower, it boasted one of the largest living rooms he'd ever seen. The room ran the entire width of the home. The main feature, though, was a screened-in front porch. Like the living room, the porch ran the entire width of the house. Inasmuch as the place was situated at the rear of the lot, a nice breeze seemed always to sweep across the porch – there being no houses, on either side, to break up any tidy little zephyr.

His grandparents used to sleep out on the porch during the summer – in a time when people could indulge in such things without fear of being fodder for whatever creep happened to be prowling the neighborhood.

That wouldn't last long! The neighborhood would change in six or eight years!

The old couple had a studio couch – which made into a double bed – on one side of the massive porch. A glider – placed on the other side – was where little Jimmy had slept, on those wondrous nights when he'd stayed over. The child had always cherished every moment he'd spent at the "Dog House".

His grandmother had always been this best buddy. His grandfather – an outwardly gruff man, with a bulbous nose and an almost-red complexion – had always scared the boy. Jimmy must have been nine or ten before he finally awoke to the fact that, inside, Grandpa was all mush. A genuinely kind man – who would move heaven and earth to have you believe exactly the opposite.

His grandfather had died in 1946. His grandmother had passed away in 1965. In 1939, though, they'd be alive and well and vital – and everything else that he'd remembered them to be! Hopefully, he would be able to strike up some sort of relationship with this glorious couple – to love and cherish them all over again. That would be so neat!

Parks Hayworth could hardly wait to see the enchanted "Dog House" again!

He pulled the Ford to the curb – across the street from his grandparents' residence. A shocker: In 1939, the immense front porch had <u>not</u> been screened in. As long back as he could remember, the porch had never been without those huge screens. He'd been certain that his memory of the place would've gone back as far as 1939. Even further. Obviously not!

He did remember, though, the swing – situated underneath the huge maple tree in the front yard. His grandfather had installed the "two-seater" – as he'd called it – for little Jimmy.

Parks turned off the ignition. He sat behind the wheel – debating whether he should try and approach his grandmother, on some trumped-up pretense. Grandpa was obviously not home. For one thing, he seldom missed a day's work. For another, his light-green '38 Buick was absent from its accustomed spot on the lawn – parked beneath the other side of the huge tree.

Five minutes passed. Twice, he'd been on the verge of getting out of the car.

Twice, he'd vetoed the idea!

What should he do?

He didn't want to simply drive off – not without seeing Grandma. Yet, his legs felt like two strands of overcooked spaghetti. His head had begun to spin once more!

A permanent condition? Dear Lord, he hoped not!

Sighing heavily – possibly another permanent affliction – he turned the ignition back on.

As he reached for the starter button, the door to the house opened! His grandmother stepped out onto the huge porch.

The heavy-set woman was lugging a large laundry basket – filled to overflowing with wet, heavy, clothes. She was younger – much younger – than he'd ever remembered. A quick calculation – through the almost-impenetrable fog – indicated that his grandmother was probably a year or two younger than Parks Hayworth. Amazing!

God! He was older than his own grandmother!

The woman began to hang the soggy clothing on the line – which had been strung from the house to the humongous tree and back to the house.

Parks thought back to the old wringer-type washing machine – in the kitchen of the basement-less dwelling. He pictured that wonderful woman – the woman at whom he was staring – as she had labored, through the years, in baling out the water from the cumbersome washer. She always had to bail the gamey water into the sink, when the laundry had been finished. It would not be until a year or two before his death, that his grandfather would finally break down and spring for a stupid pump for the thing.

Tears filled his eyes – as he watched that great lady methodically pin the laundry to the clothesline. Slowly, the dizziness began to subside. Wiping away the tear, which had trickled down his face, he got out of the car. Standing next to the Ford, he began to inhale deeply, once more.

He fought, mightily, to steady himself, as he walked across the street. He made his way up the long, uneven, narrow, sidewalk – which divided the massive front yard into two immense stretches of beautifully-maintained, almost-manicured, green lawn.

As he neared his grandmother, his knees began to sag once again. It seemed as though his body was on the verge of total numbness!

He was about twelve feet from the woman – when she became aware of his presence. She turned to face him.

What Parks felt at that moment would be impossible to describe. The raw emotion was overwhelming! Dizzying!

His grandmother smiled at him. She always smiled. Always.

"Yes?" Her voice was even richer than he'd remembered.

He groped wildly – frantically – for something to say! Anything to say! He was unable even to stammer! His throat felt as though it was made of concrete!

The woman's voice had always possessed a special quality. Hearing that unique – that wonderful – sound again, and beholding this dear woman who'd meant so much to him for all those years, was simply too much!

He collapsed at her feet!

When the blackness began to clear – about 30 seconds later – Parks was having a terrible problem, trying to force his eyes to focus! The blinding glare from the sun was not helping.

Through the haze, he could hear his grandmother saying, "Gee God!" It was her favorite expression. She'd used it often.

Parks managed to zero his gaze upon her. She was kneeling beside him – his head lying in the crook of her arm!

He raised himself to his elbows.

"I'm ... I'm awfully sorry, Ma'am." His voice was more a wheeze than anything else. "I ... I really don't know what came over me."

"Gee God! You sure did give me a scare, there, Mister. Can I get you some water or something? Gee God!"

Parks struggled to his feet. His grandmother labored to a standing position also.

She looked as though she expected to have to field him on the first hop, once more.

"I'm sorry that I ... that I gave you such a start," he said, once his underpinning seemed a little more stable. "I ... really, I don't know what ... what came over me."

"Gee God! You sure did scare me there, Mister. Is there anything I can do for you?"

<u>No</u>, he thought. <u>Just be my grandma</u>!

"Uh," he managed to say, "well ... you see ... I was just ... I was just gonna ask ... ask you if you could ... uh ... well, if you could tell me where ... where the **Tasty Bar B-Q** is located."

The woman scratched her head, as she replied, "I don't think I ever heard of that place. Are you sure that it's supposed to be around here?"

The restaurant would not come into existence for four or five years. But, Parks had to say <u>something</u>!

"Yes," he replied. "Well, maybe not. I'm really not sure. I understood that it was somewhere near to Joy Road. I just came from Joy Road ... and I didn't see it."

He hoped – fervently – that she wouldn't notice that his Ford was facing in the direction of Joy Road. Not away from it.

Once again, she scratched her head.

"Well, Joy Road, you know ... it kind of circles out to the left. Down the other side of Livernois. Crosses Grand River ... maybe a mile from here. Maybe that place ... maybe it's up there somewhere. I just never heard of it. Don't mean it doesn't exist. I just never heard of it."

Parks tugged at his earlobe. His mind was churning – in a futile effort to come up with something else to say to this dear lady. Something – anything – to prolong the visit!

"Well," he finally managed to stammer, "it's ... it's really not that ... all that important. I'll find it ... eventually. Say! Excuse me, Ma'am. But ... but, you look ... well, you look awfully familiar. You ... you're not from Minnesota, by any chance, are you?"

"Why ... why, yes. As a matter of fact, we are. My husband and I. We're from there. From Minnesota."

"What part?"

"Oh ... a little town. Outside Minneapolis."

"Winona?"

"Why ... why, yes. How did you know?"

Parks smiled – probably too broadly.

"Well," he replied, "you just ... you just look familiar. Awfully familiar. Like I should know you. It was a lot of years ago ... more than I'd really want to remember. But, you look as ... uh ... that is, much more slender than I remember."

"How long ago was that, Mister ... uh ... Mister ... ?"

"Parks".

"Mister Parks, I'd ... "

"No. No ... no, no. My first name is Parks. Last name is Hayworth ... but, I'd be honored, if you'd call me Parks."

His grandmother blushed! Amazing! Blushing! That's two in one day!

"Oh, gee God," she replied. "I couldn't do that. Gee God! How long ago are you talkin' about, Mister Hayworth?"

Parks was crushed! Hearing his own grandmother call him "Mister Hayworth" was incredibly devastating!

"Ah ... lessee." He was trying, valiantly, to rally. "About ten ... maybe twelve ... years ago."

"Nope. That wouldn't be us. Wouldn't be me. We've been down here over twenty-five years now. Probably closer to thirty."

"I'll be darned. And you do ... you look so familiar. I know it couldn't have been thirty years ago. Or even twenty-five. Must have you mixed up with someone else. I think they lived on ... on High Street."

"High Street? Well, I do have a sister that lives on High Street. Her name is Mary. Mine is Kate. Kate Swenson. Maybe it's Mary, who you're talkin' about. We do look a little bit alike. But, she's a good bit fatter'n me."

Parks closed his eyes – and uttered a silent thanks, that he'd been able to remember the name of the street on which Dolly's Aunt Mary lived.

"Why … why, yes," he blurted. "Yes. Yes, I guess I do mean her. Now that I think of it, her name was Mary! Yessir! Yes … that's who it was, all right. Mary! Wow! Small world, eh?"

He was overplaying his hand! He knew it! But, he was desperate – to keep the conversation alive. Kate seemed to sense Parks' desperation. It made her terribly uncomfortable! And just a little bit frightened!

"Well," she said, at length, "I have some things that I should be attendin' to, if you're sure you're all right, Mister Hayworth."

"Oh! Yes. Yes, of course. Yes. Go ahead. No, I'm … I'm fine. I'm … I'm really sorry to have … to have bothered you."

"No bother at all. Sorry I couldn't help you. Goodbye."

The well-known "bum's rush"!

"Uh … yes," he rasped. "Yes, goodbye. Thank you. Thank you so much. Thank you."

He wondered why he didn't just shut up! It was obvious that the woman was horribly ill-at-ease!

Parks turned to make his way back to his Ford.

While looking back, over his shoulder – at the dear, sweet, woman, who'd meant so much to him throughout his life – he tripped on one of the uneven squares in the narrow cement walk. The klutzy move hurled him, unceremoniously, in what seemed to be forty different directions at once!

He laid there – spread-eagled across the walk! He was certain that he was in the throes of terminal mortification!

He had undoubtedly skinned his knee – as he'd done so many times as a boy. On that same sidewalk. In addition, he'd probably torn a hole in the knee of his brand-new trousers. As he'd also done, on numerous occasions, as a child.

He became aware of an additional factor: His grandmother was laughing – uncontrollably!

Pulling himself, once again, to his feet, he looked back at her. Sheepishly!

It was scant consolation that he'd actually not torn his nifty, dark-blue slacks.

His pratfall made it all but impossible to make even a semi-graceful exit.

FIVE

Parks had driven away from his grandparents' "Dog House" – and had stowed his beloved '37 Ford in the huge parking lot behind the mammoth *Riviera Theater*, at the intersection of Joy Road and Grand River. About two blocks from where – some years later – the **Tasty Bar B-Q** would come to life.

He boarded one of the big yellow trolley cars. The clanging bell of one of those street-dinosaurs had heralded Jim Sidorwitz/Parks Hayworth into 1939 that morning.

Our hero was headed downtown.

Once inside the streetcar, he reveled in the décor: Parks was intrigued by the long wicker seats which lined the sidewalls of the vehicle – as opposed to the normal two-by-two's! The single seat traversed the inside wall – on both sides of the car – all the way back to the conductor's station. The elongated seats took up the front two-thirds of the car! He was amused as he watched the overhead straps – flapping from one side to the other – as the car clattered, clanged and swayed its way along.

From just inside the rear doors, the conductor supervised nickels being tossed into the fare box, made change, issued transfers to other transit units – and operated the rear doors.

From his station, to the rear of the car, the seats were the common, front-facing, two-by-twos.

Was this great or what?

The newer cars – to come in the mid-forties – would be much smaller, would have no conductor and would feature the normal two-by-twos exclusively. The new cars were nice – and would feature a far more intelligent use of space! They were <u>far</u> quieter. But, they would not have as much character! Not nearly as much!

Progress! You can't beat it!

The old trolley cars were propelled by electricity – as the newer ones would be. Electricity provided by wires that hung overhead. There was absolutely no engine noise. However, the metal wheels of the bigger, older, vehicles – rolling along, atop metal tracks, which had been anchored in the pavement below – made an exceptionally loud, almost-grinding, sound. The clattering – as the huge units swayed from side to side (causing the aforementioned straps to flap so wildly) – produced that irrepressible noise! That sound that was so loud, so bothersome, and – and so <u>wonderful</u>! All this was at about 30 miles-per-hour! It was truly a unique experience!

Sitting just behind the driver, in the weaving, almost-empty, car, Parks stared out of the side window across from his seat.

He was still amazed at the mind-boggling changes which would take place along Grand River Avenue over the next decade or two. Many of the businesses, fronting on the busy thoroughfare, were totally unfamiliar to him. They would have gone out of business or changed their names – or, possibly, made major alterations to their store's appearance – by the time little Jimmy Sidorwitz would be deemed old enough to journey downtown by himself, in the mid-forties. Amazing!

Parks was surprised at how quickly the noisy, clacking, conveyance had gotten him downtown. Maybe he was still immersed in some kind of overblown pipe dream. A time warp? He didn't really know what a time warp was – although he'd seen mention made of such things in some of the movies of the seventies.

He only knew that the time sequence had seemed totally out of whack! Ever since Mr. Horne had appeared to him. If, indeed, that was what had happened. The five hours – the period that Jim Sidorwitz had spent deliberating the efficacy of the archangel's offer – had blown right past him! It had seemed more like five <u>minutes</u>!

And now? And now, the trek downtown! <u>That</u> appeared too fast! <u>Way</u> too fast!

He disembarked at Griswold and State Streets – and hurried along State Street toward Woodward Avenue, a couple blocks away. The old emotional roller coaster was back on its way to the summit, once more.

It was wonderful – positively thrilling – to see some of the old buildings. Such as **Kern's Department Store**, at Woodward and State. "Under the clock at **Kern's**" was, far and away, the most popular meeting place in all of downtown Detroit. Up until the time the building had been demolished in the early-seventies. Torn down – along with **Sam's Cut Rate,** the large store which had been located around the corner.

The old City Hall was still standing, Parks noted. The unique building wasn't quite as dirty as he had remembered. From the time he'd been a small child – brought downtown by his mother or grandmother – he'd been convinced that the old stone building had always been a dark, grungy, dingy, grey. In the mid-forties, someone had – in the dead of night – cleaned a small area of the building. The spot – approximately six square feet – had shown that City Hall had been, at one time, a rather attractive beige.

Well, attractive by comparison, anyway. The exercise in cleaning-in-the-dark-of-night had shamed the city fathers into, eventually, having the entire building sandblasted.

City Hall had become a vision of cleanliness. And the embodiment of blandness.

Instead of beautifying the building, the massive cleaning project had – astoundingly – seemed to rob the joint of a good deal of its "character". In the late-fifties, the historic building would be demolished! (Wouldn't <u>everything</u> be destroyed?) The City Hall site would be converted to a small park – over a brand new underground parking garage. Progress! Ya can't beat it!

The city offices would be combined – with those of Wayne County – in the new *City/County Building*, a United Nations Building look-alike, further down Woodward, close by the waterfront.

Parks peered down toward the Detroit River – and the pier which housed both three-decker Bob-Lo steamers. The *Columbia* and the *Sinclair* would chug up and down the mighty Detroit River – to and from the Canadian amusement park/picnic island – until the nineties. For decades, the steamers had offered romantic moonlight cruises, on weekends – and, for decades, thousands of people had taken advantage of the dreamy excursions. Alas, late in the twentieth century – the boats would be scrapped! Would stop running to Bob-Lo. The thought of the demise of those two beautiful ships would've caused Parks great trauma! Some of the happiest days of his childhood had been spent on them. The park itself had always seemed like almost an anti-climax.

Standing out – among the dozens of storefronts on lower Woodward Avenue – were the marquees of the two burlesque theaters: *The Empress* and *The Avenue*. The house comedian at the latter – for well over 20 years – had gone by the name of "Scurvy". Parks chuckled to himself. He'd caught "Scurvy's" act! Many times! He'd never gone out of his way to publicize his many trips to "The Burley-Que".

Gazing up the other way, Parks felt a trace of dizziness once again – as he beheld so many equally-familiar storefronts! Glorious stores and buildings from his childhood.

Grinnel's had been a multi-storied store devoted to music: Records, sheet music, piano rolls, instruments! Whatever you wanted, if it had to do with music, it was sure to have been on one of the floors at **Grinnel's**. Jim had especially loved their massive record department. The wondrous store got records – before anyone else in town! Great!

One establishment that he'd totally forgotten was the old *TeleNews Newsreel Theater*. As its name would suggest, the movie house featured newsreels, documentaries and travelogues exclusively. It was from the "radio lounge" of the *TeleNews* that Harry Heilmann had described the road games played by the Detroit Tigers. In the thirties and forties, the play-by-play announcers did not travel with the team. Too expensive.

When the Tigers played in another team's stadium, Heilmann would "reconstruct" the contests from the **Western Union** ticker – at the *TeleNews*. In the fifties, such "reconstruction" would become an art form – featuring simulated crowd noises, crack-of-the-bat sound effects and other such sophistry. However, in the thirties and forties, the only background noise heard on the Tigers broadcasts was that of a ticker. A really eerie sound – when contrasted with the sounds of the crowd at home games.

In the thirties and early- and mid-forties, Detroiters were treated to two different broadcasts of their team's games – play-by-play by Ty Tyson on station WWJ and Heilmann on WXYZ. The memories of switching stations at different times of the game, brought a warm glow to the heart of Parks Hayworth. Memories long forgotten. Till that moment.

He made his way down Woodward Avenue – to *The Guardian Building* – known in 1939 as *The Union Guardian Building*. The ornate structure was, at that time, second in height only to *The Penobscot Building*.

Dolly Sidorwitz was – Parks was certain – employed by *McNeil & Wilkins*, in 1939. *M&W* was a prestigious law firm, in *The Union Guardian Building*. A check of the directory in the huge, high-ceiling lobby indicated that their offices were located on the 22nd floor – exactly as he'd remembered.

Parks thought back to one of his most frightening moments ever: The dreadful experience had taken place in the same building – when he'd been six or seven. In 1938 or 1939.

It had taken place on a bitter-cold, stormy day. His father had dropped little Jimmy off outside – giving him elaborate directions where to find the elevator. And specific instructions: He should ask operator to let him out on the 22nd floor. The boy had been quite upset at his father's treatment of him. You'd have thought that he was a baby or something. He knew perfectly well where his mother's office was – and how to get there. He'd been there many times.

However, as little Jimmy had stepped into the elevator, he had been struck by a shattering thought: Did it cost money to ride the elevator? Like a bus or a streetcar? If so, he was out of luck! He had no "elevator fare".

It would take forever to walk up 22 flights of stairs – if, of course, he was even able to find the stupid staircase. The youngster didn't really know whether the building even <u>had</u> stairs, for heaven's sake.

He'd never been so relieved in his young life – as when he had stepped out, unscathed, on the 22nd floor. Ah, memories! He was caught up in a whirlpool of memories.

A warm feeling accompanied Parks Hayworth, as he entered one of the many elevators. Maybe – just maybe – he'd gotten off his damnable roller coaster! At long last! About damn time!

On the 22nd floor, he made his way down the long, white-marbled hallway, toward his mother's office – at the very end of the corridor. Stopping just short of the frosted glass door, he stared at the ponderous, intimidating, gold-leaf, letters, which spelled *McNeil & Wilkins – Attorneys At Law*.

He thrust open the door to the reception area. It was much larger than he'd remembered.

Another surprise was the switchboard operator: Madge – the sister of his very favorite aunt. Parks had not remembered her working for *M&W*. She'd married a man from St. Louis – when little Jimmy was eight-years-old – and had moved to the Missouri city, with her husband. Jim had seen Madge, from time to time, during her infrequent visits to Detroit.

Something else to think about: He'd most certainly have to try and strike up an acquaintance with his Uncle Paul and Aunt Genevieve. The latter was Madge's sister – and a positive saint. His favorite aunt. Even more so than Aunt Juanita.

Parks closed the door – then, grabbed a hurried look at the desk in the far-right corner. It was vacant. He'd hoped – fervently hoped and prayed – that Dolly Sidorwitz would have been seated there. His disappointment had blown away the warm fuzzies he'd experienced on his way up.

"Can I help you?" Madge's high-pitched, almost-squeaky, voice hadn't changed.

"Uh … yes. Uh, well I … "

"Yes?"

"You see, I … "

Parks froze! His eyes were riveted to the figure of his mother – as she walked out from one of the inner offices. He'd been right! She <u>was</u> the most beautiful woman in the world!

He thought of the Dolly Sidorwitz he had seen just 18 months earlier – in 1978 – at his father's funeral.

Parks, as Jim, had driven up to Detroit with his oldest son, Dave, and with Cynthia and Cynthia's husband, Mike – arriving the day of the wake. Dolly had aged significantly, in the two years since he'd moved from Michigan. Yet, she still had retained a goodly portion of her beauty.

Parks – standing in 1939 and beholding the breathtakingly-lovely Dolly was completely flabbergasted! She was about 20 years his junior! Back to the old roller coaster!

He felt the floor begin to pitch and buck beneath his feet!

He was barely aware of Madge's nasal voice: "Are you all right, Sir? Is there anything I can get for you?"

Amazing! Madge – who, like his grandmother, had absolutely no idea who he was – had expressed <u>concern</u> over him! Incredible! In 1979, such things never happened! Well, or so it seemed.

He couldn't pry his eyes from the lovely form of his mother!

"No … uh … no," he muttered, absently. 'I'm … I'm fine."

Finally, the realization that there was no escaping his penetrating stare caused Dolly to look up – and lock her eyes directly on him.

"May I help you?" she asked from the far corner of the huge room. The melodic voice had changed little over the years.

"I'm … I'm sorry, Ma'am," Parks was able to stammer. "I don't think I've ever seen such … such a beautiful woman as you are. You're positively breath-taking! You really are!"

His mother blushed! Another one! Unbelievable! Three in one day!

"I haven't the faintest idea who he is, Dolly," explained Madge.

Tearing his eyes from his mother, Parks rasped, "I … I guess I'm probably in the … in the wrong office. I've been here once before … and this doesn't look very familiar. I mean … uh … I've only been in the office that I'm looking for … only been in it once before. And … and … and … and this doesn't look like it. I'm … I guess I'm a little bolixed up."

"A little what?" asked Madge.

"Mixed up."

"Well, that's certainly true," responded Madge, as Dolly approached the switchboard.

To his mother, he pleaded, "Look, Ma'am. I'm … not trying to be funny or anything, but I … "

"Well that's a good thing," interrupted Madge. "Because you're not. You're certainly not funny. Not funny at all."

"… but," continued Parks, ignoring Madge "would it be possible for you to have a … a cup of … a cup of coffee? A cup of coffee … with me?"

In the seventies, of course, such an invitation would seldom have been thought untoward! Well, not completely outrageous!

Our hero was obviously experiencing much more difficulty than he could ever have dreamed possible – in attempting the adjustment to the much more genteel era of the late-thirties. Why should that be so? A horrible puzzlement! Jim Sidorwitz had always considered himself completely out of touch with the mores of the seventies. With the customs and mores which had developed – beginning in the sixties.

He was offended by that era's "openness". He'd been certain – for years and years – that he would be far more comfortable in the more proper thirties. Yet, there he was: A terribly forward – a terribly "open" – person! Forward! Open! And bombing!

Dolly, obviously distressed, was able to half-whisper a tormented, "No. No thank you. Thank you anyway, but … "

At that point, Parks brought the most traumatic day of his life to its nadir:

He began to sob! Uncontrollably! He was overwhelmed with dizzying wave upon dizzying wave of kaleidoscoping emotions! Who knew what they were? Where they were coming from? Who knew how long they'd last? Who knew if they'd ever go away, for heaven's sakes? He had absolutely no clue! Everything seemed so – so – out of reach! Totally beyond his control! He'd "lost it"! Probably inevitably! Possibly permanently! Permanently? Dear Lord!

His 1979 mother was 67-years-old. He would never see her again. Of that, he was more than positive.

His 1939 mother – his 27-year-old mother – was the only one he had! And there he was: Causing her an enormous amount of discomfort! Exactly the opposite of his intention! The realization – the reality that it would be next-to-impossible to ever foster any kind of relationship with her – simply consumed him!

Unnoticed by Parks, a third woman had entered the reception area. Distressed at what she'd seen, she had ducked back into one of the inner offices. The lady was Loretta Zandrynski. She was almost as beautiful as his mother. Little Jimmy had had an incurable crush on Loretta – from the time he'd been four or five. She used to bring him chocolate cigarettes – whenever she and her husband, Richard, had visited the Sidorwitzes.

A minute-and-a-half later, Loretta was back—with Lawrence Albright, one of the junior partners in the firm. One of the <u>larger</u> junior partners in the firm.

"What's going on here?" Albright practically shouted – his empty-barrel voice shattering what was left of our hero's psyche!

"I'm … I'm sorry, Sir," Parks was able to murmur. "It's just that … it's just that … it's just been a … a … a horrendous day for me, and I … and I … and I … I just … well, I just … stumbled in here by mistake. Then, I … "

"Good heavens, Man! Are you all right?" A smidgen of "boom" had left the attorney's voice. But, just a smidgen.

"Uh … yes. Yes, I am. I am. I'm all right. I'm … sorry."

Looking directly at Dolly, he rasped, "And I'm especially sorry … sorry, if I caused you any … any embarrassment. I certainly didn't mean to. Quite the opposite."

His mother stood – transfixed! Totally bewildered! Completely bemused!

Parks wheeled – and burst out of the office! Blinded by his tears, he bounced off the marble walls three different times – in his frantic run toward the bank of elevators!

He waited what seemed an eternity – 15 or 20 seconds – for a car! None came!

And there was Albright – heading his way!

Parks veered into the stairway – just beyond the elevators! He trundled down the steps – two and three at a time – till he reached the 18th floor!

Hurrying out into the corridor on that level, he hit the "Down" button, once again!

When – 30 seconds later – the car stopped and the door opened, he half-expected to find Albright inside. He was not! Well, at least something seemed to be going right.

Once out into the fresh air, Parks hurried to the **Cunningham's Drugs** on Griswold – two blocks away.

Dropping onto one of the stools at the lunch counter/soda fountain, he ordered a cup of coffee. He had a lot of thinking – a whole batch of sorting out – to do. The manner in which he was botching everything – literally everything – was beyond belief.

For years, as mentioned, he'd spent an inordinate amount of time daydreaming – fantasizing almost endlessly – about just such a situation as the one in which he'd found himself. Had found himself – at that very moment. In his imaginings, everything had always gone so swimmingly! So beautifully! So magnificently!

Never had a person been so obviously "constructed" for an era! Not like Jim Sidorwitz had been "assembled" for the late-thirties! "Born thirty years too late," he'd always maintained. 1939 <u>should</u> have been his era! Especially for a man armed with all this important knowledge! Certain of so many things – from the future:

- The world would not end – at least not until after November of 1979!
- No American cities would be bombed during World War II!
- Indeed, he should be warmly secure in the knowledge that we'd won the war!

It was an interesting paradox: The first time he'd passed through that World War, he'd been far too young for the draft. The second time would find him much too old.

Some people, in the seventies – <u>many</u> people in the seventies – had decried the sad fact that, in their opinion, the Second World War would wind up being the last truly romantic period in the history of The United States. Jim Sidorwitz had been one of them.

That had been one more reason Jim had yearned to relive "Those Wonderful Years". The forties had been a very special – albeit an exceptionally scary – time:

Virtually every citizen of Detroit – "The Arsenal of Democracy" – had been absolutely certain that the day (or, more probably, the night) would arrive, when enemy planes would come and bomb the city! It was inevitable! It was also terribly frightening! Yet, they all faced up to that "certainty"! Virtually <u>everyone</u> did! Now <u>that</u> was stress! And – look, Ma – no *Valium*! No *Ritalin*!

In every school in the area, air raid drills were conducted twice each week, during the early-forties! At a minimum!

At *St. Mary's of Redford*, everybody – students and faculty alike – would find themselves seated on the hard, uncomfortable, cement floor in the corridor, on the lower level – singing patriotic songs! Songs that dotted the roster of the weekly *Your Hit Parade* broadcasts. The tunes were very popular – throughout the entire country.

In the sixties and seventies, many of those ditties had been sneered at – as "too preachy" or as "oversimplifications". "Too jingoistic"! Such stuff was considered, at best, to be "campy". It was consistently derided by the "hip" (the overwhelming number of whom had not been alive during that special time). So many people had absoutely no conception of the feelings and emotions that had been abroad in the land, back then.

Parks would always have a warm place in his heart for *Praise The Lord And Pass The Ammunition,* and *Coming In On A Wing And A Prayer* – as well as *We've Got The Lord On Our Side, The White Cliffs Of Dover, God Bless America* and *This Is Worth Fighting For*. In the seventies, a number of left-wing groups had launched a concerted campaign – under the guise of Separation Of Church And State – to keep such politically incorrect songs from being sung/performed in any and <u>all</u> schools. <u>Any</u> reference to the Deity was considered politically incorrect! Especially in (shudder) the school, in the court, or in any government building.

He grimaced – as he recalled that one of the television channels in Houston had shown the 1945 Academy Award-winning short subject, *The House I Live In*, one night, in the late-seventies. When

Frank Sinatra had belted out the title song, it had been more than enough to bring tears to the eyes of Jim Sidorwitz. Now, Parks Hayworth – six years before that movie would even be made – found himself becoming a trifle misty.

His mood hardened, once more, as he recalled the written word of the television editor of one of Houston's dailies. In his revue, the writer was practically overcome – with disgust! Virtually sent into cardiac arrest! Aghast at the "blind patriotism" that the movie – and the beautifully-written, beautifully-performed song – had evoked.

<u>It was that</u> "<u>blind patriotism</u>" <u>that saved your ass</u> … <u>so you could write such drivel</u> thought Parks. Then, he wondered if he'd said <u>that</u> aloud.

He caught himself – a split-second before he banged his fist on the counter! The reaction of the Houston editor still rankled! Still, the last thing he would need, at that point, would be to call even more attention to himself. Till that moment, he'd been a walking-talking carnival sideshow! "Step right up, ladeez and gentlemen!" He most assuredly didn't need to expand his horizons in that area!

He closed his eyes – and took another heavy pull on his coffee. It was cooling rapidly. Not unlike his experience the night Mr. Horne had appeared.

Mr. Horne! Parks wondered if he and the "boys" were amused. Was a great deal of currency changing hands up there? Certainly, Jim Sidorwitz's rich, rewarding, wonderful, dream was turning into a complete nightmare! How many of the "boys" had bet any of their coin of the realm on the utter disintegration of such a glorious dream?

Hey! That was it! He was dreaming! Had to be! What else could it be? Of course! Of <u>course</u> it was a dream! It could be nothing more than that! A damn dream!

He pinched himself. The only result was a fair amount of pain in his left biceps.

Hmmmm! Okay – maybe it wasn't a dream! Could he be on some kind of hallucinating "trip"? Without benefit of drugs?

Wait a minute! Maybe <u>with</u> drugs! Maybe that was it! Maybe someone at the rent-a-car company had slipped some "stuff" into his coffee! Maybe it had been Rita – an assistant manager at the office! She had certainly been upset at what she'd considered blatant favoritism – shown to him by Charlie Lawrence, their new boss. Maybe she'd found out about his "obscene" raise. And had reacted at the perceived unfairness of it all. Maybe <u>that's</u> what had brought all this on! Maybe he was suffering the result of Rita's "getting back" at him!

Well, whatever she may have slipped him, it should be dissipated in a while. Soon. One would hope so, anyway. Hopefully it would not be long before he returned to earth. Yes, he'd decided. Soon he would come back down to earth.

<u>Down To Earth</u>? That was the title of the Larry Parks/Rita Hayworth flick! The movie which seemed to have played such an enormous part in the whole illusion. In the whole "trip"!

He giggled! The guy across the counter was staring at him! What else was new?

He giggled again – despite an effort not to! That caught the soda jerk's eye.

He found himself almost wishing that he actually had taken LSD – or one of the other hallucinogenic drugs – at some point in his life. He'd most certainly have a better handle on what was happening to him.

From what he knew – or thought he knew – about drugs, a "trip" was not supposed to last as long as the one in which he was currently in the midst. Maybe the perverted conception of time was part of the hallucination. The clock over the fountain told him it was 3:45 PM. Could he actually have "been under" <u>that</u> long?

Not likely. He was thinking too rationally.

"By you, this is rational?" he found himself mumbling.

More people were staring at him! Wonderful! Could he not go anywhere – do one single thing – without making a total ass of himself?

He would have to concentrate now! Concentrate on his every move – no matter how minute or seemingly insignificant! Almost like a baby learning how to walk. He would have to learn – for one thing – how to talk once again. His vernacular – his entire vocabulary, probably – was out of date. Well, it was out of date – in reverse.

As stated, a generous part of his longing to return to the thirties had been his yearning for a far more genteel way of life – one in which every other word was not the "F-word"! For women as well as for men.

Certainly, in 1939, he should be deliciously within his element. Jim Sidorwitz had detested the pushiness – the uncaring selfishness – of the sixties and seventies. He'd abhorred the fact that progress – that success, in fact, sometimes even survival – were all so closely equated with the pervasive, the in-your-face, aggressiveness of the culture from which he'd come. From which he'd "escaped"?

And there he was! In 1939! And horribly aggressive! It just didn't make sense! Nothing made any damn sense!

All at once, he realized that he'd acquired a splitting headache! Looking at the back bar, he spotted the old dark-blue, transparent, *Bromo Seltzer* bottle – mounted upside down atop the colorless, cylindrical, aluminum dispenser.

He ordered a *Bromo*!

It had been years – decades – since he'd seen a soda jerk make up a *Bromo*. Pouring the erupting liquid – pouring it rapidly, that was the secret – from one glass to another. He'd forgotten that the fizzie stuff was served in a dark-blue, transparent, tumbler – with the *Bromo Seltzer* logo emblazoned, in gleaming-white lettering, on the side.

A really proficient soda jerk could stage a memorable performance. The woman who'd mixed Parks' serving rated, maybe, a C-Plus. Hell, maybe a B-Minus.

He scoffled down the fizzing liquid in one long drag – the way he'd always done. It was quite a shock – to find that the exercise had left him dazzlingly short of breath.

He was beginning to perk up again! Thank God! Another trip to the top of the old roller coaster. All part of the action! Especially in some stupid pipe dream!

On the other hand, would a pipe dream be so infinitely detailed? Even down to the logo on the side of the stupid glass? Who knew? Who the hell knew?

He sighed heavily – and tugged at his earlobe. There was only one thing to do: He would have to go home! Home! That was a room upstairs – over some damn grocery store! A room across from Helen Shaddon's bailiwick!

He raised a thumb and forefinger to his closed eyes – and gently rubbed. It felt good.

There would be ample time, he decided, to be able to see Highland Park – the little city completely surrounded by Detroit. Except for the few blocks, where it bordered on Hamtramck.

Plenty of time to make an ass of himself in Highland Park!

As he boarded the trolley for his return trek out Grand River, it occurred to Parks that most of his problems that day might have been caused by the fact that he'd probably tried to do too much. And to do it too quickly. He'd been like a child – turned loose in a candy store. There'd been so many goodies – that he'd simply gone bonkers, in an attempt to wolf down every hunk of sweetness at once. He'd have to bite off his pleasures in much smaller chunks. Chew them at a far slower pace.

When he finally disembarked from the old trolley car – the trip out had seemed three or four times as long as his schlep downtown – Parks' state of mind was evolving once more:

Maybe – just maybe – he actually <u>was</u> on some kind of remarkable journey! If so, he was playing with a deck which was much different than that of anyone else! Astoundingly different! Including that of his parents! Including that of his grandparents. And – not insignificantly – including that of Helen Shaddon.

Retrieving his beloved Ford – and being mildly surprised to find the car exactly where he'd left it – he headed further out Grand River.

As he reached Oakman Boulevard once more, it occurred to him that he'd made the purchase of a radio his first priority. He'd done everything but! Typical! He decided to stop at **Sears** and pick one up. He paid the munificent sum of $14.95 for a table model *Zenith*. America didn't know it – but, the country was on the threshold of "The Golden Age of Radio". If he was irretrievably in 1939, Parks mused, he might as well take advantage of it.

SIX

The first full night in the room above the grocery store was one to remember:

As quickly and as easily as Parks had fallen asleep on his last night in 1979, he'd experienced exactly the opposite phenomenon on his first night in 1939. He tossed about, on the strange, creaky, bed – doing his best to determine whether he was comfortable or not.

His newly-purchased cathedral-shaped radio – tuned to WJR – was of little help.

The station had signed off the air at 1:00 AM. It had not occurred to Parks that, in the late-thirties, precious few stations would be broadcasting 24 hours a day. CKLW, across the Detroit River in Windsor, Ontario, happened to be one of them. However, the Canadian station's program held no interest for Parks.

He'd padded across to the dresser – and turned his new acquisition off. He made a note to buy a bedside stand. Having the radio way over on top of the dresser was all wrong.

Crawling back into bed, he continued to reflect upon the traumatic day – his first in his new era.

It was obvious, of course, that he would be unable to withstand many more such days. He felt akin to one of those metal balls in a pinball machine – one which was being buffeted about continually. He'd ricocheted, he was certain, off of everything on the game's surface. Lying in his bed was no help. He was unable to stop – or even slow down – the whirlpool that his mind (so called) had

Returning

become! It simply kept churning! Wouldn't give him a second's respite!

The most troubling questions, of course, had to do with his mother and his grandmother. Did either of them have any idea who he was?

Of course not, he reassured himself. How could they?

As little Jimmy, he'd not recalled either woman ever speaking of some idiot who'd made a complete ass of himself – and on the same day – in 1939.

Of course, in 1939, little Jimmy had been only seven. Would Dolly or Kate have spoken of such a thing in front of him? Especially if they were afraid that someone might be stalking them? Maybe stalking the entire family? Not likely.

Of course, if he'd not taken Mr. Horne up on his offer, then neither woman would've been confronted by some idiot who'd made a complete ass of himself. Dear Lord! It was so damn confusing!

On the other hand, he'd not been seven forever. Had the situation been such an overwhelming – such a traumatic – situation for either lady, he was certain that the experiences would have come up in family discussions, when he was older. One way or another, he was positive, he would've heard about it. Besides, the way his grandmother had broken up at his swan dive, in her front yard, would indicate that she'd been anything but severely traumatized. Still …

Still, as Yogi Berra was reputed to have said: "I can sum it up on one word … ya never know".

His mother, though! His mother was a whole different story. She'd seemed terribly upset! Horribly discombobulated!

Well, there was really nothing he could do about it. He'd just have to cool it.

Yes. And he'd also have to avoid – at all costs – using expressions like "cool it".

Back to his mother and grandmother: There'd be plenty of time to plan a whole campaign to ingratiate himself to his parents and grandparents – and, hopefully, his aunt and uncle. Well, he assumed that there'd be plenty of time. However, it was painfully clear that he couldn't really know. Mr. Horne had told him that – even as an archangel – he couldn't know. Archangels had no clue about such things. Neither did the "boys'.

Dear Lord! There was so much to think about: Medical techniques, for instance! Procedures in 1939 were quite primitive – when compared to the seventies. The same held for research and development. **Bristol Meyers** made *Vitalis*, back then. They made *Ipana* toothpaste and *Sal Hapatica* – a laxative. **Squibb** made aspirin tablets. Near the end of the 20th century, the two companies would merge. The new entity would be at the forefront of R&D – especially looking for a cure for cancer.

In 1978, Jim Sidorwitz had had an appendectomy – which, in and of itself, should not have been a major surgical event. Either in 1978 – or in 1938. The latter year was when his Aunt Juanita had "gone under the knife". She had her appendix removed – with no complications. She had been fine. Home from the hospital – and bright-eyed and bushy-tailed – in a matter of days. No complications whatever.

Jim Sidorwitz's appendix had ruptured, though. And abscessed! A terrible infection had set in! He'd been on the Critical list for almost two weeks. It had taken all the doctor's skill and diagnostic expertise to keep him alive. To identify and then isolate the "bug"! Then, to prescribe appropriate antibiotics.

Antibiotics which, most assuredly, would not have existed in 1939.

Had that same ailment struck him on that very day – his first in the late-thirties – he would never have survived! Of that, he was certain.

Well, hopefully, he'd be around for awhile. He was counting on it.

The following morning, Parks awoke at 5:30 AM. Despite the fact that his "curiosity buds" had been recharged, there certainly was nothing to do or see at that hour.

He forced himself to try and go back to sleep. It almost worked.

At six o'clock, he got up and flicked on the radio.

The dial was still set at CKLW. Parks grinned broadly as *The Early-Morning Frolic* – starring Joe Gentile and Toby David – signed on! It had been one of his favorite shows! For his entire life! It had also been one of Detroit's favorites. The show was to last into the mid-fifties.

Ralph Binge had replaced Toby David in the early-forties. Jim Sidorwitz had always preferred Binge. Apparently, so did almost everyone else.

The program had been a real phenomenon. Joe Gentile – no matter with whom he was working – had kept virtually all the shows sponsors, for well over twenty years.

Ralph Binge had died in 1963. The last Parks had heard, Joe Gentile was still the public address announcer at *Tiger Stadium*.

In the late-fifties, Toby David had returned to CKLW – on the television side – as "Captain Jolly", hosting the *Popeye* cartoon show. He became a favorite with the kids.

Soupy Sales had gotten his start in Detroit, in those years – doing a show on WXYZ-TV. Soupy and "Captain Jolly" were to become the two icons in local kids' programming.

During Toby David's tenure on *The Early-Morning Frolic*, listeners constantly wrote in, requesting that Joe hit Toby over the head with the frying pan, which came across with a loud CLANG! – accompanied by an insipid cry of pain from Toby.

On those occasions when someone in the radio audience felt particularly sadistic – or had it in for Toby – he or she would request that Joe throw Toby down the elevator shaft – with accompanying, highly-outrageous, sound effects, of course.

Those fans who <u>loved</u> Toby would ask that Joe merely hit him over the head with the bottle. The sound effect was a DOINK! The cry of pain was not quite so pronounced – but, equally as idiotic.

Unsophisticated? You bet! Pure cornball? Right on!

The show was, of course, unmitigated nonsense. A far cry from the "sophisticated", the "relevant", the "pungent" (and, most usually, the highly off-color) "humor" of "raunch radio" or "shock radio", which had begun in the late-sixties or early-seventies. One such program – in early-morning – was aptly named *Rude Awakening*. It lived up to its title.

The Early-Morning Frolic had featured no "biting social commentary". And, as outrageous as this may sound, neither Gentile nor David ever "dissed" anyone! And the entire Motor City loved it! It was great fun – and didn't offend anyone!

It never would've survived in the seventies.

In addition to the lack of irreverence – and the single-entendre, potty-mouthed, "humor" of Jim Sidorwitz's seventies – the show was, for all practical purposes, three hours of non-stop commercials – broken up occasionally with the playing of a record and/or top-of-the-hour newscasts by Val Claire.

The duo's "Dramas From Real Life" were every bit as funny – and as corny – as Parks had remembered. The claims for the sponsors' products and services were so exaggerated – and so outrageous – that no one was offended by the hyperbole. Everyone recognized the show as pure nonsense.

The public – while recognizing the stretch of imagination around which the commercials were built – bought the products and patronized the services. That, of course, was before all the truth-in-advertising legislation and consumer groups began to abound. Ralph Nader would've been in cardiac arrest!

In the mid-forties – long after Ralph Binge had replaced Toby David – the show had moved to WJBK, in Detroit. And had retained virtually its entire stable of sponsors.

On Parks' second day in 1939, it happened that Joe bonked Toby with the frying pan – right at the top of the show! Parks, of course, broke up! Once more, it was a monumental struggle to stifle the potential gales of uproarious laughter! He certainly didn't want to awaken Helen Shaddon. She'd advised him, the day before, that she was a light sleeper. He especially didn't want to awaken her with an avalanche of uncontrollable laughter!

Parks spent a leisurely day – tooling about the Motor City.

After "breakfast" – two hamburgers and coffee at the sainted **White Tower** – he drove to Highland Park. He was delighted to find that it was as familiar to him as he could've hoped. It was virtually the same little city to which he, his mother and sister had moved in the fall of 1947. Some of the happiest days of his life – well, his childhood – had been spent in the apartment on Tyler Street, in Highland Park.

After lunching at the Highland Park branch of the **White Tower** chain, he piloted his beloved Ford past many familiar landmarks throughout the metropolitan Detroit area. Past homes of relatives and friends – as well as many businesses which, he knew, would not survive into the sixties and seventies.

A blessing: He encountered no one who would send him into the same sort of frenzy he'd experienced so frequently the day before.

That second day set the pattern for many more to follow: Parks would awaken early, put on Gentile/David – sometimes dozing and sometimes not – then, rise when it suited him. His life was almost like a vacation. Well, exactly like a vacation.

From time to time, he'd walk across Mansfield and attend Mass at *St. Mary's*.

The nuns had begun to filter back from their "mother house", in nearby Monroe – where all but a few would spend their summer in retreat. School would be opening soon.

Little Jimmy had not attended the school until the fall of 1941. Parks was not at all certain that Sister James Mary would have been assigned to the facility in 1939. It certainly would be nice to see her again, though.

Then, one morning in late August it happened! Wonder of wonders! He saw her!

There she was! Sister James Mary! He'd been seated ten or twelve pews from the altar, when she'd walked in! She'd made her way to the front pew and knelt. She was joined, after a few minutes, by Sister Jane Loretta and Sister Perpetua. A couple of minutes later, in strode Sister Martin Therese – a huge nun. She was every bit as large as Parks remembered. She'd put little Jimmy across her lap one time – and had used a thick ruler on him! He'd never stepped out of line in her room again!

It was old home week at *St. Mary's of Redford*!

Jim Sidorwitz – and now Parks Hayworth – had always held nuns (any nuns) in the highest of esteem. He believed – even long into adulthood – that they were all saints! Every one of them. They had to be – to have put up with him and some of his out-of-control classmates! As a group, they were so saint-like – that he couldn't imagine any of them ever having to go to the bathroom!

The presence of those dear nuns added to the warm glow provided by the Mass itself. Parks had always loved the Latin Liturgy. He'd always believed that the changes wrought by Vatican II, in the sixties, had turned the Mass into something akin to a PTA meeting. It had lost its pizzazz. There was no pomp. No circumstance. Everything which had served to make the service so special had been changed. Or discarded.

The loss of splendor – the absence of the pageantry – had been part of the reason that Jim Sidorwitz had strayed from the Church, in the late-sixties. So, it was great to get back – particularly to the beauty of the Latin Mass. Especially the grandeur of the High Mass. It had taken centuries – literally centuries – to compose and refine all those breathtakingly-beautiful Gregorian Chants. They'd been discarded – virtually overnight! A source of heartbreak for Jim! He had always been particularly upset at the newer "guitar" Masses. He'd always felt as though he'd just attended the *Peter, Paul & Mary* concert.

Throughout his life, Jim had seldom eaten breakfast. Parks, though, was another matter. He'd gotten into the habit of wolfing down a late breakfast/early lunch in that wondrous **White Tower**, at Grand River and Oakman. Hamburgers for breakfast? He couldn't get enough of them!

Virtually every day found him driving past his "Dream House", on Grandmont.

Seldom did he ever see anyone there. There had been one incident in which he'd observed little Jimmy toddling his way home from *Calvin Coolidge Elementary*.

The experience had, once more, choked him up! What else?

Obviously, he was not "ready for prime time" – when it came to making an attempt to interact with any of his family. Would he ever be?

Another time, he saw Marilyn Faffenberger's mother standing on her front porch. He'd completely forgotten what she'd looked like. A rather portly woman – but, with an exceptionally pretty face.

Then, one evening, just as dusk was falling, he saw his mother! She was seated in a lawn chair on the front porch of his exquisite "Dream House".

And that wasn't all! His father was sitting on the cement steps! It was the first time Parks had been able to observe his father – since he'd returned from 1979. Another dizzying experience!

He swerved his car to the curb – about halfway down the block – and sat for several long moments, with his eyes closed.

"Pop," he rasped to himself. "Pop."

Bernard Sidorwitz had passed away in 1978 – about 18 months before Mr. Horne's visit.

His father had been hospitalized for almost seven years, before his death! The incapacitation had been the terrifying result of a massive stroke! Bernie's entire right side had become paralyzed. His arm and leg had eventually atrophied – resulting in the amputation of his right leg! Just below the knee! Parks shuddered! How God-awful that had looked! It had been the last straw! The final indignity!

The old man had died shortly thereafter!

Parks still quivered – when he thought of the horribly-withering looks which would cross Pop's face, when he'd chance to glance down at the grotesque remains of the butcher-like amputation! Dear Lord!

Jim had seen his father shrivel from a six-foot, 245-pound, giant of a man – to a virtual 90-pound, emaciated, pasty-complexioned, skeleton! Another head-to-toe shudder overcame the badly-shaken Parks Hayworth!

Jim had moved from Detroit to Houston, in early 1976. He'd returned twice to the Motor City – putting himself "fanny-deep in hock" to do so. Each time he'd returned, the fact of his father's continued deterioration would be that much more starkly evident! That much more emphatic!

A tear trickled down Parks' cheek. As trite as it had always sounded – as trite as it would always sound – death, for his father, had truly been a blessing. He had – indeed – "gone to a better place"!

Now, though – at that almost-sacred moment – Parks Hayworth looked, once more, at his father. Bernie Sidorwitz! A strong, vital, virile, man of 33! It was enough to send him, once again, into his patented, all-too-familiar world of light-headedness!

He sat there, in his '37 Ford, for fully five minutes! Would the cobwebs <u>never</u> clear?

Once he felt he'd steadied sufficiently, he got out of the car – and walked back up the block, toward the young couple. It would be, he knew, a stupid move to let Dolly recognize him. It had been almost two months – since the disturbance in her office!

Parks glanced across the street, at his parents. Dusk was shrouding him somewhat. It was also clouding his own view. He was surprised at the flush of emotion he was experiencing toward his father.

In his childhood – on into his young adulthood – he'd not been especially close to the elder Sidorwitz. Bernie had worked seven-days-a-week, during World War II. Gone years without a day off! It was then that Pop's drinking problem had begun to control him. That certainly had not helped the father/son kinship. The relationship reached its nadir in the mid- and late-forties, when Jim had been in his mid-teens.

When Dolly and Bernie had separated in 1947, Jim had been overjoyed! The father/son relationship was to remain strained for a couple decades thereafter. It would not be until the final twelve or fifteen years of the old man's life that father and son had become reasonably close.

In some ways, Jim had ultimately become closer to his father than to his mother.

In other areas, however, the gap, which had been born – and nurtured – in Jim's childhood could never be totally abridged. Not really. It presented Parks with a strange paradox of love, and maybe not-love! Certainly regret! Tons of regret! And foreboding!

Seeing Bernie again elicited all kinds of emotions and memories – all of which defied analysis.

As Parks walked past his parents, he experienced an overwhelming, all-consuming sensation: A feeling of total helplessness! Not simply just another emotion! This one was unlike anything he'd ever known before! Who could ever imagine such a degree – such a depth – of complete and utter powerlessness! Of such impotence!

Knowing all the trials, the problems – the ravaging heartbreak – that lay ahead for the contented-looking couple, a devastating, all-pervasive, feeling of gloom engulfed him. He was so – so powerless!

So very powerless! How could he ever warn them? How would he be able to do anything – <u>anything</u> – to help them? Dear Lord!

What would that virile young man – seated on the steps across the street – think, had he known that his last seven years on the planet would be spent in a foul-smelling, public nursing home? What would he do – knowing that he would shrivel into a shell of the man that Parks was staring at? What would it do to him – to know that he would eventually lose the bottom half of his right leg? In some dreadful, depressing, urine-drenched, filled-with-despair, building? Dear Lord!

Again, Parks suffered an almost-overwhelming spasm – as the horrible image of the mangled remains of his father's leg consumed him! How would Pop ever cope with the knowledge that he would die virtually penniless? Virtually? Literally penniless!

Tears streamed down Parks' cheeks – as he reached the corner of Grandmont and Orangelawn. He dared not walk back the same way. For one thing, there was the chance that Dolly would recognize him – even in the fading light. For another, he couldn't stand the emotional impact of looking at his father again. Not at that moment, in any case.

He turned left and walked a block to Abington Street, turned left again, made his way down to West Chicago – then, back to Grandmont, and his precious Ford.

Despite his resolve to not gaze at his father again, he swung the car around – and drove, slowly, past the "Dream House".

"Like a damn magnet," he muttered aloud. "Like a damn magnet!"

He noticed his father's 1936 Dodge four-door sedan in the driveway. Pop would not buy his '37 Ford club coupe for another two or three years. Not until the family had moved into the small house on Penrod. The Dodge had been a neat car too.

Another month passed. Parks continued to scan the want ads – in all three daily papers. He'd found absolutely nothing in the way of employment opportunities! Except for the occasional clerking job – at fifteen glorious dollars a week. Each and every week. Not lucrative, by any means. But, actually, not terribly bad – for the times.

He'd applied for two positions – and, of course, had gotten neither! He'd been unable to "phony up" a synthetic work history. Employers shied away from a 47-year-old man, with no verifiable references – as though he was a carrier of the plague!

It was, most certainly, a buyer's market! In spades!

Parks had paid Helen Shaddon three months rent in advance. That had happened a week after Mr. Horne's visit – so, a roof over his head was not a panic priority. Not yet, anyway.

However, a goodly amount of panic was beginning to set in! He was down to slightly more than $125.00.

Of course, he owned his beloved '37 Ford – and gas was less than 20-cents a gallon – so he was not in dire straits in that area. Food, certainly, was cheap enough. As long as there was a **White Tower**, he was in good stead – eating-wise. He certainly needed no new clothing.

He'd been frugal all his life. His lifestyle in the fifties, sixties and seventies had demanded that he be the next thing to a penny-pincher. So, having been broke all his life, Parks had watched his expenses closely, in his new era. No matter how tight he was with a buck, though, sooner or later the money was going to run out! Then, what would he do? Well, he'd jolly-well better come up with a source of revenue! Damn soon!

Then, it hit him!

He'd been looking at the negative side all along! How twisted could *that* be?

While it was true that he possessed absolutely no mechanical skills – and did not own a degree – Parks was a man with 25 years of experience in the rent-a-car business! It was a field practically unheard of in 1939! Well, in its infancy, anyway.

Hertz was – for all practical purposes – the only rental company extant. Their Detroit operation was small – infinitesimal by 1979 standards. Parks quickly determined that his chances of catching on with "Number One" were practically nil.

The situation became scary once again!

Well, frightening – until Parks decided that his only chance at survival would be to give Ol' **Hertz** a little competition!

He was certain that he could pull it off – whatever "it" would turn out to be! It was time – way past time – to break out of all the negativism! He threw himself into contriving an irresistible sales pitch!

He tried it on eleven new car dealers! They'd all resisted!

The gist of Parks' presentation had played upon the fact that he'd worked for a mythical car rental company in Houston – for almost twelve years. Despite the fact that the company was – in Parks' pitch – no longer in business, the experience had provided our hero with the expertise to set up a profitable rent-a-car operation! Right smack-dab at the lucky dealer's location!

He'd hoped to convince that lucky dealer that a rental division would not only be an excellent source of additional revenue for the dealership – but, as a significant bonus, would provide a wonderful "feeder" for the used car lot.

Of course, Parks was not at liberty to reveal to that fortunate soul just how valuable a used car – <u>any</u> used car – would be in two or three years – once World War II would have mandated that the automobile factories convert to the war effort. To do so, of course, meant that they would stop producing cars! Obviously, existing cars would become more and more valuable, as time went on.

As stated, the eleven dealers chose not to be so lucky.

The twelfth dealership was **Keller-Dubin Motor Car Company** – a Ford store!

Parks paused, before entering the showroom on Grand River, at Schaeffer Highway. He was aware, of course, that Clark Dubin – of **Keller-Dubin** – had founded a rent-a-car company in the late-thirties or early-forties. Jim Sidorwitz had, in fact, worked for **Dubin Rent-a-Car** in the late-fifties. At that point, the company had become the second-largest entity in the industry.

Parks had not known exactly when Mr. Dubin had gone into the car rental business. In early October, 1939, though, the company did not exist!

Dare he hope? Yes, he could! Clark Dubin <u>was</u> interested!

Parks was able to sell Mr. Dubin – a tall, heavy-set, rumpled-looking, giant of a man, with a deep, booming, voice – on the idea of setting up a company, entirely separated from the dealership!

Clark Dubin was willing to crank up the company with twelve 1939 Fords – purchased by the fledgling company from the **Keller-Dubin Motor Car Company**. The fact that the 1940 models had already been introduced weighed more than slightly in Dubin's decision.

The company was christened **Dubin Auto Rental**!

Dubin's partner, Horace Keller, was not interested in the new venture! Not interested – aside from the fact that the dealership had sold the embryonic company twelve cars, from what was considered "last year's inventory".

Privately, Keller had called Dubin a complete idiot – for even thinking about investing in such a "flea-brained scheme"! In addition, Keller had insisted on – and had received – a ghastly-high rental fee for the nominal office space which **Dubin Auto Rental** would require, at the dealership's location. The demand had upset Clark Dubin! Had upset him – to the point that Parks was certain that his new-found connection was destined to die aborning!

However – to Parks' immense relief – Dubin advised him that, having come that far, he would not be derailed by an obscene rental fee!

Sooner or later, Keller would pay!

Parks indoctrinated two of the ladies in the Title & Accounting Department into the "drive yourself" business. Once Miss Ellis – and her assistant, Gertie – and been sufficiently trained, our boy was free to get out on the street! And begin hustling!

It didn't take long to get the new company launched! The market, of course, was nowhere nearly as lucrative – nor as pervasive – as it had become in the fifties, sixties and seventies. The other side of the coin, however, was the fact that competition was not nearly as fierce. In fact, there was no competition!

Hertz, had been so long entrenched that management apparently had felt no need to aggressively promote their service. Everyone knew who they were – and where they were located. In a veritable monopoly, it isn't difficult to become complacent.

Parks beat down the door of every insurance company and every collision shop upon which he was able to blunder. Within two weeks, a minimum of ten of **Dubin's** cars were on rental – at all times! Frequently, the operation would be out of cars altogether.

Parks' founding of **Dubin Auto Rental** was the supreme irony: As Jim Sidorwitz, he'd started in the business in 1957 – as a rental agent for **Dubin Rent-a-Car**, as the company would become known. Jim's mind would've boggled – on that day in January, 1957 – had he known how the company had begun!

Needless to say, Clark Dubin was ecstatic with the early results. In 1939, Dubin knew little about the business. It was his plan to add another twelve cars in mid-November. Parks advised him not to act in haste. Historically, from Thanksgiving Day – until the middle of January – the car rental industry is exceptionally flat. Parks assumed that, in 1939, the period would be all-too-similar to the disaster area it had always been, in the fifties, sixties and seventies.

He was certain that he could maintain a satisfactory utilization percentage, with the twelve cars – but, would be hard-pressed to increase business during that period. A fleet of 24 cars, at that point, made no sense.

When, in December, Dubin noted that utilization had dropped slightly, he was not alarmed. Parks had prepared him for the small decrease – and had assured him that business would most certainly pick up again in the latter weeks of January. True to Parks' projection, revenues took a sharp upswing in the third week of January.

Dubin Auto Rental doubled its fleet in February – and more than doubled its revenue! And its profits!

Our hero's expertise in the field so impressed Clark Dubin that, in the spring of 1940, he gave his rising star *carte blanche* over the entire operation. He removed himself from day-to-day oversight of the company. Parks was in total charge!

The arrangement worked well. While Dubin was becoming more and more fascinated with the business, he recognized that Parks – at that point, anyway – possessed "far more car rental smarts".

Dubin could not have known, obviously, that, in less than two years, the country would be at war! There would be precious few 1942 automobiles! And absolutely no 1943, 1944 or 1945 models! Used cars, as previously noted, would become extremely valuable!

Parks had determined, of course, that the larger his fleet at the end of 1941, the better off **Dubin Auto Rental** would be. He also knew that – with the advent of gasoline rationing – a car rental company would be severely restricted.

The automobiles themselves, though, would be worth plenty!

Further, Parks assumed that Clark Dubin would not be adverse to "sticking it to" his partner, in the dealership. Horace Keller had thrown every roadblock imaginable in the path of the car rental entity – beginning with the astronomical office-space rental fee.

Thus, when the 1940 and 1941 models would become invaluable, Parks was certain that Dubin would not hesitate to charge the dealership astronomical prices for the rental cars – as fodder for the used car lot.

The dealership would, obviously, still realize a tidy profit on the units – even after paying a king's ransom for the vehicles. Parks imagined that Dubin might even consider selling them retail – totally independent of the dealership.

Taking advantage of the fact that Dubin had left him to his own devices, our boy set about making preparations for World War II – almost two years before Pearl Harbor Day! As he built his fleet – slowly, but steadily – the company began to turn even more substantial profits!

In June of 1940, Clark Dubin rewarded Parks Hayworth with 20% of the company – along with a substantial raise in salary! Considering the economy of the era, the new wage was more money – by far – than Parks had ever earned in his life.

Even more – after cost of living adjustments – than in 1979; his last raise from Charlie, his new boss, notwithstanding! Yes, even more than he would've been taking home – after his "obscene" raise in pay!

SEVEN

Though Parks' earnings had quadrupled by the summer of 1940, he had remained at the room above the grocery store on Grand River and Mansfield. It was becoming a source of some concern to Clark Dubin – himself, very much a *bon vivant* – that his "rising star" would not move to more luxurious (or, at least, less austere) living quarters.

Parks' reasoning, of course, was two-pronged:

First, he was endeavoring to invest every available dollar in the stock market, secure in the knowledge that the war boom – and the mind-boggling postwar expansion – would eventually pay him a more-than-handsome return, in the mid- and late-forties.

Many, many dollars! He could count on many, many dollars! If he lived that long!

He was feeling more and more secure in the belief that he would "last awhile". He <u>must</u> have been gaining confidence! For he had become fearful of entering his dotage without "a few bucks".

So, as an additional option, he began looking into buying real estate – warmed by the knowledge that land values would also skyrocket after the war. Of course, it would be awhile before he'd be able to inaugurate a full-fledged real estate portfolio. Hopefully, he'd have time to wait it out. Hopefully!

He'd been so broke – for so long! Becoming as affluent as possible – as quickly as possible – had become an obsession with our hero!

The other – and equally important – reason he'd remained in his tiny room was the lady who was ensconced across the hall.

Beginning in the fall of 1939, Helen Shaddon and Parks had begun to see more and more of one another. Their paths had crossed, once or twice, on Sunday mornings – as each had walked across the street to *St. Mary's* to attend 9:15 AM Mass.

Helen could hardly help but be impressed that Parks would bother to attend church. She'd heard so much about single men: Mostly, how they never went to church. A bunch of pleasure-seekers – interested in nothing but luring a poor unsuspecting woman into bed. Parks certainly did not fit that profile. In addition, she was touched by her boarder's total immersion in the service itself. It was almost as though he was afraid that the Latin Mass would, somehow, be taken from him. That, of course, was impossible. How silly.

From time to time, they would repair to **The Blue Ribbon Café** – a rather nondescript little restaurant on Grand River, just a few blocks from the **Keller-Dubin** dealership.

The "dates" – and that particular restaurant – had been Parks' idea. Not only was the eaterie handy to his office – for weekday lunches – but, it was not far from "Helen's Building".

Further, the place held a lot of "warm fuzzies" for our boy.

The Sidorwitz family – Bernie's and Dolly's family – had gone to dinner there, virtually every Sunday evening, through the early- and mid-forties. Almost since they'd moved from the "Dream House" to the little house on Penrod, in late-1939. Especially, once Bernie had begun to work those back-breaking seven-day weeks, during the War.

Sunday evening was the only time the family could be together.

As a little boy, Parks had enjoyed the weekly meals – despite the fact that, for a while, they'd been the source of further difficult feelings between him and his father.

One of many:

There had been one incident – just after they'd moved to the bungalow on Penrod – when little Jimmy had teased for a candy bar, while shopping with Bernie, in one of those new-fangled "super markets" (where you actually served yourself – picked your stuff right off the shelves. What would they think of next?)

Bernie had so berated the child – in front of all those other patrons – that Jimmy had resolved <u>never</u> to ask his father for <u>anything</u> again! Ever! And, even on those occasions when his mother was present – like at **The Blue Ribbon** – he still refused to ask for anything. As long as Bernie was around, the little guy simply never asked! Ever!

So, as he got bigger, the usual single hamburger simply did not suffice. But, the little boy steadfastly refused to ask for another.

Dolly must, somehow, have perceived that her son wanted more – or, maybe, needed more. So, she explored the wonders of a hamburger steak platter with little Jimmy – for which he'd been eternally grateful. That had been the only problem with the Sunday dinners, though – and it had gotten resolved. Eventually. So, on balance, the boy had thoroughly enjoyed them.

Now, during his second passage through 1939, going to brunch or dinner at **The Blue Ribbon**, with Helen, was especially nice. They spent hours there – talking. Helen seemed to enjoy their conversations at the café. Enjoy them immensely. To even, one could almost say, treasure them. Much more than Parks ever would've imagined.

His landlady had changed, since Parks had moved in. Changed enormously. Had "loosened up" – considerably. For her part, Helen attributed the sea change in her attitude and personality – and, as time went on, to her vernacular – to getting to know her "star boarder" better.

"You know?" she observed, one Sunday morning at the eaterie. "You have a way of drawing people out. I certainly never thought I'd turn into such a blabbermouth."

"Oh, Helen. C'mon. You're not a blabbermouth."

"There's times when I really feel like it. Like I feel that I am … really am an old blabbermouth. And I think that my whole … what's the word you always use? Vernacular, is it? I think my whole vernacular has changed a whole lot. Thanks to you."

"Awwww," he gushed, patting her hand. "You're just trying to brighten my day. And, you know what? You're succeeding!"

Like most Americans, Helen had become distressed as Hitler had begun his relentless march across Europe. Her son, Jeff, had enlisted in the Navy, the previous year, following his father's death.

In 1939, the war seemed to be coming closer and closer. In November, Helen had informed Parks that Jeff had been stationed on the *USS Oklahoma* – a battleship, which operated out of Pearl Harbor. Parks was certain that the "battlewagon" would be hit in the cowardly Japanese sneak attack, in December of 1941.

Once she'd informed Parks of the lad's assignment, the look of dismay, which had engulfed Parks, had set off an alarm – deep inside Helen. A sensation she would be at a loss to explain. Jeff's duty station was fast becoming a sore point between the two. Their lengthy conversations at **The Blue Ribbon** finally reached a point where they notably avoided any reference to the young sailor. The situation left Helen totally bemused.

Of course, no one in the United States – in the general population, at any rate – had a way of knowing that a <u>second</u> war was brewing! In the <u>Pacific</u>!

Jeff's military situation to the side, what had begun as a mostly dining arrangement was fast becoming something more. Something much, much deeper.

When the couple did not drive to **The Blue Ribbon**, Helen would invite Parks in to her "apartment", for dinner. Hers was the only room in the building with cooking facilities. As much as Parks enjoyed those home-cooked meals, he usually insisted that they eat out. Helen's life with Walter Shaddon had been terribly Spartan. Much more – substantially more – than had his own, as Jim Sidorwitz.

Things, it appeared, hadn't changed much for her, since she'd become a widow.

A meal in a restaurant was a real treat – a genuine delight – for her. Parks had never tired of beholding that special "Christmas Morning" look she took on whenever they dined out. He reached a point where he was so moved by her heart-felt pleasure at restaurant meals – that he insisted they eat out two or three times during the week.

Most usually, they'd go to a slightly more-swank eaterie. However, on Sundays, it was always **The Blue Ribbon**. Mostly mornings – but, an occasional evening. It had become a tradition. A nifty tradition.

One Sunday evening, in 1940, Parks had almost fallen out of his chair! Literally!

His mother and father – along with his infant sister Dee – had entered the restaurant. They'd had little Jimmy – eight-years-old – in tow!

Parks had tried – valiantly – to relate to Helen, during the meal. But, he could not! He tried – valiantly – not to look at the Sidorwitzes. That effort was equally unsuccessful. His mind seemed to resemble a bowl of oatmeal. Or maybe eggs. Yeah, that was it. Eggs. Scrambled eggs!

Helen, of course, was caught up in a strange – almost overwhelming – sense of unease. It began to gnaw at her! The same squeamish feeling she'd experienced the afternoon she'd told Parks of Jeff's assignment to the *Oklahoma*. She had no idea why Parks should be so distraught! On either occasion!

And she had no clue as to why she should be so troubled by his demeanor. On either occasion! All she knew was that it was terribly eerie!

With those notable exceptions, Parks and Helen were getting along famously.

Parks was, of course, a compulsive talker. Helen, while by no means shy, usually wound up doing much more listening than she did talking. She would occasionally tell him how "funny" he still talked. Usually when he was excited. Or upset.

It had taken great effort, but our hero had managed to divest himself of most of his seventies vernacular. He was able, for the most part, to adapt his style and manner of speech to the year in which he'd been transplanted.

Helen, as noted, had begun to speak much more fluently. And much more "Parks-like".

"I really think that the way you talk is rubbing off on me ... more and more," she'd said, one Sunday morning, with a hearty laugh.

They'd been standing in the hallway – having returned from breakfast at **The Blue Ribbon** – as Helen unlocked the door to her "apartment".

"Everyone," she continued, "all my friends ... they keep talkin' about how I don't talk the way I always did. They keep askin' me, 'Who's the guy?' They figure some guy's got to be responsible for the change. The change in my ... in my vernacular."

"What do you tell 'em?"

"Well, I start to tell 'em about you ... then, I get kinda embarrassed."

"Helen, you have to realize that ... for all those years ... you seldom got out of the house. All those years with Walter. Now, since he's passed away ... rest in peace ... you're an entirely different woman. In an entirely different situation. You're in an entirely different environment. Besides, you don't have to be embarrassed about us. It's perfectly normal for a healthy, vibrant, young woman to keep company with ... ahem ... a healthy, vibrant, young man."

"I guess that lets us both out," she answered, laughing heartily.

He cracked her, smartly, across her bottom!

"Boy," he observed. "You're getting awfully damn persnickety in your old age."

Evenings were usually spent holding hands – and listening to the ponderous floor-model *Zenith* radio Parks had bought for Helen. The set had taken up a goodly portion of one wall in Helen's "apartment" – which was, in reality, a large room, partitioned into kitchen/living/sleeping areas.

Helen had never been exposed to what Parks had always described as his "schmaltzy" music. Seldom had a musical program – of any sort – poured forth from the tiny, cheap, garish-red, plastic, radio in the Shaddon home, while Walter had been alive.

Like a large portion of her personality, Helen's tastes had begun to change – as her relationship with Parks had begun to deepen.

Together, the couple would spend entire evenings, listening to such programs as *The Bayer Album of Familiar Music, The Kraft Music Hall* – which starred Bing Crosby – as well as *Waltz Time* – featuring Frank Munn, "The Tenor With A Tear In His Voice".

A particular favorite was *Your Hit Parade*. The program was in its pre-Sinatra days. The singing star was Barry Wood. The show also included Mark Warnow's orchestra and – as the "girl singer" – Joan Edwards. Then, Bea Wain. Then, Joan Edwards again. Miss

Edwards was the niece of Gus Edwards – "Ukulele Ike" – the voice of Jimminy Cricket in Walt Disney's fabled *Pinocchio*.

As time went on, some of the music seemed to "get" to Helen. Certain lyrics would, in fact, move her to tears. Usually the same songs which made Parks misty.

He bought her a phonograph – and about 30 of the big, clunky, 78 RPM records of the day. Parks joked that he was afraid that he'd contracted a hernia – carrying the "platters" upstairs. The heavy load was the equivalent of a mere two or three long-playing albums of the future. Could, eventually, be condensed onto one single 90-minute cassette audio tape – which weighed mere ounces.

Parks' favorite radio program was Crosby's. Helen was partial to *The Fitch Bandwagon* – which starred Dick Powell, when he was still a singer. The show played between *The Jack Benny Show* and *The Chase & Sandborn Show* – which featured Edgar Bergen and Charley McCarthy, with Ray Noble's orchestra – on Sunday nights.

Sunday became their special radio night: In addition to Benny, Powell and Bergen/McCarthy, the never-ending parade of quality shows included *One Man's Family* and *Manhattan Merry Go Round*, which showcased tenor Thomas L. Thomas. All of these preceded *The Bayer Album of Familiar Music*, with Evelyn McGregor and Donald Dame. The star-studded evening was rounded out by *The Hour of Charm* program with Phil Spitalne's "All-Girl Orchestra" and featured "Evelyn And Her Magic Violin". (The latter was Mrs. Phil Spitalne.)

The more time the couple spent together, the more peaceful – and, paradoxically, the more fretful – Helen became.

She had never – she'd confessed to Parks – been so happy in her life. He was the answer to all her prayers. "Once I finally figured out that I should be praying for such things," she'd elaborated.

There were, though, the many things which disturbed her – although she was unable to explain why. Even to herself.

It was terribly upsetting to her that Parks seemed preoccupied with such minutiae as the shape of coffee cans. They were round and wide – and not very tall. What was the big deal? Or the tin *Log Cabin Syrup* cans – which were shaped like a little log cabin. You poured the syrup from the "chimney". Why was he so taken with the shape of the *Nabisco Shredded Wheat* box? Even the cardboard cards – which separated the layers of cereal biscuits – seemed especially to intrigue him.

In addition, her "star boarder" was – irrationally, she thought – enraptured with the commercials on the radio. "Plug uglies", as he'd called them.

Why should <u>anyone</u> be thrilled with jingles which extolled the virtues of such things as *Spud* cigarettes or *Old Dutch* cleanser? Or *Super Suds*? Or *Chipso* soap powder? Or *Campana Balm* skin lotion? Or *Odor-O-No* deodorant? Or *High-Speed* gasoline? Or *Ipana* toothpaste? Or *E&B Beer*, for heaven's sakes?

"Every time I see you getting all wrapped up in a *Teel* commercial," she'd admonished, referring to a red-liquid dentifrice, "I just get the most terrible feeling, Parks. Like … just like that night at **The Blue Ribbon**! If I live to be a hundred, I'll never know what came over you that night. Some things about you … there are some things about you, Parks … that they bother me. Really bother me. Scare me, don'tcha know. Frighten me. I wish I … "

"If I live to be a hundred, Helen, I probably won't know what came over me that night at the restaurant, either. I sure can't explain it … even to myself. And the commercials? Everyone … everyone, Helen … they have their own little quirks. Their own little idiosyncrasies. I happen to get bent out of shape over stupid commercials. Don't ask me why … because I really don't know why."

"There you go again," she groused. "You and your Texas talk. Parks, I've never heard anyone say 'bent out of shape' before. Never."

"Like I said, it's … it's a whole different world down there. A whole different way of talking."

"I'm sure that what you're telling me is true. But, Parks! It seems like you only use your language from Texas when you … only when you get upset. When you get all flummoxed."

"Flummoxed? I'm not flummoxed!"

"Oh, yes you are," she answered, pushing back a strand of grey/black hair. "Yes you are. I'm gettin' to where I can tell. Where I can tell pretty good."

She was right of course. She was becoming far more perceptive. A troubling thought!

It would not be until Christmas Eve of 1939 that they would become intimate!

Prior to that enchanted evening, they had held hands a lot. But, beyond that, they'd barely done much more than to share a kiss or two. Parks had sensed that – had he "pushed" too far, too quickly – he'd have scared the bejeebers out of Helen.

When the latter learned that Jeff would be unable to get leave – would not be home for the holidays – she'd become exceptionally morose.

The most joyous time of year – and there was Helen. Terribly blue!

She was, of course, no more melancholy than Parks. This would be his first Christmas without his children! His seven wonderful children!

He'd spent many hours – as the holidays had approached – parked outside the little bungalow on Penrod, to which the Sidorwitzes had moved. He was, by that time, authorized to use company cars for his personal use. He did his best to vary the models and colors – so as to avoid being noticed by his parents. Or little Jimmy himself.

Other times, he would spend hours at **Freddie's Bar** – at the corner of West Chicago and Burnette. A half-block from his grandparents' "Dog House". He'd look for his grandfather's light-green 1938 Buick outside the tavern. When he spotted the car in front of the beer garden, he never failed to stop in.

Usually his grandfather was by himself. During those times, Parks was able to talk at length with the wonderful man who'd so terrified him, when he was a child. The old man was exactly as Parks had remembered him: Gruff exterior – and all mush underneath.

Grandpa had always been interested in baseball and hockey. The bulk of the conversations had to do with the Tigers and Red Wings. Parks saw to that. Well, every now and then, there would be a question about Kate.

On the few occasions that his grandmother had accompanied Grandpa, things were – without exception – very difficult. Extremely tense. The dear woman, of course, remembered the episode wherein

Parks had fainted in her front yard. As a consequence, she was always apprehensive – terribly uncomfortable – in his presence. How sad.

And this had been his best buddy. His dearest friend. Sad – beyond words!

Still and all, it was wonderful to be able to see his grandparents again. Especially at the holiday season. It was just a honking tragedy that the relationship couldn't be much closer. Much, much closer.

Well (sigh) maybe someday.

On Christmas Eve, in Helen's "living room", it was a terribly morose couple which sat on the davenport – another word Parks had come to reacquaint himself with – and listened to the radio, silently holding hands. The gloom was pervasive enough that they'd left the dishes – filled with half-eaten food – on the table. Unheard of! Helen was a certified "clean nut"!

As beautiful carol after beautiful carol after beautiful carol poured out of the loudspeaker, each of them found themselves wiping away tears. More and more tears – as the evening had progressed.

Holding both of her hands between his palms, Parks began to kiss away her tears.

It was too much! She began to cry! To sob! Uncontrollably!

As Parks found himself caught up in Helen's sorrow, his own loneliness seemed to lessen. He held her tenderly against his chest – running a hand through her grey-streaked hair.

After ten or twelve minutes, she appeared to have cried herself out.

He continued holding her tightly, stroking the back of her neck – and gently kissing the top of her head. She would tense – then, relax. Press up against him – then, almost deflate. A few seconds later, the sequence would begin all over again.

Finally, looking up at him, she blinked her eyes – an heroic attempt to see through the blur of her tears – and rasped, "Parks? Who are you?"

It required a goodly amount of effort – for the question had rattled him – but, he nuzzled his cheek against her left temple and responded, "What do you mean by that, Pretty Lady?"

"You ... you're so ... so strange sometimes. Sometimes ... sometimes, I feel like you were ... were sent to me. Sent to me ... by heaven. By God himself."

The statement – coupled with her "Who are you?" question – had caught him completely off-guard.

"Aw g'wan with ya," he'd managed to respond. It had taken a monster-effort for him to maintain even a semblance of steadiness in his voice. "I'll bet," he continued, "I'll just bet that you say that to all the handsome, debonair, *bon vivant,* young men you share your davenport with."

"Stop kidding, Parks."

He was becoming more and more apprehensive by the second. Especially when she straightened into a sitting position – and began fussing with her hair.

"This moment," she said, "is not for kidding. With you ... when I'm with you, Parks ... there's times when I feel so ... so strange."

"Strange? What do you mean ... strange?"

"Just what I said. Strange! Why, just the looks you get sometimes. There's times when I almost feel like you're ... you're from ... well, almost, from another planet. From another world, for heaven's sakes. Don't ask me why ... because I can't tell you. It just seems like ... well ... when I was at my loneliest, you came along."

She forced a smile – and wiped away a renegade tear.

"I thought," she half-whispered, "that there was something special about you ... the first day you ever got here. Even though you were laughing like a lunatic."

"Funny you should mention that." He was rallying – and had even manufactured a sort-of grin. "I was just gonna say that was exactly when I decided that you were something special yourself. I told you then that you were the most charming woman I'd ever met. I meant it then ... and I mean it now."

"No you didn't," she sniffed. "You didn't say I was the most charmin' woman you ever met. You just said I was charmin'."

"My, my," he clucked. "We do have a good memory, don't we? Well, listen, My Little Chickadee, if I didn't say that you were the most charming woman I'd ever met ... well, I sure as hell meant it."

"Is this love, Parks? Could it be love, do you think?"

"I ... I don't know, Helen. I ... I feel something for you. Something earth-shaking. Something wonderful. Something I've never felt before."

"Well, that's just what I was thinkin' about you. Sometimes, Parks, what I feel towards you is just ... is just ... well, pure contentment. Like I know that you'd always take care of me. Always."

"It's true, Helen. I would. I always would. Be there to take care of you. For always and ever. I swear it."

"But there are times," she said, "when I get awful frightened. It's like a bell rings inside me. A bell. Way down deep. And I just..."

"Is there a bell ringing inside you now? Way down deep?"

She laughed – a most-welcome sight!

"No," she replied. "But, I think I've got a siren going off in my head."

"That's <u>my</u> natural state, Pretty Lady. Especially when I'm with you."

"Now, you g'wan," she replied. "I've never heard such malarkey in my life."

"Stick around. You'll probably hear more. I'm doing my best, y'know."

He raised her head and kissed her. Gently at first. Then, more urgently.

Twice, she attempted to break away. But, he held her fast – as his ardor built.

When the kiss ended, he was still clinging to her – desperately! Helen's chest was heaving – frantically! She tried to catch her breath! She wasn't having much luck!

He began to fondle her bosom – through the ever-present housedress and apron. He was amazed at the firmness of her breasts. He was even more incredulous – at the fact that he'd paused to evaluate them.

She'd seldom worn a dress which flattered her figure. On those few occasions when she had – it only served to reemphasize to Parks just what a beautiful woman she actually was.

His klutziness, on that Christmas Eve, was incredible! Parks found himself exploring her body with his hands – as though he was a high school sophomore!

Helen, of course, resisted! At first, she resisted! Attempted, even, to push him away! Her emotional wall, however, began to crumble – as he began to kiss her neck lightly. Then, to nibble softly at her earlobes! He darted his tongue into and out of her mouth!

Her resolve evaporated! She melted against him.

He found – quickly – that his groping was not the only sophomoric aura which surrounded him. He was all thumbs. He struggled – mightily – to undress her. He couldn't even get her apron untied.

She smiled. For a fleeting, frenetic, moment both of them feared she would laugh – deflating one of the most beautiful, most tender, moments in both of their lives!

Instead, she moved both of his hands up to her head – and kissed him with great tenderness.

Then, she reached behind her and unfastened the apron – as well as the many buttons on her dress. The latter would've presented a formidable task for the fumbling Parks. Button upon button. They ran from the top of her bottom up to the neckline.

She hesitated – for what seemed an eternity. Then – after having fought a thousand battles – she unhooked her brassiere. (They didn't call the garment a "bra" in 1939.)

He moved his hands slowly, softly, tenderly, down past her neck – working the apron, dress, and brassiere down to her waist. He gasped – totally unprepared for the unmitigated beauty of her pink-tipped breasts!

Then, he lowered himself – so as to kiss her over her entire bosom, running his tongue around each nipple! She began to moan – as she experienced the hardening, in response to his flicking tongue!

Parks began to undress her!

Then, he found himself kneeling on the floor, beside the sofa. Helen was, by then, reclining on her back – completely nude! Parks ran his tongue up and down her body! From her navel to the tip – then to the top – of each gorgeous breast!

He was in the process of trailing a path downward – when an alarm clattered inside his subconscious! He could have no way of knowing how prevalent oral sex might have been in 1939. Or whether the sheltered Helen would react positively to the technique. It might just scare the bejeebers out of her.

Of course, he'd had no clue that the subject would become Topic A in the last few years of the twentieth century – thanks to a president and an intern. Every 8-year-old kid would know from such things.

It didn't take long for the thought of oral sex to become academic. It was more than evident, from the manner in which she was moaning – and writhing, in a ceaseless, beckoning, rhythm – that she was ready for him to enter her!

He surprised himself – with the proficiency with which he was able to continue kissing, fondling, and caressing her – while he was disrobing! It hadn't _all_ left him!

As he lowered his body onto her – gently penetrating her – he half expected her to become a raging torrent of raw, pent-up, emotion! However, as he began to lovingly probe, and then withdraw, he found her clinging tightly – desperately – to him!

It was an incredible display of tenderness – when sheer animal passion would seem to have been in order!

EIGHT

As the brand new decade of the forties dawned, Parks was quite at peace with himself – and with practically everything around him. **Dubin Auto Rental** was doing exceptionally well – and Parks was investing every dollar he felt he could spare into stocks, and a few parcels of land, all of which he was certain would skyrocket in value over the next decade.

He no longer drove his beloved 1937 Ford. Why should he? He was able to use company cars. Why not extend the life of his prized '37 as long as possible? Keep it into the sixties! Maybe even the seventies – if he lived that long! It would be worth a fortune 25 or 30 years down the road. Especially with so few miles on it.

He kept the car behind the building in which he lived. Eventually, he would have to buy a building – in which to house the glorious vehicle. He'd tried mightily to find a garage, in the neighborhood – one in which to domicile his "baby". Unsuccessfully. But, he'd find one eventually. No sense in exposing it to the elements for all those years.

Besides, it made sense for our hero to begin collecting cars – ones he knew would become classics in the world of the sixties and seventies. Certainly, he'd need a place to store those acquisitions. To protect what he envisioned as a sizeable investment.

Of course, in 1960, he would be 68-years-old. Would he still be alive? If he did survive to that age, he felt certain that he'd be married – hopefully, to Helen Shaddon.

Mr. Horne had <u>mentioned</u> another relationship. Even posed the possibility of Parks siring more children. Well, having kids was probably out of the question. But, certainly not a marriage to – and a fulfilling relationship with – Helen Shaddon.

Did this mean that he was turning his back on his own kids? On those seven wonderful children – "back" in 1979? On Kathleen? Maybe <u>this</u> was why there'd never been a largesse for Jim and Kathleen!

He shuddered – and tried to eliminate such thoughts from his consciousness. It took a good bit of effort to concentrate on his cherished landlady. All the things that he would do with her. And all of the things he would/could do <u>for</u> her. He'd be able to leave her a rather tidy stock portfolio and some valuable real estate – as well as, hopefully, a fleet of classic cars. It would be a nice bequest.

He would have to take care that she would be aware of the value of those things.

As 1940 hurried past, Parks became more and more enraptured with Helen. They'd spend hours in her living room – talking, laughing, listening to the radio and thoroughly enjoying one another. In addition to their Sundays at **The Blue Ribbon**.

Helen had been an only child. Her father had died when she was six-years-old.

Her mother had struggled, mightily, to overcome a plethora of monumental hurdles – financial and emotional problems, as well as physical weakness – to simply survive. Survive – and raise her daughter. She'd managed to hang on till Helen had turned fifteen.

Although, ostensibly, Helen had been raised, from that point, by her paternal grandmother, she'd been, in truth, left to shift for herself. The young woman had retreated into an emotional shell.

She'd married early in life – for the stability and security that the family unit of those days represented. She would later admit to Parks that he – her "star boarder" – was the first man to whom she'd ever "opened up". The <u>only</u> man to whom she'd ever "opened up". She'd shared many things with him – some of them quite intimate. Others were "merely" very private.

"Stuff that I'd never dare to mention to Walter".

Her life with Walter had been adequate – but, she'd, obviously, never felt the sort of emotion that Parks evoked in her. She was forever advising him of that fact.

"I can't tell you," he would respond, "how happy it makes me ... that I was able to open a door or two for you".

Twice Parks asked her to marry him: Once after their first intimate encounter – Christmas Eve, of 1939 – and again in March of 1940. She had declined both times.

Having wed for purely pragmatic reasons the first time, she wanted to be sure of a second marriage. Be certain that it would be emotionally rewarding. That such a marriage would be totally fulfilling. A life with a second husband would have to be everything that her first marriage was not – "and then some".

"There's times," she'd say, "when I think I'm shootin' too high."

"Oh, I dunno," Parks had replied on one occasion. "You might be surprised to find out that I'm Young Lochinvar ... or maybe Saint Francis of Assisi."

"Nothing about you would surprise me. Nothing."

Her rather chilled response had troubled him. Had bothered him – greatly. There was that worrisome tone of voice again.

"I ... I don't know what you mean," he'd responded – trying, valiantly, to rally.

"Yes. Well, I don't either, Parks. It's just that sometimes ... well, sometimes ... you seem to be ... to be ... someone else. I don't know if that makes any sense to you. I don't even know if it makes any sense to me. You just seem to be ... well ... off in another world sometimes."

"I don't mean to be."

"I know. I'm sure that you've got a lot on your mind. But, Parks, there are times when ... times when ... you seem to be so ... so awfully strange. Don't get me wrong. I enjoy bein' with you. I think I probably love you. I know that you've done so much for me. I talk much better now ... for one thing. I know that I've got more confidence in myself. Walter never much listened to what I ever had to say. Just shut me out ... I guess you could call it. Oh, he was good to me ... and all that. A good provider. But, he didn't much care about what I ever thought. Jeff seemed to be a baby ... and then, all at once, he was a man. And gone away from me. You've helped me, my dear Parks. Helped me in so many ways. Helped me improve my outlook on life. And my vocabulary."

"How 'bout your vernacular?"

"Yes. By all means, my vernacular. But, there's other things. You've gotten me to where I read the papers ... listen to the news on the radio. Stuff like that. I love to ... well, just sit with you. Sit with you and ... and talk."

"Among other things," he leered. She blushed.

"I wish you wouldn't do that, Parks," she groused. "Say those things."

"Can I help it? I love to see you blush. Where I come from, nobody blushes."

"Yes," she answered, almost under her breath. "Yes, I know. You keep saying that. Sometimes, I wonder just where it is you do come from."

One troubled island – a horribly troubled island – in a sea of serenity was the fact that Helen's son, Jeff, was stationed on the *Oklahoma*.

Parks found himself wishing – desperately – that he'd had time to have done some serious research, before coming back in time. An impossibility, of course, given the short time he'd had in which to make his decision. Probably by design.

He'd have to rely strictly upon his memory – which, he'd always prided himself upon, was better than average. However, he'd not been blessed with total recall. Perhaps, if he had, it would've disqualified him for his trip to the thirties.

The last time he'd been in 1940, he'd been eight-years-old. Besides, who could have predicted that he'd fall in love with a woman whose son would be stationed in Pearl Harbor? Still, it was terribly upsetting to him that he had absolutely no recollection of the damage the *Oklahoma* may have suffered on that "Day of Infamy".

He was fairly certain that the battleship had, indeed, been hit. But, how badly?

There was only one solution: He had 18 months to get Jeff off that ship!

Another consideration – one which had never occurred to him, before – was the fact that he was now meeting other young people. Youths who'd be eligible for the draft. Nice kids – most of whom he'd met at the dealership. How could they know what fate awaited them? Dear Lord! What would become of them?

As an eight-year-old, he'd, of course, had no such concerns – beyond his father and a couple uncles; all of whom, it turned out, were too old to be inducted.

It was a heavy burden for Parks – not unlike the burden of knowing the God-awful circumstances under which his father would die.

The burden became particularly heavy in September of 1940 – when Congress passed the *Selective Service Act*.

As 1940 neared its end, Helen finally agreed to marry Parks. Finally! They planned to announce their betrothal on Christmas Eve – a year to the day after they'd first become intimate. They would be wed in the spring of 1941.

Spring would be a logical time. Things were going well at **Dubin Auto Rental**. Parks' portfolio of stocks was not setting world records – but, it didn't figure to. Not with the economy – and *The Great Depression* – being what they were. Eventually, Parks knew, his holdings would "take off".

By the spring of '41, our hero was certain that the happy couple would be more than able to buy a house. They'd buy a house – and keep "Helen's Building" on Grand River. Owning a house would be important – critical even. He wanted Helen to have the security of owning a home – along with the knowledge that she could keep her beloved building.

Equally important: Within the next two years, Detroit would become the "Arsenal of Democracy" – and would experience a severe housing shortage. Property values would wind up "on the moon"! For a man who'd "never had two nickels to rub together", real estate would become a monumental consideration.

Was he becoming obsessed with money? Probably. But, having been so broke for so long, he wanted to assure that his intended would never face financial uncertainty. Ever!

Jim had subjected Kathleen to too much financial uncertainty! Far too much!

He'd see – by God – that the same thing would <u>never</u> happen to Helen!

Over the summer, Parks had bought a 1931 Model A Ford, a 1934 Ford roadster, 1934 DeSoto (the "twin sister" of the world-famous Chrysler Air-Flow), a 1936 Chrysler New Yorker and a 1940 Lincoln Zephyr. It had taken some doing. He'd had to trade some of his stocks to purchase the Lincoln, but the price was simply too good to pass up.

He'd managed to pay cash for each vehicle – and had gotten each at a bargain price. The country would not come out of the depression – really come out of it – until about halfway through World War II. Each of his newly-acquired cars would be of exceptional value in the sixties and seventies.

His fleet – including his cherished '37 Ford – were domiciled in a building near Dexter Avenue and West Grand Boulevard. He'd finally managed to lease a building to house his classics-to-be!

All of this raised the eyebrows of Clark Dubin! While he was impressed with his employee's rent-a-car expertise, he found his financial dealings to be most curious.

It had been Thanksgiving Day, 1940, when Parks and Helen experienced their first real disagreement. Misunderstanding would be a more accurate term.

To spare Helen the "grief" of preparing dinner, Parks insisted that they dine out – and not at **The Blue Ribbon**.

Their Thanksgiving feast consisted of turkey, "with all the trimmin's", at **Shore's Restaurant**, on Warren Avenue – almost a shrine in Detroit in those days. The eatery specialized in roast turkey, chicken and duck. The place was swarming with people, of course. It was Thanksgiving – "Turkey Day" – after all. The meal was delicious.

As they devoured their dinner, the couple spent most of their time discussing their pending marriage. Helen was enthused over the fact that Jeff had written her – advising his mother that he had cleared leave time with his officer-in-charge.

He would definitely attend the nuptials.

Returning

Jeff! Parks was no closer to getting Helen's son out of harm's way, than he'd been when he'd first learned of the lad's ill-fated assignment!

December 7, 1941 was coming with a rush! Barely over a year in the future! A feeling of terrible foreboding swept over Parks – resulting in a violent, involuntary, shudder.

He had finally met the young sailor just four months before – when Jeff had come home on leave. Helen had never rented the vacant room in her building. It made a dandy billet for her son's stay.

Ever since the youth had returned to his ship, Parks had wracked his brain – in a futile attempt to come up with an idea. Some dazzlingly-brilliant brainstorm which would get him off the *Oklahoma*.

His campaign included speaking to Clark Dubin's brother-in-law, when the man had stopped by the dealership. Dubin had introduced him to Parks.

"This is my wife's brother, Ben Lozen," Dubin had said. "He's a lieutenant commander ... or some damn thing ... in the Navy. Conceited bastard. Skipper of a cruiser."

Lozen had laughed heartily. "Destroyer", he corrected.

"Cruiser. Destroyer. What the hell's the difference?" Dubin had barked.

Parks, of course, was more than slightly interested! Ben Lozen might be the answer – the avenue off the *Oklahoma* for Jeff.

"What port do you operate out of?" Parks had asked.

"Norfolk."

Parks had smiled. Jim Sidorwitz had been stationed in the Virginia city in the early-fifties. He loved the place.

"Is Norfolk really as bad as everyone makes it out to be?" he'd inquired, of Lozen.

"Nah. Not to me, it's not. I've always enjoyed it there."

Parks had managed to pull Lozen off into one of the sales cubicles in the show room – and had engaged him in a serious discussion of Jeff's situation. He'd almost stated it as a "problem" – but, that would've been unwise. He couldn't tell <u>anyone</u> of the upcoming cause for such a "problem".

The only avenue that the officer had been able to offer was a suggestion that Helen declare that – as a widow – she needed Jeff at home. To help support her. Under those circumstances, the youth might be able to terminate his enlistment – and receive a hardship discharge. Parks winced at the word "hardship".

After having fought a thousand battles within, Parks had made a monumental blunder! He had broached the subject to Helen. She'd looked at him as though he'd lost his mind!

Why would she possibly even think of such a thing? It was obvious that she was doing all right for herself. Maybe she wasn't living high off the hog, she'd snapped. But, she was certainly comfortable enough. Besides, she went on, Jeff loved the Navy. He wouldn't want to leave the service. Why would Parks even suggest such a cockamamie thing? Such an outrageous thing? What a stupid suggestion!

It had taken three days before the huff had worn off.

Obviously, the hardship discharge avenue was verboten!

What would he do? What could he do? How would he ever get Jeff out of danger?

During Thanksgiving dinner at **Shore's**, the matter came to a head: He'd blurted out his latest brainstorm! He'd have done better to have thought it through!

"I know what, Helen!" he exclaimed.

"What do you know?" she asked, around a mouthful of dressing and gravy.

"We'll get married December first. Or thereabout."

"First of December? Are you out of your mind? That's just a week away! We'd never be able to get things arranged in time. What on earth could've ... ?"

"No. No, I meant the first part of December ... next year. Nineteen forty-one."

"Nineteen forty-one? Why? Parks ... why on earth would you want to wait so long? Haven't you been the one who's been wanting to get married as soon as possible? Now you want to put it off? For a whole year? Why? What's wrong? Is there someone else?" Her eyes filled with tears. "If there is ... " she tried to continue.

"No! Of course not, Helen! Of course not! There's no one else! How could there be?"

"Sometimes I wonder. Sometimes, when you're gone for hours and hours and hours, I don't have the foggiest idea ... as you always say ... of where you are."

She was, of course, referring to the many times Parks would sit down the block from the little house on Penrod. Or when he would "tip a few" with his grandfather (and sometimes his grandmother) at **Freddie's**. Mostly, it was the former – Penrod. He enjoyed watching himself, as a young boy, learning how to play baseball – rather clumsily, to be sure – in the vacant lot in the middle of the block.

"Oh, Helen," Parks managed to reply. "You know me. I sometimes stop at **The White Tower** for a cup of coffee ... read the paper. You know how I get lost in the newspaper. Especially *The Times*."

"That's another thing I don't understand. You make a big thing out of *The Times*. Didn't you miss *The News* and *The Free Press* when you were in Texas? You'd think *The Times* was the only paper in the whole world."

"Of course I missed the other papers." He started to shovel a forkful of turkey into his mouth – then, thought better of it. "It's no big nefarious thing," he continued. "Everybody likes one paper better than the other two. I happen to like *The Times* best. I stop off and get a cup of java ... and just get lost in the stupid paper. The time just flies on me. You know what a lousy judge of time I am."

"I guess I do," she sighed. "But, I certainly don't know why you want to postpone our wedding."

"Just so that Jeff'll be home for it."

"That's the dumbest thing I've ever heard. Parks, he's gonna be home anyway. You saw the letter. I showed it to you. His commander ... or whatever ... promised!"

"You can't be locked-and-loaded sure of that."

"Locked-and-loaded? I've never heard anyone say that before," she responded. "But, I'm pretty sure. He's pretty sure. Besides, you couldn't be any more certain that he'd be home next December. The way Hitler's goin', we could be in a war by then ... God forbid."

The thought sent a shudder through her.

"Well," he was struggling to sound convincing, "I just thought that, if we waited maybe a little bit longer, he'd have a much better chance of actually locking in his leave. Put in for it way ahead of time, and all that."

"That's the silliest thing I ever heard. Look, Parks, if you don't want to marry me, why, just say so and I'll ... I'll ... "

"No! No. Of course I want to marry you. I love you. It's just that ... "

"It's still the damndest thing I ever heard."

Her face reflected the shock she felt at having used a "swear word" – especially in public. Seldom did she ever use "damn" or "hell" – except in the Biblical sense. She looked quickly around – blushing, of course – to see if anyone might have heard her.

"It's not an excuse, Helen. I wouldn't use an excuse ... wouldn't hide behind an excuse. If I didn't want to get married, I'd say so. I've got balls enough to ... "

Her face turned scarlet!

"Don't you ever use that kind of language in front of me, Parks," she seethed. "Especially when we're in public."

"I'm sorry, Helen. I just got a little upset. But, what I'm trying to say is that I don't need an excuse. If I didn't want to get married, I'd up and tell you. I'd say so. It's just that, by postponing it a tad, we could ... "

"A what?"

"A tad ... a little."

"One of your words from Texas. You certainly seem to use 'em a lot ... especially when you get upset. I still don't understand why we would have to wait until a year from next month. And don't tell me that it has to do with Jeff being able to come home. I don't believe that! Not for an instant!"

He shrugged. He wished that he hadn't. He was certain that it had come across as an insipid gesture – or, perhaps, one of indifference.

"Okay," he said at length. "All right. Let's drop it. We'll get married in March ... like we planned."

"No! Certainly not! Not if you don't want to get married. I don't need you, y'know."

"Well, I need you. It was a stupid thought, Helen. I was just thinking out loud. You know how I do at times. I should start running some of this stuff through my brain ... before engaging my mouth."

Helen set her fork down on her plate – with a loud clatter. Everyone in the eaterie seemed to hear the clank. Everything seemed to come to a screeching halt. It appeared as though every other pair of eyes in the place had zeroed in on them.

"There are times," she said, sighing deeply and looking directly into Parks' eyes. "There are times," she repeated, "when I don't think I know you. That I don't know you at all. Like now. You're an entirely different man sitting there. Entirely different. I really don't think you need me all that much. Sometimes, I think you're just using me to satisfy some far-out need, and ... "

"Where'd you get that expression?" he interrupted.

"What expression?"

"Far-out."

"From you. You've said it once or twice. I got it from you. Where else would I get such a ... ?"

"I've said that?"

"Of course. I've just about picked up your entire vernacular. I don't believe the way I talk, sometimes. Where'd you think I got it from? Walter Winchell?"

She smiled at last. It was faint – but, it was a smile! The storm warning seemed to have been taken down! The fury had passed – he hoped!

"No," he answered, "it just sounded funny ... coming from you."

"Well, it sounded just as funny coming from you. Leastways the first time I heard it. I thought it was just more of your Texas talk."

It was his turn to sigh.

"You're right," he half-whispered. "It is. It's part of the language from where I came. Helen, look. I'm really sorry about suggesting we postpone our wedding. I can't imagine what I was thinking. I love you. I really and truly do. I'd be lost without you. It was just a stupid thought ... that just happened to be passing through my alleged mind. Forgive me?"

She sighed – and ran a hand through her hair.

"Yes," she said – after what seemed an eternity.

Parks reached across the table and took her hand in his.

"Yes, of course," she continued. "But, I'm tellin' you, Parks ... I'm tellin' you. You sometimes worry me! You worry the fool out of me."

"I know. I sometimes worry myself."

"Really worry me! Parks ... that was the most ridiculous suggestion I think I ever heard."

"I agree. Totally ridiculous."

"But, that's the thing that worries me, y'see. Really worries me. And do you want to know why, Parks?"

"Something tells me that I really don't want to know."

"The reason is ... the reason is ... that you never make ridiculous suggestions. Ever. Even if I think something you want to do ... or something you want me to do ... is idiotic at the time, it always turns out ... turns out, without fail ... that it made sense. It always turns out that whatever you think is gonna happen ... no matter how far-fetched it may seem ... it always happens. Always!"

"Ohhhhhh." He tried to dismiss her statement. "Like what?"

Oh, like the Tigers winning the pennant, this year. And that hockey team ... the one from Montreal ... going out of business."

"The Maroons?"

"Yes. Everyone was surprised by it. But not you. And no one really expected the Tigers to win this year."

He smiled nervously – and fiddled with his mashed potatoes.

"Wasn't all that unexpected. I just happened to think that the team was a whole lot better than people gave 'em credit for. Del Baker ... he's a brilliant manager. Besides, we didn't take the *World Series*."

"That's right. But, you seemed to know that Cleveland ... "

"Cincinnati."

"... that Cincinnati was going to win it."

"Did I say that?"

"No. You didn't say it. Not in so many words. You just ... just seemed to know. You seem to know a lot of things, Parks. Lots and lots of things. That's what scares me! Scares me to death! Now, here you are ... all wrapped up in getting Jeff home next December! Next December ... instead of this spring. Why? Why next December? What's going to happen next December?"

"What's going to happen? Helen, how would I know what's going to happen then?"

"Well, it seems to me that you ... that you must ... must know something. You even wanted me to tell the Navy that it was essential for Jeff to be here with me ... to support me. Why? You knew ... you know ... that's not true. Why did you want Jeff and me to do something like that? What do you know, Parks? About Jeff? About the Navy? Is something bad going to happen to him? Something awful? Something really bad? A year from this December?"

Her eyes, all of a sudden, filled with tears.

Parks felt an icy shiver begin at the base of his spine! In an instant, it had rushed to the top of his head! He could feel the color begin to drain from his face! He hoped – desperately, he hoped – that Helen was not able to gauge his condition!

"No," he finally rasped – his voice much weaker than he'd have preferred. "No, of course not. Of course not! Nothing's going to happen to Jeff! Nothing! I give you my word, Helen. He'll be fine. I'll see that he's gonna be fine. Trust me."

"I do, Parks." Suddenly, she seemed terribly deflated. "I do. At least I think I do. It's just that there's something about you ... something about all of this ... which makes me so ... so uneasy. Terribly, horribly uneasy."

Once more, the chill shot up Parks' spine!

Payday before Christmas – and Parks went off his austerity program. Temporarily, anyway. He bought his fiancée a host of presents. Most of the gifts were of a practical nature: A *Mixmaster*, a new vacuum cleaner (he was shocked at how Neanderthal the "dirt suckers" of that era were), a set of expensive china, sterling silver flatware – and an ornate floor lamp.

On the more frivolous side, he presented her with a beautiful, ruffled, bedspread – and a fur coat. In addition, he gave her gift certificates from **J.L. Hudson's** and **Crowley's** – two of Detroit's largest and finest department stores. Along with the certificates came the admonition to pick out some pretty – dress-up – dresses. And – not the least of the admonitions – she should lay in some sexy underthings.

On Christmas Eve, he took her downtown – to the *Statler Hotel*– for dinner.

Helen had wanted to spend the evening at home – as they had the preceding December 24th. But, Parks had insisted on the more opulent evening.

"Well," he explained, "we're announcing our engagement ... even if it's only to our-own-selves. Ergo, we gots to do something to make it memorable."

She smiled – and semi-blushed.

"Well," she laughed, "we did something pretty memorable last year."

The remark surprised Parks – probably no more than it shocked Helen.

"You bat, Keed," he replied, with a broad grin. "We could never duplicate last year. We shouldn't even try. It happens like that ... just once in a lifetime. You can never go back."

"You always say that," she responded, her manner growing more serious.

"Well, I always mean it. So, instead of trying to top last year ... which is un-toppable ... or even equal it, what do we do? We add to it. We compliment it. Who knows? We just might wind up renting a room upstairs ... and doing the same thing we did last year."

He succeeded in upgrading her semi-blush into the real, full-fledged, thing.

NINE

With the coming of the new year – 1941 – new problems arose. Problems which Parks should have foreseen – but, did not:

In planning their March wedding, our hero was unable, of course, to produce the various documents that the Catholic Church, of that era, required in order to announce the banns of matrimony.

He'd not given any thought to the fact that he would need a baptismal certificate – as well as first communion and confirmation documents. In addition, he would need to furnish information pertaining to his parents.

The Church was much more rigid then. Much more invasive – and much more unyielding – in the forties than in the seventies. Ever-so-much more than at the new millennium.

The documentation would have to be provided, or the pastor at *St. Mary's* simply would not consider marrying the couple. And, Parks was certain, Helen would never consider any other wedding. She would never wed outside the Church.

His only out was to try and convince the pastor that he'd never belonged to any organized religion. He would be required to take instructions, of course – then, be baptized, confirmed, etc. etc. etc.

Fortunately, the pastor bought it!

Helen, though, was another story!

"It doesn't wash, Parks! It just doesn't wash! You can't get over the fact that the Mass is in Latin ... the way it's always been! It's almost like you were on another planet, somewheres. Some place where you couldn't get the Mass. Parks, we've gone to church every

Sunday. Every Sunday since you moved in, for heaven's sakes. I don't understand it! Don't understand it at all! You love the Mass! You're always ravin' about the Latin Mass! The Latin Mass! The Latin Mass! Like the Mass wasn't always in Latin."

"Oh, it is. It is. It's just that I never got exposed to Catholicism ... till I moved from here, down to Houston. I never pursued it, actually, down there. Not formally, anyway. Mainly, because I never had anyone to pursue it with. It was just one of those things. One of those things that I was always going to ... "

"Yes. It seems like it's <u>always</u> 'just one of those things'. Always."

"Well, I wish now, of course, that I'd gotten myself involved down in Texas. I just never got around to it. You know how I tend to procrastinate."

She shook her head – vehemently!

"I don't know, Parks. I just don't know."

"Helen, it's ... "

"I dunno, Parks. Maybe we'd just better call the whole thing off! There's just too many things, Parks! Too many things ... that just don't jibe. You say you were in Detroit till nineteen thirty-four?"

"Thirty-five."

He knew that she was trying to trap him. He'd told her ... many, many times ... which year he was purported to have left The Motor City. She had a much better memory than that.

"It was thirty-five," he repeated. "What's that got to do with anything?"

"Well, you ... you just never talk about your past. Not here. Not in Texas. Not anywhere. That wouldn't bother me so much ... except that you're so nostalgic otherwise. You talk on and on about ... well, the Latin Mass for instance. Or even *The Times*. Or even sillier things ... the *Hi-Speed* gasoline signs. Or that *Sinclair* sign ... the red-and-green one with the big H-C in the middle. You even remarked, one time, how gas stations look. A gas station is a gas station ... a little building with gas pumps out in front and one of those do-hickeys they use to raise cars. Those things are all stuff I've always taken for granted. So has everyone else I know. Except you!"

"Oh, Helen. You're exaggerating."

"No I'm not! I'm not! Everyone takes that stuff ... all that stuff ... for granted. But, not you. Why? Why, Parks? In heaven's name, why?"

"No special reason. They don't have *Hi-Speed* gas in Texas ... and very few *Sinclair* stations. I've just always had a soft spot for some things."

"Exactly what I mean," she snapped. "My point exactly. Stupid things ... like gas stations ... mean a lot to you." She pushed away a strand of grey hair. "They must remind you of something ... or someone. Something or someone out of your past! Otherwise, they wouldn't mean anything. Yet, you've got nothing ... absolutely nothing ... to tell me about your past! Nothing! Not a thing!"

"Helen, look! I just ... "

"Were you in ... in jail or something? Or maybe the nuthouse? If so, then I should know. It wouldn't make any difference ... not in the way I feel about you. I swear it. But, I've got to know. Got to know ... what it is you're hiding."

He tried to embrace her – but she pulled away!

"Helen, I wish you wouldn't even think about canceling our wedding! Or even postponing it."

"Why not? Isn't that the pot calling the kettle black? Parks, you were the one who wanted to postpone it! Postpone it ... till way next December! Next December, for heaven's sakes! That's something else I don't understand."

"You're making a big thing over nothing, Helen! Over nothing! All right! Nostalgic I am. I'm also hokey ... and sentimental. I'm also very half-assed. You know that's true. You've told me as much ... many times."

She smiled in spite of herself.

"Well," she muttered. "Not quite in those words."

"Maybe so. But, you still said as much. Listen, the reason I've never told you about ... never spoken of ... my parents is because ... is because ... well ... they were killed! In a fire! When I was ... when I was eight."

He hoped, desperately, that he'd be able to invent a plausible story. Come up with something believable – "off the seat of his pants"!

It was something he should have had in readiness.

"I was pretty well kicked from one aunt-and-uncle to another," he continued. "I was with my maternal grandparents for awhile. But, they couldn't keep me. So, I really didn't have much of a childhood."

Helen shook her head.

"That may be true," she responded. "But, if you went to Texas in thirty-five, you'd have been ... what? ... forty-three? That's an awful long time, Parks. An awful long time ... between childhood and forty-three. Were you in jail? What did you do? And who did you do it with?"

"Helen, look. I haven't ... "

"We might as well get these things thrashed out now, Parks. I could never rest easy ... not being married to a man I don't know. And ... when you come right down to it, Parks ... I really don't know you. I don't know you at all."

"I ... I never realized that you had all these questions. Ones that needed answers."

"I can imagine," she said, icily.

He took a deep breath. It was a situation that he most certainly should have foreseen – and prepared for.

"I was never married, Helen," he began. "I promise you that. You can search all the records ... here and in Texas, or anywhere else ... and you'll never find a marriage between Parks Hayworth and anyone else. I swear that to you."

Parks felt a substantial tinge of guilt at the oath! Technically, what he'd told Helen was true. But, the overall falsehood was taking its toll. In his unique situation, though, what else could he do?

"I went with a few ladies," he explained, "but, it doesn't pay to go into what I may or may not have done with them. I didn't know you then. I wish I had ... but, it wouldn't have done me any good. You were married to Walter. And I was a confirmed bachelor. Then, I got hung-up on a lady."

"Hung-up?"

"Yeah. I fell in love with her. At least, that's what I thought at the time."

Visions of Alice – his "Veteran Fiancée" – began to race through the movie projector of his mind. He rubbed his chin, nervously, and then worried his earlobe.

"Looking back," he rasped, "I was probably just infatuated with her. It was late in life for me ... or, at least, I thought it was. My late-thirties. Before that, I sort of just kind of knocked around. But, this lady ... her name was Alice. And I tried my damndest to please her. You'd never believe some of the things I did to try and make her happy."

Parks' sincerity – as he spoke of the very real Alice – seemed to move Helen.

"Maybe," she soothed, "maybe I shouldn't be hearin' any of the things you did to please her."

Parks was quite wound up.

"In truth," he said, "she was the reason I moved to Houston. I worked for **Stark Hickey Ford** ... down Grand River. One of the guys there ... one of the management guys ... was moving to Houston. He asked me to go with him. Things with Alice had reached a point to where I just couldn't continue. Couldn't go on with the relationship."

"I ... I guess I understand."

"It's like that old line: You can't live with 'em ... and you can't live without 'em."

"Old line? What old line? I never heard it."

"Well, things had gotten to the point where I felt the only thing I could do was ... was to get the hell out. I decided to move down to Houston. It worked ... to a point. It was a sonofagun ... trying to get her out of my mind. But, at least, I was far enough away to where I wouldn't ... couldn't ... go crawling back to her, like I'd done so many times before. So damn many times before."

He couldn't tell if he was getting through. She'd folded her arms –not an encouraging sign.

"Why did you come back to Detroit?" she asked, coldly.

"Mostly because the company I was with down there wasn't doing very well. It was a little car rental company ... a spin-off of the dealership I'd left **Stark Hickey** to go to work for."

"Spin-off?"

"Yeah. They'd set up a separate company. I understand that they're completely out of business now. Mainly, though, I felt as though I'd gotten Alice out of my system. And I really wanted to come home."

"I guess I can understand that," she acknowledged.

"Stupid as it may seem, I missed things like the *Hi-Speed* sign. The *Sinclair* sign. I missed Harry Heilmann and Ty Tyson doing the Tigers games. I missed the Saturday football games ... with the University of Michigan. I missed the Red Wings. They never even heard of hockey down there. I even missed the Lions."

In the thirties and forties, the NFL was not a big deal. Far and away, the college game was a much bigger draw.

"I even missed," he droned on, "*Harold True And The Day In Review*". He was referring to Detroit's most popular local evening news broadcast of the day. Lowell Thomas – and his national nightly newscast – probably had a larger Detroit audience. But, Parks was convinced, he was the only one.

"Wasn't your move back here awful sudden?" she pressed. "That's what that fellow ... what was his name? ... that's what he said. That's what he told me ... when he rented the room for you."

"Gabriel Horne?"

"Yes. Mister Horne."

"Yeah. It was one of those things that just came up all of a sudden. I thought that I had a connection with **Hertz** up here. And it was a situation where I had to do something ... awfully damn soon. In a real hurry. I'd known Gabe Horne for a long time ... and I was able to get him ... and a couple other guys ... to help me out."

"You were gonna go to work for **Hertz**? You've never mentioned that."

"Well, it fell through. Learned that the whole thing had evaporated ... the second day that I was back here. Uh ... up here. So, the whole trip back ... up ... was for naught. Or it would've been ... if I hadn't met you. That turned out to be the best thing that ever happened to me, Helen. You turned out to be the best thing that ever happened to me."

She appeared to have been moved by the sincerity of Parks' obvious love and/or infatuation toward Alice. His emotion had come naturally. He had been deeply in love with Alice in the early- and mid-seventies. Well, maybe it <u>had been</u> infatuation! Who the hell knew?

He'd been truthful in that part of his explanation. He had, indeed, moved to Houston to force an end to his relationship with Alice – as well as to be near his children, once Kathleen had moved to Brownsville, in South Texas.

Because of the fact of his deep love (or overwhelming infatuation) for his "Veteran Fiancée", the things he was telling Helen had an unmistakable ring of sincerity.

"Just one thing," Helen pressed. "Where is Alice now? Is she the one you go to see ... when you disappear for hours on end?"

"No! No. No, I swear to you. I haven't seen Alice ... not one time ... since I've been back. Back up here. Never! Not one time!"

"You're sure? Don't lie to me, Parks."

"No. I've not seen her. I understand that she's married again."

"Again?"

A bad slip! There were few divorcees in the early-forties. A divorced woman was a fallen woman. Bore a horrible stigma.

"I guess I should've mentioned that she was divorced," he muttered.

Surprise and disappointment were etched in Helen's face.

"Divorced? You ... you went with a divorced woman?"

He nodded.

"Didn't seem to matter much," he explained. "Neither of us were Catholic. I'm a bit of a fatalist, though. I'm convinced that it was never meant to be ... Alice and me. I was convinced of that ... that's why I took off for Texas. I never had any reason to change my mind. In any case, she's married again. And, I hope that she's happy."

"You're sure ... you're absolutely sure ... that you're over her?"

"Absolutely. I've been over her ... over her for a good while. I'm not gonna try and tell you that she didn't have a hell of an effect on my life at one time, though."

Helen smiled softly.

"I can see that," she allowed. "That's why I wonder if it was really infatuation. Or if you're still in love with her."

"It was infatuation," he answered – probably much too quickly. "But, nine- or ten-years-ago, I wouldn't have said that. You have to realize that I was in my late-thirties ... and I'd never really felt all that much for a woman ... any woman ... before. Then, along comes Alice, and ... for whatever reason ... she really knocked me on my fanny. It's got to affect a person ... any person ... at that age. It sure as hell affected me. I was so taken with her that it wasn't ... it couldn't be ... a legitimate relationship. It was all one way ... headed in her direction. Going her way ... always. Finally, I managed to wise up. Wise up enough to break it off. But, for a couple or three years, she was everything. My every thought and deed ... all of them were wrapped up in Alice."

"I have another question," prodded Helen.

Just what Parks' needed. He had absolutely no idea if any of his semi-true/semi-false explanation was getting through to his intended. What could this next question be? What could it bring? Would his entire house-of-cards collapse?

From one-too-many questions?

"What question is that, Dear Lady," he finally asked.

"Did I ... do I ... knock you on your fanny?"

"You bet you did. You bet you do. I'm still there. Hopefully, I'll never get up. I love you, Helen."

He kissed her tenderly.

"Parks, I'm sorry," she whispered softly, her head pressed against his chest. "I'm just so sorry. It's just that ... there were so many things went through my mind. I'd always promised myself that I'd never ask 'em. That I'd never pry. But, this thing with the Church ... it was just too much! I had to know! I can see, though, how painful it was for you. How awful it was, for you to dredge up all those ... all those memories. I know ... in my heart of hearts ... that you couldn't play-act all those things. All those things that

Alice meant to you. I didn't mean to bring out all the ... well, all the pain ... you must've felt. Maybe still feel. But, I simply couldn't, Parks. I couldn't marry you. Not with all the doubts I had. Does any of this make sense?"

"Of course it does," he answered. "It's not really as painful as you might think."

"Now, that I don't believe. I could see the tears in your eyes."

"Ahhhh. You know me, Al." A slight smile crossed his face. "I cry at parking meters and baseball games.".

"Not quite. Almost ... but, not quite. I know that you must've felt a great deal for her."

He nodded once more.

"I feel much more for you, Helen. In a whole different way. A much healthier way. I love you very much. I want very much to be your husband. I just hope that you'll understand me ... understand the fact that I'm half-assed ... and make allowances for it. That's one thing that Alice could never do. Or would never do. One thing I promise you: I promise that I'll always love you. I'll never step out on you. Never cheat on you. I'll always ... always and ever ... devote myself to you. To making you happy. Can you believe that?"

A tear trickled down her right cheek.

"Yes, Parks. Yes, I can. I can believe it. I do believe it. I love you too. I just hope that what I feel for you ... well, that it isn't infatuation. Some of the things you described ... about your feelings for Alice ... well, they describe, perfectly, what I feel for you, at times."

"Have no fear. It's totally different. Trust me. I've been there before. Totally different."

"I have one more question for you."

Here it comes. One more bolt from the blue. He'd dodged the bullet so far. All the bullets – so far. Would this one last question be the one which would trip him up?

"What question?" he asked. "What question, pray tell?"

She smiled warmly.

"Would you make love to me?" she asked.

TEN

On March 3, 1941, Parks and Helen were married at *St. Mary's of Redford* Catholic Church.

Helen's son, Jeff, had, indeed, attended the wedding; had given the bride away.

Arriving a week before the ceremony, the youth did much of the legwork for his mother and stepfather-to-be.

Parks had grown to love the young man. He would lie awake – literally every night – desperately seeking a way to keep the lad from his date with almost-certain holocaust.

There was, of course, the possibility that Jeff could escape injury in the sneak Japanese raid – but, Parks didn't like the odds. The young sailor's chances would be much brighter, obviously, in a port such as Norfolk.

Norfolk! Of course!

Why hadn't he thought of it before? Clark Dubin's brother-in-law, Ben Lozen, was commanding officer of a Navy destroyer. Parks had spoken with Lozen at some length about Jeff's assignment to the *Oklahoma*. But, he'd never asked the officer, specifically, whether he could (or would) see to having Helen's son transferred to his ship. He'd gotten sidetracked on the ill-advised Hardship Discharge issue.

The morning after he'd come up with the bright idea of getting Jeff transferred off the battlewagon, Parks put in a call to Norfolk. He spent the entire morning trying to track down the skipper. After three futile, frustrating, hours, he was advised that Lozen's ship was at sea. No one seemed able – or willing – to inform him when the ship would return to port. But, they'd see that he got the message to return Parks' call.

When Lozen's call had finally come – four days later – he advised Parks that it would be impossible for him to request a specific man. In addition, the field in which the young sailor was specializing was more indigenous to a battleship – than to a destroyer.

"Besides," Lozen had gone on, "why would anyone in his right mind want to give up Hawaii for Norfolk?"

"But, Ben! You said that … "

"Don't get me wrong, Parks … I love Norfolk. But, I'd give four fingers and my left nut for duty in Pearl. It's beautiful out there, Parks. Gorgeous. Simply breathtaking! So very, very, very beautiful."

Beautiful, indeed.

Parks thanked the skipper – then, once again, set about the whole frantic process of trying to devise another plan. Back to the old drawing board.

He was, though, able to put Jeff's plight on a back burner, long enough to enjoy his honeymoon a – two-week trip to New York City.

The scenery – especially through the mountains in Pennsylvania – was breath-taking. (Like Hawaii? He was back to thinking of Jeff again.)

Parks had chosen a brand new, dark blue, 1941 Ford convertible for the trip. Convertibles, though practically legislated out of existence in the sixties and seventies, had been one of Parks' special loves. He kept the top down virtually throughout the entire trip east.

The happy groom, of course, had been accustomed to driving the Pennsylvania and Ohio Turnpikes. In 1941, neither toll road existed. Another situation which typified the differences in the forties – vis-à-vis the seventies: The oil had to be changed – twice – on the way to New York and three times on the trip back. The lubricants of the day were primitive in comparison with the motor oils from where Parks had come.

The couple stayed in picturesque little tourist homes, in quaint little towns. There were no Formica-laden **Holiday Inns** or **Ramadas** in 1941.

New York City was not as different as Parks had imagined. One monumental difference: The lack of pollution. Well, of course, the glass skyscrapers, along Park Avenue, did not exist. Also conspicuous by their absence were the ill-fated twin towers of the *World Trade Center*.

How big a change could there have been in the *Empire State Building*? Well, the high barrier, which fenced in the observation deck a few floors from the top of the building had not yet been installed.

The *Statue Of Liberty*, *St. Patrick's Cathedral* and the *Radio City Music Hall* had changed precious little. Of course, the *United Nations Building* had not yet been built.

The real shocker had been *Times Square*: It was remarkable what the smut peddlers of the sixties and seventies had done to it. The theaters on 42nd Street – which had become skin show/porn houses in the sixties – featured top-flight movies of the day, in 1941. Three of the houses presented live stage shows – accompanying the flicks. Usually big bands. Johnny Long's orchestra was playing in one of the theaters and Woody Herman's aggregation was ensconced in another.

There was a bountiful number of other pluses: Parks was able to take in such landmarks as *The Polo Grounds*, *Ebbetts Field* in Brooklyn and the old *Metropolitan Opera House* – as well as *Tony Pastor's* in Greenwich Village. All were in their more-or-less heyday!

The newlyweds attended two Broadway shows: One was *Panama Hattie*, featuring a vivacious, rising young star – Ethel Merman. The other production was Rodgers & Hammerstein's immortal *Oklahoma!*. Parks attributed his obvious unease, during the performance of the latter, to the fact that the title of the show was a constant reminder of Jeff's situation.

The happy couple stayed at the *Waldorf-Astoria*, for a fraction of the cost of a room at a **Holiday** Inn or a **Howard Johnson's** in 1979.

"Can we afford all this?" Helen had asked, as soon as Parks had tipped the bellhop – and they were alone – on their first evening in Manhattan.

"No," he'd answered. "They'll probably cart my fanny off to debtor's prison. But, you can warm yourself ... on those cold lonely nights ... with the glow that comes from the knowledge that you've slept at the *Waldorf*."

"Parks?"

"Whatcha want, Lady?"

"You know that I've never delved into your finances. I don't know all that much about them ... even now. I know that you rent cars for a living. Well, I know that you work for a company that rents cars. I don't know how much you make. I was brought up that the husband took care of the money ... the finances. I never knew anything about Walter's situation ... and I had a few surprises, when he went and died. A couple weren't very pleasant. With you, well, I always kind of figured that you were ... that you were ... that you were doing well. Pretty well, anyway. But, you always stayed the same. Exactly the same."

"What do you mean, 'stayed the same'?"

"Well, you didn't seem to be living any differently. Same room. Same clothes. Same everything. Except for the cars. You always bring home different cars. Now, all of a sudden, you're spending money ... like a drunken sailor."

"Where'd you get that expression?"

"From Jeff. He's not very fond of it."

"Well, Pretty Lady, truth to tell, I have. I've been doing pretty well. The company is going great. I don't guess I told you, but I own twenty percent of it these days. There are a great many things in store ... that should make my stock extremely valuable. Exceptionally valuable. I've been putting as much away as possible. I've invested in the stock market ... pretty heavily. Those cars that I've picked up? They're going to be worth a lot of money someday. Or at least, I think they will. Mainly, though, the reason I've stayed in my same little room is that I'm madly in love with my good-lookin' ... my well-built ... landlady. If I'd have moved out ... to more posh diggin's ... "

"There you go with your funny talk again. You must be upset. I'm sorry, Parks. I didn't mean to upset you. I probably shouldn't have brought up such a touchy subject. I seem to be gettin' pretty good at it, though."

"I'm not upset, Helen. Honest. If I'd have moved out, though, we might not be here right now ... having this conversation."

He was worried that the expression, "having this conversation" had crept in.

"I've never been happier," he hastened to add. "Never been happier to be anyplace ... other than to be here. Right here ... right now. Be here right now ... with you, My Little Chickadee. When we get home, I'll go over the whole financial thing with you. But, for the moment, content yourself that we're doing all right. I promise you ... we can afford this. I should've realized that you'd be concerned about money. I really should've gone over the whole shot with you ... long before this. I'm the one to apologize."

"I really don't mean to pry, Parks. If you'd rather ... "

"What pry? Of course you should know where we stand. I was wrong in not filling you in on these things before we got hitched. I hope that you can forgive me. For the moment, though, Me Proud Beauty, it's important for you to not worry about how much anything costs. We're gonna have a helluva honeymoon. I wouldn't have it any other way. Take my word for it ... we're all right. I wouldn't lie to you."

He kind of wished he'd not made that last statement.

The newlyweds returned to Detroit – and set about buying a home.

They found what Helen had called <u>her</u> "Dream House" – on Prevost Street, near McNichols and Greenfield Roads. The place was seven-years-old – and, marginally, similar to Parks' own "Dream House". The one on Grandmont. But, just marginally.

Less than a week after Parks and Helen had closed on their home, the house next to little Marilyn Faffenberger's became available. Parks had missed out on a chance to live just a few doors away from <u>the</u> house – the one which had meant so much to him.

<u>Well, you can't live in the past forever.</u>

As spring became summer – and rolled, relentlessly, on into fall – Parks and Helen seemed to be in heaven. Old cliché – but, in this case, apt.

"Not only are we outrageously happy," Parks had said to his wife, on many occasions, "we're abusing the privilege."

She was everything he could've hoped for – the epitome of the devoted, caring, loving wife. The house was always immaculate – but, never uncomfortable. Despite the fact that Helen usually spent about half of each day, cleaning at "her building", dinner was always on time. Parks, a confirmed workaholic, altered his life-long pattern – and was seldom home later than six o'clock.

The sainted **White Tower** – even that – had been forsaken. But **The Blue Ribbon** still loomed large. Each and every Sunday morning, the couple had continued to repair to the café – after Church, of course.

He bought her a brand new 1941 Ford coupe, a model he knew would be exceptionally valuable in the future.

The United States was gearing up for war!!!

It was everywhere. The general feeling – abroad in the land – was that going to war was simply a matter of time. That it would not be long, before the country became embroiled in the European theater. Hitler had the entire continent within his grasp!

The brave people of London braced – night after night after night – for the inevitable bombings! Dear Lord – all the destruction!

The incredible courage of those people! Filing into the shelters! Every night! Not knowing <u>what</u> would be left, after the Luftwaffe had done its worst! Unable to know what would've survived – once the bombers would have returned to their base! Impossible to envision the condition their houses or flats – once the gallant, valiant, citizens were able to go home. They couldn't know whether their homes would still be standing.

No one gave much thought to the Japanese!

As a result of the first stirrings of the war effort, prosperity was coming – albeit slowly – to Detroit. Helen had been able to rent every room in "her building" – and, indeed, had begun to compile a waiting list.

And, at Parks' urging, she was able to bring in much more money than she'd ever dreamed possible. Parks advised her to charge at least $20.00 per month for each room – and a minimum of $30.00 for her "apartment". He didn't insist, of course. It was, after all, "her building". She took his advice – with much trepidation – and was surprised at the ease with which she got her price.

She drew the line at raising the rents of existing tenants. She simply couldn't bring herself to "do such a thing". Our hero never pressed the matter.

Obviously, the thought of war held much more significance for Parks than simply room-rental rates or the scarcity of automobiles or the escalation of property and stock values. He had to get Jeff Shaddon off the *Oklahoma*! Out of Pearl Harbor!

As October pushed into November – a scant month before the "Day of Infamy" – Parks was becoming more and more frantic! Night after night, he would lie awake – desperately groping for some brilliant, ingenious, plan which would see his stepson removed from the oncoming devastation!

He prayed! He prayed – continually! He asked Mr. Horne – and "the boys" – if they wouldn't intercede! Nothing came! Ever! A total blank! Always!

To suggest that Helen intercede was out! She was already too sensitive about his concern for Jeff's presence in Hawaii.

Well, maybe he'd have to get her involved. We are, y'know, talking about a human life, here!

A day never passed without Parks frantically searching through his memory – hoping to flush out any little glimmering of the *Oklahoma*, and how badly she may have been hit. He fervently wished that he'd paid more attention when it had actually happened.

He knew that the *California* had been badly hit! A classmate, in the fourth grade, had lost a brother on that battleship. Of course, everyone knew how badly the *Arizona* had been devastated. As Jim Sidorwitz, he'd always wanted to visit the monument to the ship, in Hawaii. Try as he might, though, Parks could not remember the exact fate of Jeff's ship. He was certain that it had not been good!

When Thanksgiving came, he knew that he could no longer stand aside. He had to see that the boy got out! It had to be done – no matter what the cost!

It was the couple's first Thanksgiving as man and wife – their first Thanksgiving in their new home. He looked across the table at his new wife. She was the picture of contentment. He thought back one year – to their confrontation at **Shore's**.

He would let her enjoy her Thanksgiving. But, he would have to do something!

And do it quickly!

On the following day – Friday – as the couple sat reading and listening to the radio, Parks began to speak.

However, he was cut short as – Frank Munn, on the *Waltz Time* radio program, began to sing Jerome Kern's beautiful *The Song Is You*. Helen was dewy-eyed at the lyric – and completely taken with Mr. Munn's performance! As he sang, "Why can't I let you know the song my heart would sing," she looked across at her husband – and smiled, warmly. She was so filled with love for him! That was so evident!

Once again, Parks could not bring himself to spoil a special moment – and broach the gut-wrenching subject to his wife. He would have to think of something else.

Each day – when no brilliant idea had formulated – Parks would attempt to summon courage enough to do what he knew must be done.

Each day, he was simply unable to blurt out what he knew must be said.

And December seventh was approaching! Relentlessly! With a rush!

He began suffering terrible headaches! They were caused, of course, by the God- awful burden he was carrying.

Jim Sidorwitz had always been known as a procrastinator. He had joked that he'd have postponed the bicentennial a couple of years, if he'd thought he could get away with it. The line had always brought a chuckle from his friends and family.

But, the situation with Jeff was no laughing matter!

Finally, on December 5, 1941, Parks made his move!

George D. Schultz

As the couple was doing dishes – Helen washing and Parks wiping, as usual – she asked him, "Why so quiet, Honey?"

"Oh?" He tried to keep the nervous twitter from his voice. "I ... I wasn't aware that I was being all that quiet."

"If I've learned anything about you, Parks Hayworth," she responded with a laugh, "I've learned that ... unless you're talkin' a mile-a-minute ... there's something wrong. There's something up. C'mon, now. What is it?"

Her voice was so bright! So full of spring!

He sighed deeply.

"Oh, nothing," he responded. "No! Wait! Yes! Yes, there is too something! Helen ... you know how you've always said that ... that it's as if I always seemed to know what was going to happen?"

"Yes. Yes, of course. But, what's that go to do with any ... ?"

"Well," he interrupted, "the truth is ... "

Suddenly – as though he'd been pole-axed – Parks dropped to the gleaming kitchen floor! The cup he was drying shattered into a million pieces.

The horror on Helen's face screamed the expectation that her new – her wonderful – life with Parks had also been shattered! Along with the cup!

She dropped to her knees! She took his head in her soap-laden hands!

He was gasping for breath! Clawing at his collar! Frantically, she unbuttoned it!

Helen's eyes seemed to be protruding from her head! She tried to scream! She tried to speak! She could do neither! It was as though her throat had seized up! She watched her husband become more and more frenzied!

She knelt there – petrified in the icy grip of terror!

He looked up at her! His expression was of both love and sorrow!

Then, his eyes glassed over – and he went limp!

Frantically, Helen scrambled to her feet! She ran to the telephone – in the living room! Her voice returned! It must have!

She was screaming!

In her frenzy, she was able to dial "O"!

When the operator came on the line, Helen hysterically tried to explain her predicament!

Telephone operators in 1941 were much different than the robots the phone companies, across the nation, seemed to produce in the seventies. The voice on the other end assured Helen that everything would be all right. She managed to verify Helen's address – then put in a hurried call to the police and fire departments!

Within minutes, an ambulance, two police squad cars and a shiny red 1940 Chevrolet coupe from the fire department were speeding toward the house on Prevost!

Parks remained virtually comatose – for four days!

He regained consciousness on Tuesday, December 9th – the day following Franklin Roosevelt's impassioned "Day of Infamy" address to the Congress!

Two days after the actual "Day of Infamy"!

Parks didn't slowly surface from his unconsciousness! His eyes snapped open – as if they'd been equipped with springs! He didn't pause to ponder his condition – or his whereabouts!

For a fleeting moment, he was terrified that he'd been sent back to 1979!

"Jeff!" he shouted – as he sat bolt upright in bed. "Jeff! Oh my God! Jeff!"

He looked about frantically! His eyes darting in a frenzied search for Helen! Or – hopefully – for Helen and Jeff!

He was alone! In a private room! In a hospital!

He sprang out of bed – and dashed into the corridor!

He was halfway down the hallway – headed toward the nurses' station – when one of the young resident physicians shouted, "Stop!"

Parks never broke stride! His hospital gown flailed in the air behind him. He'd built such momentum that he practically ran over the counter at the station! The two startled, clad-in-white, ladies behind the wooden separation jumped to their feet!

"Quick!" he shouted. "Quick! Where's my wife? Where is she? I've got to know! Got to see her! Where is she? My stepson! Is he all right? For Christ's sakes! Don't just stand there! Where's my wife? Where in the name of Christ is she?"

At that moment, the young doctor – half Parks' age – caught up, breathing heavily. He'd not come close to catching up with the distraught patient!

"Mister Hayworth!" the young man panted. "Mister Hayworth! You must get back to your room! You're a sick man! Please, Sir!"

Parks paid him no attention!

"My wife!" he continued to shout at the two nurses. "My wife! Where is she? I gotta know where my wife is! Where, in God's name, is she?"

"Well now, Mister Hayworth," began the young man, still terribly short of breath. "It's all right. Everything is all right. Now, let's get back to our room, shall we?"

"God damn it!" Parks slammed his fist on the wooden counter top! "Will you, for Christ's sakes, tell me where my wife is? Or do I have to tear the whole fucking building apart? Now, cut the bullshit! Tell me where my wife is!"

Then, turning to the young doctor, he screamed, "I'll break your fucking head!"

The young man paled! His eyes opened to monumental proportions! He wheeled around – and raced, frantically, down the long corridor!

Three or four patients – and/or their visitors – poked heads out of their rooms!

Parks turned back to the two nurses.

"Look," he panted, "I'm sorry. I didn't mean to get that shook up! I apologize for the language! I never use those words! But ... you've got to understand ... I've got to see my wife! Speak with my wife! Talk to my wife!"

The older of the two women reached across the counter and took one of Parks' hands into both of her own.

"Mister Hayworth," she began, "there's no easy way of telling you this: Your wife is dead!"

Parks grabbed for the counter with his free hand! He almost missed! He tried to speak! Nothing came!

"I'm sorry, Mister Hayworth," the nurse continued. "I hated to have to tell you like that. But, the way you were acting ... there was no other way."

"Here," she went on, walking around the counter. "Here ... let me help you back to your room. I'll try and tell you about it. I'm sorry, Sir. Just as sorry as I can be. Please believe that. She was a fine lady ... a wonderful lady."

Parks nodded absently – as the nurse took him by the arm. He was surprised at the extent to which he found himself obeying – meekly obeying – the heavy-set, matronly woman. In his entire life, he'd never been as docile as that. Ever!

As she guided him back to his room, the young resident barreled toward them, from the opposite direction! The doctor and two huge, black, attendants – one of whom clutched a straightjacket in his immense lunch-hook of a hand!

"There!" shouted the young physician. "That's him! Right there! Get him!"

The nurse laughed – and spoke to the older black man.

"He's all right, Sam," she assured. "He's fine. Just let him be. Just forget it."

"You sure, Miss Elizabeth?"

"Positive. See? He's just as docile as can be. Wouldn't hurt a flea."

"Yes'm, Miss Elizabeth."

The resident was turning beet-red!

"What do you mean he's all right?" he bellowed. "He was running up and down the hallway ... like a mad man! He even threatened me!"

"He was just a little upset," Elizabeth answered, with a smile. "He's fine now. Aren't you, Mister Hayworth?"

Parks was totally nonplused.

"What?" he finally responded. "Oh. Yes. Yes, I'm fine. I'm sorry if I ... "

"Perfectly all right," soothed Elizabeth.

Then, to the resident and the two attendants, she continued, "Now, if you'll excuse us, I have to get Mister Hayworth back to his room."

"Well," muttered the young man, "I want him sedated!"

"We'll handle it, Doctor," Elizabeth replied firmly.

She led him to his room and ushered him back into bed. Then, she tucked the covers in around him and stood over him, gazing down into his ashen face.

"Please," he asked, tears streaming down his face. "Please ... won't you please? Please, Miss! Please ... tell me about it."

Elizabeth sighed deeply.

"Well, Mister Hayworth," she began, "as I say, I'm sorry that I had to be the one to tell you. We'd planned it to where Doctor Lodewig ... he would be the one. But, no one knew when you were going to come out of ... out of your coma."

"Yes, yes. I understand all that. But, what about Helen? Where is she? What happened?"

"Well, they brought you in last Friday."

"Last Friday? What ... what day is this?"

"Tuesday. Tuesday ... December ninth."

"Nineteen forty-one?"

"Yes. Of course. What year would it be?"

"I'm ... I'm sorry," muttered Parks. "I'm ... I'm just a little upset. I didn't mean to interrupt you. Go ahead ... please!"

"Well, like I said, they brought you in on Friday. Darndest thing that any of us have ever seen. Doctor Lodewig too. Had all the earmarks of a heart attack ... or maybe a stroke. But, every time we'd pursue one course of action or another, it always turned out negative. Doctor Lodewig said he really didn't think you had either a stroke or a heart attack. But, he sure didn't know what it was you did have."

"Yes, Ma'am." Parks was surprised to find that he'd twisted the top hem of the sheet into a misshapen mass. "But, could you please ... please ... tell me about my wife?"

Elizabeth nodded.

"I was coming to that," she said. "I've got to tell you these other things ... because, to tell you the truth, so much has happened since they brought you in. If I didn't tell you gradually, you'd never be able to put it all together."

Parks did his best to keep the flaming rage within him. His hands found two virgin areas on the sheet – and began to twist once more.

"For one thing," continued the nurse, "we're in a war! A big one! On Sunday, the Japs bombed Pearl Harbor. That's in Hawaii. Oh, that's right. You already knew that, didn't you?"

Parks scrunched his eyes closed.

"Yes," he mumbled. "Yes, I knew that."

"Well, the Japs ... they bombed Pearl Harbor. No one was expecting it. Jeez! I couldn't believe it. Nobody could."

"Yes Ma'am. Look. I'm trying to remain calm. I think I know what it is you're going to tell me. But, please! Won't you ... please ... go ahead and say it?"

"Well, Mrs. Hayworth ... she spent the entire time with you here. Right here in the hospital. She never left the building."

If such a thing as a heart-broken smile exists, that was what crossed Parks' face.

He nodded slightly. "My wife wouldn't," he rasped.

"She didn't. But, when the Japs hit on Sunday, she got awfully worried. Your son is there, you know."

"I know."

"Well, the boat he was on got hit. Pretty bad, I guess. Mrs. Hayworth ... she couldn't find out anything on Sunday. Nothing! Not a thing! The stations ... they all went off the radio ... at about ... I don't know ... one-thirty in the morning. Maybe two o'clock. And she still couldn't find out anything. Poor thing. She was half out of her mind with worry. Spent half the night in the phone booth, down the hall. Between every call, she'd come back ... she always did ... to see if there'd have been any change in yourself. Then, she'd go back to phoning. I guess she tried everything ... and everybody ... she could think of. The *Navy Department*... or whatever it is. But, they couldn't help her. She called the newspapers. Same thing. Japs caught everyone by surprise ... like I said."

"Not everybody," he replied, cryptically.

"What?"

"Nothing. I guess I'm still a bit groggy."

"Anyway, I guess that ... along about four in the morning ... she was able to get through to someone in Washington. I think it was Senator Vandenberg. Either him or Senator Ferguson. Anyway, whoever it was ... he found out some things for her."

Parks closed his eyes – and nodded his head. That had been positively brilliant of Helen. She was a smart lady. He couldn't think of another person who'd have thought of calling their United States senator. Then, the inevitable: Tears continued to course down his cheeks – only faster now! And more of them! The numbness had begun to subside. In place of the impact – the horrible shock – a terrible void began to consume him.

It was at that point that he began to realize just how much he would miss his beloved Helen! His wife! His friend! His lover! She had been a remarkable woman. He loved her deeply.

All of their friends had told Parks – at one time or another – how they'd admired the way that he and Helen had never stopped "playing house".

"And we never will," Parks had always replied.

Now, she was gone! She would be there no longer! No more "playing house"!

It was also at that point that he realized the staggering – the overwhelming – proportion of his failure! How horribly he'd failed her! Failed her miserably! Failed her – and her son! Failed her – and <u>their</u> son!

He began to weep.

" ... ship the boy was on," Elizabeth was saying, "was hit. Hit bad. It was the *Oklahoma* ... or something like that. Anyway, whatever ship it was, it took something like six torpedoes."

Six torpedoes! Parks' fear of the worst had been well-founded!

"My God," he sobbed. "Six torpedoes! The ship had to have gone down."

Elizabeth nodded.

"It was more like it capsized," she explained. "Or it went and rolled over or something. A lot of boys were killed. But, I guess they figured that ... maybe if there was an air bubble in there ... they figured that ... some of 'em, anyway ... could maybe be alive. No one seemed to know much of anything about your boy."

Parks pulled at his earlobe. Maybe no news was good news.

"Finally, this morning," Elizabeth continued, "they got word. He was killed. They couldn't never confirm it ... not till this morning. But, he was dead. Goddam Japs!"

"Oh, God," gurgled Parks. "Why him? Why ... of all people ... him? He was such a ... such a good kid."

Parks broke down completely – his body wracking hysterically in convulsive sob after convulsive sob!

Elizabeth did her best to console him – but he was totally implacable. She simply pulled a chair over to the bed and sat down – patiently waiting for her patient to "ride it out".

It took almost ten minutes.

At length, he was able to ask, "Are ... are they sure?"

She nodded. "Absolutely positive." Her voice was as husky as his.

"And ... and my wife?"

Elizabeth shook her head slowly.

"She just couldn't cope with it ... poor thing! First you ... and then the boy! She just simply collapsed! Never regained consciousness! Just too much for her! Too much for her heart! Doctor Lodewig said that she'd had a history of heart problems. Went back to when she was a child ... as I understand it."

Parks shook his head. Looking at Elizabeth, through tear-filled eyes, his voice was a husky whisper. "I never knew. She never told me. But, then, she wouldn't. I ... I don't know what I'll do without her. How can I ever go on without her? She was everything ... everything ... to me!"

Once again, he broke down.

"She was the best thing that ever happened to me," he wailed. "And I failed her! I failed her ... badly! I goddam well failed her! She'd be alive, if I hadn't ... ! Why did it have to be her? And Jeff? Why'd it have to be Jeff? Why couldn't it have been me? Why not a piece of shit ... like me? Why Helen? Why Jeff?"

"Well, Mister Hayworth, it was just God's will. That's all. Just God's will."

"Yeah," he sneered. "Shit! God's will!"

"Sometimes, we can't understand these things, but ..."

Parks raised a hand.

"Please," he snapped. "Please. Spare me the sermon. If it's a sermon I want, I'll listen to Bishop Sheen."

"Bishop who?"

"Never mind. You never heard of him."

Elizabeth took his hand into both of hers, once again, and, in a soft whisper, she said, "I'm truly sorry, Mister Hayworth. I really and truly am."

He made several futile attempts to wipe away the tears.

"I know," he muttered. "I know. I'm sorry. I apologize. I didn't mean to snap at you ... bite your head off. And the language ... please excuse my language."

She massaged the back of his hand.

"No apology necessary," she replied. "It must be a terrible, terrible, shock for you. I'll have them bring you a sedative. That'll help you to ... "

"No! Please, no! I'd rather not! What time is it?"

"About quarter-after-three. In the afternoon."

"I've ... I've got to get out of here. Has anyone made arrangements? For the funeral? For the funerals? For my wife? For my wife ... and my son?"

ELEVEN

In the days and weeks that followed the deaths of his wife and stepson, Parks managed to survive. Just barely.

There were, of course, the funeral arrangements to be made – and the agony of Helen's wake. The funeral director was a blessing. He'd put everything together. Parks seemed to simply follow along behind, as in a trance – nodding his head, absently, or shaking his head, blankly, as the coffin was chosen, floral arrangements selected, grave site purchased, newspaper announcements composed and legal papers prepared and filed.

Parks had become violently ill – sick to his stomach – upon realizing, as he'd looked at the various coffins, on display in the basement of the mortuary, that his beloved Helen was probably behind one of the many doors he'd walked past.

Dear Lord – maybe she was even being embalmed at that very moment!

He'd had to beat a hasty retreat to the men's room a second time!

The first time Parks was able to lay his eyes on his wife was the day of the wake. There she'd lain! In that damn coffin! She looked so – so pasty! So lifeless! Certainly not the vibrant Helen he'd loved so deeply. Once again, he became terribly sick! The beginning of another tradition?

Despite the fact that Helen had virtually no family, he was surprised at the number of people who came to pay their respects. It really shouldn't have been such a shocker. Although essentially a private person, there had been very few lives that Helen had touched – in which she'd not left a lasting mark. An indelible impression.

Another surprise came when Parks noted the number of cars lined up behind the limousine for the damnable procession from the funeral home to the church – and then on to the cemetery. He'd expected few – wondered if there'd be any. More than a dozen vehicles made the long, bleak, somber, trek.

The day before Helen's funeral, Jeff had been buried at sea.

Parks had been, of course, unable to attend the memorial services planned by the Navy. Not only had he to see to Helen's situation – but the government had slapped all manner of travel restrictions on the civilian populace. Parks didn't press for any sort of exemption. He'd never have been able to withstand another funeral.

Death was all around him! It permeated everything he touched!

Helen's friends – some of whom Parks had never met prior to his wife's passing – did their best to involve him in as many of their undertakings as possible.

Loving tribute to Helen's lifetime of giving and caring.

Jim Sidorwitz had always cherished his private moments – seven children notwithstanding. Parks Hayworth – the widower – was grateful not to be left alone.

He felt singularly guilty, of course, for not having prevented Jeff's death – when he'd known full well what was coming! Had known for years! Literally years! And still the young man was lost! The loss of Helen, obviously, compounded his deep sense of guilt – and the overwhelming despondency that accompanied his monstrous sin! His unforgivable sin!

He seemed on the verge of suicide! Every day!

He was "escorted" to a Christmas party, at the home of two of Helen's friends.

The couple, Pam and Larry Hollis, had flat-out invaded Parks' sanctuary on Prevost, and – once Larry had literally dressed Parks – the pair had physically hauled him off to their home for a raucous party.

Pam and Larry lived next door to the home that Helen had shared with Walter, for so long. They'd kept in touch with Helen over the three years since Helen had sold the house. Neither the Hollises nor the rest of their circle were given to hell-raising parties – such as the Christmas Eve get-together, in 1941. Certainly, the neighbors must've had their own thoughts about such a spirited (and raucously loud) celebration – so soon after the United States had found itself at war.

The entire production, Parks would discover later, had been staged exclusively for his benefit. What greater tribute to Helen?

While he had been unable to join in the merriment, the camaraderie that filled every room had, mercifully, taken the edge off his loneliness – and the monumental guilt which had become his constant companion. To a degree, anyway. And only temporarily.

Probably, it had pulled him through those horrid, almost unbearable, days!

As the New Year approached, Parks found it impossible to remain in the house on Prevost. His and Helen's "love nest". Her "Dream House". He decided to look for a single room. Good enough for the likes of him. Certainly, he could've "bumped" one of the tenants from "Helen's Building". However, he could no more live there – than in the house he'd shared with her. Besides, she wouldn't like that.

He managed to find a room. He rented it by the week. The rent – reflecting the times – was outrageous for such a positive hovel. Once again, he found himself living upstairs over a row of stores on Grand River. His new residence was in the middle of the block – between Pinehurst and Mendota – a few blocks from the dealership.

His "diggings" were exceptionally Spartan. To the point of being depressing; furnished with an old bed, two even-older chairs – neither of which came close to matching the wobbly table of the same vintage – plus a grime-laden stove, which had to be coaxed to light, and a clattering refrigerator, both of which had seen much better days.

This was all he required, he told himself. This was all he deserved.

Despite the fact that Parks could not bear to live in the cozy place on Prevost, he couldn't bring himself to sell it. In a raging housing shortage, the home sat vacant.

He was tempted to sell the building on Mansfield and Grand River – but, he decided against that too. It was – when all was said and done – a very valuable property.

Besides, it was "Helen's Building"!

He contracted with the wife of the gentleman who owned the grocery store downstairs – to keep the place clean and to collect the rent generated by the rooms on the second floor. Although he'd been sorely tempted to raise rental rates across the board, he resisted.

Something else Helen wouldn't have liked.

Finally, with an acute housing shortage hammering – unrelentingly – at him, Parks decided that he'd be a fool not to, at least, rent the home on Prevost. He would be extremely selective – and screen the applicants most carefully. It was, after all, a seller's market. And it was Helen's "Dream house".

The couple he ultimately selected seemed ideal:

Hector LaCroix was an engineer from a small town in France – one which had been overrun by the Nazis. In 1942, he was involved in a top-secret defense project at the **Ford** Rouge plant. Hector never – ever – spoke of his job.

He and his wife, Renee, moved into the house in July.

Since Helen's and Jeff's deaths, Parks had thrown himself, helter-skelter, into his work. The easiest means, he knew, of escape.

With the advent of gas rationing, it became feasible to cut back the rent-a-car operation. **Dubin Auto Rental** wound up selling the bulk of the company's immense-for-the-times rental fleet to **Keller-Dubin Motor Car Company** – at an obscene profit.

Clark Dubin's revenge!

While, technically, Parks was still administering the car rental company, there was very little left to administer. With the insistent (and persistent) backing of Clark Dubin – and over the violent objections of Horace Keller – Parks took on additional duties, within the sales department of the dealership.

The sales situation answered two of Parks' needs:

1. The profit potential was enormous – leading to a goodly number of rather staggering commissions.
2. He could spend all day – and half the night – at the dealership.

It was escape – pure and simple.

Even after six and seven and eight months had passed, Helen's death continued to foster the constant, depressing, miasma – the constant funk – that consumed the man.

Virtually every night, he would lie in the old bedstead – fists clenched – and snarl such things as: "Mister Horne? Are you there? Well, fuck you, Mister Horne! Fuck you ... and all your 'Boys'!" More often than not, he was on the verge of screaming the epithets!

As a sop for his despair, he found himself fiercely aggressive, when it came to his sales techniques. He became – far and away – the Number-One Salesman in the entire dealership! The commissions began to pile up! Money was pouring in!

Jim Sidorwitz had lived beneath the poverty level – all of his life. Parks Hayworth found himself accumulating wealth – faster than he'd ever dreamed possible.

At the dealership, he was a dynamo! Indefatigable! He escalated his investments in real estate. Primarily, he bought land outside of what was then the central city – property he knew would skyrocket to many-times its early-forties worth, once the migration to the suburbs would begin in the fifties.

He bought no more cars. This was no time to invest in automobiles.

If Parks was conscious of a definitive change in his personality – and he could hardly have been unaware of such a transformation – he appeared totally unconcerned.

His strictly-business, aggressive, approach (a "throwback" to the seventies?) was a contradiction of his personality prior to Helen's death. He'd always told anyone who'd listen that he suffered from "terminal schmaltz".

He'd taken Helen to every **MGM** musical he could track down. Pictures such as *"Maytime"*, *"The New Moon"*, *"Naughty Marietta"* and *"Rosemarie"* – each of which had starred Jeanette

MacDonald and Nelson Eddy. Each was the embodiment of the term "schmaltz"!

When Helen was alive, he'd anxiously awaited the release of his all-time favorite picture – *Going My Way* – which would feature Bing Crosby as a priest. Although most contended that Barry Fitzgerald, as the crusty Father Fitzgibbons, had stolen the picture, Jim Sidorwitz had been enchanted by the *Metropolitan Opera* star, Rise Stevens. It had been, as stated, his all-time favorite movie – and he could hardly wait to take Helen to see it. They'd shamelessly hold hands! It'd be one of the high points of his entire life! An answer to a prayer!

But, of course, that was all gone now!

Jim Sidorwitz had always found it terribly frustrating, that Kathleen had never enjoyed such movies. Wonderful woman that she was, she'd attend them – because she knew how much they'd meant to him. As often as not, though, it had been a monumental struggle for her to stay awake. Of course, Jim had encountered the same problem, when he'd humor her – and accompany her to a western.

Motion pictures seemed to epitomize the lack of common interests between them.

"*Going My Way*, made in 1944, had never played at a movie house near him, during Jim's marriage to Kathleen.

However, it had shown twice on television. The first time, Kathleen had fought valiantly to stay awake – and had lost. The second time, when shown at an earlier hour, the TV station had so chopped-up the movie that it was barely recognizable. That one "didn't count".

"Why didn't you advertise it as <u>excerpts</u> from *Going My Way*?", he'd asked, in an angry letter to the station's general manager!

During their marriage, Jim and Kathleen had gotten along passably well. After their divorce, they had remained close (although not intimate) friends. Over the ensuing years, they'd grown much, much closer.

The marriage had lasted 18 years. Except for the seven children, though, the union had not been especially rewarding – for either spouse.

Jim had often said, "When I'm called to that big rent-a-car counter in the sky, I will have left the world a hell of a lot better place than when I found it ... by dint of the fact that I've sired those seven wonderful kids."

As a husband/wife relationship, the marriage, as stated, had never been very satisfying for either Jim or Kathleen. Consequently, it withered and died. The shriveling had been gradual. Had taken years. But, the marriage had, after 18 years, "dried up".

Jim, from the time he'd separated from Kathleen, maintained that he'd never stop searching for the woman who would be Jeanette MacDonald to his Nelson Eddy. Or Judy Garland to his Gene Kelly. Dolly Sidorwitz had not been that far from the truth.

Until he became Parks Hayworth, he'd never found his Jeanette – or his Judy.

By the summer of 1942, Parks Hayworth had lost every trace of "schmaltziness". His fantasies had turned to dust. The dream world – where he'd spent so much time throughout his life – had come to mean nothing. There <u>was</u> no dream world!

His visions of returning to the thirties and forties – and picking up on all those wondrous movies and those glorious radio shows had all turned to ashes. In the seventies, he couldn't lay his hands on enough cassettes of *Fibber McGee & Molly* and *The Bob Hope Show* and *Duffy's Tavern* and *Amos N' Andy*.

How wonderful it would be, he'd thought, to be able to enjoy them first hand. In their element. When they were fresh and new.

But, without Helen? Without her, it meant nothing! Nothing! Absolutely nothing!

No longer did he drive past the little house on Penrod – in hopes of looking in on young Jimmy. No longer did he drive past his grandparents' "Dog House". He never looked for his grandfather's new 1941 blue-and-white Buick outside **Freddie's Bar**.

His thinking had become completely turned-around. Jim had been so broke – and while money had always been a major consideration (how could it not be?) it had never been the be-all and end-all.

With the affluent Parks, it became his uppermost priority! A massive sea change.

He spent scant time away from the dealership – and those precious-few hours were likewise devoted to the accumulation of wealth. When he was not out in the suburbs, examining a choice parcel of land, he was lying awake in bed – well into the night – concentrating upon the vast font of trivia still stored in his memory.

How to put that minutiae to use? Well, there were always bookies around. The New York Yankees had been upset by the St. Louis Cardinals, in the 1942 World Series.

That little nugget should bring in a few dollars.

The St. Louis Browns would win their first – and only – pennant in 1944. They would have to sweep the season's final series from the Yankees, to beat back the Tigers.

Even with the blowout of "The Bronx Bombers", Detroit would have to lose the final game to – of all people – the Washington Senators. The "First In War/First In Peace/Last In The American League" Washington Senators. One of the Tigers aces – Dizzy Trout – would be on the mound! And he'd <u>lose</u>! All of those gems of knowledge could be converted – when the time was right – to more than a little coin of the realm.

It would even be possible to clean up on the first game of the '44 *Series* – if he picked his bookies with enough care. Although the heavily-favored Cardinals would go on to win the World Championship, they'd lose, in game one, to the Browns. Lose to a rather obscure pitcher – named Denny Galehouse.

His beloved 1945 Tigers would have a tough time winning the pennant. He remembered an especially crucial series against the hated Yankees – at *Yankee Stadium*. It seemed to him that the Tigers had swept three or four games. But, he wasn't quite sure. He'd have to be awfully careful with his bets, when '45 season rolled around.

His memory, obviously, was far from total recall – witness the *Oklahoma*!

He did remember the most crucial game – in that exciting series with the Yankees, in 1945 – being won on a pinch hit by another obscure pitcher, Detroit's Zeb Eaton.

Once the pennant race had been settled, the New York club had utilized a seldom-used technicality to waive their pitching ace – Hank Borowy – out of the league. The formidable Yankee pitcher had wound up with the Chicago Cubs – the Tigers' opponent in the *World Series*. Young Jimmy Sidorwitz had been furious at the transaction!

The addition of one of the best right-handers in the *American League* vaulted the Cubs to favorites in "The Fall Classic". Especially after Borowy defeated the Tigers' ace – Hal Newhouser – in the *Series* opener!

The Cubs still lost. Sixty years later, they'd never found their way back to "The World Serious"!

The betting potential was unlimited! A lot of money to be made!

TWELVE

As 1942 turned into 1943, Parks became even more reclusive. Helen's friends, couple by couple, had long since begun to wash their hands of attempting to persuade him to participate in social and family functions. To them, he'd become a lost cause.

He, by then, was spending virtually every waking hour at the dealership. He'd become terrified at even the prospect of missing a possible sale. His marathon days at the showroom limited the time available to devote to the necessary legwork required to search out possible real estate windfalls.

So? He hired an agent!

Elliot Voorhees had, at one time, been a bookkeeper at **Keller-Dubin**. An up-and-coming star, he'd gone on to establish his own financial consultant business in the summer of 1941. Voorhees had handled the personal finances of Clark Dubin since he'd hung out his shingle.

Dubin introduced Voorhees to Parks – and recommended the two get together.

They'd hit it off immediately.

Parks rather surprised himself when he found himself instructing Voorhees to keep an eye open for any house for sale on Grandmont – between Orangelawn and West Chicago. Maybe some of the "schmaltziness" had remained. Or was possibly returning?

Was it possible that it hadn't all died?

Although his "Dream House" had failed to appear on the market, two months after Parks and Elliot had met, the home in which little Marilyn Faffenberger had lived became available.

"Grab it!" Parks half-shouted. "Slurp it up!"

"They want too damn much money for it, Parks," Voorhees had cautioned. "It's not worth that kind of money."

"I don't care! Get 'em down as far as you can ... then, grab it! I want it! I want that house!"

"But, Parks! It's just a damn house! There are a million others ... just like it ... that'll ... "

"I don't care. Buy the thing! Get it for me, Elliot."

Once he'd acquired the Faffenberger home, Parks put it up for rental. The list of applicants was, of course, overwhelming!

He didn't spend a great amount of time checking out the family to whom he rented the place. They seemed nice enough, though. His new tenants were an Irish family named Brogan. He was a mechanic and she was a housewife. With three children – a considerable burden in the rental marketplace of that (or any other) era – they'd been unable to find housing.

Parks could relate. Jim Sidorwitz had experienced a goodly number of adventures – most of them horribly unpleasant – when his seven kids were growing up. The Brogan children seemed well-behaved. Besides, there <u>was</u> the name Brogan – it sounded so much like Hogan, his name for Cynthia.

For Cynthia (sigh) in "another life". He was comfortable with the Brogans.

As time passed, Clark Dubin had become more and more concerned with Parks – and his never-ending obsession with his finances. With making money!

"Take a break," he'd admonished. "Take a vacation, Parks. Some goddam thing. You're not a spring chicken, y'know. You're gonna burn yourself out ... quicker'n shit! You mark my words, you asshole! You'll burn yourself out!"

Even irascible old Horace Keller, Dubin's partner, got into the act. "Slow down, Man! You're already makin' more money than either Clark or me, f'God's sakes. You don't need it all! Leave some for the rest of us! You're goin' to wind up bein' the richest man in the whole damn graveyard."

It wasn't just the two owners: One of the ladies at the office expressed her concern:

Gertrude Potter, who had worked in the accounting office since early 1939 – and who, along with Miss Ellis, had performed most of the paper work while Parks was "out hustling" business for the car rental entity – cornered our boy one day, near the water cooler. It was a week before Christmas – 1943.

"Mister Hayworth," she'd expounded. "I'm surprised. I thought you never took a break."

"Don't let it get around," he replied with as near as he ever got to a smile. "Could ruin my reputation ... as a money-grubbing S.O.B."

"S.O.B.? What does that mean? What's an S.O.B.?"

Parks reflected on the naiveté of the period once more – something on which he'd not dwelled, in a long, long while.

"Well," he stammered, "it's ... uh ... it ... well, it sort of means son of a bitch."

She blushed! Parks was certain that he'd stopped noticing ladies blush. For all he knew, ladies simply didn't blush anymore. If they did, he surely hadn't noticed.

"Well," Gertrude replied, "you're certainly not one of those. But, we are worried about you. All of us. You work harder than anyone. Are you going to take any time off for Christmas?"

"Christmas?" He struggled to keep the contempt from his voice. "I doubt it. At the risk of sounding like ol' Scrooge himself, I've really got no family ... and so, really, Christmas isn't all that special to me. Not anymore, it's not."

She lowered her soft brown eyes.

"Yes, I know," she responded, in a whisper. "I know. I know about your wife and son. We all do. I'm sorry."

He looked at her. Stared at her. He wondered why he'd not spoken to her in such a long time. She and Miss Ellis – her boss – had, after all, been the first two employees he'd ever trained, in the wonderful world of the rent-a-car business.

Oh, he'd exchanged pleasantries with her once in a while – but, had gravitated away from any of the office people as the rental company had grown. Then, of course, when Helen had died, he'd "dug a hole – and pulled it in after him".

Since the early days, he'd barely noticed her. She was attractive – in a plain sort of way. A little on the short side, maybe. She couldn't be much more than five-one or five-two. Pretty face. And long blond hair.

He'd long since stopped noticing such things.

"That's nice of you, Gertie," he finally replied. "Nice of you to care."

"Look, Mister Hayworth, if you don't have anyplace to go ... anyone to be with ... on Christmas ... why, you'd be more than welcome at my mother's place. My son and I ... we live with my mother. We don't have much ... but, you'd be more than welcome to share what we do have."

"Your husband? In the service, is he?"

"Uh ... well, he was. He was killed, you see. At Pearl Harbor."

It was Parks' turn to lower his eyes.

"I'm ... I'm sorry. So very sorry. I didn't know."

She attempted a smile.

"He was on the *California*," she rasped.

"I'm sorry. It must be very difficult for you to try and raise the boy. How old is the little guy?"

"Going to be two. He was born about three months after his father was killed."

Parks winced.

Shaking his head, he replied, "Never got to see his son. That's ... that's tragic. How very sad."

"Well, Charles is still a baby. We ... you know ... we make out all right. But, I can certainly sympathize with you."

"That's nice of you. You're a nice lady. It's also sweet of you to offer me your hospitality at Christmas. But, I'll be all right. I'll be fine. I'm honored, though ... totally honored ... that you'd invite me. You don't really know me all that well. I don't know you all that well either, for that matter."

"What difference does that make? It's Christmas. The time to be with people ... people who care about you. It's really not a time to be alone. For anyone to be alone."

Once again, Parks marveled at the genuineness of the people at Christmas time.

In the forties, Madison Avenue hadn't had a chance to turn the season into a red-and-green sales curve – yet.

Upon reflection, Parks wondered if he'd actually be able to cope with being among others – in a family situation – at Christmas. He had – surprisingly enough – poked his head from his self-imposed hole, for the briefest of heartbeats.

But, then he immediately retreated – back into his refuge.

Parks didn't break out of his shell in 1944 either. He steadfastly refused to deviate from his 12-hour work regimen. The money, of course, continued to roll in.

From time to time, he would reflect upon his lack of sensitivity. All through his life, he'd always considered himself to be a caring, empathetic, unselfish person. It was obvious that he had changed – dramatically. The only thing that bothered him – was the fact that his loss of compassion didn't bother him.

All those war songs! The ones that had meant so much to him – the first time through what he'd considered the last romantic era of the twentieth century – hardly moved him. He simply never listened to them. Never listened to the radio. Never played a record. Had neither a radio nor a phonograph in his hole-in-the-wall living quarters.

Such tunes as *Stage Door Canteen, This Is Worth Fighting For, We've Got The Lord On Our Side* and *There's a Star Spangled Banner Waving Somewhere* moved him not at all – on his second excursion through the period.

The war, of course, was going well for the Allies. It would be a matter of another year or so before V-E Day – and then V-J Day. Parks simply could not get himself "up" for the coming celebrations – another situation, he knew, that should concern him.

But, it didn't.

Returning

Then, 1945! At long last, a weary world witnessed the end of the bloodiest war in history! The Third Reich had been obliterated! Then, that glorious V-J Day! Japan had surrendered – unconditionally!

That glorious year! And it brought little change in Parks' personality. Or his life.

V-E Day and V-J Day came and went! The entire country found itself – literally – dancing in the streets. An era of unparalleled prosperity lay ahead. That, of course, intrigued Parks. The automobile manufacturers had begun to assemble cars, once again.

Gas rationing had become a thing of the past. No longer were ration coupons and/or tokens required to buy meat, sugar, coffee – and even shoes. Vegetables were packed, once again, in real tin cans – not glass jars. Toilet tissue could, as before, be shipped round – rather than flattened (by government edict) – to save valuable shipping space. The wonders of the post-war era were everywhere!

Soon, it would be time to revive **Dubin Auto Rental**!

The Tigers were poised to win the pennant and the *World Series*. It would be the final chance for Parks to see his all-time favorite ball club. The team had featured such worthies as Hal Newhouser, Dizzy Trout, Rudy York, Eddie Mayo, "Doc" Cramer, Roy Cullenbine, Skeeter Webb, Bob Swift and Paul Richards. Eventually, Hank Greenberg and Virgil Trucks would return from the military – and contribute to the pennant race.

1945 would be the final year for "Wartime Baseball".

In 1946, the Joe DiMaggios, the Ted Williamses, the Bob Fellers, the Bobby Doerrs, the Birdie Tebbetts, the Bill Dickeys would all return and claim their rightful positions from their wartime replacements. Many of those substitutes would never be heard from (or heard of) again.

The St. Louis Browns – who, bless their hearts, would become the Baltimore Orioles in 1954 – had even employed a one-armed outfielder named Pete Gray.

After 1945, it would be 23 years before Detroit would, again, participate in the "World Serious".

Parks, who – when transplanted to 1939 – could hardly wait to see "his" team, missed the entire 1945 season. He could not have cared less.

The first postwar cars to come rolling off the assembly lines were listed as 1946 models. **Studebaker** produced a few '46 autos. Then, the company made a huge splash – when they came out with their completely redesigned '47 line in late-spring of 1946.

Kaiser - Frazier listed their initial models as 1947s.

A new car – of any pedigree – was hard to come by. Every dealership in the country had a voluminous waiting list. And they gave away nothing! Not a penny off full retail price. Virtually every customer would gladly accept whatever make, model and color as became available. Conversely, most new car buyers were on virtually every waiting list in town. It had become quite a game.

It was, as stated, a wildly lucrative time for dealerships – and car salesmen!

Parks association with Clark Dubin, of course, gave him a leg up on the rest of the sales force. For the most part, though, he was simply working harder than his peers – and was far more successful! He was making money faster than he could count it.

He continued to invest wisely – and, with the post war prosperity firmly in place – his entire portfolio began to "take off".

The dreaded, evil, income tax didn't take nearly the bite in 1945-46, as had become the case in the seventies. Parks, by the summer of '46, became wealthier than he'd ever dreamed possible – even in 1979 dollars!

As the year droned on toward its end, cars began to become slightly more plentiful. Customers could afford to be just the slightest bit more choosy. It was still, positively, a seller's market. However, the days – in which a salesman's job was the equivalent of a license to print money – were plainly numbered.

It was at that point that Clark Dubin and Parks decided it was time to "get seriously back into the rent-a-car business".

Parks relinquished his sales position – and climbed back into the saddle as rent-a-car manager, at a salary approximating his wartime earnings.

It didn't take long to resurrect the car rental entity. It was simply a matter of reactivating a small-but-efficient operation. One which had been "sleeping" for a few years.

The new cars would come in slowly, of course – but, they would come in. By the middle of October, 1946, **Dubin Auto Rental** was back in business. As the supply of the shiny new automobiles became more than a trickle, Parks began to open new offices – and to hire personnel. The company was beginning to expand – in spades!

A supreme irony befell Parks, when he hired Al Pilnick to handle the brand new, staggering-for-the-times, operation at *Willow Run Airport*. Pilnick was the person – city manager, at that point – who had hired Jim Sidorwitz to work as a rental agent at **Dubin's** downtown rental station, in 1957.

The *Willow Run* operation consumed more of Parks' time than the automobile sales situation ever had. Although the airport was some 30 miles outside Detroit – closer to Ypsilanti – it served The Motor City's growing air traffic needs till 1958.

There were never-ending, high-pressure, negotiations for counter space inside the terminal – as well as wash facilities and parking slots close by the terminal. **Hertz**, by then, had become much more competitive – and much more combative. Sensing, for literally the first time, that they would be in competition for the traveling sales reps' buck, they pulled out all the stops. Played hardball from the very beginning.

It would take all of Parks' expertise to negotiate **Dubin Auto Rental** into the airport at all. It would not have happened, he was certain, had Clark Dubin not had an "in" with two of the regents at the *University of Michigan* – which owned the airport.

Until the airport operation had been safely finalized – and each of the complicated contracts signed, sealed and delivered – Parks seldom put in less than an 18- or 20-hour day. Sunday – his only day off – was not nearly enough to recharge his batteries.

His complexion was taking on a pasty hue. His legs seemed to weigh 700 pounds each. He found himself constantly short of breath. His hair – his pride and joy (till then, he'd not lost any) – was beginning to turn grey. His forehead got slightly "higher".

As Christmas, 1946, approached, Clark Dubin summoned Parks to his office. Our hero was certain he'd sensed a definite change in Dubin's usual jolly demeanor – as he sat, uncomfortably, in the huge leather chair across from his employer's massive, battered, always-cluttered, desk.

"Parks," Dubin began, "it's still two weeks to Christmas ... but, I thought I'd give you your present a little bit early."

"Clark, you shouldn't ... you certainly ... "

"You'd better let me finish. You may not like the present. At least, not for the moment."

"Not for the ... ? What're you talking about?"

Dubin leaned back in his high-backed leather chair. The creaking sound, at the base, was almost deafening.

"You're fired, Parks!" he barked.

"Fired? Fired? What the hell for? I put **Dubin Auto Rental** on the goddam map! Clark! We ... we're just starting to get this thing off the ground! Into the big time! I'm sure that ... when the *Willow Run* thing gets going full blast ... I'm sure that ... "

"I know, Parks. I know. I'm positive that's the case. Just as sure as I can be. This ... what we're talking about here ... has nothing to do with business. Well ... it does and it doesn't."

"What the hell is that supposed to mean?"

"Parks, what you've done for the company ... and for me, personally ... is just ... is just ... well, I can never repay you for it. But, maybe I can start."

"By firing me? Oh, thanks a batch! Helluva start!"

Dubin sat straight up! Folding his hands on his desk and narrowing his penetrating stare on his employee – burning two holes into Parks' own eyes.

"Goddam right it's a great start," he responded. "Otherwise ... you son of a bitch ... you're gonna fucking kill yourself!"

"What difference does that make?"

Dubin slammed his fist on the desk – causing his pen to literally catapult out of its holder.

"It wouldn't make a goddam bit of difference," he shouted. "Not a fucking bit of difference ... if I didn't give a shit about you! You've made me a boodle of money ... and I'm aware that you certainly could continue to do so. I don't even know who the hell I can get to replace your ass! To expand the business! To hit the heights I think we ought to hit! No fucking idea!"

"I ... I don't understand what you're ... "

"Dammit! That's why my present is probably more generous than you realize. I'm aware of the fact that ... with your expertise, with your track record ... you could go down the street to **June Chevrolet** and set up Old Man June in the car rental business. Or ... with the money you've accumulated over the past few years ... you could probably open your own company! Kick me right square in the ass ... business wise!"

"Clark! Don't be silly! I wouldn't ... "

"Probably not. I'm sure not. That's not like you. But, Parks, I'm not gonna have you kick the goddam bucket on me! I'm sure as hell not gonna be responsible for that."

"I see. I see what you're getting at, Clark. But, it's crazy. I put in the hours that I do because I want to. It has nothing to do with you."

"Yes and no. If you didn't have a goddam job here ... if you didn't work here ... then, you couldn't work all those apeshit hours. All those idiotic hours. Not for me, anyway."

"Oh. I see." Parks was bristling. "Then, you'd be off the hook ... as far as your own pissy-assed little conscience is concerned."

"That's right," boomed Dubin. "I'd be off the goddam hook! Parks ... it's time someone talked to you like a Dutch uncle! I realize that you've never gotten over Helen passing away. Or Jeff. I know that. Do you think I don't know that?"

All the wind left Parks' sails. He slumped back into the chair – seeming to deflate before Dubin's eyes.

"Did ... did you have to bring those things up?"

"Yes!" Then, Dubin's tone softened. "As a matter of fact, yes I did. It's about time someone took you in tow ... and told you how things are. Everyone ... including me ... has given you a wide fucking berth! Till now!"

"I ... I haven't asked for anything."

"I realize that, dammit. I'm not saying you have. But, everyone ... fucking everyone ... has just left you to your own devices. I guess we all figured that ... sooner or later ... you'd come out of it. On your own. You'd figure it out. But, now? Now I'm not so sure any of us were doing you any goddam favors."

"You figured I'd come out of ... of what?"

"Out of what?" mimicked Dubin – in a high-pitched, nauseating, nasal voice. "You know goddam well 'out of what'! You've been in this hung-dog snit for five years now! Five years, Parks! Five fucking years! She's dead! She's dead, Parks! The kid is dead! They're both gone! I know how much you loved 'em ... but, they're both gone!"

"I still love 'em," sniffed Parks.

"Of course you do, you son of a bitch! I know that! You ... you're about to cry. I'm sorry. I didn't mean to be so abrupt. So ... unfeeling. But, God knows ... this is the first time you've shown any kind of emotion! In five years! Five shittin' years!"

"I know, Clark. It's just that ... "

"Parks, you're the one who used to get all choked up at hokey movies and radio programs ... and all such shit as that. Since Helen and Jeff died? Nothing! Not a goddam thing! You're like a goddam robot! Hell bent on making money! On making a bundle! Okay! Okay ... you've made your fucking bundle! Besides which, you've got twenty-percent of the goddam company. You keep that, of course. It's yours. Even if you go stick your nose up Old Man June's ass ... or open a shit-assed company of your own. It's still yours ... no matter what."

"What do you mean, I've made my bundle?"

"Oh, cut the shit, Parks. You and I have the same agent. Remember? Elliot has told me what you've been doin' ... how much you're rakin' in."

Parks sat bolt upright!

"That's a piss-poor thing for him to do," he hissed. "Where the hell does Elliot get off? Telling you about my ... about my ... about my ... "

"Don't blame Elliot, Parks. I put incredible pressure on him. He had to tell me. Again, I wouldn't have bothered ... if I didn't give a shit about you. Parks ... you could fucking retire! Retire tomorrow! Retire today ... tonight! Especially if the company, here, really takes off!"

"Yeah," he groused. "But, look how inflation has hit us."

"Granted. But, you ... yourself ... said it would abate. I don't know how you know such things, Parks ... but, I've never gone wrong listening to you. Even taking into consideration that inflation'll always be with us, you could still retire. And retire in comfort. And with your twenty-percent of **Dubin Auto Rental** ... and with the stock market taking off ... you'd be more than comfortable."

"Can't do it, Clark."

"Don't want to do it ... that's what you really mean, Parks. How the hell long are you going to keep banging your head up against the frigging wall? Like that old joke ... it does feel good when you fucking stop."

"I'm not banging my head up against the wall."

Once again, Dubin slammed his ham-hock fist on the desk! The pen rolled off, onto the floor.

"God damn it!" he fumed. "Yes you are! Listen to me, you ornery bastard! Instead of me firing you ... which I didn't want to do in the first goddam place ... why don't you just take a vacation? A long vacation? A hell of a long vacation? Two or three months! Hell, six months, if need be. A whole fucking year! Whatever! With pay!"

Parks smiled – in spite of himself.

"Man," he said. "You're really anxious to get rid of me ... to run my ass off ... aren't you?"

"If I don't get rid of you this way," Dubin's voice was barely a whisper, "I'll be getting' rid of you through the undertaker's establishment." It was his turn to deflate. "Do you realize," he continued, his voice a husky whisper, "that you're aging like nobody's business? You used to amaze me. Never looked anything like your age. Still don't. But listen, you sorry bastard, it'll just be a matter of time. If you don't do something ... and do it fucking quick ... you're gonna look older than Methuselah. It's not that far down the road."

"Look, I appreciate what you're saying Clark. I really do, but, can't you see ...? "

"Not saying, Parks! Doing! One way or another, your ass is gone!"

Sighing heavily, Parks leaned back once more – allowing the chair to swallow him. He closed his eyes. All the fight – all the feistiness – had left him.

"Okay," he responded, at length. "Okay, Massa. I'll go quietly."

"Hah!" growled Dubin, grinning broadly. "You never do anything quietly. But, that's good. Now, get your sorry butt out of here."

Parks labored to pull himself out of his chair.

"If you need some money ... quick-like," added Dubin, "have Miss Ellis or Gertie to cut you a check. For whatever you need. And I'll take it from there."

"No," responded Parks. "No. That's okay. Just deposit my checks. Deposit 'em into my account. Over at **National Bank of Detroit** ... where the corporate account is."

"Good! Fine! Wonderful," said Dubin – with a broad grin. "Now, I want your ass out of this vale of tears! Don't even worry about cleaning out your desk. Don't worry about a goddam thing. I'll handle it. We'll all manage ... manage to muddle through ... somehow. Oh, I would make one suggestion."

"Only one?"

"Oh, go to hell, you wise bastard. This is what I think: I think you should go somewhere. Some place far away. Get the hell out of town for awhile."

"Boy! You really do want to get rid of me, don't you?"

"It'll give you a whole new perspective, Parks. Who the hell are you gonna leave all that money to? You're knocking yourself out ... killing yourself ... building a pile of dough. For what? You'll kick the goddam bucket ... and the goddam government'll get it all. Enjoy your money, Parks! Enjoy the hell out of it."

"Yeah." Parks was back to being dejected. "Sure."

"I'm serious, you asshole. Enjoy your money ... while you can still have a fling or six. You owe it to yourself ... to do something outrageous! Something fucking scandalous!"

"Yeah. I just see me doing something scandalous."

"I mean it. You really are entitled, y'know. I'm aware that you've always ... in some warped way ... blamed yourself for what happened to Helen and Jeff. But, that's all bullshit! All bullshit, Parks. Total bullshit! I'm as positive as I can be that this is why you've been punishing yourself all these years."

"Punishing myself? Some damn punishment. I have managed to pick up a buck or two, along the way. Or hadn't you heard?"

"Big deal. You've still been punishing yourself. You're running yourself right into the ground. You live in that stupid-assed hovel of a room ... as though you don't deserve anything better. Either you're punishing yourself ... or you've got some kind of shithead death wish. One's just as stupid as the other."

"Clark, look. I've ... "

"Listen, Parks! You've paid the goddam toll. You've worked it off! What's left ... it belongs to you, Parks. You can't bring anyone back to life ... whether you like it or not."

"I'm not saying I can. But ... "

"All you can do is kill yourself!" Dubin had built up an impressive head of steam. "And ... whether you realize it or not ... that's exactly what you're doing! And you're doing a helluva good job at it. Now, get your ass out of here ... and don't come back till you're completely charged! To the fullest! Full of piss and vinegar! Understand?"

Finally, Parks broke out into an enormous grin! It had taken long enough!

"Understand," he said – reeling off a crisp, military salute! "Merry Christmas, you son of a bitch! It really is a helluva present you're giving me. I guess I really needed someone to kick me in the ass."

"Consider your ass booted!" Dubin's eyes clouded over. "And merry Christmas to you too ... ya bastard!"

Isn't that what the Christmas season is about? Good will toward all?

THIRTEEN

Clark Dubin's "gift" had, of course, caught Parks completely off guard.

As he sat alone in the dreadful room he called home, on that evening – reviewing his "financial profile" as someone on Madison Avenue would one day call it – our hero began an agonizing reappraisal. It was the first time in a long time that he'd allowed his attention to wander from the figures on the battle-scarred ledgers and journals in front of him, on that rickety old table.

He leaned back, in the rickety old wooden chair, and ruminated about the fact that, for the first time in memory, he wasn't totally wrapped up in his finances – whatever that may signify. Up to that point, money had been the exclusive – the only, the single – measuring device by which he'd assessed literally every facet of his life. Since Helen's death, he'd never allowed himself to think of anything else.

Talk about Ebenezer Scrooge!

He let his gaze wander the scruffy, dank, room. For the first time, it occurred to him that the place always seemed to have a musty smell to it. The bed was ready for the happy hunting ground. The antiquated stove and the dilapidated refrigerator, all of a sudden, depressed him – terribly.

He scrunched his eyes shut. Despite the fact that the room's furnishings were out of his sight, he felt the presence of each and every single item of furniture, or appliance! They'd begun to exert a stranglehold on him! Sucking the very breath out of his body!

He was unable to break the death grip of utter dissatisfaction! It was the first time in – literally – years that he'd even <u>tried</u>! Suddenly, it hit him:

Parks didn't want to live there any longer!

Gathering up the financial documents, he stuffed them back into their well-worn accordion folder! Grabbing his coat from the tiny pasteboard "closet", he threw it on and bolted from the dismal room – barreling down the steps two- and three-at-a-time!

Jumping into his car, he cranked the brand new '46 Ford club coupe into action – and headed down Grand River.

It took practically no time to get downtown. The swift trip was a duplicate of that first trolley ride, upon his return to 1939. Time-wise, anyway. The entire drive was a haze. He pulled up in front of the stately *Statler Hotel* – and sat behind the wheel for three or four minutes, staring at the imposing edifice.

He sighed deeply and shrugged – then, got out of the car. Pushing his way out of the December cold, and into the posh lobby of the resplendent *Statler*, he became unsure whether he actually wanted to carry out his plan – the plan he'd so suddenly hatched.

It was academic: The hotel had no vacancy.

That removed any doubt. He <u>had</u> to have a room for the night! Any room! Well, not really <u>any</u> room! It had to be a nice one!

He hurried back out into the cold night air and drove the few blocks down Washington Boulevard – to the *Book Cadillac Hotel*, Detroit's other opulent hostelry. The "Book" was another fine old house, which – after having been part of the **Sheraton** chain in the fifties and sixties – would fall upon hard times in the seventies.

The "Book" had a vacancy!

Ten minutes later, ensconced in a smaller-than-expected room on the 10th floor, he drew a hot bath. A very hot bath. Throughout his life, whenever he had wanted to relax – really "unlax" – he had always opted for a good old hot bath. It had never failed to prove out-and-out therapeutic.

"Sometimes, I feel like I ought to have a prescription," he would mutter to himself, when a good soaking had been particularly satisfying.

What better way to begin his "new life"? Whatever that may be!

In the depressing room in which he'd been living, such a luxury had not been available. The drab bathroom – which he'd shared with four other tenants – had offered an always-grungy stall shower, but no tub. Every time he would enter that grimy enclosure, he would half-expect to have his shower interrupted by Norman Bates, in drag, with a very large knife! How long would it be, before Alfred Hitchcock's *Psycho* would appear – "to scare hell out of everybody" – on our friendly, neighborhood, movie screens?

The facilities at the "Book" offered a refreshing change. Highly uplifting. Once immersed in the steaming water, Parks leaned back and closed his eyes. The tub had one of those "old fashioned" tapered backs. Well, not "old fashioned" for then. It seemed to him that all tubs, in that epoch, featured a tapered back. Was that great – or what? He liked the shape. Easy in which to lie back. Not many of those glorious tubs remained in the seventies.

He could feel the tension begin to ooze – ever so slowly – out of him. It almost seemed as though the tenseness had found itself intermingled with the steam – which wafted its way toward the ceiling. Locking his hands behind his head, he allowed himself another deep, languid, luxurious, sigh.

Clark Dubin had been right, of course. He usually was. Parks had so immersed himself in the building of his financial empire that he'd done so to the exclusion of everything – and everybody – else. That, of course, had been evident to one and all.

Why hadn't Parks seen it?

The answer, obviously, was that he did see it. He simply refused to do anything about it.

His thoughts wandered to Pam and Larry Hollis. He wondered where they were. What they were doing. He hadn't been very nice to them – nor to the many others of Helen's friends. They had tried to do so much for him – and he'd refused to let them. How sad. A real pity. He would have to make it up to them! Pam and Larry – and all the others!

He yawned. Suddenly, he felt very fatigued. More so than at any time in the past few years – 12-hour-days at the dealership and the tenuous *Willow Run* negotiations notwithstanding.

Once more, he sighed. God! How I've screwed everything up!

The basis, of course, for his dream of returning to the thirties had been to enjoy all those wondrous things! The glorious things that he'd been too young to appreciate the first time around. Well, when Jim Sidorwitz had been too young or – once the fifties would roll around – when Jim had been too wrapped up in trying to eke out a living.

From 1957 or '58, he'd literally needed to work two or three jobs to support his family. On a few occasions, four and five jobs – if one counted his early-morning paper routes. At one stretch, in the late sixties, he'd gone almost three years without a day off.

He'd so run himself into the ground, physically, that, in January of 1970, he'd contracted pneumonia. Had been in bed for a week.

In Jim Sidorwitz's mind, the number of jobs – and the ghastly number of hours – had been "no big deal". He'd merely done what he'd had to do. "The kids didn't ask to be born," he'd always maintained. He was most grateful that his health had been such that he'd been physically able work those many hours. His main regret had been that he had missed a goodly amount of fun, with his kids.

Married in 1954, he and Kathleen had begun their marriage – by producing four children in the first five years.

A contented smile gradually appeared on Parks' pink-from-the-steaming-water face, as he thought back to those days. Days which would not begin for eight years.

He and Kathleen had bought "the whole Catholic line". They'd never used any form of birth control – until after their seventh child, Clancy, had put in an appearance, in 1966.

"God will always provide for you," they'd been taught.

The couple had believed it – and had accepted it – on blind faith. Though Jim Sidorwitz had expressed a goodly amount of doubt in the sixties – when the financial vise was at its tightest – Parks Hayworth wasn't so sure that he didn't still believe it.

They were right and I was wrong.

Jim and Kathleen had come upon exceptionally hard times – just after the birth of their first daughter, Cynthia, in 1959. Cynthia, whom Jim had always called "Hogan", had followed three boys: Dave, Doug and Dan.

Although, the couple "hadn't used anything", Kathleen had gone almost four years – after Hogan – before becoming pregnant again. Their belief that "God will not send you any children you cannot afford" had been reinforced during those four difficult years.

Sure enough, God had not sent them any more children.

In 1963, God obviously had felt as though they could handle another baby – and sent them Donald. He'd been named after one of Jim's best friends – who'd served with him in the Navy, in the early-fifties. Don was the first of three more children – in four years. The final two had been girls – Duffy and Clancy.

About the time that Kathleen had found herself pregnant with Tracey (Clancy), the marriage had begun to deteriorate. When Clancy was born, in March of 1966, it was agreed that there would be no more children.

Jim had found himself under a tremendously heavy financial burden – and could see no way out. While the three and four jobs were critical to support his family, they were also a means of escape for him. Working 20 hours a day left him very little time to wonder about the future – or to grapple with the problems within the marriage.

The other side of that coin: It had been an heroic struggle for Kathleen – to not buckle under the sheer weight of raising seven children. Especially given the Sidorwitz's precarious financial situation. Through the years, it has always been the mother, after all, who has traditionally been involved with the children on a day-to-day, event-to-event, trauma-to-trauma basis. Much more than the father. It was ever thus.

In Jim's and Kathleen's case, each parent had felt, at one time or another, that he or she would eventually crumble under the awesome weight of their responsibilities. Fortunately, each had been able to "reach back" and tap some unknown reservoir of strength.

Once Jim had begun working three and four jobs, he was virtually never at home – except to sleep. About three hours every night.

The obvious result of such a schedule was the placing of an even more enormous burden on Kathleen, who, of necessity, became mother, father, counselor and confessor to the seven offspring.

It might have proved to be too heavy a load – even for such a lady as Kathleen – to handle. However, Cynthia had stepped into the breach. Jim had always referred to her as his "saint". From the time she was nine, "Saint Hogan" had taken her three younger siblings under her wing. They'd been five, four and two at that point.

Later, in the seventies when they were in their pubescent years, Don, Jeanine and Tracey had never failed to take their problems and concerns to Cynthia – before they would consider approaching their parents. Hogan, you see, was not "a member of management".

Despite the fact that Jim and Kathleen had always gotten along tolerably well, they decided – in the months after Tracey's birth – that, eventually, they would separate. It was a mutual agreement. An "Armed Truce Treaty", as Jim had always referred to it.

As the children had become more independent – and as Jim had done slightly better in the rent-a-car business – the pressures finally began to diminish, albeit slightly, for Jim and Kathleen. Once they would have discharged their responsibilities toward their children, each felt as though he or she would be better off moving on – to, hopefully, a more rewarding man/woman relationship.

Jim had often wondered what would've happened – what the marriage would've been like – had he and Kathleen been more comfortable financially. Undoubtedly, they would've been better able to relate to one another more satisfactorily – without the constant, almost-debilitating, pressures of scratching and scraping for practically every nickel and dime.

The conclusion Jim had reached most often was that it was entirely possible that he and Kathleen would've been much better off in a more stable financial situation – but, "Maybe the kids would've turned out rotten".

"Looking back," he'd said, on numerous occasions, "I don't think I'd have changed one thing. It's almost miraculous the way the kids all turned out so well. Turned out so magnificently. You've got to wonder what the odds against that would be. If things had been different with the money stuff ... well, who knows?"

The marriage had been typical of the early-fifties: If a person was close to 22 or 23, and not married, then, something was drastically wrong. Therefore, without really knowing one another well enough, Jim and Kathleen had wed – and had set off down the primrose path of married life. It would be *The Donna Reed Show.*

Once the realization set in that the union would never be *The Donna Reed Show* or *Ozzie & Harriet* – or even *I Love Lucy* – they were, as Jim would say, "fanny-deep in kids". The couple had, though, hunkered in – and done their best to raise their offspring.

When, at last, the older three were virtually on their own – Danny, Number-Three Son, was a senior in high school – Jim and Kathleen reached the decision that the time to part had arrived. They had said, through the years, that they would know when the time was at hand.

The younger three – whom Jim had, good-naturedly, dubbed "The Dirty Rats" – were still quite young: Ten, nine and seven.

While any separation is never accomplished without some trauma, Jim's and Kathleen's parting was far from unexpected. The children had been conditioned that the parting – and the divorce – was inevitable. They'd, of course, reacted like champions.

As the months went on, and the children – especially "The Dirty Rats" – could see that Jim was still around, any uncertainty which may have existed wound up being put to rest. As improbable as it may sound, Jim actually was able to do more things with the younger three. More than when he'd actually lived in the same house. His "being around" made the separation progress even more smoothly.

It was "a divorce made in heaven": Each parent related better to the children, when the other parent was not around. In addition, the fact that Jim and Kathleen had remained close – albeit not intimate – friends was a most-critical positive, for the kids.

The divorce had become final in 1973.

Some six months after the parting, Jim had taken up with his "Veteran Fiancée".

He had fallen for Alice – fallen hard – and was certain that he loved her deeply.

However, Alice's temperament was explosive! She would fly off the handle at the most innocent of situations. She was cynical and suspicious – constantly looking for an underlying, nefarious, motive! Even in the most charitable or unselfish of acts.

After three years of the tumultuous relationship, Jim had had enough.

It coincided with Kathleen's decision to sell the house in Detroit – awarded her, of course, in the divorce proceeding – and move down to Texas. The sale of the home would consume almost an entire year. Ironically, Kathleen would be the last one – along with "The Dirty Rats" – to relocate in The Lone Star State.

Kathleen had been born in Detroit and had lived in The Motor City until 1950 – eight months after Jim had joined the Navy.

In February, of that year, her parents had decided to move down to Texas. To Brownsville – at the southern-most tip of the Lone Star State.

Her father had inherited a three-acre parcel of land on the outskirts of the South Texas town, many years before. He had lived in the Rio Grande Valley as a child – and was certain that his family would enjoy themselves in the semi-tropical locale. He was right. His wife and daughter had come to love Brownsville.

Jim and Kathleen had conducted their entire "romance" and courtship by mail.

He'd been stationed in Norfolk, in the fall of 1950 and had begun writing to the 15-year-old Kathleen. She'd returned letter for letter. Each letter – over the next three years – had become just a little more romantic. A little more serious.

By the time he was discharged, in the spring of 1953, Jim had not seen 18-year-old Kathleen in four years. He hitchhiked from Norfolk to Brownsville – a trip which took three days – and spent most of a month "freeloading" with Kathleen and her folks.

Her family had taken to him – and it seemed the best of all possible relationships.

A true "story-book romance"! Just "schmaltzy" enough to appeal to Jim.

The one fly in the ointment: Kathleen had promised her parents that she would finish her high school education before marrying. She would not graduate till June, 1954.

The couple had become engaged in the spring of 1953, during Jim's "freeloading" days in the Rio Grande Valley.

After 3½ weeks in Brownsville, he'd hitchhiked up to Detroit – another three-day trip – to secure a job, buy a car (his blessed, beloved, '49 green DeSoto) and ready himself for married life. Prepare himself to live *The Donna Reed Show.*

The happy couple was wed September 12, 1954. A year to the date after a young United States senator – named John Fitzgerald Kennedy – married a beautiful young woman named Jacqueline Bovier.

In the lives of Jim and Kathleen, it had mattered not to either bride or groom that – from July of 1949 (when Jim had joined the Navy) till September of 1954 (when they'd wed) – they'd been in each other's company for less than a month. Didn't matter!

It should have! It should have set off all kinds of alarm bells! But, it didn't!

The lack of familiarity would, of course, prove to be a fatal stumbling block. It would be the primary cause of their separation after 18 years.

Once they had parted, Kathleen had resolved to remain in Detroit – in order that her children could be close by their father. However, after some three years – and with her parents in failing health – she'd decided to move back down to Brownsville.

The decision proved to be the kickoff for the migration of the entire Sidorwitz family to Texas:

Doug – Number-Two Son – would be the first; settling in Houston, to take advantage of the "boom town" employment possibilities.

Six months later, Jim had moved in with Doug – the apartment Mr. Horne had visited. Doug had taken another apartment four months after Jim had moved in.

Number-Three Son, Danny, had moved down to Brownsville – a week after Jim had arrived in Houston. Living with Kathleen's folks, Danny went to work at a pizza restaurant. Within a year, he would manage the place.

Days after Danny's relocation, Dave – Jim's eldest, just discharged from the Air Force – had moved down to Houston, where he met and married a beautiful young woman. One who also was from Detroit – but, one whom he'd never met till their paths had crossed in the Texas city.

Eight or nine months after Doug and Jim had first become roommates, Kathleen – having sold the house – arrived in Texas, with Cynthia and the "Dirty Rats" in tow.

The five of them spent a week in Houston – before four of them pushed on to Brownsville. It was a few months after Doug had decided to take a much larger apartment with his best friend.

Inasmuch as Doug had moved out, 18-year-old Cynthia ("Saint Hogan") decided to remain in Houston – and live with her father.

In the blossom of young womanhood, Hogan had experienced some trouble relating to her mother. The final three or four months in Detroit had been rather turbulent. The younger woman was not thrilled with the prospect of moving away from Mike, her boyfriend.

Cynthia spent almost two years with Jim – before marrying Mike, her fiancé from Detroit. The newlyweds then bought a condominium three blocks from Jim's place.

Once in Brownsville, Kathleen had no trouble in finding a job. That was, of course, before the staggering devaluation of the Mexican peso – which caused such a devastating ripple (more like a tidal wave) in the economy of the entire region.

Jim would make the 700-mile round trip to Brownsville every fourth or fifth weekend to visit his "Dirty Rats". During the summer, Don, Jeanine and Tracey would spend most of their school-free days with their father at his beloved-though-austerely-furnished apartment – sleeping on the living room floor.

Once in Houston, Jim had dated a few ladies. He'd never found anyone for whom he'd cared as much as he had loved Alice – despite her cynical nature. He had, it was true, many happy memories of his life and times with Alice. It always came down to the question of whether all the "wonderfulness" was worth the every-other-week turbulence!

"Ah Jim," muttered Parks, as he sponged his forehead with a soft, fluffy, pink, washcloth. "You did all right. You really did."

The memories seemed to evaporate – as a sudden chill enveloped Parks. The water had gotten cold. Well, lukewarm. Could he have been reminiscing <u>that</u> long?

He turned on the hot water, once more, and, as the steaming liquid gushed out of the ornate faucet, he began to ruminate over the life and times of Parks Hayworth – successor to Jim Sidorwitz.

His first inkling had been an attempt to compare his love for Helen to what Jim had felt for Alice. Bad move. There was absolutely no similarity. None! He had never experienced the overwhelming emotions that he'd felt for Helen. He doubted that he ever would again. He'd always believed, though, that Jim's love for Alice could have grown and blossomed! Could have bloomed into "one of the great loves of all time" – had she only returned his love.

As Helen had.

He shook his head – frantically – from side to side.

It was no good. Helen was dead. Had been for five years. Five years? Dear Lord! Five whole, entire, years! An eternity.

He began to reflect on the changes which had come over him in those five years:

He'd abandoned – completely deserted – every one of the neat things he'd resolved to accomplish upon his return to "the last romantic era". Instead? Instead, he'd thrown himself into his job – working at a relentless, merciless, pace.

What irony! What sheer irony! He'd come back in time to live a much more leisurely life – to get away from the frantic pace of the seventies. Yet, there he was:

Working harder than he'd ever labored as Jim – a man with a wife and seven kids to provide for.

It was at that moment – soaking in a tub of water, rapidly turning cool once more, on the tenth floor of the *Book Cadillac Hotel* – that he resolved, at age 54, to take control of his life once again.

Fifty-four! He'd not thought much about how old he was. Not until Clark Dubin had observed that he'd begun to age – age rapidly! Had begun to look much older.

What was the sense? He had all the money he needed. His investments should provide him with a more-than-satisfactory income for the rest of his life – inflation notwithstanding. What was he trying to prove? If he became a millionaire – not likely, given his age – what would he do with all that money? Dubin had hammered home a most-telling point: When he died, to whom would he leave all that loot?

He was certain that he'd never make it back to 1979. Probably not even close!

Maybe it was just as well. How would he ever explain to his children or Kathleen – or even Charlie Lawrence, his boss – that he'd aged 40 years? In just one single night?

He sighed deeply. He'd never see his children again.

Wait a minute! That wasn't necessarily true. His spirits perked up as he remembered Gabriel Horne advising him that he might be able to observe his kids from afar – possibly enjoying them in a way that would've been impossible the first time around.

He sighed once again. His exuberance deflated – as quickly as it had come.

Parks was in 1946 – almost 1947. Dave, his first-born, wouldn't arrive till June, of 1955 (precisely nine-months-and-four-days after he'd wed Kathleen.)

What would he do till then?

Well, he certainly wasn't dead – even at age 54. There were things he could still do! Many things! He had missed his beloved 1945 Tigers (damn!) – but, there were other attractions! Stuff he could enjoy – at his leisure! The idea – suddenly – held great appeal for Parks!

Then, once again, his high spirits diminished. He was – equally as suddenly – very tired, once again. Back to the old roller coaster, was it?

What kind of man had he become? Not one to be proud of, he knew.

He wondered why he'd not told Clark Dubin that he could never accept the offer to continue Parks' salary. He could never accept that – for which he did not work.

"God," he mused, aloud. "I really was all wrapped up in myself. Wrapped up in the whole damn money thing. Dear Lord!"

He would phone Dubin the next day – and advise his benevolent former employer that he could not accept the salary.

The 20% of the company, though! That was something else. Parks knew that **Dubin Auto Rental** – soon to become **Dubin Rent-a-Car** – would thrive and prosper. Clark Dubin was already talking of going national. Actually, Parks had channeled Dubin's thinking along those lines. The company would, of course, be a resounding success. It would make a millionaire of Clark Dubin. And it certainly wouldn't hurt Parks Hayworth.

He closed his eyes, sloshing onto his left side.

Possibly, he thought, he could contrive a way to get some of his money to his children. As before, the exhilaration evaporated.

That was no good. If he could've devised a plan – in 1946, or even in the fifties – to get money to Kathleen or the kids, Jim most certainly would've seen the results, by 1979. Sooner than that. There had been no money. Ever! Not one damn red cent!

Sometimes (most of the time?) knowing the future isn't all it's cracked up to be.

Witness Helen and Jeff.

He thought of a movie: *It Happened Tomorrow.* The main character – whom his memory told him was Don Ameche – was able, somehow, to obtain the next day's paper. Parks was unable to recall how the phenomenon had come about. He would have to see the picture, once it was released – unless it had made the rounds of theaters during his self-imposed exile. That would not be a big surprise.

Seeing into the future had been such a rewarding situation for Ameche – until he read of his death in the final "tomorrow's paper".

Was Parks beginning to doze? It seemed as though he'd nodded off once or twice.

The water was cooling once more.

Maybe he <u>would</u> make it back! All the way to 1979! In that case, he would have his wealth – and would be able to distribute it to his family, at that time! Personally! He would, of course, see that Kathleen was well taken care of.

Naw! He was grasping at straws! Was he trying to gloss over another failure? A failure – one which would rival the size and dimension as that which had caused the deaths of his wife and stepson? He shuddered again – from head to toe!

"Damn," he grunted, as he shifted position once again, "that doesn't hold water either. Making it back to seventy-nine! Just as stupid as every other cockamamie idea I've ever come up with."

He simply could not conceive of his passing, though. Could not imagine dying – and not making some provision for Kathleen and their offspring.

Yeah! Right! Just like you took care of Helen! Helen and Jeff! Right on!

What would've happened had he suffered a fatal heart attack in the past five years? Who would've known? Who could've ensured that Kathleen and the kids would have gotten all his money? Gotten any of his money? How would his family ever have claimed their rightful inheritance?

Had he made it to 1953 or 1954, he was certain that he'd have found some way to get money to Jim and Kathleen. Simply put, no money had ever been forthcoming. Ever! Not one penny! Obviously, he would never make it back as far as 1955. He would never see his kids again!

Hell! This is where I came in!

In 1955, he would be 63-years-of-age. Could he reasonably expect to live that long? One would think so! Yet, he had to face up to one unshakable – rock-solid – truth:

He had to acknowledge that, when all had been said and done, there had been no largess for the young Sidorwitzes!

His life now seemed purposeless. Never had he felt so alone. The only person he'd really known, as Parks Hayworth, was Helen. And she couldn't help him.

All of his many friends were in 1979.

Well, that wasn't quite true. Clark Dubin had certainly been a friend. A wonderful friend. Parks couldn't imagine any employer – in the seventies – who would've done nearly as much for any employee.

What to do?

Well, for openers, he must restore some purpose to his life. Indeed, he had to begin living again. Who knew how much time he had left?

Heaving himself out of the tepid bath water, he stood, dripping, on the plush pink bath mat. With leaden arms, he reached for a fluffy pink towel.

Once dried, he padded out of the bathroom. Fetching his wristwatch from the nightstand, Parks was shocked to find that it was almost midnight. He'd spent – literally – hours in the tub! Hours! How about that? The time had gone so fast! Sound familiar?

Not unlike the night that Gabriel Horne had appeared to him in Houston.

He was, obviously, beyond wondering whether <u>that</u> whole thing had been a dream.

Parks dressed and made his way downstairs to the nightclub on the ground floor. At the bar, he ordered a *Vernors* ginger ale – the beverage Jim had always referred to as "The Nectar of The Gods". He got the fisheye from the bartender, but the short, bald, man finally set a large glass of the "Nectar" on the bar.

Our hero had not been in the club a half-hour, when he was approached by a prostitute – a very beautiful one. The price would've been $30. Pretty steep – even for 1946 – but, a tab he could've afforded.

On another night, he might've been tempted.

On that night, though, it was definitely not the thing to do.

FOURTEEN

As 1946 became 1947, a whole new era dawned for Parks Hayworth.

Following Clark Dubin's advice, he began indulging himself – beginning with an extended vacation:

New York City, once again. Surprisingly, it was not the excruciating experience he'd expected – now that he was without Helen. Maybe he was making serious progress.

One could hope!

He leased an apartment – for three months – in the Brighton Beach area of Brooklyn. He wanted to stay away from the "standard tourist stuff" – and found himself enchanted by the predominantly Jewish neighborhood. It was a simpler time – and the people were out-and-out delightful.

The streets were still safe. Parks enjoyed taking invigorating, long walks, in the refreshing – non-polluted – night air.

He promised himself that he'd return during the summer – and take in a few Dodgers games. The Brooklyn team would win the National League pennant in 1947, he knew. In one of the *World Series* games – which was to become a classic – Cookie Lavagetto would break up the no-hitter that Yankees pitcher Floyd Bevans was throwing.

Parks was determined to see that game.

He reflected, sadly, upon the fact that – although the good people of Brooklyn couldn't know it, they would lose their beloved Dodgers! In just ten short years! This was, probably, the sport's first real commitment to the almighty dollar – and to hell with the fans! Seeing the citizens so caught up in the team – even in the off-season – was most depressing to our hero. How sad.

"If you only knew," he'd sigh to himself, after an especially spirited discussion with one of the multitude of true fans. "Dear Lord, if you only knew."

At the same time, he also promised himself that – if he were still alive – he'd attend that wonderful 1954 *Series* game, at The Polo Grounds, in Upper Manhattan. The one in which the Giants' Willie Mays would make that incredible, over-the-shoulder catch of the long, screaming, ball – off the bat of Vic Wertz, of the Cleveland Indians.

The "new and improved" Parks Hayworth was going to see everything he could possibly see. As much history in the making as could be witnessed. Too much time had already been wasted.

In Manhattan, he took in a number of New York Rangers hockey games – at the old *Madison Square Garden*, on 8th Avenue. The team was the least-talented of the six clubs which comprised the exceptionally-competitive *National Hockey League*, of those days. Despite their consistent occupancy of the *NHL*'s cellar, the team boasted a number of true stars – such as Edgar LaPrade, Buddy O'Connor and Don Raleigh.

However, the team's real attraction was goalie Chuck Rayner – as fine a netminder as existed at that time. Some pundits referred to Rayner as "The Lone Ranger" – or to the team as "The New York Rayners". Despite the fact that the New York defense was anchored by the wondrous, prematurely-graying, Neil Colville, the Rangers' "D" was unable to protect their goal adequately. The result found the opponents' forwards using the New York net as a shooting gallery. The beleaguered Rayner was, most usually, called upon to stop two- and three-times as many shots as his opposite number, at the other end of the rink.

Parks also attended a number of Broadway musicals:

Finian's Rainbow – with the delightful Ella Logan – was one such production.

Parks had always loved the Original Cast album of the show – and had always regretted the fact that, by the time the motion picture studios had finally deigned to make a movie out of the production (in the sixties) Miss Logan was too old to star in the flick.

She had died shortly after the movie was released – silencing that charming, lilting, brogue! She'd possessed one of the most beautiful, most alluring, voices that Parks had ever heard.

He also took in *Annie Get Your Gun* – which featured Ethel Merman as Annie Oakley. The ebullient star had changed little since Parks and Helen had seen her in *Panama Hattie*, on their honeymoon.

Parks had attended the performance amidst much trepidation. The opening of old wounds posed a terrible worry. However, he found himself caught up in the sheer dynamics of Miss Merman's performance – and entranced by Irving Berlin's glorious musical score. As had been the case throughout Jim Sidorwitz's life, the beautiful *They Say It's Wonderful* brought tears to the eyes of Parks Hayworth. If he could survive a Merman show without Helen, he felt certain that he could handle anything.

He was cured!

It certainly had taken long enough! Somewhere, he was positive, Helen was nodding her approval – and smiling down at him. Maybe even applauding! It was entirely possible that Jeff was doing the same thing!

Dear Lord – he hoped so! He sure hoped so!

Up and down Broadway Parks trekked – attending production after production.

Brigadoon was an enthralling musical. His favorite song, from the Lerner and Lowe score had always been the beautiful, *Come To Me, Bend To Me*. He appreciated anew the beauty of the song. Till then, however, he'd never been enraptured by the ballad that "Tommy" and "Fiona" had sung when they'd parted – *From This Day On*. What a remarkable song! It was a shame that he could not have shared the poignant ballad with Helen, during their brief time together.

In the sixties, he'd come upon a recording of *Come To Me, Bend To Me* by Fred Waring's orchestra – featuring a remarkable soprano soloist, named Patti Beems. Parks (as had Jim) had always yearned to share it with someone he'd love – someone with whom he could relate! Relate closely! He could hardly keep the tears at bay – when he looked at the short, fat, bald man sitting next to him, while the song was performed on the stage. When *From This Day On* was being sung, all our hero could do was to close his eyes – and let the sobs come.

On a happier note, *Allegro* was still around. The only non-success that Rodgers & Hammerstein had ever penned. Our hero had never stopped loving the two ballads – *A Fellow Needs A Girl* and *So Far* – from the score of the show. He'd always thought it was a wonderful production.

Critics – BAH!

Up In Central Park was more enrapturing than he could ever have imagined. It was heart-warming to listen, once again, to the very beautiful *Close As Pages In A Book.*

Part of the lyric said: *Darling, as the strongest book is bound/ We're bound to last/For your life is my life/And while life beats away in my heart/We'll be close as Pages In A Book/Never to part.*

If only. If only.

Toward the end of March, Parks began to feel the pangs of homesickness. He believed that the three months in New York had allowed him to recharge his batteries – as Clark Dubin had put it.

He put in a call to Dubin, asking for assistance in procuring an apartment – or some manner of living quarters – for his return to The Motor City.

"If you're too busy, Clark," he'd said, "maybe you could ask Elliot Voorhees ... or even Gertie Potter ... to see what they can do."

"Not on your life, you horse's ass. If I don't personally see that you wind up with a decent place, you'll wind up living in the goddam city dump. I've seen the places you pick out. No sir! You just get your sweet ass back here ... and see what plush quarters ol' Clark has done promoted for you."

"You're scaring me, Clark. I don't need the Taj Mahal, y'know. Just a simple apartment. I don't need for the rent to be on the moon."

"Fear not, Dear Boy. When Dubin does it, he goddam well does it right."

"Yeah," muttered Parks. "That's what I'm afraid of."

While Parks sat by the darkened window of *The Empire State Express* – as the train steamed its way across upstate New York and Ontario, Canada – he seemed more at peace with himself than he'd been in years. He was convinced that now – finally – he'd gotten a handle on his life. It was about damn time!

Helping, of course, was the warm glow of solvency. Money, he knew, would never be far from his consciousness. He doubted that he'd ever assume a blasé attitude toward financial stability. He'd struggled too long – and strained too hard – for it to be otherwise.

He had arranged – before leaving Detroit – to have the woman who'd been collecting rent from the tenants at "Helen's Building" to expand her duties: She also collected from the Brogans, in the old Faffenberger house on Grandmont – as well as from Hector and Renee LaCroix on Prevost.

She would forward the money to Gertrude, the young bookkeeper at the **Keller-Dubin** dealership. Parks had contracted to pay Gertie $200 per month – which she'd considered a windfall – to watch over his financial affairs. Record keeping – simply posting entries and producing balance sheets – was no longer Elliot Voorhees' schtick.

Still, even with all his "ducks in a row" financially, Parks wondered what he'd do with his life. He was determined that attending to his finances would never take up the overwhelming preponderance of his time. Never again!

On the other hand, with no job to go to – his decision to retire was iron-clad – he would be at loose ends, most of the time. How would he use all that leisure time? How would he fill his life? How would he deal with the emptiness?

How would he cope with the still-existent void that Helen's death had left?

Parks' first order of business, upon his return to Detroit, had been to drive past the "Dream House" on Grandmont. Could it possibly be for sale? Available – and Elliot had missed it?

He'd hammered at his agent – for two or three years – to keep his eye open for that house! If, as and when the place ever came on the market, Voorhees was admonished to grab it! Price would be no object! If Elliot knew nothing else, he was spectacularly aware of the fact that Parks wanted that house!

It wasn't available! Our hero was mildly surprised at his disappointment.

He headed up Southfield Road to Davison – and turned left. Three blocks later, he found himself on Penrod. The little house – to which his family had moved in 1939 – seemed almost deserted, although there was no <u>For Sale</u> sign in the front lawn.

Did the Sidorwitzes still live there? It didn't appear so.

The family had moved to a huge, rickety, old house on Prairie – a block away from his grandparents' "Dog House" – sometime in 1947. Had the move already taken place? Apparently, it had. Another disappointment.

<u>I guess that must be a step in the right direction. At least, I'm feeling stuff now</u>.

At the end of the block, he turned right on Schoolcraft. As he drove past Rosemont – the next block east – a <u>For Sale</u> sign seemed to jump out at him. He lurched his '46 Ford to the right – and headed down the street. Well, five doors down the street.

The house was a small, white-shingle place – laid out in exactly the same configuration as the little house on Penrod. The only difference was in the siding. Parks was somewhat familiar with the house. One of little Jimmy's young playmates – Joseph – had lived there. The place struck a significant chord within our hero.

Should he buy it? All at once, he found himself longing for a home of his own – a real house. He certainly was not going to return to the home on Prevost. The "Dream House" was, to all extents and purposes, beyond his reach. Probably for the foreseeable future. Damn!

Clark Dubin had gone to great pains to find him an apartment – no small accomplishment in post-war Detroit. It was a nice three-room place on Ohio Street, near Grand River and Oakman (and, significantly, **The White Tower** – which was back in our hero's good graces).

It was also not far from the dealership. Was there a message there?

What to do? He found himself lusting after the little, white house on Rosemont.

And for no apparent reason.

Hell, even if I stay on Ohio, I can always use the house as a rental property.

He ordered Elliot Voorhees to buy the home.

Gertie had done an excellent job of "minding the store" – finance-wise. Parks discovered that he was in much better shape, than when he'd left for New York.

So much for all my hands-on expertise!

Hmmm. Hands-on. Seventies words. He'd not used an expression from the future, since – since he-couldn't-remember-when. He wondered what that little factoid could mean.

Sitting in the accounting office at the dealership – a week after his return – he invited Gertie to dinner. It was the least he could do.

She would be getting off in two hours. Parks was certain that it would take him that long – at least – to work his way through the dealership, renewing acquaintances and looking in on his baby – **Dubin Rent-a-Car**.

The car rental company had expanded! At break-neck speed! Had even "gone public"! Clark Dubin, the newly-minted chairman of the board, was, of course, ecstatic.

Dubin offered Parks the presidency of the new corporation! The presidency!

Parks declined – despite the fact that the position carried a salary he'd never allowed himself to dream possible. Even in 1979 dollars.

Seated in the mammoth chair, across from Dubin's, cluttered, gridiron-sized, desk, his eyes had practically crossed, when his former employer made the mind-warping offer!

"Clark, as Jane Ace ... of *The Easy Aces* ... would say, 'You could've knocked me over with a fender'. But, really, I have to decline ... with thanks. More thanks than you can ever know. I've semi-retired."

"What do you mean, 'semi', you bastard? From what I understand, you haven't done a damn thing since last December. Nice work, if you can get it."

"Aw c'mon, Clark. You could buy and sell me! Out of your petty cash drawer."

"Not so, ol' Buddy. I've got all my money tied up in expansion. We're gonna be truly nationwide ... in just the next few months. We're opening in Cleveland next month. Chicago the month after that. In fact, I just … last Wednesday … I just bought a hotel, in Chicago. One across from *Midway Airport*."

"A hotel? In Chicago?"

Dubin nodded.

"The only way I could operate there," he groused. "My esteemed competition has *Midway* ... the terminal building ... all tied up. Got a damn exclusive, they have. Of course, they're headquartered in Chicago. And they got more damn money that I could ever hope for. But, here's the busiest airport in the whole damn country ... maybe in the whole damn world ... and I can't even set up a goddam card table in the goddam lobby."

He smiled, closed his eyes – and leaned back in his massive chair.

"Helluva nice hotel, though," he continued. "Almost new. Cost me an arm and a leg, but it's wonderful."

Parks whistled. "Man, you don't fart around, do you? I can't leave town for a minute ... without you sneaking off and opening your stands all over the country!"

"That's why I need you, Parks. I've got a franchise program going now. Got so many goddam inquiries, that I can't handle 'em all. Franchises! That's one reason I was able to expand so fast."

"You're not trying to handle the whole thing yourself, are you Clark? It's a physical impossibility. You'll spread yourself too thin."

"No," laughed Dubin. "In fact, that's how I was able to get you that apartment."

"My apartment?"

"Yeah. The guy you're subleasing it from ... Phil Bormann ... is in Washington, even as we speak. I'm moving him there ... poor bastard. I've really got him running. We'll be opening there in a few weeks ... maybe a month."

"Holy mackerel! You're really pickin' 'em up and layin' em down, Clark."

"I'm not layin' anything, Asshole. I don't have time. I'm gonna set up a whole regional office in Washington. Let ol' Phil run it for me. Run the whole damn region! Listen, Parks! I've got live ones ... for franchises ... in Philadelphia and Baltimore. Probably Wilmington and maybe even Richmond. Just got inquiries the past day or two for franchises in Pittsburgh and Boston. God only knows what'll be in the mail tomorrow. Had a feeler or two for Saint Louis ... and a couple nibbles for Cincinnati."

"Those are great, Clark. But, how about New York City? You gotta be in New York! Simply gotta! No other way to go! You have to be there!"

"Yeah. I keep having trouble in New York. Two or three times I thought I had a deal ... but, the thing always kept falling through. Those people want too damn much. I think I'm gonna open a company store out there. Just need to find someone to run it. That's another place where you'd be a big-assed help for me, Parks."

"Count me out, old tycoon buddy of mine! I'm happy right where I am."

"Well, hell. I guess that figures. How d'ya like the apartment, by the way?"

"It's great! Couldn't believe it when I saw it. I just couldn't imagine just how you did it ... in this housing shortage. Furnished and everything."

"Well, that's how I did it. Poor Phil. I just packed his ass off to D.C. Practically with only the clothes on his back. He didn't have time to dispose of anything. So, I just sent a couple guys from the service department over. Put his personal stuff in storage ... and had Ernie's wife clean up the joint ... somewhat."

"Well, I really appreciate it, Clark. Thanks. Seems like that's all I'm doing these days ... thanking you. You've been so damn good to me. I'm most grateful. I really am. I'll always be grateful to you. You're a wonderful friend ... and a helluva guy! I'm truly grateful."

"Grateful, shit. You've earned it, Parks. If you hadn't drug your ass in here ... and held my feet to the fire ... I'd still be just a hack car dealer. Now I'm a big-assed business executive ... with extensive holdings, as they say. If you hadn't sold me on rent-a-car, none of this would've happened. Some shit, hah?"

"Clark, you've never been a hack! Never! At anything! Not on your worst day."

"We've taken on another ten or eleven new employees, just here in Detroit," Dubin explained. "Just since you left. Since you began cooling your heels in New York. Had to ... had to put 'em on ... the way things are blooming around here."

"I can feature that. But, I've really got to pass on the presidencity, Clark. I made a resolution ... the night you fired my butt ... that I was gonna begin to enjoy myself. Put my life ... what's left of it ... back together. Nose-to-the-grindstone days are all behind me."

"Yeah. You son of a bitch. You did it the right way. You've got everything under control. Okay, you're not making a million bucks. But, you're comfortable. Right? Of course right. But, me? I got a goddam tiger by the tail."

"You're breaking my heart, Clark."

"No, really. I don't know how I'm gonna handle it."

"You'll handle it the way you've always handled things. Magnificently. You're going to let it make you a millionaire ... is what you're gonna do with it. Couldn't happen to a nicer guy. Who are all these brand spanking new employees? And where the hell are they?"

"Ahhhh. Some of 'em you know. They're from the dealership here ... Al Fontenato, Harry Grimes and Bobby Dallman. I hired one guy from **Hertz**. Kind of a know-it-all, smart-assed, guy. But, he's good. And I need someone in Cleveland ... right away. Got a sharp kid ... really sharp kid ... who was an assistant manager at **Simmons & Clark** ... the jewelry outfit. Gonna make him manager downtown. Picked up a hell of an accountant ... from **T.B. Rayles**."

"The sporting goods store?"

"Yep. Hell of a whiz with figures. I'm even trying to talk Hal Bowen into leaving the dealership ... going to work for the rent-a-car thing. Horace Keller's so pissed off at me right now that ... well, he can't see straight. If Hal leaves," Dubin permitted himself a slight chuckle, "Horace'll flip his ever-lovin' cork."

"Well," responded Parks, with a broad grin, "Hal is ... was ... a damn good sales manager. How *is* your glorious partner, by the bye?"

"Like I said ... pissed. I mean, he's really upset. The car rental thing is doing a hell of a lot better than the dealership, y'know. Not even close. Even though we're still getting a small fortune for every car we retail."

"Still?"

Dubin nodded.

"Still," he affirmed. "Those days are numbered, of course. But, they're still with us ... thank God. Soon, though, we're gonna have to roll up our sleeves and compete. Actually work for a damn living. And you know, Parks? I don't know if Horace can psyche himself up to operate like we did before. Operate in the coming real world. I think I'm probably gonna buy his ass out. He's getting' damn nigh impossible to live with, these days."

"Surely you can't be talking about loveable ol' Horace Keller. Why, that sainted man has got the milk of human kindness by the quart in every ... "

"Spare me," interrupted Dubin. "Yes ... difficult as it is to believe. Part of the problem is that he can't forget that he told me what an asshole I was for getting into the rental business, in the first damn place. Funny ... he used to talk, all the time, about buying *me* out."

"Yeah. I know. It was the number-one rumor on the corporate grapevine ... for lo, those many years."

"I really think that Horace is running out of gas," responded Dubin, his voice a study in seriousness. "I think he'd like to take the money and run. Retire. God bless him ... he deserves it. He's worked hard. He really has. I'm gonna wait awhile, though ... before I start tangling assholes with him over that. The rent-a-car thing is just simply too big ... too important ... right now. Taking up all my time. My time and my energy. But, I love it. I really jolly-well love it, Parks. Once we get the franchise bullshit in gear, we'll get together ... Horace an' me. In the meantime, ol' **Dubin Rent-a-Car** is really rollin'."

"I'm sure you are. Franchising is the way to go ... at this point. But, once you get established ... on a grand enough scale ... start buying 'em back. Start buying back the franchises."

"Buying 'em back?"

"Right," Parks nodded. "Franchises are the way to get the ball rolling. But, with franchises, you don't have nearly the control you're gonna need. Look, when your corporation becomes a true giant ... nationally and internationally ... you don't want to be fighting all those internal battles. And with a whole shitload of licensees ... believe me ... you'll have more conflict than you need. So, you start buying the franchises back. Give 'em a good price ... a fair price. Let 'em make a few bucks ... more than a few bucks ... on the deal. But, get the franchises back. You're gonna need all the control you can get."

"Yeah." Dubin's gaze wandered off to the far wall. "Yeah," he continued. "Makes sense. Makes real sense."

"The control you'll have ... with all company stores ... that'll make it well worth your while. Well worth the money. Especially, when you get to where you're renting cars one-way ... city to city. If you get a couple or three uncooperative franchise-holders, you can lose cars. A lot of cars. Faster than you can shake a stick at them. Believe me when I tell you."

"Hmmmmm. Yeah. Never thought of that. Never really thought of renting 'em one-way."

"You would've, Clark. You would've. The possibilities of renting a car from here to ... say ... Philadelphia and then having Philadelphia rent that same car to Charlotte, North Carolina, or Portland, Maine ... or, hell, Portland, Oregon ... would be too delicious for you to pass up. If you were hamstrung by franchises, well, you might just be opening a can of worms."

Dubin rapped the desk with his fist – and smiled.

"Parks," he asked, laughing boisterously, "where the hell do you get your expressions? I never heard anyone who talks the way you do." He was down to giggling. "Can of worms. I like that. Can of worms. Wonderful."

"Aw c'mon, Clark. The expression isn't that ... that unusual."

Parks was glad that he'd caught himself before he'd used another expression from the future – such as "off the wall" or "that far out".

"I still don't see all that many changes around here," Parks added, hurriedly. "Where are all these new people ... this massive throng ... that you've hired?"

"Oh, we're moving into posh ... to use one of your words ... new offices! Downtown! Downtown, don'tcha know!"

"Downtown?"

"Downtown," answered Dubin, with a wide smile. "Right downtown! *Penobscot Building.*"

"Well, dip me! I'll tell you what your money's all tied up in, Clark. It's all tied up in more money."

"How long has it been since someone bade you go to hell?"

"You know, Clark? You really ought to hire Gertie Potter ... at a generous wage, of course. I had her working on some of my personal finance stuff ... rents and mortgage payments and that sort of thing ... and she did one helluva job for me. She really did. I'd never really noticed her before. Not that much. I don't really know why I asked her to do my day-to-day stuff. Well, of course, she was a quick study ... when I was setting the car rental thing up. She and Miss Ellis picked it right up. In fact, looking back, Gertie, I think, caught on even a little better than Miss Ellis."

"Well," acknowledged Dubin, "they both did a helluva job. Lucky for us."

"I suppose," said Parks, "that ... if I'd have put the arm on Elliot ... I could've gotten him to do it. The bookwork, I mean. But, it's such small potatoes for him."

"So, why'd you ask Gertie?" Dubin asked, with an obscene leer.

The question caught Parks off guard. He was unable to respond immediately.

"Hah! Threw you a curve there, did I?" pressed Dubin. "Couldn't be because she's the prettiest girl out there, could it?"

Parks smiled nervously – and shook his head.

"Good try, Clark. I appreciate the compliment ... left-handed though it is. Naw, I guess it was because she invited me out to her house for Christmas one time. Back when I was so busy being a complete horse's ass. In any case, she really dazzled the hell out of me with her expertise. Her expertise ... regarding my financial records."

"You sure it was just the financial records? Like I said, she's a pretty lady."

"Of course it was the records. What'd you think? Hell, I'm old enough to be her father, for God's sakes. You might give some thought to hiring her, though. And, like I said, pay her a decent salary, you bastard. She's got a little kid ... little boy ... dependent on her."

"I think you've got the hots for her, Parks."

"You're out of your tree, Clark. Me? Have the hots for her? She's just a kid."

"A kid, huh?" responded Dubin with a laugh. "She's a kid ... that already has a kid of her own. She's something like twenty-six or twenty-seven. Twenty-eight, maybe."

"Yeah," muttered Parks. "About half my age. A lot of things I may be ... a cradle-robber I'm not."

Parks and Gertrude went to dinner that evening. They drove out to Frankenmuth, Michigan – a little more than an hour from Detroit – and filled up on *Frankenmuth Inn's* famous roast chicken.

The banter, for the most part, was light. Once they'd finished dinner – and languished over coffee – Gertrude seemed to retreat into some sort of shell.

"What's the matter," he asked.

"Oh ... nothing."

"C'mon, Gertie. You were fine ... till a few minutes ago. What happened? What gives?"

"Nothing. It's just that ... just ... it's just ... "

"Just what?" he persisted.

"Well, you ... you don't have to be so nice to me."

"I suppose I don't. I don't imagine that anyone truly has to be nice to anyone ... if they really don't want to be. What's that got to do with you being so upset?"

She lowered her soft brown eyes. "I'm not upset," she answered, in a half-whisper.

"Well, you're something. Gertie ... what was all that I-don't-have-to-be-nice-to-you remark all about? You've got me worried now."

She sighed – and locked those fawn eyes onto his. "I'm sorry. I didn't mean to worry you. It's just that ... it's just that ... no one is ever this nice to me."

"Oh, how can you say that? I've noticed you around the office. I've never seen anyone give you a hard time. Except for Old Man Keller. He's a pain in the fanny to everyone."

"That's at the office."

"So?"

"So ... away from the office, people treat me like dirt."

"I find that difficult to believe," he replied. "What people? Where? How do they treat you like dirt? Give me a f'r instance."

"Well ... well, with fellows I've gone out with. They always take me out to dinner ... some really nice place. Like this one. Or, we'll go to some fancy nightclub or something."

"I'm not much the nightclub type," he responded.

"I know. I'm really not either. But, they take you to these ritzy places ... and then they give you the bum's rush."

"That's probably because you've got such a nice bum," he replied, with a laugh.

Bad move! Gertrude obviously saw no humor in Parks' remark.

"You're making a joke out of it," she said, with a mirthless laugh. "But, it's really a pain. They act as though they've bought ... and paid for ... you. With a big-deal night out. I've always kind of admired you. Everyone thinks that you've always worked too hard. But, I never looked at you as being ... well, as being ... truly a money-grubbing man. I always felt you were a nice guy."

"And you're afraid that I'm gonna put a move on you?"

"I've never heard that expression before. But, if that means are you going to try and lure me to bed? Then, yes. I guess that's what I'm afraid of. I don't really know if I'd be all that offended. I wouldn't go, of course ... but, I don't know that I'd be terribly offended. At least, I wouldn't ... unless you didn't want to take no for an answer. You don't seem to be one of those who ... one who thinks ... thinks that a girl owes it to him. To go to bed with him. In payment for a night's entertainment. They're the ones who really upset me."

She half-smiled.

"It's been a nice evening," she went on. "A really nice evening, Mister Hayworth."

"Parks."

"... Parks. I guess that I'm just afraid that something might happen ... to louse it up."

He smiled broadly.

"Be it known, forever more," he announced, "that this night shall remain un-loused. I really hadn't planned on trying to seduce you."

"I didn't think you had. I really wouldn't have mentioned it ... if you hadn't kept at me about it. I haven't dated all that many men ... despite my age. First of all, there was a noticeable shortage of men, during the war."

"I hadn't noticed."

She laughed. A soft, rich, lyrical laugh. To Parks, it was most becoming. Most enchanting.

"Well," she said, "I did. I noticed. For a girl ... woman ... of twenty-seven, I guess I must be awfully naïve. Seems like the few guys that were around ... well, they had so many women fawning all over them ... that they figured their body wastes don't have an offensive aroma."

Parks' laugh was boisterous enough to be heard – all across the restaurant.

"I like that one," he said. "The line breaks me up."

"Breaks you up?"

"Breaks me up," he nodded. "You're a lady after my own heart. I intend to steal that line ... use it liberally. Nothing prideful about me. You know, for years, one of my favorite expressions has been, 'He doesn't know one of his vital body openings ... from an excavation in the ground'."

"I know. I've heard you say it. Many times."

"Yeah. I'm a man of few words. Trouble is, I keep saying 'em over and over."

"Well, truthfully, you're kind of co-author of my line. I ... uh ... adapted my line from your line."

"Ah-HAH! We're probably one of the great literary teams of all time."

She smiled once more. Her eyes sparkled.

"Anyway," she said, "before I was so rudely interrupted, I was about to tell you about my love life ... or lack thereof. The guy who wrote the song, *They're Either Too Young Or Too Old* ... he sure knew what he was talking about. Or what she was talking about. Whoever it was ... they positively knew their onions."

"You're talking about the part where she says that, tomorrow, she'll go hiking with that Eagle Scout unless ... she gets a call from Grandpa for a snappy game of chess?"

"Uh huh," she answered with a nod. "So, I never really dated all that much. Now that the guys are all back from the war, they also seem to think they're entitled to fall into beddie-bye ... with any dame that they deign to bestow a little attention on."

Parks stroked his chin – then, began to pull at his earlobe.

"I never thought much about it," he observed. "But, I'd have to imagine that it's a pretty accurate statement."

"It's a damn accurate statement."

Her comment took Parks aback. He'd never heard her use a word like damn or hell before. Not unlike Helen. Obviously, the subject under discussion was terribly upsetting to her.

"Well," he said, at length, "put your mind at ease, Me Fair Beauty. My name is Hayworth ... and I'm English. You won't have to worry about my Russian hands and Roman fingers."

It was her turn to laugh loudly.

"I've never heard that one before," she said.

"I got a million of 'em," he answered, in his best Jimmy Durante voice. "A million of 'em."

She grew serious once more.

"Are you coming back to work at **Dubin**?" she asked.

"Why? What brought that on?"

"Oh, there are rumors flying around the dealership ... like you wouldn't believe."

"You mean ... like the boarding house that blew up? Roomers are flying?"

She made a mock scowl.

"Ouch," she groaned. "That one I've heard. It's just as terrible coming from you ... as it is from anyone else. Besides, I like the song ... *Rumors Are Flying.*"

"Ah," he soothed. "Frankie Carle. Did you know that the girl who sings the song on the record is Frankie Carle's daughter? Her name is Marjorie Hughes. She also did *Oh What It Seemed To Be*, and a number of other records ... with her father's orchestra."

She favored him with an indulgent smile.

"I guess I knew that," she said. "If not, it's been duly noted. Now, stop dodging the question. Are you coming back to work at the rent-a-car?"

"I don't think so. Why?"

"Because we all miss you."

"That's nice of all you. I'm honored. Honestly."

She reached across the table – and patted the back of his hand.

Then, she pulled back – and dropped her own hand into her lap.

"Since I was able to sneak a look at some of your financial holdings," she explained, "I can understand why you wouldn't be all that anxious to get back into the day-to-day grind."

"Gee, God." He was surprised to hear himself use his grandmother's pet expression. "The way you talk. You and Clark Dubin. You'd think I was one of the Rockefellers or something."

"No. Nothing like that. I just never dreamed that you had so many holdings. And I'm sure that I'm not even aware of the real scope of your ... your financial empire."

"Some financial empire. Whatever chintzy little progress I've managed came from the Judeo/Christian work ethic, M'Dear. Shoulder to the wheel. Nose to the grindstone. Ear to the ground. And ... if you don't think it's pure hell to stay in that position, for any length of time ... I've got a serious bulletin for you."

"Oh, Parks! Be serious."

He was surprised that she would use that expression. It was his recollection that such a line hadn't come along till the fifties.

"Why be serious?" he asked. "Do you want to marry me for my fabulous wealth? If so ... well, then you're not as adept with figures as I thought."

"Cut that out. No, it's just that I'm concerned about you ... and I'm interested in what you do. How you do. Really, I am. Of all the people who've come rolling through the dealership, I guess you've always been my favorite. Well, you and Mister Dubin. Mister Keller is a wretch. I don't like him."

"Join the cast of thousands, Keed."

"I guess I just don't want you to leave," she went on. "I've always admired you ... even when you didn't know I was around. Ever since I came to work there ... seven or eight whole years now ... I've never seen anyone ... anyone ... who'd worked as hard as you've always worked. I guess that's what I've always admired about you. I know that part of it stemmed from when Mrs. Hayworth passed away. Everyone says that you worked all those dippy hours ... so that you wouldn't have time to think about Mrs. Hayworth."

"Call her Helen. She'd have liked that."

Tears began to glaze his eyes.

Once again, Gertrude reached across and patted his hand – letting her own linger atop of his for five or six seconds. The gesture was quite moving – and just the slightest bit unsettling.

"I'm sorry," she rasped. "I didn't mean to bring up painful things. It's just that we were all so ... so worried about you. I'm certainly aware that you don't have to come back to **Dubin's**. In a way, I guess I hope you don't. I'll miss you. We all will. I just hope you'll be able to enjoy yourself a little bit more now."

"That's sweet of you, Gertie."

He was surprised at the huskiness in his voice.

"Me?" she responded demurely. "Sweet? Sweet of me?"

He brightened, somewhat.

"Yeah," he answered. "You. The one with the nose. I don't know a hell of a lot about you ... except that you're an exceptionally nice lady, whose husband was killed at Pearl Harbor. And ... you've got a little boy."

"An exceptionally nice lady? Me? Oh, Mister Hayworth! This is so sudden!"

"Yeah. Smooth-talker that I am. No, I mean it, Gertie. I asked you to kind of watch over my stuff, because you seemed ... more than any of the other girls in the office ... to have your head tightened on a little better. Hell, much better. I'm grateful to you, for handling my affairs ... you should excuse the expression. Again, though, I really don't know that much about you. How old is your boy now?"

"Five."

"Five! God! Boy, the time really flies when you're havin' fun. What was his name again?"

"Charles."

"Oh, yeah. Charles. Nice name. You seem to have survived pretty well. In fact, I think you've done a much better job of surviving than I have. Than I ever did."

"Well, I was able to get over my husband's death ... if that's what you mean. Or, at least, I've pretty well gotten over it. I don't know that you can ever put it behind you. Not completely, anyway." She sipped her coffee – and grimaced. It was cold. "That's an apt word, though," she continued. "Survive. After awhile, you get to where you want to do more than just survive. I'm sure you'll find that out ... sooner or later."

"I guess I've been finding it out over the past few months, Gertie. I just kept on wounding myself. Shooting myself in the stupid foot."

Her laugh was bittersweet.

"We all do," she mused. "We all do. I did. Maybe there are times when I still do. But, sooner or later, you realize that there's not really much you can do about things."

"You can say that again," he said bitterly.

"Just pick up the pieces," she continued. "Just pick 'em up ... and go on. Sounds trite, I know. But, it's true."

Parks caught the waiter's eye – and ordered fresh coffee for both of them.

"Yes," he sighed, at length. "It's just that I'm not too smart. Took me longer than most to figure that out."

"Not necessarily. Have you stopped to consider the possibility that you may have loved Mrs. Hayworth ... Helen ... more than I loved Frank? I loved him. I loved Frank, of course. But, something tells me that very few people have ever felt what you felt ... what you feel ... for your wife. And ... with your son being killed at the same time ... you had more than double my loss. Way more than double my loss. When you factor in those kinds of things, you're really not doing all that badly. Not badly at all."

She reached across – and took his hand in hers.

When she touched him, the third time, it became much more than merely unsettling. Parks felt something electric – a surge of high voltage – course through him.

He wondered if it had been something in his reaction which had caused her to let go – suddenly – and fold her hands on the table in front of her.

Maybe it had been the waiter! He appeared out of nowhere, to set cups of fresh coffee in front of them.

"Can I ask you something personal?" he half-whispered, once the waiter had left.

"I don't know," she answered with that soft smile. "It depends on how personal, I guess."

"Your name. Somehow, you don't fit the ... the image I've always had of a ... of a Gertie."

"Well, it's better than being called Gert. Not much better, though."

"I guess it must be. I had a great aunt who lived in Minnesota. I was just a little kid, the first and only time I saw her in my life. Aunt Gert. Now, she looked like a Gert. She didn't look like a Gertie."

"What ... what do you mean?" She seemed ill at ease.

"I don't know. And I apologize. I didn't mean to make you feel self-conscious about your name. It's a nice name."

"No it's not. I've always detested it. But, it's the moniker I got stuck with. And there's really not much you can do ... to clean it up, I mean. As bad as Gertie is, Gert ... or Gertrude ... is seven-thousand times worse. Especially Gert!"

"Doesn't need to be cleaned up. But, how 'bout this? Have you ever thought of using Trudy? Going by Trudy?"

"Trudy?" She brightened measurably. "What made you think of Trudy?"

She smiled – and seemed to relax slightly. It appeared to have been touch-and-go, for a moment.

"Well," he answered, "I guess I've always been kind of enamored with the name ... ever since Trudy Irwin was on *The Kraft Music Hall*, with Bing Crosby. Someone told me, at the time, that her name was a derivative of Gertrude. To me, you look like a ... exactly like a ... a Trudy. I'm sorry, but that's the way I see it. So saying, I'm gonna shut my trap ... which I never should've opened in the first place."

"Trudy!" she said – in an almost sing-song tone. "I like it! Trudy! I wonder why I never thought of it."

"Can't think of everything. You've pretty well had your hands full ... throughout your young life. I'm sure you wouldn't have had time to have gotten all caught up in something so trivial."

"No. Really. I really should've thought of it. Trudy." She was rolling the name around on her tongue. "Trudy. I really like it. Really and truly. I've never liked my name ... but, I like Trudy. First time in my life ... that I really like my name!"

He took a long pull on his coffee.

"So do I," he replied.

FIFTEEN

They drove back to Detroit. The time was 10:15 PM, when they pulled up in front of the newly-named Trudy's mother's bungalow, on Appoline Street, between Schoolcraft and Grand River. It was a tiny, quaint, wooden home. The front porch sagged a little bit – and the house, Parks could tell (even in the dark), badly needed a coat of paint. At the very least.

Trudy invited our hero in – to meet her mother.

Amanda Chamberlain, prepared a pot of tea and served Parks the first home-made apple pie he'd tasted in years. It was delicious. On a par with his grandmother's. A higher compliment he couldn't pay anyone – or anything.

Amanda – heavy-set and built almost in the identical mold of his Grandma Swenson – had, undoubtedly, sampled her own pastries often. It was easy to see from whom Trudy had inherited her peaches-and-cream complexion. And soft brown eyes.

Little Charles, of course, was in bed – fast asleep.

Parks asked if he might at least see the boy.

The trio tip-toed into the tiny bedroom at the rear of the small house.

Charles was a blond-haired, fair-complexioned, boy. He was sleeping in a crib, pushed flush against one wall. It was obvious that he'd outgrown his sleeping facility.

There was barely enough room for the three to stand between the boy and Trudy's single bed – wedged up against the other wall.

Tears formed in Parks' eyes. He smiled. A flood of memories inundated him – soft, fuzzy, visions of each of his seven children. His seven children. The ones in his other life.

"He ... looks so cute," he rasped. "So innocent."

"They all do ... when they're sleeping," responded Amanda, with a laugh.

"At that age," added Trudy.

They repaired to the living room – and another cup of tea. Their visitor spent 45 minutes at the little home. It was supposed to be "socially out to lunch" to stay as late as Parks had remained – but, as he told himself on the way home, he couldn't help it.

It had been a delightful visit.

Well, there had been one uncomfortable moment – when Trudy had advised her mother of her name preference.

"Trudy?" Amanda had asked. "Trudy?" The older woman's brown eyes seemed to harden. "Where ... where on earth did you ever come up with ... with Trudy … for heaven's sakes?"

"It was Parks' idea! And I think it's a good one! I think it's a great one! I love it."

"I dunno," the older woman responded. "Hmmm. Trudy."

"You're not going to be upset by it, are you Mother?"

Amanda's face became a picture of confusion – and dismay. She, most certainly, was fighting a battle within. An epic battle, Parks believed. Then, at length, she forced a smile. The author of the new name believed, though, that it had been touch-and-go.

"No, Honey," she half-whispered. "If ... if you want to be called Trudy, then ... then, that's what we'll call you. You just kind of took me by surprise ... is all. I didn't know that your name was all that big a deal."

"Well, it's not," insisted Trudy. "It's just that ... just that ... given my choice, I prefer Trudy."

"Sold," conceded Amanda Chamberlain – with a goodly amount of grace, Parks was forced to admit. Forced to admire. He wondered if he'd have shown as much class.

The classy lady ran a hand through her grey-streaked hair. It was the picture of a gesture Parks had seen Trudy employ a few times. A motion he'd seen Helen perform – many, many, many times. The bun, in back of the older woman's head, was beginning to lose its hold. She turned to Parks.

"Do you have any more ... any other ... uh ... brainstorms, Mister Hayworth?"

"No, Ma'am. I probably should've kept my big mouth shut with this one. What an upset that'd be."

"No you shouldn't!" The forcefulness in Trudy's voice surprised Parks. "You couldn't have given me a nicer present," she said, firmly – looking more at her mother than at Parks. "You're a dear, sweet, man," she continued, looking up into our hero's eyes. "A dear, sweet man."

When it came time for Parks to leave, he thanked both women – profusely. It had been years – literally years – since he'd spent such a delightful evening. Nothing, certainly, that he'd experienced in New York could've come close.

The only rub had been Amanda's many pointed references to the disparity in the ages of Parks and Trudy. The barbs seemed to have upset Trudy – much more than their obvious target. Over the course of the evening, Trudy had never brought up the age factor.

Probably more to show Amanda her displeasure with the constant references to age than anything else, Trudy pointedly stood on her tip-toes – and kissed Parks, as he was getting ready to leave. A heart-warming surprise!

And a beautiful end to a beautiful evening!

As had happened – when she had touched his hand at the restaurant – Parks experienced another highly-charged, crackling, bolt of extreme voltage, when her lips met – and lingered upon – his own! It took a copious amount of self-control – to refrain from pulling her close! From clasping her tightly to him! From clinging to her! Clinging desperately!

From kissing her – deeply!

As he drove to his new apartment, Parks was doing his best to try and cope with what he'd begun to feel toward this woman. This Trudy. It was beyond cold analysis.

It certainly defied logic: She was about half his age – a fact which was quite at the forefront of Amanda Chamberlain's thinking. Quite obviously, a major concern for the woman.

Certainly, Parks shouldn't be going through some kind of big emotional "thing" – like some damn schoolboy. Still, he'd not felt these things since – since – since Helen?

Perhaps he was going through some sort of "awakening" – after having been "out of circulation" for so long. Who knew?

He had dated once, after spending the night at the *Book Cadillac*, and before leaving for New York. In addition, he'd gone out with three different ladies in Brooklyn – one of whom had lived across the hall from his apartment in Brighton Beach.

He'd never been intimate with any of them. Had, in fact, felt no desire at all.

Had any feelings – all feelings – for the opposite sex gone? Left? Had they totally disappeared? For good? Was there to be no form of arousal for him? Was his sex life finished? Ka-poot?

If that was the case, then why the sudden shock wave with Trudy? From one kiss? From just touching her hand, for God's sakes?

Again, who knew?

Parks was in the midst of a terribly disquieting night! Trudy seemed to monopolize his every thought!

During the infrequent periods – when he was able to grab fitful snatches of troubled sleep – he found himself dreaming of her.

Twice, during the night, he arose and brewed a cup of tea.

He spent a goodly amount of the restless night – staring out of his living room window. The apartment was on the fourth floor – of a six-story building. It was one of six large apartment houses on Ohio Street. Parks' quarters were in the rear of his building.

The night was gorgeous! Brilliantly moon-lit! Parks gazed out across the alley – and at the two-story frame houses on Cherrylawn, the next street over. The back yards were illuminated. He was surprised at the extent that he could appreciate, once more, these comforting symbols of the times:

There were swings, rose-lined trellises – and bicycles left outside, next to the garage in most cases. In the seventies, it would've been sheer folly to leave a bike outside – even in your own back yard. It would be gone within minutes. Within seconds, maybe. Within seconds, probably.

From time to time, he'd make a concentrated effort to apply the brakes to his swirling mind! His so-called mind! That brain of his – which was careening! Lurching out of control. It was, of course, a futile exercise. Trudy was never far from the surface.

A myriad of thoughts, images – and fantasies – maintained their constant, continuous, unrelenting, bombardment. None of them – none of <u>it</u> – made much sense.

It would be a struggle, he knew – but, he was simply going to have to channel his thoughts, in a more orderly, more logical, manner. Concentrate on his economic game plan. Another term he'd have to watch: Game plan. No one would use that expression for decades. What? Had he not admonished himself about that term before? Probably.

He thought of the little white house on Rosemont – where Joseph had lived during their childhood. It was funny: He'd never thought of it before, but the kid had always been "Joseph". Never "Joe" or "Joey" – or anything else. "Joseph".

Obviously, Joseph and his family had just moved away. Parks knew not where.

When the Sidorwitzes had moved from Penrod – moved to that spooky, old house on Prairie – young Jim had lost contact with all of his old acquaintances and playmates.

He'd just bought Joseph's house. Hmmmm. Joseph's house. He couldn't remember the boy's last name. How about that? He wondered if he'd ever known it.

<u>Should</u> <u>I</u> <u>stay</u> <u>here</u> <u>and</u> <u>rent</u> <u>Joseph's</u> <u>house</u> <u>out</u>? <u>Or</u> <u>should</u> <u>I</u> <u>move</u> <u>in</u> <u>out</u> <u>there</u>?

He wondered what Trudy would think of living there! Living in that house!

<u>Oh,</u> <u>this is stupid</u>!

He tugged on his earlobe.

"Better make up your mind, Hayworth," he said aloud. "Ya gonna live here … or out on Rosemont?"

Whether he rented the house or not would affect his financial set up. He'd better concentrate on that. On his finances. On money – and nothing else. For the time being, anyway.

"Boy," he mused, under his breath, "she sure has beautiful eyes."

At one point or another, Trudy always managed to intrude into the reverie-of-the-moment. It was as though he was a school kid – with a crush on some unattainable movie star or something. Or maybe Miss Graybell, his simply gorgeous homeroom teacher in the seventh grade. As unavailable as that!

"Ahhhhh, this is stupid," he repeated. Only, this time he'd said it aloud. As though the spoken word would carry much more impact. "I'm old enough to be her damn father," he prattled on. "The way things have gone with my life, I might actually be her damn nephew or something. Who can tell, anymore?"

The next morning, Parks called the dealership – and invited Trudy to lunch.

She declined. It was a terrible let down for him. More so than he wanted to acknowledge.

He got into his car – and drove to his grandparents' "Dog House". It looked deserted. Parked across the street, he could see the old-fashioned steel latch positioned across the screen door and sash, in front. It was padlocked. Same immense padlock as always. He'd always wondered where Grandpa Swenson had ever found a lock as huge as that one.

He put his hands on the top of the steering wheel – then, rested his head on his forearms. Nothing seemed to be going his way.

He was certain that the Sidorwitzes had actually moved to the big house on Prairie Street, by then. He'd always called it "The Barn". Often! Every day! His grandmother had always referred to it as "The Haunted House".

The most unhappy days of Jim's childhood had been spent there. The only advantage had been the close proximity to his grandparents.

During the years that he'd lived on Prairie, Jim had been bullied – unmercifully – by a bunch of young punks, a few years older (and a good bit bigger) than he. The gang made terrorizing the neighborhood a way of life. They were very good at what they did.

Returning

The leader of the crew of cut-throats was a young thug named Art Sarnes. Parks would never forget him. He was absolutely ruthless!

When Parks had been returned to 1939, he'd halfway promised himself that he'd "do something" about Art Sarnes. However, as he had become more and more taken with Helen – and had immersed himself in building his portfolio – he'd lost any thought of vengeance. In fact, he'd practically forgotten the creep. Then, of course, the grief from Helen's death had made any thoughts of retribution a complete non-starter.

Sighing deeply, he pulled away from the curb and headed down Burnette the half-block to Westfield, turned right and crossed the railroad tracks – then, turned left onto Prairie.

The ominous old house sat on the left, about two-thirds of the way down the block toward Dover Street – the next intersection.

He pulled over to the curb – across the street from the place – and sat, staring at the joint.

His father's 1937 Ford sat in front of "The Barn". Pop had kept the car into the early-fifties. The presence of the automobile meant that his father was still working the midnight shift, in the maintenance department, at **Bryan Incorporated** – a huge factory on West Chicago, near Schaeffer Highway.

It also meant that 15-year-old Jim would not be home for lunch, in all probability.

Jim had, as mentioned, never gotten along with his father! Not until the last 12 or 15 years before Pop had died.

The youth had attended *St. Cecilia's* in the 8th and 9th grades. The school – located at Livernois and Burlingame – was a little more than a mile from "The Barn". It had been a long way to come home for lunch. But, young Jim had hated to carry his lunch (in the standard brown paper bag). He'd detested those room-temperature bologna or jelly sandwiches. Abhorred them, to the point that he would jog home each noontime – just to eat. The school had no hot lunch program – nor anything to drink. No Coke machines. No cold milk. Hell, no warm milk. Nothing to wash down those miserable, cotton-dry, sandwiches. It meant dozens of trips out into the hallway – to sip tepid water from the fountain, outside the girls' lavatory.

A couple months into his first semester at *St. Cecilia's*, Jim was chagrined to learn that Pop would begin working nights. It wouldn't have been so stressful for Jim – had his father devoted his days to sleeping.

At the time the family had moved into "The Barn", Dolly's and Bernie's marriage was disintegrating. Big time – as they'd say in the future. His father, a by-then-incurable alcoholic, usually spent most of his mornings at some saloon – usually two blocks away, at **Freddie's Bar**. But, dammit, he'd always made it a point to arrive home about the time that young Jim would be eating lunch. Boy – talk about a "power lunch"!

Pop's constant tirades – wherein his sole reply to any statement made by Jim was "Horseshit!" – drove the youth to carry his lunch. To grapple with the dreadful, dry, warm, sandwiches. And all those trips to the stupid water fountain by the girls' john.

Parks leaned his head back against the cushioned upholstery. Why was he doing this to himself? Memories of "The Haunted House" had always depressed him. Always.

It would do no good to hang around. His mother still worked downtown in the *Guardian Building*. She wouldn't be home till almost 6:30 PM. Young Jim wouldn't get there till four or four-thirty – depending upon where he may have decided to stop off.

Dee, his sister, went straight from *Ruthruff Elementary School* – on West Chicago, between Livernois and Stoepel – to a girlfriend's house, where she stayed until Jim picked her up. The young man usually postponed that chore. Got to Louise's house – as late as possible.

Suddenly, the door of the ponderous, old "barn" opened – and his father emerged.

That gave our hero a bit of a start! The old man had aged! He looked so <u>old</u>!

As Bernie walked into the street – and climbed into his Ford – he looked directly at Parks! It was a chilling – withering – sensation. Pop had been only 10 or 12 feet away. His gaze seemed to linger on our boy – for a terrifyingly long time!

Could his father have recognized him? No! Of course not! That would've been impossible! Still, what had made Pop stare at him like that? He shuddered!

As his father drove away, heading up Prairie, toward West Chicago – and, probably, **Freddie's Bar** – Parks took off in the opposite direction, toward Joy Road.

Crossing Dover Street, he shook his head – and blinked back the tears. He'd been certain that – by 1947 – he would've become immune to totally unraveling. To utterly disintegrating – every time he saw himself or a member of his family.

He really hadn't dwelled on such things – since Helen's passing.

His father's cutting stare had plunged him back into a condition for which there might not be any cure.

Maybe he should've taken Clark Dubin up on his offer of the presidency of **Dubin Rent-a-Car**.

<u>At least, when I was working my butt off, I didn't have time to think. Must be a moral there, somewhere.</u>

As the summer of 1947 approached, Parks did his best to search out activities in which to busy himself. He managed to get caught up, somewhat, in Tigers' baseball games. Rare was the day that he didn't venture down to *Briggs Stadium* – later to be dubbed *Tiger Stadium* – at Michigan Avenue and Trumbull Street.

In 1946, the Tigers had sold and/or traded off such stalwarts as Rudy York, Pinky Higgins, Birdie Tebbetts and Hank Greenberg. Despite the fact that his beloved 1945 team had been decimated, Parks became a staunch, rededicated, fan – even though the hated Yankees would win the 1947 American League pennant. Indeed, he knew that the Tigers would not reach the World Series again, till 1968.

The team, in the forties, was owned by kind, generous, industrialist Walter O. Briggs. When school was in session – at the beginning and end of each baseball season – a staple at the stadium would always be the contingent of literally hundreds of "Safety Patrol Boys". These were the school-crossing guards. The "Safety Boys" were always seated in the lower leftfield grandstand on school days

– the guests of Mr. Briggs. For free! "Sowing the seeds," the old gentleman had always called it.

For Parks, in the summer of 1947, the Tigers had become an escape. He had been spectacularly unsuccessful in his many clumsy attempts to date Trudy. He had long abandoned the effort to put her out of his thoughts.

Clark Dubin had convinced Trudy that she should leave **Keller-Dubin** and go to work for the car rental entity – at a significant raise in salary. A <u>significant</u> increase!

Parks would "drop in" at the new offices in the *Penobscot Building*, from time to time – ostensibly to look in on the operation. Trudy would talk to him – be most gracious to him – but, without the warmth that had glistened through, in bountiful quantities, that evening in Frankenmuth and, more significantly, later at Amanda Chamberlain's house.

Finally, one stiflingly hot day in July, Parks confronted her.

They were alone in the Car Control office. It had been one of those days when Parks had found himself badly missing the air conditioning he'd grown so accustomed to – had, indeed, taken for granted – in the sixties and seventies.

"Why are you upset with me?" he'd asked, mopping his brow, with his limp, moist, handkerchief.

"Upset with you? I'm not upset with you. What makes you think I'm upset with you? I'm not upset with you, Parks. There's no reason, God knows, for me to be upset with you. I'm not upset with you."

"Yeah? Methinks that thou doth protesteth too damn mucheth. What is it, Trudy? What's wrong? What's ... ?"

"Nothing." Her manner became noticeably subdued. "Nothing, Parks." Her voice seemed about to fail her. "Nothing ... really."

"Are you afraid that I'm trying to get serious with you? That our age differences would get in the way?"

She averted her eyes – still the soft doe eyes he'd grown to admire. Grown to love?

"Well ... no. No. Not really." She was trying to rally her voice, but without much success.

"Would it upset you so terribly, Trudy?" His voice was just this side of pleading. "Would it be that upsetting to you ... if I were to get serious? I guess that must sound incredibly stupid. You're already upset ... and I haven't done zilch."

"Haven't done what?"

"Zilch. Sorry. My funny Texas talk."

"Yes. Mister Dubin says that you use it when you're nervous ... or upset or something."

"Mister Dubin talks too much sometimes. Look, the point I'm making is ... I haven't made a play for you."

"Haven't put a move on me?" she replied, with a wan smile.

"You've got a good memory."

He mopped his forehead, once again. Why was he sweating so profusely? It wasn't <u>that</u> hot! And he <u>had</u> been able to cope without air conditioning for eight years.

"Yeah," he advised her. "I've never put a move on you."

At that moment, Sue Blair, who managed the Car Control section walked in – just back from lunch.

"Trudy?" pressed Parks. "Please let me take you to lunch. Okay? Will ya? Huh? At no time will my fingers leave my hands. I promise to return you safe ... and in reasonably good shape. Please? Huh? Will ya? Huh? Please?"

Trudy lost an internal battle – and, in spite of herself, smiled broadly!

"Oh, for the love of heaven," she replied, with an overdone sigh. "All right. Let me go to the little girl's room. I'll be right back."

Every restaurant in downtown Detroit seemed to be jammed!

Parks talked her into riding out Grand River with him to **The Blue Ribbon** – the eatery that he and Helen had frequented so often. Where he'd become so badly unraveled – on the night when he'd seen himself as a child. Since Bernie and Dolly had never frequented the restaurant, once they'd moved to the big house on Prairie, he'd have no such worries.

Trudy, it appeared, was worried enough for both of them.

"Now, then," he began, immediately after they were seated, "I want you to know that ... goofy though it may seem, given the differences in our ages ... I can't get you out of my alleged mind.

I'm sorry if that's offensive to you. I don't really do very well at these things ... at saying stuff like this ... me being a first-class putz and all."

She closed those fawn eyes – and shook her head slowly.

"You're not a putz, Parks. Far from it. And I'm ... I'm not offended. As a matter of fact, I'm very flattered. How could I not be? Honored, if you will. It's just that ... it's just that ... well, Parks, you really are old enough to be my father. What my mother keeps harping on is ... well, it's true. It's true." A tear trickled out of her right eye. "Damnably true."

Parks nodded – almost imperceptibly. He swabbed his brow, once again, with the napkin. His handkerchief had long-since given up the ghost.

"I know," he said, his voice barely audible. "I know. She's worried about you. She has to be. I would be too. She can't be too thrilled with me."

"Oh, she thinks you're a nice enough guy. She just doesn't want any more heartache for me."

"And you? What do you want? What does our Trudy want?"

She sighed. Her eyes misted slightly.

"I ... I want to be happy," she said, at length.

"That'd make a great title for a song," he chuckled. "Trudy ... we all want to be happy. What would make you happy?"

The eyes snapped from one side to the other – then, rolled back toward the top of her head. She sighed two or three times. Twice, she started to respond to his question.

Finally, she blurted it out: "You! You ... being twenty or twenty-five years younger! That'd make me happy!"

He nodded.

"Yeah," he muttered. "Me too. But, that's impossible ... dammit."

"Nothing's impossible." Her answer seemed to come from far away.

"What do you mean by that?" he asked, his eyes assuming Bette Davis proportions.

"Just ... just what I said. Nothing ... is impossible. I find myself wishing for impossible things all the time. Things that ... if I let myself think they were impossible ... well, I'd have a tough time surviving. Am I making sense? Any kind of sense at all?"

"I don't know. I guess so. What kind of things?"

"Oh ... things. Just things. Things like my husband being alive. Stuff like that. Sure, they're impossible to some people. But, if I accepted them as being impossible, I'd have one terrible time trying to get by. I know that it's impossible for Frank to be alive. But ... oh ... I think that, what I'm saying is, there's always hope. So ... to me, it's not impossible. I don't know ... maybe I've been seeing too many 'Topper' movies. I keep hoping that someone like Mister Jordan'll appear and ... "

Parks dropped his napkin to the table!

"Mister who?"

"Oh," she replied. "Just a movie I saw the other night. Sue and I went. Real fantasy-type thing. This Mister Jordan ... he was kind of a heavenly ambassador for Rita Hayworth. A go-between, I guess you could say. She was the goddess of the dance and she'd come down from heaven. And this Mister Jordan had to ... you know ... keep her on the straight and narrow. By golly, you should love ol' Rita. Same last name as yours and all."

Parks wondered whether the fact that Miss Hayworth's costar was named Parks had made any impression on his luncheon mate. Apparently not.

"She fell in love ... you know ... with some guy," Trudy continued. "A mortal. He was in show business. A hoofer ... and a song writer. And ... well, you can guess the rest. They fell in love."

"Sounds like my kind of flick."

He was upset with himself for using the word "flick". He didn't think it was a 1947 word. More than that, though, he was shocked at the weakness in his voice. He wondered if she'd picked up on it. What kind of message would it have sent?

"Anyway," she went on, as though he'd said nothing, "I keep hoping ... ever since I saw the movie ... I keep hoping that Mister Jordan would appear to me ... in the same heavenly-blue suit he was wearing in the picture ... and say, 'Gertrude, old girl, I'll grant you any wish you want,' and I'd ask him to send my husband back to me."

An ironic smile crossed her lips.

"Impossible?" The question was directed to herself – more than to her dinner partner. "Impossible?" She still seemed to be talking to herself. "Yeah. Yeah, it's impossible." She was back to talking to Parks. "I know that. I'm aware of that fact. But, if you could realize how I've ... how I've fed off that dream ... that silly wish ... ever since I saw the movie, why ... "

"And before the movie?"

"I don't know. I guess I just sort of pictured that Frank would kind of walk in. Tell me that it'd all been a mistake. Maybe he'd swam to one of those deserted islands out there." She laughed, self-consciously. "I don't even know if there are any deserted islands out there. I ... maybe he would've gotten amnesia or something. Had just gotten his memory back! Got it back that very morning ... and he'd come running right back to me. Stupid?"

"Beautiful."

"Anyway ... oh, provider of lunch ... that's why I say that nothing's impossible. I'm sure that I never loved Frank anywhere near as much as you loved Helen. But, I've missed him. And it's strange. I don't think I could live without the thought that ... someday ... he'll come back. Maybe through the amnesia thing. Or maybe Mister Jordan'll actually appear. Come to me at night ... and do all sorts of wonderful things for me."

"Boy! Are you leaving yourself wide open with that one."

"Oh ... poo! You know what I mean. Worse than that ... I know what you mean. Stop it. You're embarrassing me."

At that point, the waiter appeared, took their orders, then, the picture of discretion, he disappeared.

"What about now?" persisted Parks. "Are the wishes ... are the dreams ... are they still the same?"

"Yes. The wishes mostly."

She sighed – and cast those eyes downward. She seemed to be studying one of the spoons. Intensely.

"The dreams have changed ... slightly," she augmented – this time, speaking more to the spoon than to Parks.

"Oh? How so?" Once again, his voice seemed to be failing him.

She picked up the spoon, turned it over two or three times – still fastidiously inspecting the utensil.

"I shouldn't be telling you this," she began. "But, the dreams ... the dreams have been of you. Have been more and more ... of you."

"I'm honored. Me as me? Or as some virile Young Lochinvar-type?"

"I'm afraid that I don't know who Lochinvar is ... but, I can guess. No ... the dreams are about you ... as you."

"Now I'm really honored. Wrinkles and all?"

"You don't have any wrinkles. Well, none to speak of, anyway. You wouldn't have those, I don't imagine ... if you hadn't knocked yourself out all those years. But, yes. I do dream of you from time to time ... just as you are."

"I ... I surprise myself by asking you this, but, why won't you see me? Especially if you dream about me?"

"From time to time."

"Okay. From time to time. That still means that I made some sort of impression on you. I'm glad of that ... tickled pink, if you can picture such a thing."

"I think I'd be afraid to. To picture such a thing ... as you tickled pink."

He retrieved the napkin – and began, once more, to dab at his forehead.

"I never really felt," he began, "never really felt as though I really had any kind of chance to ... uh ... you know ... go with you. Maybe I still don't. Probably don't." His voice cracked when he'd uttered those two words. "But," he pressed on, "till now ... till just a few minutes ago ... I never allowed myself to even entertain the thought that you might ... that you would ... "

"I know," she responded, setting the spoon back in place on the tabletop. "That's why ... why I've been doing all the dodging of the luncheon invitations. Or, at least, that's part of it. The rest of it is ... well, the rest of it is ... is that I feel something. Some kind of affection, you know. For you. Dammit. Parks, we can't! We simply can't!"

"Why? Why, in heaven's name? You, yourself, said that nothing's impossible."

"It's not. I mean, if Mister Jordan ... or Michael the Archangel or someone like that ... were to come down and touch you with a magic wand or something ... and you'd become twenty-eight or thirty again ... then, I might ... "

"You may not have liked me at twenty-eight or thirty."

"Oh ... I think I'd have liked you at any age. But, Parks! Can't you see? We simply can't get serious about one another. What would people say?"

He banged his fist on the table – much more loudly than he'd intended.

"Ah-HAH!" he spouted. "That's the crux of the whole damn thing! I frankly don't give a rat's ass what anybody thinks! I don't! I could care less! Hell on 'em!"

A couple phrases from the future! He'd have to be more careful! What else was new?

He felt himself about to launch into a tirade on the whole age question. He was on the verge of pointing out the fact that Bing Crosby had married Katherine Grant – despite the fact that she was a year or two younger than Gary, Bing's eldest son.

He managed to catch himself. Dixie Lee Crosby was very much alive in 1947. Gary was still a few years away from recording the best-selling *Play A Simple Melody* and *Sam's Song* with his father.

Parks was unable to come up with an alternate example of a May/December romance that he could apply – celebrated or uncelebrated. He was upset with himself! He should've had a ready example. Certainly such a situation did exist. It must exist! Even in 1947. Why had he not prepared himself?

The waiter returned with their orders – and placed the steaming plates of fish-and-chips, the house specialty, in front of them.

Once he'd departed, Trudy smiled – and asked, "What's going on in that devious little mind of yours, Mister Hayworth? I can smell the wood burning from here."

"That's my line."

"I've never seen a copyright. Besides, I know exactly what you're thinking. I'm telling you, Parks, it just simply will not work.

We'd have too many things going against us. Not the least of which is Charles."

Parks' face brightened at the mention of her little boy's name.

He swallowed a mouthful of fish – prematurely – and asked, "How is he these days?"

"Oh, he's fine. A pistol. Like always. You ... you do realize that you're almost fifty years older than he is, don't you?"

"I can't fault your mathematics. I don't know as I agree with your logic, though."

"I've always wanted ... always wanted someone who could ... you know ... play ball with Charles. Take him to ballgames. That sort of thing."

"Well, there've been fifty-five-year-old men who've gone on to live normal, useful, lives. Where do you think I spend most of my afternoons, these days? Inasmuch as a certain gorgeous lady ... who shall remain nameless ... won't go to damn lunch with me. Or dinner either, for that matter."

"Where?" she asked – around a mouthful of fish.

"Where indeed? *Briggs Stadium*. That's where. I'd love to have company. Teach him the game ... and all that. I may have lost a step or two ... but, I can still hit fungoes pretty good."

"Whatever fungoes are."

"Baseball. You take the ball and throw it up in the air. Just a little bitty. Then, when it comes down, you whack it with the bat. Theoretically, the kid out in the field catches it. I used to be pretty good at hittin' 'em."

He thought back to the many such occasions he'd undertaken with his own sons – especially with Dave, Doug and Dan; before the necessity of having to work so hard – take on so many jobs – had arisen. Poor Donald had gotten shut out in that area.

"Well," muttered Trudy, skeptically, "even if you're able to do that sort of thing now, Charles is only five. In another five years, he'll be ten ... and you'll ... you'll be sixty."

He sighed heavily. Was he fighting a losing battle?

"Look, Keed," he responded. "I've been hitting a lot of fungoes for a lot of years. I doubt that I'll ever lose my interest in sports."

"I can think of one time that you did."

He nodded slowly – and sighed once more.

"Touché," he said. "But, Trudy ... that wasn't me! It wasn't! It really wasn't!"

"Yes. But, Parks! You might not be you again."

"Entirely possible. Like you said ... so eloquently ... nothing's impossible. But, I'll tell you this: It's highly improbable. Look, you get no guarantees. Neither do I. No one does, Trudy. Absolutely no one."

Her eyes seemed to soften – as she lowered them.

"I know," she rasped. "I know."

"Now, as to what people are gonna say? We'll make 'em so damn envious of us that they won't be able to say anything! Not a damn thing! Well, nothing but nice stuff, anyway. Trudy? Trudy ... I love you!"

Everything seemed to stop! A hush seemed to envelope the entire restaurant. Never had the sounds of silverware clacking on plates vanished like that..

"I ... I'm surprised I said that," he muttered – after what seemed an eternity. "I don't think I intended to say that right then. It just sort of slipped out. But, I'm not sorry. Nor do I apologize. Mainly, because it's true! I guess I must've known something was up ... from the first time we touched! That night out in Frankenmuth."

Once again, she lowered her eyes.

"I know," she replied, in a husky whisper. "I know. I felt it too."

"And ... gee God! When you kissed me that night ... "

"That was for my mother's benefit."

"Yeah. I was aware of that. I knew you were sending her a message. But, that's a hell of a delivery system you've got there. Prettiest messenger I've ever seen. Or kissed, anyway. Trudy, if you only knew the message I got out of that whole thing ... "

"I do know! I got the same one ... God help me."

"Really? You really did?"

She smiled, softly – then, nodded.

"Really," she affirmed.

"Then what the hell are we doing? Wasting all this time?"

"What about my mother?"

Returning

"Trudy ... Trudy, I realize that you're concerned about what your mother says ... and what she thinks. Believe it or not, I'm concerned about it too. Your concern for your mother is probably one of the reasons I love you. One of the reasons that I'm in love with you. One of many, by the bye. And, having just met her ... for even that short a time ... I can tell that she's a great lady. A fine lady."

"She is, you know. She really is."

"Of course she is. Obviously, she's worried about you. Like I said, I would be too. But, Trudy! You're a big girl now. You're capable of making your own decisions."

"I'm not sure that's true, Parks. I don't know that I've ever made any kind of big decision. Ever."

"You have, Keed. Believe me, you have. You make decisions every day. A big decision is almost always the culmination of a whole bunch of little decisions. I realize that this is a gigantic decision for you. Someone once said that you can't make it across a wide canyon in two short jumps. You can't reach second base with one foot on first, and all such stuff as that. I got a million of 'em. But, they all apply. They're all apt. Apt as hell."

"I don't know that we can use your clichés on my mother. They may be inspiring to you ... and even to me. But, my mother's going to have a whole batch of them too."

"I'm sure that she'll be grossly upset. I would be too, if it were me. But, don't forget, Keed! We've got an ace-in-the-hole."

"Ace-in-the-hole? What ace-in-the-hole?"

"Us."

"Us?"

He nodded emphatically.

"Yeah," he said. "We got us. Us'll make it work. You know we're not talkin', here, about a couple of schleppers, here. Not chopped liver, y'know. Us are of sterling character."

She laughed – heartily.

"I don't know about sterling," she replied. "You're certainly a character, though. Character enough for the both of us."

He clucked his tongue.

"Tut tut," he admonished. "Don't tell me that we're about to have our first spat."

"I was wrong, Mister Hayworth. You're not a character."

"Well," he huffed. "That's better."

"You're not a character," she repeated. "You're an idiot. A fathead!"

His laughter filled the restaurant.

"One of those things I love about you, Goit, is that you're such a sentimental, romantic, fool."

SIXTEEN

Trudy and Parks were married in August, of 1947.

Little Charles – Charlie, as Parks had begun calling him – was ring bearer ("ring bury-er" as the boy called it).

Clark Dubin gave the bride away.

Amanda Chamberlain, of course, had been livid. She'd steadfastly maintained that she would never attend the ceremony. However, as the day of the wedding came ever-nearer, she'd relented and, had not only attended, but – at long last – had given the happy couple her blessing.

Another wide, yawning, canyon crossed!

Parks bought Amanda a beautiful, rich-blue, gown – which the older woman and her daughter had selected. She looked resplendent at the ceremony.

"It's not fair," Dubin had whispered to her at the beginning of the ceremony. "It just ain't fair … that you'd show up your daughter this way. Being so beautiful and all."

The remark had made Amanda's day.

The newlyweds journeyed to New York City for their honeymoon. The selection of the city had created a good deal of trepidation. Parks and Helen had honeymooned in New York. Trudy would rather have traveled to Niagara Falls. But, Parks had insisted on the place which would become known, a couple of decades later, as "The Big Apple".

In an overwhelming example of what would become a popular expression in the nineties, Parks "pushed the envelope"! He insisted that they bring little Charles along.

As the big day had loomed, larger and larger, Trudy had become more and more apprehensive. Especially, when her intended had insisted on including the boy in their honeymoon plans.

"I'm just afraid," she'd confided to Sue Blair, "that this is only the beginning of the problems we're going to have with the age difference. I love Charles to pieces, of course. I'd better. I am his mother, after all. But ... taking him on our honeymoon?"

"As I'm understanding you," Sue had responded, "what you're telling me is that ... that you're afraid that Parks isn't going to be able to satisfy you. Satisfy you ... ah ... sexually. Is that what you're saying?"

Trudy lowered those eyes.

"Well ... yes. I guess I am," she muttered. "You know, my mother's had a lot of things to say about the gap in our ages ... and that was one of the things that she's hammered at. Hammered at, pretty good. In fact, you might say that she's really belabored the point. To where I'm ... well, I'm downright embarrassed. I mean ... what a subject to be discussing! To be discussing all the time. It makes me blush! And in front of my own mother, for heaven's sakes."

"I can imagine,"

"No you can't. She just keeps harping on the subject, Sue. Just ranting on and on. She kept saying that, even if he's up to the ... uh ... situation now, he's going to be sixty, when I'm thirty-five. That'd be asking a lot, she says. And, when I'm forty-five, he'd be seventy. She says that ... for him to be ... ah ... 'operative' then ... well, that's darn nigh impossible."

"Well ... she may have a point."

"Oh, Sue! I don't know which way to turn ... what to believe. I really haven't the foggiest idea what to expect. And now? And now ... he wants to bring Charles along to New York. Let me tell you ... it's really a worry. It's beginning to get to me! Get to me ... that maybe there's not going to be anything in that ... uh ... area for me. Nothing at all! And right from the very start!"

"Oh, I think you may be borrowing trouble, Trudy. You don't know ... not for a fact ... that he's not ... uh ... interested. Or that he ... ah ... can't perform. As I understand it, a lot of men ... women too ... are active right up into their sixties. Even their seventies. Some, I guess, go right up into their eighties. If it were me, I think that I'd be more upset about going to New York. Isn't that where he went with his first wife?"

Trudy laughed – nervously.

"Well," she said, "I guess I was at first. Was upset, you know. But, he was so ... was so ... so interested. I finally got to thinking, 'What the heck ... he doesn't ever put any real demands on me'. He's been so good to me, Sue. So very good to me. I'm as convinced as I can be that he loves me ... truly loves me. I believe that he loves me very deeply. I don't imagine there can be any doubt about that. Even if his wanting to go to New York were to have some deep-rooted significance to his marriage to Helen ... well ... I guess that I can indulge him. It took me long enough to figure it out, but love's a two-way street. And I do love him. So ... New York it is."

"Well," maintained Sue, "I think that'd bother me more than this sex thing."

Trudy laughed, once again. Laughed nervously.

"Oh, Sue! It's not a ... a sex thing. It's a legitimate concern. I haven't been to bed with a man since ... since nineteen forty-one. With my husband. Frank's the only man I've ever slept with."

"You mean that you and Parks ... you don't ... ?"

"No. He's never made a serious pass at me. 'Put a move on me' is what he calls it. A little necking ... maybe some heavy breathing. The occasional pat on the fanny. But, that's been ... that's been it."

"Yeah," answered Sue. "Then, I guess that would be a bit of a worry to me."

"Well, it's bothering me! Really bothering me! Sue, it may be that I'll ... that I'll never know what it's like. To have a man make love to me ... again. Ever again."

It was a very real – monumentally serious – concern.

To the point that she was on the verge of advising Parks that she was seriously considering canceling the nuptials – a week before the wedding was to take place. It would've been, of course, earthshaking news to the prospective groom.

His fiancée might have followed through on her threat – had not Parks dispelled her fears! Put them to rest – five days before the ceremony! Not a moment too soon!

Our hero had never moved into the little two-bedroom, white bungalow – Joseph's house. Nor had he put it up for rental. For some inexplicable reason, the place had remained vacant and unfurnished all those months – while Parks had stayed put in the apartment on Ohio Street.

Once Trudy had agreed to marry him, he had asked her if she would consider moving into the house on Rosemont. One look – and she'd fallen in love with the place.

Parks, of course, asked her to decorate it. Furnish it – from top to bottom. She'd jumped into the assignment – with great exuberance.

Once the place was ready – five days before the wedding – the bride- and groom-to-be dropped by to inspect the results of Trudy's handiwork.

Everything was in place. They'd toured the entire single-story dwelling, winding up in the basement. The cellar was still unfinished – and the couple was trying to decide exactly what to do with it.

The cement block-walled basement ran the length and breadth of the house. The "fruit cellar" extended out under the front porch. The coal furnace took up almost a fifth of the floor space – directly across from the coal bin. The "stationary tubs" were pretty well situated out of the way – in the far corner, in the rear.

As the couple had started back up the stairs – Trudy, standing on the first step, while Parks remained on the cement floor – he turned her around. The added height of the stair made his fiancée almost as tall as he. He looked deep into those warm, brown eyes.

"You know?" he began, in a surprisingly-husky voice, "the eyes are the window of the soul. You have a beautiful soul. You're a beautiful woman."

"Oh, stop it. You're getting me all embarrassed. Besides, I'm not beautiful. I could stand to drop a few pounds."

"So could I. But, I figure that ... if we were all a little fatter, we'd all be a little closer."

"You're an idiot," she replied, laughing. "A total fathead."

"I know. You told me."

"Well, it's true."

He smiled – and kissed her on the nose.

"Well," he said, "you're just as much a squirrel as I am. Maybe even more so."

He kissed her tenderly. Kissed her long! Kissed her deeply!

Her body melted against him.

"You know," he rasped, "it's been a good while, since we've had a decent necking session."

She kissed him back – on the nose.

"I thought you hadn't noticed," she observed.

"Am I made of wood? From the neck up, yes. But, otherwise?"

He kissed her full on the lips – letting his tongue dart into and out of her mouth.

His hands dropped to her buttocks – gently rubbing and patting, in unison with his tongue's little adventure between her lips.

Trudy clung, tightly, to him – moving her head lightly around his tongue. Then, biting softly – and stroking it with her own. He worked his hands up between them – and unbuttoned her blouse. Reaching both hands inside, he tenderly caressed her brassiere-bound breasts. The couple had never "gone that far" before.

Her breathing became more and more labored. Her body began to weigh down upon him – as her legs became more and more rubbery.

He picked her up – and started to ascend the steep stairs.

"Parks! What're you doing, you big lug? You'll hurt yourself! Put me down!"

"All in good time, M'Dear," he replied – in what he fervently hoped would be a strong, virile, non-labored, non-breathless, voice.

He strove – mightily – not to show the struggle he was experiencing, negotiating her up into the kitchen. Despite the fact that Trudy was ever-so-slightly overweight, she certainly was not a large woman. Parks was determined to prove to her that he was as masculine as a younger man! A much younger man!

He carried her all the way through the kitchen and into the dinette. He could've set her down, in that location, he felt – and he would've proved his point. But, he made a bold decision to go "the whole way".

With his wife-to-be still in his arms, he turned toward the living room. Once in the front room, he made another right turn and lugged her down the hallway – to the larger of the two bedrooms, in back. To their bedroom!

It required a Herculean effort to set her down, ever so gently – bottom-first – on the bed.

Climbing up with her – striving vigorously to conceal his labored breathing – he began kissing her ears and neck.

He removed her blouse. He was surprisingly adept in unhooking her bra! Tossing the lacy, filmy, undergarment onto the floor, he ran his tongue over her full, lush breasts – pressing hard against the beautiful, soft-pink, nipples. The urgent pressure, the soft moisture and the breathless warmth caused them to harden – immediately!

Fumbling with the zipper of her skirt, he managed to lower it – in bumbling fits and starts! His futile effort to tug the skirt down over her hips brought a smile to the lips of his intended!

She assisted him! Well, she took over the project! She pulled the garment up over her head!

She was moaning, slightly, as he peeled the silken, opaque, white panties down over her satin-smooth hips!

He beheld her! Reveling in her beauty! She was, at that point, clad only in black nylon stockings – held in place by a pair of frilly, black, elastic, garters, with tiny red roses located in the center – and a pair of red leather pumps.

It was the most sexually stimulating sight he'd ever seen.

Parks began to remove his own clothing – thinking, all the while, how he used to be much more adept at this sort of thing. His hands fumbled at the buttons of his shirt.

Trudy smiled at his plight. Taking his hands from the shirt, she placed them upon her breasts. Then, she finished undoing the buttons.

Once she'd helped him out of his shirt, she unbuckled his belt. Then, she unzipped his slacks. Reaching inside, she found his rigid penis! Gently stroking him, she used her free hand – to assist him! To help him divest himself of trousers and undershorts – after he'd managed to kick off his shoes!

Then, once both of them were clad only in stockings (somewhere, in the exercise, she'd "lost" her shoes), he returned to her heaving breasts – tenderly kneading them with his hands, pressing his tongue, once more, against the erect nipples, then, softly, biting on them!

At that magic moment, Trudy was mere seconds from the first orgasm she would ever experience! Ever! In her entire life!

When Parks trailed his tongue down across her tummy, her navel, then her lower abdomen – to flick at her clitoris – she was ready to explode! All it took was two or three passes at the super-sensitive, throbbing, membrane to send her "over the top"!

Her passion erupted – in dimensions she could never have dreamed possible! In 1947, not much was said or written about such things as oral sex. Monica Lewinski was not anywhere on the horizon – to make every eight-year-old kid spectacularly aware of such things.. Trudy, of course, had not been exposed to the new "openness"! Not even to all the "honest" "relevant" stuff of the sixties! She'd been totally unprepared for what had just happened to her.

Parks continued to lavish her down there! His bride-to-be continued to become lost – swept up in wave after wave, spasm upon spasm, of unbridled passion! The trembling of her body, plus the soft – then, not so soft – moans spoke volumes!

Parks basked in the confirmation! There could be no doubt that she was so lovingly caught up in whirlpool after whirlpool of sheer, orgasmic, ecstasy!

Each time she appeared to reach a point where she was certain she'd be physically incapable of withstanding further climaxes, her husband-to-be would increase the sensual stroking with his tongue – sending her to even higher, wholly undreamed-of, plateaus!

Finally, he ceased the oral stimulation!

Trudy had long-since passed the stage of simply writhing around – and bounding about – the extremities of some far-off, overwhelming, climax-laden, Shangri La.

She was, by then, shaking violently! Uncontrollably! From head-to-toe! For a wrenching second or two, Parks feared she'd become delirious! He was certain he'd heard her mumble, "How can I be so cold? On such a hot night?"

It was obvious that she was unaware of the glistening perspiration – which coated her still-gyrating, shivering, body.

It was at that moment that Parks entered her!

Lowering himself slowly – invading her ever-so-gently – he began to press into, then pull out of, her with great care! With exceptional tenderness! The action was enough to rekindle Trudy's fire! Within seconds of feeling the warmth – and the rigidity – of her intended inside her, she dug her nails into his back, then wrapped her legs around his gyrating, pistoning, buttocks!

Parks could sense that Trudy was soaring, once again, to the heights she'd scaled only moments before!

Suddenly, he stiffened! His entire body began to quiver! He moaned three or four times – and deflated! Then, he simply laid on top of her – panting desperately!

Totally spent!

After five tranquil, placid, minutes, Parks raised up slightly. He kissed Trudy warmly – first on the mouth, then on the nose.

Then, he rolled off her, and onto his back. She turned onto her right side – facing him. A deep, satisfied, smile crept onto her lips. She began to stroke his forehead.

"Hey!" Her voice was a husky whisper.

His eyes opened slightly, as he replied, "Whatcha want?"

"Whatcha doin'?"

"Just waitin' for a streetcar."

"Know something?"

"Not a hell of a lot," he answered with an insipid smile.

"I've never been so thoroughly laid in my life Mister Hayworth. Did you know that?"

"I haven't taken a survey ... if that's what you mean."

Returning

"Seriously, Parks. I've only ... been with ... one man. My husband. But, I've never had a what-do-you-call-it? Never had one of <u>those</u> before."

"An orgasm?"

"Yes. I've never even come close. Today ... tonight ... I couldn't keep track. I honestly lost count."

"Well," he said, brightly. "I'm glad I was invited."

"Invited?" she answered, laughing heartily. "You were the whole party!"

There went Trudy's thoughts of canceling the wedding!

Further, she was no longer apprehensive at the prospect of including Charles in their honeymoon plans.

Parks would – most certainly – think of something!

They spent six happy weeks in New York City.

Parks' insistence in including little Charles bore fruit! Our hero was able to obtain *World Series* tickets to the almost-no-hit game that Floyd Bevans, of the New York Yankees, would pitch – against the Dodgers, at *Ebbets Field*. It would be a once-in-a-lifetime opportunity for the youngster to witness one of the true classics of baseball history.

The boy would be unable to fathom the total import of what he would see, of course, at that tender age. However, as the years would go by, Charles would, Parks hoped, eventually, realize how fortunate he'd been to have attended the epic game.

The youngster – as well as his mother – had been impressed by the pomp and ceremony, which preceded the opening pitch. As the game progressed, however, they'd lost Trudy.

However, Charles seemed uncommonly attentive during the course of the contest. Surprisingly, the lad had not become wrapped up in a quest for hotdogs or peanuts or any of the other goodies purveyed by the many venders – to Parks' delight.

As the game progressed into the ninth inning, Parks experienced a mild scare:

Bevans still had his no-hitter. Had he picked the wrong game? Was his memory totally gone? No! It <u>had</u> to be the right game! He was certain that there had never been a no-hitter thrown, in *The World Series* – until Don Larson had pitched his perfect game in

1956. He was positive that he'd not "lost it", memory-wise. Not totally, anyway. Why, he even remembered how Larson had gotten the final out in his "Perfecto"! (Dale Mitchell had struck out!)

Still, his recollection had been that Bevans had lost his no-hitter before the ninth inning. He'd thought it had been in the seventh. Certainly no later than the eighth.

As the home half of the ninth began – three outs from a no-hitter (which would still be something for Charles to have witnessed) – Parks did his best to hammer home to his new wife and stepson the importance of the situation. The boy was making a concerted effort to understand. Trudy was not impressed.

The leadoff hitter for Brooklyn, Carl Furillo, walked. Burt Shotton, the Dodger manager, sent in Al Gionfriddo to run for "Skoonj".

Parks leapt to his feet – as Gionfriddo stole second. The action was a throw-back to his younger days – when he was a "sports nut"; before his disillusionment with virtually all athletes had set in. Before his distaste for almost all athletic endeavors had overtaken him. He'd become disgusted with almost all jocks – as they'd come to be known. He'd held nothing but contempt for almost all the owners – and literally all the umpires.

In 1947, though, sports was still about having fun! Not about bazillions of dollars – and in-your-face, overpaid, underachieving, celebrities! Before "talking smack" had become such an integral part of the game. Any game.

Bucky Harris, the Yankee manager, had ordered Bevans to walk Pete Reiser. Dodger runners at first and second!

Parks' heart began to pound! He could feel the blood coursing through his body – the pounding at his temples!

<u>This</u> <u>is</u> <u>it</u>! <u>This</u> <u>is</u> <u>it</u>!

As dramatically as he could, he tried to set the scene for Trudy and Charles:

"If this next guy ... this Cookie Lavagetto ... if he gets a hit, not only could the Yankees' pitcher lose his no-hitter ... conceivably, he could lose the whole ball game!"

Trudy still seemed to be unmoved by the situation.

Charles, though, appeared to have a glimmering of understanding!

Sure enough, Lavagetto slammed a double off the right field scoreboard and two runs scored – wiping out the one-run New York lead, breaking up Bevans' bid for fame and, not incidentally, winning the game for the home team!

The crowd, of course, went insane. It just simply didn't get any better than that!

As the newly-minted Hayworth family left the ball park, Parks was taken with the flushed, delirious faces of those around him. He felt a God-awful sadness – a sadness, born of supreme irony. In 10 short years, their beloved Dodgers would belong to Los Angeles. How tragic! Who – among that arm-waving, cheering, hoarse, flushed crowd – would ever believe it? The Los Angeles Dodgers? Blasphemy – in Flatbush, anyway!

So as not to be "tied down" by Charles, Parks was able to "farm him out" – to an elderly Jewish lady, who'd lived down the hall from the apartment he'd taken in Brooklyn's Brighton Beach neighborhood, the previous winter.

With Charles attended to, Parks and Trudy were able to take in a number of Broadway shows – most of which Parks had attended on his previous trip – and to see the sights. It also gave them ample time for lovemaking!

Parks had, indeed, "thought of something".

The new groom hadn't been so happy in years. When Helen had died, he'd been certain that he would never again love anyone. Certainly not as much as he'd loved his dear wife. And he was equally as positive that he could never hope to find someone who could love him as much – as deeply – as Helen had. Or be anywhere near as good to him.

He'd been wrong! On both counts!

The love he felt for Trudy was, of course, much different. For one thing, it was much more physical! And at his age! Plus, It was every bit as rewarding!

More rewarding – in some aspects!

The couple had discussed, on a number of occasions, the reasons they were so compatible in bed. Parks believed that he'd been able to satisfy her so completely – because, as he'd matured, he'd learned the value of patience.

"A younger man is just simply not going to have the patience to explore what makes a woman happy," he'd told Trudy, after their celebrated initial session, in the white house on Rosemont.

"Are you telling me that you're exceptionally experienced?"

He shook his head emphatically.

"No!" he half-shouted. "Not at all. I haven't been to bed with all that many women! Believe me, I haven't. But, when you're younger, you're always in a hurry to ... how shall I say? ... get there. As you get a few years ... and a few barnacles ... on you, it becomes obvious that getting there is half the fun. I think most people give too much significance to their orgasm. They're great ... don't get me wrong. I'm not knocking orgasms. You've never seen anyone more pro-orgasm than me. But, they're not the be-all and end-all. If you get yourself all wrapped up in that ... in that alone ... you're missing out on a hell of a lot of other neat stuff. It takes awhile to learn that ... or, at least, it did for me. A little retarded, I guess. Hopefully, I've got it surrounded by now."

"Oh, boy," she'd responded – clapping her hands – "have you ever got it surrounded!"

The Hayworth family returned to Detroit and set up housekeeping in the little white house on Rosemont.

Trudy seemed happy. Her concern with "the age gap thing" seemed to diminish by the day. Over lunch, with Sue Blair, Trudy confided that her concern in that area had practically evaporated.

"Your worries about his being able to ... uh ... perform were unfounded?" asked Sue, with an obscene laugh.

Trudy nodded – emphatically.

"Were they ever," she affirmed. "At the risk of telling tales out of school, I never should've been worried about it in the first place."

Sue reached across the table – and placed her hand atop Trudy's, leaving it there for 10 or 15 seconds.

"See?" she enthused. "You see? It just doesn't pay to borrow trouble. I guess that could be a lesson to all of us. I know that I'm terribly susceptible to it. How's your little boy adapting?"

"Oh! He's loving it! He really is! He loves that house. Well, for one thing, he has his own bedroom ... instead of sharing that tiny one, at my mother's house, with me. He's just as thrilled as he can be! Has a couple little playmates down the block. Seems to be getting along well with 'em."

"Sounds ideal. Couldn't happen to a nicer gal ... or to a nicer guy. I don't really know Parks all that well, but I can see the effect he's had on you. I can't tell you how happy I am for you. For both of you. Do you have Charles in school yet?"

"He's going to kindergarten ... over at *Peter Vital School*, on Westwood. Seems to be doing pretty well. I guess the biggest bonus of all is that I get to stay home with him. To raise him. Watch him grow up."

"I know. We all miss you at the office."

Trudy smiled warmly. Those eyes, however, seemed to cloud slightly.

"I ... I miss you guys too," she said. "Say hello to everyone for me. But, I ain't a-comin' back! I'm having too much fun. Besides, I think it's best for Charles to be away from my mother."

"How's that? Don't you and your mother get along? I always thought that ... "

"No! Of course we do. But, you know. She's getting on in years ... and really doesn't have the patience she used to have. Not like when I was little. Plus, we can't always agree on discipline ... things like that. Besides, it's her house, y'know. And living there ... "

"I see what you mean."

"I used to worry about Parks and Charles ... how they'd take to one another. He's almost my mother's age ... and, like I said, older people sometimes don't have all the patience in the world."

As soon as she'd said that, Trudy remembered what Parks had told her about young men not having the patience to ascertain what it takes to satisfy a woman.

She rolled the soft brown eyes back – toward the top of her head.

"In some areas, anyway," she hastily amended.

"I'd never thought much about it," replied Sue, around a mouthful of **The Blue Ribbon's** famous fish and chips.

"It was the cause of some concern for me ... obviously," advised Trudy. "But, Parks and Charles get along famously. Parks calls him 'Charlie' ... but, Charles doesn't seem to mind. Parks always refers to the two of 'em as 'us boys'."

"From what little I know of Parks," replied Sue, "he should get along great with Charles. I've heard him say that he's the world's biggest kid. I've heard him say it more than once. My guess is that he's right ... that he probably is the world's biggest kid. He and Charles should do just fine."

It had become obvious to the new Mrs. Hayworth that Parks did enjoy children.

Whenever they would dine out, he was forever "mugging" at babies and toddlers. He seemed captivated by them. The feeling, most always, seemed to be mutual. From time to time, he would talk to them – advising them, usually, that he was "The World's Tallest Baby".

"Have you ever seen a baby ... who's taller than me?" he'd invariably ask.

The youngster would always eat it up – even if the child couldn't quite fathom exactly what Parks was saying.

Trudy usually tried to hide an obvious feeling of being ill-at-ease, at such times. And she didn't know why. Her husband's enchantment with kids most always seemed to be a source of discomfort to her. Why?

Well, why would a man – so obviously thrilled with children – never have fathered any offspring of his own? It was a real puzzlement. It was also a bother.

Trudy had confided to Sue that she was concerned that Parks' affinity for children could be an indication that he may have sired a number of kids – in some secret, hidden, perhaps-nefarious, life.

Sue merely advised her friend that she – as before – was borrowing trouble.

Still, the discomfort seemed to surface for the newly-minted Mrs. Hayworth – each time her husband sailed into his "World's Tallest Baby" routine.

As Thanksgiving, 1947, approached, most of Trudy's misgivings had appeared to vanish. Seemingly, she was happy to be the wife of Parks Hayworth. Her new neighbors had accepted her – an important aspect. She'd never really been able to rid her mind of the what-will-people-say? syndrome. Not totally, anyway. But, when it became obvious that her "scandalous" marriage to a much older man had had absolutely no effect upon her relationship with her new-found friends in the neighborhood, whatever problems she may have had, in that area, seemed to disappear.

As frosting on the cake, Amanda Chamberlain had never again mentioned age. Not once the wedding had taken place.

Amanda and Parks got along famously. Parks was forever buying his mother-in-law some little trinket – for herself or for her house – and insisted that Amanda accompany them out to dinner once or twice a week. Every time he bought tickets for a stage show or a concert, he always included Amanda.

Twice, between the time they'd returned from New York City and Thanksgiving, Parks and Trudy had taken off for four or five days: Once to Chicago and once to Michigan's beautiful Upper Peninsula. Amanda had been happy to keep Charles for them. Even to driving the boy out to school, every day – in her rusty 1939 Studebaker.

A week before "Tom Turkey Day" Parks bought his mother-in-law a brand new 1948 Ford club coupe.

The lone cloud over Parks' head concerned his grandparents. He'd given up any thought of establishing some sort of relationship with his parents. He was certain that his mother would freak out completely, should he attempt to approach her. Even after eight long years! Especially with her marriage disintegrating! He'd been able to see her – to view her from afar – precious few times.

The same went for his father. Especially after that long gaze from Pop, on Prairie Street. Was our boy just being paranoid? It had, after all, only been a glance. Still –

Parks had watched little Jimmy play ball on Penrod a few times – and maybe some sort of acquaintanceship with the lad could be possible in the future. But, to all intents and purposes, any situation with his parents was out of the question

.

That being the case, he'd always entertained the possibility of interfacing with his grandparents. But, his grandmother had always reacted so coldly to him – always so aloof – during their "chance" meetings at **Freddie's Bar**. It was heart-breaking!

Then, of course, the "chance" meetings had stopped – when Helen had died.

He'd lost touch with his grandparents altogether. How could he have been so insensitive?

Numerous times, after having sorted his life out (in the bathtub at the *Book Cadillac*) he'd driven past the tavern and the "Dog House". His grandfather's new Buick had most usually been parked on the massive lawn, by the maple tree in front of the "Dog House". Never at the saloon. He couldn't remember any interval when Grandpa had gone on the wagon. He knew of no disagreement with Freddie or any of his bartenders.

Many times, he was terribly tempted to simply "pop in" on them – in their "Dog House". Three times, before his marriage to Trudy – and three or four times afterward – he was on the verge of calling on his grandparents. He wanted to introduce Trudy to them. He wanted – desperately – his grandmother's approval of the woman he loved.

His grandfather would, undoubtedly, make an off-color remark about the size of Trudy's bosom – when she was out of earshot, of course. But, hey! That was Grandpa.

Each time, Parks had driven to the little house, at the back of the lot, he had gotten cold feet. He was certain that Trudy had experienced numerous misgivings, on those occasions when he'd driven past the little, unique, "Dog House", with her in the car.

However, she'd never made any untoward remark – or questioned his motive for driving down Burnette Street so often.

Three nights before Thanksgiving, he drove past the bar and the "Dog House". The Buick was in neither place. Every light, though, seemed to be lit at the residence.

That was odd!

It finally hit him: Grandpa must've passed away! Yes! He'd died! But, how long ago?

Parks scrambled through his memory – frantically attempting to dredge up exactly when the old man had died! His recollection told him that it had to have been 1947! A year almost gone! A year wasted! One of many, dammit!

Actually, it had been not-quite-<u>two</u> years that had been wasted. His grandfather had died in 1946. Parks – still in his post-Helen doldrums – had not been paying attention. It was not until he'd missed Grandpa's Buick, under the maple tree, that the truth had hit him! Had hit him between the eyes! Blasted him – with all the subtlety of a sledgehammer!

It had taken Kate Swenson almost 15 months before she'd had "enough gumption" to sell the car.

Parks had blown yet another golden opportunity! What else was new?

"Shit!" he shouted – his voice ricocheting off every inch of the interior of the car. "Shit!" He banged both hands on the steering wheel. "Shit! Shit! Shit! Shit! Shit!"

Just when he was sure that he'd finally gotten control of himself, he let go another top-of-his-lungs bellow:

"Shit!"

The drive home was excruciatingly long.

Parks reflected, bitterly, upon his resolution to make up for lost time. He certainly had missed the boat, where his grandfather was concerned. He just didn't know by how much! Didn't know how long ago the ship had pulled out!

Another withering realization: With the death of her husband, Kate Swenson had become the next thing to a recluse – seldom venturing from the inner sanctum of her precious little "Dog House". She'd constantly "hid out" in the tiny place – until she'd sold it in 1952. If it had been improbable before, a relationship with his "best buddy" had become "damn nigh impossible"!

Both of his paternal grandparents had died before Jim Sidorwitz had been born.

The realization of his grandfather's death – plus the fact that he would be hard-pressed to see his grandmother again – ever – left our hero with a dull, bleak, void in the pit of his stomach.

What would he do? What could he do? Should he reconsider his reluctance to attempt to establish a relationship with his parents? Perhaps with his Aunt Genevieve (Madge's sister) and his Uncle Paul. It was something, certainly, to think about.

On Thanksgiving morning, Parks took Charles downtown to watch the **J.L. Hudson Company's** parade. The lavish spectacle had been sponsored for decades by what was then Detroit's largest department store. The festivities marked the official arrival of Santa Claus. It would be difficult to determine who enjoyed the parade most – Charles or his stepfather!

The puppets and the floats and the balloons were as colorful, as unique, as ornate, as funny – and as beautiful – as Parks had remembered them, from his youth. He had lugged a stepladder along – and our hero had placed the boy on top. The youngster had a great seat. Parks had a bit of trouble seeing a few of the clowns and puppets. But, watching little Charles' face light up – with that special brightness that only little kids seem to possess – was every bit as entertaining and rewarding. More so!

As Santa's float made its way past their vantage point, at *Grand Circus Park*, Parks, once more, reflected on how much less-commercialized Christmas seemed in 1947. The feelings and expression of good cheer seemed much more genuine. Much less hollow.

When he was still Jim, and living in the seventies, our hero had begun to wonder if his memory – of the thirties and forties – had been playing tricks on him. Maybe he'd become cantankerous in his old age, but Christmas, in the seventies, seemed to have lost its special meaning. He half-expected that, in the eighties, Santa would arrive in a giant red-and-green firecracker – on July 4th.

He couldn't know that, in the new millenium, there would be a move afoot to refer to it merely as "The Winter Holiday". To ban manger scenes from public property. To outlaw the singing of Christmas carols in the public schools. And he was unaware of the fact that he wasn't far off – with his sarcasm about an Independence Day kick-off to the Christmas season.

He liked Christmas, 1947, better.

No one enjoyed Christmas Day, that year, more than Parks Hayworth. He went completely overboard – buying gifts at a level which bordered on the ridiculous. He hadn't intended to, of course.

By necessity, when he was Jim – father of seven – Christmas had, most years, been rather sparse. He and Kathleen had done as well as they could. There had never been a Christmas when each of the kids didn't receive two or three new gifts – no matter how small or inexpensive.

In the long run, he felt, the austerity had never really hurt the children. What they had gone on to acquire for themselves, in later years, they seemed to appreciate more.

Jim Sidorwitz had always maintained – boasted, almost – that, even had he been wealthy, he would never go overboard in buying gifts for family and friends.

In 1947, Parks Hayworth had gone completely and utterly overboard!

Time and time again, he would staunchly vow that the present he was in the process of buying – usually for little Charles – would be the last. Definitely! No question about it!

"No more," he would insist – to himself and/or Trudy. "That's gonna be it!"

It would be, too! Until, of course, he ran into another irresistible gadget.

On Christmas morning, Charles was in his glory. Never had Santa been so good to him. The fat man with the white beard and red suit had always managed to find his grandmother's house – but, never had he left so many wonderful things.

Charles was thrilled! Almost as thrilled as Parks!

"You're sitting three feet above your chair," observed Trudy, from the sofa, across the room.

"Who writes your material? That's my line."

"Not any more. Community property, don'tcha know."

"Happy?" he asked.

"Ecstatic. Oh, Parks! You've been so good to me … and for me. And for Charles."

"Charles? Charles? Never hoid of him. There's a kind of dopey kid over there ... named Charlie. Mayhap it is him ... to whom you refer? Mayhap?"

"My. Aren't we formal today? 'Mayhap'? You say 'mayhap'? But, seriously, Parks ... "

"But seriously folks ... "

"Will you <u>be</u> serious, you fathead?"

"Serious?" he asked. "Serious? On Christmas Day, I should be serious? What are you? Some kind of religious nut? How can you sit there ... amidst the ruins of what Santa Claus hath wrought ... and even talk about serious?"

"C'mon, Hayworth. Christmas time is the time when you count your blessings. I have two. You and Charles ... Charlie."

He got up and walked over to her. Bending down, he kissed her – tenderly.

"I'm the one with all the blessings," he rasped.

Looking deep into his wife's fawn-like eyes, he whispered, "The eyes, y'know, really and truly <u>are</u> the windows of the soul. And yours is still beautiful. Very, very beautiful. Fanny's kinda cute too. I'm a very lucky guy. I don't deserve you."

"That's right. You deserve better."

"Ain't none better."

"You know what?" she whispered in his ear.

"I'm almost afraid to ask. No ... what?"

"I'd like to make love."

"Me too."

Charles was still enthralled with his Electric Baseball game, that Santa had brought.

"Honey," his mother said to the youngster. "Daddy and I have a few things to talk over in the bedroom. You play nice, here, and we'll be right back."

The boy seemed barely to have heard her.

His parents repaired to the bedroom – where Parks took Trudy, while they both had their clothes on. It took slightly more than five minutes.

"Sneaky little devils, aren't we?" he observed, grinning broadly – as he climbed off her.

"Yeah," she replied, breathlessly. "Sneaky ... but, fun-loving."

"Beats hell out of *Monopoly*," he said, with an overdone leer. "Or even Electric Baseball."

"Beats hell out of any kind of baseball," she replied.

When they returned to the living room, Charles was still engrossed in his game.

"Ah," reflected Parks. "The innocence of youth."

SEVENTEEN

As 1948 dawned, Parks resolved to get a handle on the whole "money thing" once again. He had, surprisingly enough, neglected his finances since the previous summer – just prior to his wedding. Now, he was going to "get back in the game".

When the Hayworths had begun to make their arrangements for the nuptials and the honeymoon trip, Parks had reached a decision to put the routine, day-to-day, portion of his portfolio in the hands of Ruth – another accountant at the dealership. The one who'd replaced Trudy.

"I don't know if I like that idea," Trudy had admonished. "I remember what happened the last time you left your stuff with some shameless little hussy from **Keller-Dubin**. You wound up in bed with her."

He fashioned his most lewd grin – and tweaked the edge of an imaginary *Snidely Whiplash* moustache.

"Hoo boy," he responded in his most sinister voice. "Did I ever!"

Parks found himself wishing that the results – the non-intimate ones – had been the same, as when Trudy had been in charge. Ruth, as it turned out, did a terrible job of keeping things in order.

Had Elliot Voorhees not pulled a number of chestnuts out of the fire – and had Clark Dubin not gotten his finger into the situation on one or two occasions – Parks' plight could've been much worse.

Ruth had let a number of payments slip – almost causing our hero to default on three different potentially-valuable properties! It was only through the intercession of Elliot, that they'd remained in Park's name. Elliot, then, alerted Dubin to keep an eye on things – as much as would be possible. Preferably on a day-to-day basis.

"It's just between us," Elliot had proposed. "No sense in worrying our happy groom."

Upon his return, Parks had found himself too caught up in his new marriage, his new wife, his new son, the realization of the death of his grandfather and – ultimately – Thanksgiving and Christmas. The sum total of these distractions had been sufficient to keep the usually-money-oriented Parks from immersing himself back into his financial empire.

He should've been warned – all kinds of flares should've gone off – when he, himself, had to extinguish a couple fires created by Ruth's administration.

There had been other diversions: Trips to Chicago and Michigan's U.P. They'd been most satisfying. Very fulfilling. But, they were – well – diversions.

The rents had continued to pour in from "Helen's Building". Our hero had always referred to the place by that name. Trudy seemed not to mind. It had become second nature.

The house on Prevost, though, was another matter:

Parks had rented the house to Hector LaCroix and his wife Renee. Hector had been involved in a highly-secret government project at the **Ford** Rouge Plant, during the war. Parks had, though the years, been able to collect a rental charge, far higher than market value, from Hector and Renee.

For the duration of the war, there had never been a problem. Hector had been taking home an excellent salary – and was simply never late with the rental payment. He had, in addition, absorbed the cost of all maintenance and repairs to the property. Parks had never had to worry about the place.

However, by the summer of 1946, the ordnance project had been phased out.

Despite the fact that the job market, in Detroit, had remained bullish, Hector had been unable to find another position approximating the salary to which he'd become accustomed. For almost 18 months, he had drifted from job to job – each time, dropping a notch or two in status! And – more importantly – dropping a couple or three notches in salary!

He began drinking heavily!

Parks had been unable to determine whether the drink was leading to Hector's employment difficulties – or if it was the other way around. It was classic "the chicken or the egg?" routine.

In addition, Parks' renter had begun resorting to violence – virtually always when he was drunk. Twice, he had beaten Renee! Beaten her severely! The second beating had sent his wife to the hospital!

He had suspected her, wrongly, of cheating – and, in a drunken stupor, had accused her of unfaithfulness! Renee had denied the charge – and Hector had gone berserk!

He had literally ripped her clothing from her body – and punched her repeatedly; splitting both lips, breaking three teeth, dislocating both shoulders and fracturing her jaw!

As his fury had built, he'd removed his belt, and strapped her – mostly on her bottom, but also on her thighs! Had strapped her – unmercifully!

Incredibly, Renee had refused to press charges! However, she did retain an attorney – and filed for divorce! Although the woman had not pressed for alimony, the court awarded her virtually every asset she and Hector had acquired, as man and wife!

The marriage had produced no children.

Once Renee had received her settlement, she liquidated her holdings – and returned to France.

Whatever infinitesimal chance Hector might have had at turning his life around vanished with Renee's departure! He was drunk all the time! He virtually never worked!

In addition, he virtually never paid his rent!

Parks hadn't the heart to evict him over the holidays – despite the fact that Hector had paid no rent since the previous August!

Finally, the first week in January, our hero forced himself to the house on Prevost – to perform the inevitable, the heart-wrenching, task of evicting his tenant. He'd driven past the place a number of times during the preceding months and weeks – and had witnessed the gradual seediness the home was taking on. It had broken his heart. He hoped Helen had not been looking down, during those months. Had not been forced to witness the condition of her "Dream House".

Parks was totally unprepared for what he found inside!

The place, of course, was a complete mess! There was almost no furniture. Renee had liquidated all but a few beaten-up, run-down, sticks.

The walls were full of holes! Parks couldn't imagine one person smashing that many holes – in that many walls! The drapes were beyond salvage. The Venetian blinds – what was left of them – were deceased!

The kitchen sink was clogged! The stench from the garbage-laden water was almost debilitating! The carpets were soiled and stained – beyond recognition. The stair runner had been pulled asunder – leaving the steps a hazard to navigation.

In one of the bedrooms, upstairs, the chandelier had been pulled out from the ceiling! The door to the linen closet – at the end of the hall – hung, precariously, on one hinge!

Not one room had been spared Hector's wrath!

Parks walked into the bathroom, and – immediately – he began to vomit!

In the bathtub – in a semi-solid pool of dried-and-hardened blood, lay Hector LaCroix! Both wrists had been slashed! He had been dead – the medical examiner would later determine – between seven and ten days!

That, of course, had done it! Parks would keep that house not one second longer than he had to! Than was absolutely necessary!

He phoned Elliot Voorhees: "Whatever it takes," he'd half-shrieked. "Fix it up! Do it right! I'll pay whatever it costs to put it in top shape! Fix it completely ... top to bottom! Inside and out! Replace whatever has to be replaced! Whatever it takes! Then, sell the fucking thing! I don't want to lay eyes on it again! It's a fucking Jonah! Get rid of it! Get it out of my life! Don't haggle over price! Just get rid of the fucking thing!"

It would take six months to restore – and sell – the house! During that time, Parks – true to his word – never laid eyes on the place! The sale did nothing to salve Parks' wounds. But, he did realize a tidy profit from the transaction. Real estate prices had, of course, zoomed since he and Helen had bought the place.

The other rental house – Marilyn Faffenberger's childhood home, on Grandmont – had also proved to be a profitable investment. He'd rented the place to the Brogan family; a mechanic, his wife and three children.

However trouble was also brewing in that paradise!

When Parks dropped by to inspect the premises for the first time – two weeks after the debacle on Prevost Street – he'd been upset to discover the place had been anything but properly maintained. The children had been allowed to run willy-nilly. Something highly unusual during those much-less-permissive times. Especially when the family was so large.

The house was not badly in need of repair – but, Parks foresaw a good deal of trouble, if things were not turned around, immediately. Whatever indulgence, toward renters, with which he may have been blessed had long evaporated – with the LaCroix fiasco!

Our hero warned Mrs. Brogan – in a voice that was probably a few-hundred decibels louder (and a couple pitches higher) than he'd preferred – that the family had until the tenth of February to restore the place! To get it back to the condition that had existed when they had taken possession of it! Otherwise, he would evict them!

The threat – the promise – worked! Two weeks later, Mrs. Brogan called her landlord – asking that he return and inspect the premises. The place was in mint condition! Rental property was still in exceptionally short supply. It was evident that the Brogans had been horrified at the prospect of trying to find other housing.

The entire episode turned out to be most fortuitous for Parks! As he'd pulled away from the curb – in front of the Brogan home – he spied the large For Sale sign, imbedded in the middle of the front lawn of his "Dream House", up the street!

He lost no time in phoning Elliot Voorhees!

"Get that house! I've got to have that house!"

Where had Elliot heard that before?

He got it! Parks paid much more than Elliot would have liked for him to spend – but, he got it!

He was thrilled! The macabre discovery on Prevost had begun to fade! The Faffenberger house was back in tip-top shape! He was back on top of his financial affairs! And – wonder of wonders – he now had his beloved "Dream House"!

In the days it took to close the transaction, he was continually "antsy" – as Trudy would say. She made a mighty attempt to share his enthusiasm – but, it wasn't easy.

Especially, once her husband had advised her that he'd like to move into his new addition. Move into the place – as soon as possible!

She confessed to a myriad of misgivings: She'd been extremely happy in the little house on Rosemont. Happier than she'd ever been, in her life. For that reason, she was reluctant to leave it. The classic "If it ain't broke, don't fix it" mind set.

However, it was unmistakably obvious that her husband yearned – more than she'd suspected was "normal" – to move into the big house on Grandmont. She was unable to understand the attraction – but, she'd have to have been a total dunce not to have seen the almost surreal attraction the place held for Parks.

"He can't stop talking about it," she told her mother. "It's like … like … like an obsession with him."

"I think you're probably making a whole big thing out of nothing," Amanda replied. "He's always treated you well … no matter where you've been. And you've always been good to him. You'll just go on being good to one another … and good _for_ one another. Only in a different place. I don't have to tell you: I had my reservations at first. But, I truly think you're the perfect couple. If it's that important to him … then, go ahead. Go ahead … and indulge him. I'm sure you'll be glad you did."

"I guess you're right, Mother. In fact, I'm sure you are. It's just that I'm concerned that … if this house isn't all he's hoped for … I'm just afraid that it could possibly affect his relationship with Charles. And (she sighed heavily) with me."

"Nonsense! He's so hopelessly in love with you … both you and Charles … that nothing could ever shake it. Anyone can see that. I really think you're just borrowing trouble."

That had been the same expression Sue had used – on more than one occasion. In fact, on the day after she'd spoken to her mother, Sue had told her the same thing.

From that point on, Trudy was more agreeable – if not totally sold on the project.

Parks never ceased his sales pitch: One advantage was *Calvin Coolidge Elementary School* – just a block away. It had been a one-mile walk for Charles to attend *Peter Vital School* on Westwood Street. Parks had paid three of the older girls in the neighborhood to see that the boy got safely to and from school, each day. In inclement weather, Parks or Trudy would drive the group to *Vital*.

On Grandmont, there would be no need for such an arrangement.

In addition, the place would be an excellent replacement for the ill-fated house on Prevost. Our hero never ceased to broach that position to his wife.

His eyes, she noted, would take on a special glow – as he related his plans (his many plans) for their new home:

He'd use the smallest bedroom – the one in which his Aunt Juanita had slept – as an office. He needed one anyway. He had, he advised Trudy, been entertaining thoughts of leasing office space in one of the buildings on Grand River. Having purchased the larger home, there would be no need.

Obviously, he could never share with his spouse the startling fact – that he'd actually lived in the home, when he was five, six and seven! The house was far too new!

Instead, he told her a story. A fabrication: He'd been with his broker – the night the house had been sold to another family, in 1940 – and he'd fallen in love with the place. He couldn't explain the attraction – but, that very night, he had dreamed of the house. Dreamed that he'd climbed up into the attic – through a remarkable hole in the ceiling in the linen closet – and, in his dream, he'd found a heaven up there!

He presented the dream as a "wonderful omen"!

"In any case," he concluded, "I've wanted that place ever since I first saw it. There's just something about the joint that speaks to me. I can't define it. It's one of those things … one of those silly things … that you just can't rightly explain. Why would I dream a dream like that? Who knows? I certainly have no clue. Why that particular house? Dunno. Ever since I first saw it … I just had to have it. Just had to!"

Once the move was made, Trudy's fears were put to rest. It was obvious that the place was everything her husband had hoped it would be – even if his heaven-in-the-attic dream had been kind of cockamamie. She delighted in his happiness.

The living room! He loved that living room! Well, he loved the entire place – but, especially the living room. It ran from front to rear – took up about 40% of the entire first floor, on the left side. Outside the rear living room door – ta-DAH! – a patio.

When his parents had owned the property, they'd left the patio unfinished – just a clump of earth. It had been ideal for little Jimmy and Marilyn to run their sleds down, during the winters. Something else about the house for little Jimmy to have loved.

The place had changed hands twice since his family had moved to the little house on Penrod. The people who'd bought the house from his parents had put in a cement deck – effectively removing the area from consideration for future sledding. The subsequent owners had enclosed it – adding, in effect, another room. Nice! Wonderful room! Light! Airy! Windows on three sides! Lots of windows on three sides! Great!

Parks had been tempted to use the patio room as an office. But, once he saw how thrilled Trudy was with the light and airy spot, he decided to stick with "Plan A" – and use "Aunt Juanita's Room".

He bought a brand new *Stromberg-Carlson* floor-model radio/phonograph for the patio room – as well as two rocking chairs and a long, brown, leather sofa. The latter looked as though it had been born for the sole purpose of nap-taking.

That would be the room in which he and his wife would spend the most time.

When the Hayworths moved from the house on Rosemont, they put the little white home up for rent; listing their Grandmont address in the newspaper ad. They would screen applicants from the "Dream House".

They interviewed almost two dozen candidates, during the first week. They would be most selective in their choice of tenants: Most selective. No more Hector LeCroix-like problems.

Midway through the second week of interviews, Parks was shocked when he answered the door – and found himself face-to-face with Loretta Zandrynski – the woman with whom his mother had worked at **McNeil & Wilkins**, in the *Union Guardian Building*. With her was her husband, Richard.

Parks' thoughts reeled back to that emotional day – his first in 1939 – when he'd gone to the offices of the law firm, and had wound up sobbing uncontrollably. It had been Loretta, who had vanished into the back offices – to fetch one of the junior partners.

Could Loretta have recognized him? After almost nine years?

It may have been his imagination, but there seemed to have been a mere flickering of recognition, when he'd pulled open the door.

"I thought I recognized the address, when I saw it in the paper," Loretta said. "I used to work with the lady who bought this house … when it was brand spanking new … ten or twelve years ago."

On the drive over to Rosemont, Parks had the uneasy feeling that Loretta's eyes were burning two holes in the back of his head – from her position in the back seat.

Loretta and Richard fell in love with the little home. From the moment they'd stepped out of the car, Loretta had to have it! Parks, though, was experiencing a goodly number of misgivings at the prospect of renting to someone so close to his mother. He sensed potential trouble.

Wouldn't you know? Trudy practically insisted on the Zandrynskis as tenants!

The more the two women had talked, the more Trudy appeared certain that Loretta should be the one to whom they should entrust "her house"!

Parks just wished – more than anything – that Loretta would stop her constant, persistent. prattling about having worked with the lady who had owned the "Dream House", at one time.

The arrangement with Loretta and Richard worked out well. The rent was never late. The rental fee was almost twice the size of the mortgage payment. There never was a problem with upkeep.

Richard – who owned and operated a **Shell** gas station, on Greenfield Road – was exceptionally handy with a set of tools.

As 1948 drew to a close, Parks paid off the mortgage on the Brogan house – just down the street. He owned the place and "Helen's Building" free-and-clear. He foresaw ownership of the little white house on Rosemont within a year – 18 months at the outside.

In addition to the rental properties – and the vast number of vacant lots Parks had picked up through the years – he'd bought a sprawling, one-story, building, which he used as a storage garage. His 14 cars were stored there – including his beloved 1937 Ford. He'd recently added a 1935 Packard and a 1936 Buick. The latter was a monster four-door sedan – featuring wheel wells in both front fenders.

The new facility – on Telegraph Road, just south of Plymouth Road – had previously served as a warehouse for an outfit which had dealt in welding supplies. The cement-block building had a most efficient gas furnace – allowing our hero to set the new-fangled thermostat and forget it. No concern over the ever-more-valuable cars freezing up in one of Detroit's snowy, blustery, winters.

Once he'd taken possession of the building, Parks did something he'd never done before: He bought a brand new car – and immediately put the vehicle in with the rest of his fleet. The automobile was a gorgeous 1948 Chrysler Town & Country car – a convertible, with real wood paneling. The car featured fenders, hood and dash – done in deep, exceptionally rich, blue.

Trudy, of course, questioned his acquiring so many cars – most especially a brand new one, which, it appeared, he would seldom drive. He explained that he simply had a feeling that those particular cars would be extremely valuable, in the future.

"Well," she said, "I think it's kind of goofy. But, you've always been right."

They were seated on the sofa, in the patio room, listening to Jo Stafford and Gordon MacRae, as they sang Frank Loesser's beautiful *My Darling, My Darling*.

"Oh, not always," Parks responded. "You make it sound like I'm some kind of genius or something. And that just ain't so."

"You are some kind of genius, Hayworth. How much money did you make on the election?"

"Oh ... a few bucks."

"C'mon, Hayworth. Don't kid the troops. I know that you won a hundred bucks from Richard Zandrynski."

"How'd you know that?"

"Loretta. She told me. She was madder'n a wet hen."

"Oh? Do you and Loretta talk ... often?"

"Not really. Every now and then. She says there's something familiar about you ... and she can't quite put her finger on it. Should I be jealous?"

"Nah. If we'd have tangled fannies, she'd have remembered me. I'm sure she's mistaking me for someone else. She doesn't look all that familiar to me. Did she call ... just to tell you that Richard dropped a hundred simoleons on the election?"

"No. She wants me to come to a bridge party over there, some night. I think it'd be fun. I've always loved that house, y'know. Almost as much as you love this one.'

"Are you unhappy here?"

"No. Of course not. I love it. And Charlie ... damn, now you've got me calling him that ... he loves it too. No, I just thought it'd be kind of great to be able to go back over there for an evening. That house, y'know, signaled a great big, fat, change in my life. You ... you don't mind, do you?"

"Hell no. Of course I don't mind. I was just a little surprised that you and Loretta are that thick, is all."

"Oh, we're not all that thick. She's nice. I enjoy her. But, we're really not what you'd call bosom buddies."

"With a bosom like yours, Trood, I'm glad that I'm your buddy."

Trudy's mood became serious: "Parks? How did you come to bet all that money on President Truman? No one thought he was gonna win."

"Well, for one thing, Richard kept insisting. I happened to make a remark ... when he brought the rent over. Told him that I thought it was gonna be a lot closer than everyone said it was gonna be. Told him I thought that ol' Harry might even have a chance to win the thing. I didn't want to take Richard's money ... but, dammit, he kept insisting. Wouldn't take no for an answer."

"But, everybody ... simply everybody ... thought that Dewey'd be the winner."

"Nah," he responded, shaking his head. "No. Dewey was being too damn lofty ... and intellectual. He really wasn't getting through to the regular guy ... the dirt-under-the-fingernails guy. Those are the ones who gave the election to Truman. Ol' Harry had a way of getting through to the common folks. I happened to be able to read that. I did. Richard didn't. Richard tends to get a little greedy. He thought he was betting on a sure thing. I guess a lot of people did. I probably should've given him some kind of odds or something. But, it was Richard, y'know. He just kept insisting on betting. Not me."

"It wasn't only Richard. I don't mean to meddle, Parks, but I know that you had over a thousand dollars bet on the election. I know that that Benny character ... he's a bookie. A few years ago, I'd have had a stroke ... at the thought of my husband risking that kind of money. On an election of all things. But, with you, I don't have any reason to worry. You're just simply never wrong. Never! I also know that you picked up a few bucks ... as you always say ... on Dewey getting nominated in the first place. I thought it'd be Stassen. Everybody did."

"Aaaaaah. That was just pin money. Just trying to keep things interesting. Not too many people, usually, who'll bet on a stupid nomination."

"Yes," she persisted. "But, you never miss."

"You give me too much credit."

She got up and sat on his lap – encircling his neck with her arms.

"I could never give you too much credit," she rasped.

He began to pat her on her bottom.

"I love you, Goit," he said. "Whatever hokey little things I may have accomplished, I owe to you. To you ... and my son. By the bye, I'm glad you finally figured out the kid's name. It certainly took you long enough."

"I love to hear you call him Charlie. I love to hear you call him your son."

She pulled his head down to her breasts.

"For surely that is his position," was his muffled reply.

"Position has nothing to do with it. It's still nice of you. He really is your son, Hayworth. And he's getting more like you ... with each passing day. At first, I have to admit, I had all kinds of doubts. But, last summer, when you'd take him to all those Tigers games ... and all the times you'd go over to the playground with him and play ball with him ... I just can't thank you enough."

"Hey, Lady! You givva me watta you call the swelled head. I've loved every minute of it. I love him. I love you. Always be with me, Trudy. Always! Please! I doubt that I could survive without you. Everything I hope for ... everything I dream of ... revolves around you. Around you ... and Charlie. You're both so vital to me. Like my heart beating or something. Everything I do, I do for you ... and Charlie."

She kissed the top of his head.

"I know," she said softly. "I know."

"You know, Trood, that I've never dwelled on our age difference. You have ... but, I haven't."

"I did," she whispered. "But not any more."

"I know you don't. And I'm pickled tink that you don't. But, nonetheless, the disparity is there. I'm pushing fifty-seven. I can't do a lot of things I usta could. Sometimes, though ... after a spirited game of catch, with ol' Charlie ... I have to drag my soggy old butt in here and plop it down. Take a little coronary break, y'know."

"You'd never know it in bed," she said, with a soft laugh.

"If I wasn't being so gloriously smothered in your boobies, I'm sure that I'd see the most scandalous leer in the world, on your pretty countenance."

"That's what I like about you, Hayworth."

"Whazzat?"

"You think I'm pretty."

"Of course I think you're pretty. I may be old ... but, I'm not dead. Unless you know something I don't. It doesn't take too much brain-power. I'm-a look atta you with my eye ... I'm-a see a pretty lady."

"No, Hayworth. I mean it. You always tell me that I'm pretty. That I smell nice. That you like my dress."

"You forgot one thing: You got a cute fanny."

"That's what I mean. You'll say it. You'll tell me that you love me. And ... when you look so deeply in my eyes ... I sometimes get the shivers. Just the look on your face ... and the way your eyes grow ... the way they grow soft."

"Like I told you ... eyes are really windows. You got a great soul, Goit. Fanny's not bad either."

"Will you ... for heaven's sakes ... be serious?"

"Very well," he answered. "I will ... at this time ... be serious. Wanna screw?"

The reply broke her up.

"Not that serious," she responded, laughing.

EIGHTEEN

Parks got caught up in the sweeping automotive styling changes in 1949. Virtually every car manufactured in the United States underwent radical alterations in body style – as well as suspension systems and engineering, that year. The few exceptions – Cadillac, Packard, Hudson and the "Futuramic" Oldsmobile – had been remodeled the previous year.

Studebaker, had produced a few 1946 models. They were – as were all the car makers' products – replicas of their under-produced 1942 line! Then, the Indiana manufacturer produced a startling new line! The cars were advertised as being of "modern design". Though this was early in 1946, the models were introduced as '47s.

Shortly thereafter, **Kaiser-Frazier** had produced their first models – also of "modern design".

Our hero had always believed that his 1948 Mercury convertible was one of the most beautiful cars ever built. Despite the fact that the introduction of all those brand new '49 models would prove a most invigorating time for him, he refused to take the plunge.

He would be perfectly content to drive the Mercury until **General Motors** would introduce the industry's first line of what were referred to as "hardtop convertibles" – in the spring of 1949. Those pioneer models would be the Cadillac Coupe DeVille, Buick Riviera, Oldsmobile Holiday, Pontiac Catalina and Chevrolet Belaire.

That original Riviera had, in Parks' mind, been even more beautiful than his Mercury. Arguably, the prettiest car Buick had ever produced – before or afterward.

He would wait for one of those!

He'd been tempted to buy a new 1949 DeSoto. Jim Sidorwitz's first car – in 1953 – had been a dark "gun metal green" four-door sedan. He'd paid the munificent sum of $725.00 for the car. Parks doubted, though, that he would drive a new DeSoto – preferring to tool around in his convertible. If he were to stash another brand new car in the building on Telegraph, it would raise too many questions from Trudy.

He would wait for the Buick.

When, in April of 1949, Parks was able to lay his hands on the exact Riviera he'd always wanted – yellow body and white top – he sprung! Snapped it right up! He retired the Mercury convertible to the building on Telegraph.

Clark Dubin accused him of being a traitor! Parks had always driven **Ford** products – despite the fact that he'd acquired other makes, for his collection. Dubin had been slightly nettled, when Parks bought his Mercury. But, the car was, at least, a member of the **Ford** family.

"A Buick? A goddam Buick?"

"Simmer down, Clark. It'd take something special to turn me into Benedict Arnold. I happen to believe that the forty-nine Buick is gonna be a classic."

"There you go again ... with that word 'classic'. I've never heard anybody else talk about cars in the terms of them being classics. Sometimes, I really wonder about you, Parks. How'd you know that those cars ... those 'hardtop convertibles' ... how'd you know that were coming? I didn't know they were coming. Al Daniels ... over at **Bellfort Buick** ... even he didn't know they were coming. But Parks Hayworth ... he knew they were coming. How come? How'd you know that, Parks?"

"C'mon, Clark. What makes you think I knew something? Knew anything?"

"Come off the bullshit, Parks. You always buy a car ... a new one ... right after introduction day. This year? You wait till almost goddam summer. Now, don't bullshit a bullshitter. Don't tell me that you didn't know something."

The direction of Dubin's questioning was taking on a dimension which made our hero uneasy. He'd become used to Trudy's occasional prodding along those lines. He'd most certainly accepted Helen's constant probing about his past. But, this was the first time that Dubin had ever out and out accused him of having inside information.

"Well," he said (firmly, he hoped), "I didn't know anything. Honest." His tone softened. "The main reason I waited is that ... is that I loved that Mercury. I just thought I'd let everyone get all the bugs out of their radical new designs ... before I took the plunge. Sorry to disappoint you, Old Friend, but there's nothing more sinister than that. Then, when I saw that Riviera? Man ... when I saw that Riviera, I simply had to have one. Fell in love with it."

Parks managed to put the brakes on his dissertation. He'd almost launched into one of Jim Sidorwitz's favorite diatribes: How he'd never forgive Buick for "screwing up" the Riviera – well, for "screwing up" the entire Buick product line – in 1950.

Dubin Rent-a-Car was, by the summer of 1949, established as **Hertz's** strongest competitor – although the Johnny-come-lately entity was still dwarfed by the car-rental giant.

The rent-a-car operation had long outgrown the dealership – and Dubin had, at long last, bought out Horace Keller. Despite the fact that the dealership had become the rent-a-car's "little brother", the "**Ford** store" continued to flourish.

Dubin bought a mansion in Grosse Pointe – then, a 35-foot cabin cruiser. Virtually every weekend found him ensconced on the craft – sailing the length and breadth of Lake St. Claire. Monday through Friday, though, he was still the dynamic, shirt-sleeved, 12-hours-a-day, indefatigable, administrator.

As the fifties dawned, **Dubin Rent-a-Car** had established locations in virtually every city, town and village in the nation – and Clark Dubin was beginning to talk about going international.

With the dawning of the new decade, Parks had begun to worry more and more about the amount of time he had left. The subject, of course, had never been far from the surface. With the realization that Dave – his first child – would be born within five years, the Grim Reaper seemed to lurk behind each piece of furniture! In every corner!

Parks had become certain that, had he lived past 1954, he would've done something to have helped Jim and Kathleen! Especially since he was painfully aware of the hard times that would lie in wait for the couple! Like some kind of ambush!

On the other hand, had he been successful in aiding the Sidorwitzes, there would have been no financially difficult times. No travail over which Parks could/would drive himself nuts. Good move to ignore Jim's and Kathleen's plight? The family did, after all, survive. Maybe it would've been a mistake – one of monumental proportions – to have upset what was a delicate balance. Oh, who knew? Who the hell knew? It was all very confusing. A brain-warper – leading, most usually, to a ferocious headache!

<u>Maybe I will survive for awhile … for a long while. Maybe it'll turn out that the reason I didn't do anything to help was because of the possibility that it could screw up the kids. Maybe I'll arbitrarily decide … somewhere down the line … that Jim and Kathleen and the kids would all be better off for having gone through all the poverty bullshit</u>!

He certainly wouldn't want to do anything to substantially change any of his seven children. They were the accomplishment of which he was most proud.

Most proud? <u>Hell, it was my only accomplishment. As Jim, anyway</u>.

A sudden realization: Parks remembered a man whom his children had known as "Mister John". This man – built along the same dimensions as Parks – had come into their lives in the late sixties. When Jim was working all those jobs. Consequently, he'd not come face to face with "Mister John" more than three or four times. The elderly gentleman had come around numerous times. Kathleen had spoken of him – often. And lovingly. His "Dirty Rats" had grown to love him. Well, so had the older four.

That had been during the lowest point, emotionally, financially – and in every other way – for Jim and Kathleen. The old man had not given the Sidorwitzes any money. None that our hero was aware of, anyway. Apparently, though, he was quite affluent.

Could it be possible that "Mister John" was actually Parks himself? Initially, the prospect excited him! As stated, he'd only met the man three or four times– and "Mister John" didn't seem to resemble what Parks imagined he, himself, would look like, at that age. But, in reality, who could tell? Again, who the hell <u>knew</u>?

Kathleen had advised her husband that "Mister John" was a jeweler. He had, in fact, given Kathleen a beautiful gold ring, with a quietly-elegant jade center. He would take the three younger children – the "Dirty Rats" – to the ice cream parlor, on the corner, and buy them sodas, malted milks, sundaes and the like.

Parks reflected upon what little he actually knew of the man. Precious little! He had not the foggiest idea how the old man had found the Sidorwitzes. The only thing he really knew about the "seventy-something" man was that he was a stickler for politeness – not unlike the way Jim had always been. Especially, while his children were growing.

"Mister John" would've been the perfect persona for him to have enjoyed his children – especially the "Dirty Rats". As "Mister John" he would've been able to relate to the kids – "from afar" – as Mr. Horne had suggested. Maybe from not quite so "afar".

If the old man had, indeed, been Parks, why had he not chosen to call himself "Mister Parks"? The name would've meant nothing to the kids – nor to Jim or Kathleen.

Ah-HAH! It would've meant everything to our hero, himself! The first time that he'd gazed at his driver's license – on that long ago first day in 1939! He'd have known that he'd survived – at least into the late-sixties! Knowing that, why would our boy not have made it a point to have used the "Mister Parks" name? If, indeed, he'd turned out to be "Mister John". It sure would've prevented a lot of worry for him. A helluva lot of worry.

Well, maybe Mr. Horne and "the boys" had done something to convince him to not use that handle. But, how? When?

And that opened another can of worms! Could Mr. Horne and "the boys" have known that "Mister John" was actually Parks? If, indeed, he'd turned out to be Parks?

That didn't make much sense. If that crowd up there knew who "Mister John" was – especially if it had been Parks – then, they'd have known how everything their guinea pig had gotten involved with had worked out. Would've prevented a whole lot of "currency" from changing hands up there! Or was that whole "betting" routine a farce?

Well, apparently, "Mister John" was not Parks. If he had assumed that identity, why would he have waited so long to make his presence known? Could he have been disabled for an extended period of time? It was, of course, possible. But, "Mister John" had seemed awfully fit – indeed, really robust – for a man his age.

Another chilling thought: "Mister John's" wife – "Miss Honey", as he'd always called her – had passed away in 1967 or 1968. The old man had told the "Dirty Rats" that she'd been sick – terribly sick – for along time. Could it be that Trudy would turn out to be "Miss Honey"? Would she be "terribly sick"? Would she suffer? Suffer horribly? Would he lose her? As he'd lost Helen? He shuddered – head-to-toe!

Dear Lord! A withering, bleak, prospect!

He was back to ferocious headaches, once more!

Our hero usually wound up the troubling mental calisthenics convinced that he probably would not live past 1955. Probably not long enough to see Dave enter the world. The only logical course of action, obviously, would be to put everything in Trudy's name. Involve her as heavily as possible in the family finances. It was paramount that, when the Grim Reaper did come to call, she and Charlie be provided for.

His wife had certainly proven her capabilities in that area, when she'd handled his finances, during his lone-wolf New York sojourn.

An additional detail to be cleared up: Would little Charlie consent to being adopted by Parks? He'd broached the question to Trudy one evening, as they sat in the patio room.

"You want to adopt him, Parks? You really do?"

"Of course. He's my own son. You've said … said it on a number of occasions … said that he's getting more and more like me, every day."

"That he is. Is he ever."

A Little Bird Told Me, Evelyn Knight's delightful hand-clapping recording, came to an end – and the record changer kicked in. The next of the clunky seventy-eights dropped with a resounding KLACK! *Far Away Places*, by Margaret Whiting. Pretty ballad.

"I'm honored," said Parks. "I'm really thrilled that he seems to be taking after me. I love him Goit. I honestly do. I don't know what I'd do without him."

Her soft brown eyes glistened.

"I know," she replied. "I know. I'm happy as I can be that you want to adopt him. I'll let you in on a little secret. There have been times when he's asked me why he doesn't have the same last name that you and I do. I just usually tell him that … while you've become his father, you weren't his daddy when he was born … and so he still has his biological father's name."

"Dammit! Dammit, dammit, dammit!"

"What? Did I say something wrong, Hayworth?"

"No, dammit! I did something wrong! Well, actually, it's more like I didn't do something right! I should've thought of the adoption thing … should've thought of it, a long time ago. Of course he'd wonder why he has a different last name. Of course he would. It just never occurred to me. To me, he's Charlie Hayworth … my son. I just simply don't think, sometimes. I could kick myself … right square in the arse! Let's … please … let's tomorrow go down to the courthouse and rectify the whole thing."

She leaned over and kissed him.

"I don't know if it's that easy, Hayworth … just going to court," she responded. "But, we'll get the trusty old lawyer on the case … and, if you really want to adopt him, we'll get him adopted. As fast as the creaky wheels of our vaunted justice system'll let us."

She got up and sat down in his lap. Putting her arms around his neck, she kissed him tenderly. Her doe-eyes filled to overflowing. He began to pat her lightly on her derriere.

"Such affection, Goit." His voice was hoarse. "Such affection."

"That's because I luff you. Charlie luffs you. He'll be as thrilled as he can be with his new last name. You're sure, now, that you want to do this, Hayworth?"

He cracked her smartly on her bottom!

"Ouch!" she exclaimed. "That hurt!"

"Then," he admonished, "let's hear no more of this 'Are you sure?' crap. I've never been so sure of anything in my life. I'm just not too smart, that's all."

"You're smart enough for the likes of me, Hayworth. After all, look who you married."

Once the adoption had taken place, Parks experienced the warm glow of knowing that he'd placed "one more duck in the row" – in the event of his death.

It was vitally important – critical – that the transition move forward smoothly.

He'd taken to asking Trudy hypothetical questions: If he were to pass away, would she consider remarrying? If so, would it be to someone nearer her own age? Would the manner in which the prospect related to Charlie be the major yardstick? Would it be the only yardstick?

"My God," she responded, on one occasion. "You're sure a nosy son-of-a-biscuit."

They'd been in the Buick. Parks had pulled out of the parking lot, next to the *Avalon Theater*, where they'd just taken in *Tea For Two*, with Doris Day and Gordon MacRae. He negotiated the short distance on Linwood – and turned left onto Davison.

"No, seriously," he persisted. "I want to know."

"Why?" Her voice betrayed a bit of a nervous twitter. "You'll probably outlast me … and maybe Charlie too."

"Oh, I doubt that." He hoped that she'd not picked up the slight degree of dejection in his tone.

"I don't," she answered. "You keep saying that you're slowing down, Hayworth. But, I saw you out in the back yard … playing catch with Charlie. Guys twenty years younger would've had a tough time keeping up with you. I know your fanny was dragging a bit, though, when you came in. You should maybe take it a little bit easier."

"Why? I'm gonna outlast you … and Charlie too."

He wished he hadn't said that! A frightening spasm – a horrifying chill – overtook him! Thoughts of "Miss Honey" ricocheted through his consciousness!

Trudy seemed not to notice the brief shudder. She put her left hand on the inside of his right thigh – as she often did, when he was driving.

"You probably will," she said, at length. "But, I do worry about you ... frolicking and cavorting, as you sometimes do. I know that you love Charlie. What's more important, Parks, the kid knows you love him. He tells me every night, when I hear his prayers, that the *Angel Of God* prayer is Daddy's prayer ... because you taught it to him. He always God-blesses you before he does me."

"Kid probably figures I need more help nor you."

She pinched the inside of his thigh and laughed.

"Oh, Hayworth! Be serious."

"Okay. Very well. I will ... herewith ... be serious. Wanna screw?"

"Right here? In the middle of Davison Street?"

When Korea erupted, in the spring of 1950, Clark Dubin had been totally rattled! Parks could not remember seeing his friend so nonplussed.

"God damn it," he seethed. "Just when things are starting to go so well! Now we've gotta go and get ourselves into another goddam war? I never even heard of goddam Korea! Now we're gonna fight a goddam war there? It's gonna be just like goddam World War Two! God damn it! They'll start rationing gas again ... and I'm in fucking big trouble!"

Parks shifted uneasily, in the monster chair across from Dubin's massive, messy, desk.

"Oh, I wouldn't worry about it, Clark," he soothed. "I doubt that they'll ever go to rationing gas. Not this time."

"How do you know that? What makes you so goddam sure?"

"Nothing. I'm not goddam sure. It's just that I don't see it reaching the scope of Double-U Double-U Two. Nowhere near it. For one thing, China'd have to get their fingers into it ... and I really don't think they can afford to. Even if they did, old Harry'd be ready for 'em." He was speaking of President Truman. "I just can't see the thing approaching 'The Big One'."

"Well," Dubin muttered, "you've always been right before. I imagine you must know what the hell you're talking about this time. I sure as shit hope you do, anyway. I've never gone wrong listening to you about such things, ya horse's ass."

The Korean "police action" had triggered many memories for our hero: As Jim, he had been in the Navy – stationed, at that point, at the *Naval Air Technical Training Command*, on the *Naval Air Station*, at Millington, Tennessee, just outside Memphis.

He had attended *Aviation Storekeeper's School* on the base. His class had been scheduled to graduate, three Fridays after the skirmish in Korea had broken out. (Jim had never heard of Korea either.)

The war had started – as wars always seemed to – on a Sunday. Every man from *Aviation Storekeeper's School* – each man who would graduate the following Friday – would be sent to the Korean theater! The same held true for each of the other graduating classes! From the entire compliment of twelve schools on the far-reaching base! Each and every man – to Korea! A bitter omen – for one who's class was to graduate two weeks later..

Jim was certain that his entire group would, likewise, be sent to Korea! So was every other member of his class. No one, at that point, could have a handle on the extent of the Navy's involvement in the war – ahem – in the "police action". (A "police action" which could, obviously, get you killed just as dead – as if it had been an actual war!)

Jim had been so positive that he would be sent into combat, that his mother had flown down to Memphis – the weekend before his graduation. It had been the first time that a member of his family had ever flown. The airline was called **Chicago & Southern**. The plane had been a tiny – exceptionally tiny by today's standards – DC-3. One of those "oldies" where the tail-wheel actually sat right down on the ground.

Dolly Sidorwitz and Jim had spent the entire weekend at the *Peabody Hotel*, in downtown Memphis – one of the finest houses in the entire South.

Parks remembered that, on that Saturday night, Jim's girlfriend, LuAnne – as well as his best friend, Jerry Kerns and Jerry's girl, Amy – had joined Jim and his mother. The five of them had made a futile attempt to get into the very popular – and very crowded – nightclub on the roof of the *Peabody*. They'd not come close.

Instead, the group had settled for the smaller lounge off the main lobby – on the ground floor. Ahhhhh! That had been a nice weekend.

Suddenly, Parks was hit with a brilliant idea! At least, he so considered it!

Trudy and he could take a trip! He had always been curious as to what Houston had looked like before it had begun to boom in the late-fifties. Obviously, a trip to Houston – by way of Memphis – would be a cover. He hoped it would be an effective one.

He wanted, desperately, to be in Memphis – on the Friday, Saturday and Sunday before Jim's class would graduate. Suddenly, he was terribly anxious to look in on his mother! And pining to see himself – as a young sailor!

The Riviera drove beautifully. Parks appreciated the advanced suspension system. After having been spoiled by the luxurious ride of virtually all of the cars in the seventies, it had taken a good while to become accustomed to the older coil-spring ride.

All the '49 models had marked a major advance in automotive suspension engineering. The cars, themselves, were, of course, lower and more aerodynamic – which added to the ease of handling. Actually, Jim's beloved DeSoto had been – as had all the **Chrysler Corporation** models – a little on the boxy side.

Parks had decided to continue driving the 1949 Riviera – although, he'd been sorely tempted to break out the brand new '48 Chrysler Town & Country convertible.

Nah! He'd bought the Buick late in the model year. It was barely a year old. He was still in love with the car – and still mad at **General Motors** for screwing up the '50 models.

Having, once more, "farmed out" Charlie to Amanda Chamberlain, Parks and Trudy arrived at the *Peabody* some three or four hours before Dolly and Jim would've checked in – as our hero had recollected it.

Trudy was impressed with the *Peabody*. She loved it! Even after having stayed in such luxurious houses as the *Waldorf-Astoria* in Manhattan and the *Drake* in Chicago.

Parks knew that it would be futile to attempt to seek out Jim and Dolly on Friday night. It was his recollection that they'd spent the entire evening in their room – talking.

That being the case, Parks and Trudy went to dinner at the posh – and packed – nightclub on the roof.

They got in, of course. Poor 18-year-old Jim hadn't known from such things as slipping the *Maitre d'* ten bucks. But, even if he had been that "sophisticated", he could never have afforded it. Neither, actually, could Dolly. The plane fare – and half the room fee – had been sufficient to have broken her fragile bank account.

After a luxurious dinner, the Hayworths had danced to the "sweet band" music of Hal McIntyre's orchestra – until almost two o'clock Saturday morning.

Trudy seemed ecstatic with the night out. She was especially intrigued – when the band did a half-hour "remote" broadcast from eleven-thirty to midnight. The opening announcement – and the style of the deep-voiced announcer – were classic:

"From high atop the roof of the *Hotel Peabody*, overlooking beautiful downtown Memphis, Tennessee ... a stone's throw from the mighty Mississippi River ... the **Mutual Broadcasting System** brings your way the melodic offerings of (pause) Hal McIntyre and his orchestra. Stay with us, won't you? As Hal opens with a rousing arrangement of that old favorite, *Begin The Beguine* ... followed by the current favorite, *Mona Lisa*, with that mighty dynamo of song, Frankie Lester, handling the vocal."

It was a typical hokey, schmaltzy, lead-in for the times – almost a parody. Trudy was surprised to note that "that mighty dynamo of song, Frankie Lester", was all of five-feet, six-inches – and probably weighed 120 pounds. His smooth-as-silk, crooner's voice sounded as though it was coming from a much larger man.

Noting his wife's enjoyment – she'd been thrilled, the entire evening – Parks remonstrated with himself for not having taken her out more often. He'd neglected her – despite the fact that she'd never complained at being a "stay at home".

He vowed that he would correct that shortcoming.

Try as he might, Parks could not remember when Jim and Dolly had eaten breakfast on Saturday morning. He was almost certain that they'd eaten at the hotel's coffee shop. Almost certain. It was also his recollection that they'd taken a walk around the block – or maybe two or three blocks – before breakfast. That, of course, meant that they could've eaten elsewhere. Some other restaurant that they would've blundered into on their stroll. It was hell, for Parks, not to be certain where the meal had been taken.

Complicating the situation even more, was the fact that our hero couldn't remember if they'd slept late or had gotten up early. No idea! He wished that his memory had not failed him!

At 9:00 AM, Saturday morning, Parks slapped Trudy, lightly, on the backside – and urged her to get out of bed. He was hungry. Although mildly surprised, she accommodated him. 9:45 AM found the couple ensconced in the coffee shop – eating breakfast and drinking coffee. Lots of coffee.

Trudy did a masterful job of reining in her impatience.

"Are you upset at something, Hayworth?" she asked, at length.

"Upset? No. Why?"

"I ... I don't know. You just seem ... well ... ill-at-ease. For some reason or another. I've never seen you in quite this mood. Even when you were working all those gooney hours ... after Helen had passed away. I just don't remember seeing you quite so ... quite so ... so preoccupied."

"Uh ... no. I'm fine, Goit. Really."

"Well, you know ... your attempts at conversation ... well, they're really quite ... quite stilted. And ... and you seem so ... so reluctant to leave here. We finished eating an hour or so ago. I like coffee, y'know. As much as the next person. But, my God! What've we had? Five cups? Six? I don't mind, Hayworth. Don't mind at all. I just wish that you'd ... that you'd tell me what's up."

"Nothing. Nothing really. I guess I'm just kind of lost in thought. I'm trying to picture what Houston is going to look like.

Haven't been there in so long. I've really forgotten what it's like down there."

"With your memory?"

She lifted her coffee cup to her lips – but, made a face when the aroma accosted her nostrils, and set the half-filled cup back down.

"Do you want to leave here today?" she asked.

"No!" Parks wished he'd not answered so quickly – and so definitively!

Trudy appeared not to have noticed.

"I have no idea how long it'll take us to get there," she said. "But, we'd be there a day or two sooner … if we left today. I wouldn't mind. I had such a nice time last night … that you could take me anywhere! Do with me what you will!"

"That sounds promising. Wanna screw?"

"Sounds fine to me. But, I have a feeling that you're all wrapped up with other fish to fry."

Her eyes took on a far-away look – as she pushed away her cup.

Our boy decided – at long last – that he'd subjected his wife to enough of the coffee shop. He just hoped that his bitter disappointment in not seeing his mother and/or himself was not too apparent.

The Hayworths spent the afternoon and early evening shopping – returning to the hotel shortly before 6:00 PM. They hopped into bed – for what was to be a short nap.

At 9:10 PM, Parks lurched awake!

He wanted to go downstairs – to the lounge – he advised the sleepy-eyed Trudy.

Once more, she indulged him.

"I can't imagine you wanting to go to a bar … of all places," she told him, as they showered. "You don't even drink."

"Oh, a Brandy Alexander … every now and again," he replied, as he soaped her back and bottom. "I'm not much on bars … but, the waitress, at the coffee shop this morning, she mentioned what a great place the hotel lounge was. Sounded like it might be fun."

"I don't remember her saying anything like that … anything about a bar," she replied, curtly – turning to face him.

"Uh … well … it might've been while you were in the john."

"As much coffee as I drank, Hayworth ... it's a wonder I didn't spend half the morning in the john. I always wondered what happens when I'm in the little girl's room. Now I know. Waitresses tell my husband about the hotel bar. Anything else of import?"

He didn't have to be a rocket scientist to detect the slight edge in her voice.

He handed her the soap, as he replied, "Naw, that's just about it."

She began to lather him.

"Now that I think of it," he broke the uncomfortable silence, "I probably asked her where a nice place to take a lady would be. One that was close by. She suggested the bar here. Right off the lobby."

"Like a good employee should," his wife observed – also curtly.

"Yeah. I suppose so. But, she really made it sound like a nice place."

Trudy reached around – and slapped him on his wet left buttock! The thundering sound ricocheted off all four walls of the tiled bathroom!

"Okay, Massa," she replied. "If that's where you want to go." She slapped his other bottom cheek – just as smartly and just as loudly. "Then," she said, "that's where we'll go."

The smacks had been quite severe – especially for a woman of Trudy's size. He looked at the two red hand prints on his wet posterior. Well, at least the flesh was drying – rapidly – where she'd whacked him!

Was there some meaning to be found in the stinging flesh?

Emerging from the elevator, on the ground floor, Parks and Trudy made their way to the lounge. It was crowded to the rafters. Parks wondered how Jim, Dolly, Jerry, LuAnne and Amy had ever managed to crash the joint – especially when they'd been unable to get into the nightclub on the roof "overlooking beautiful downtown Memphis ... just a stone's throw from the mighty Mississippi River".

Trudy was far from thrilled! Was he opening a can of worms? His bottom still stung slightly. Was she aware of how hard she'd slapped him?

"Oh Hayworth," she groused. "This is too much. Let's ... let's go somewhere else."

"Well, I really don't know of anywhere else. If this place is jammed, I'm sure the roof'll be like a sardine can or something. Why don't we just duck in here ... for one drinky-poo? If it gets to be too much, we can go looking ... or go back up to the room, if you prefer."

"I'd prefer not to have come down here in the first place," she muttered.

Parks found the *Maitre d'* and slipped him a twenty. He really needed to be not standing outside the lounge. Not with his spouse becoming more and more impatient.

Once seated, Trudy came off her snit – a little bit, anyway. It was abundantly apparent that she was not enjoying herself, though. Parks kept a constant watch for Dolly, Jerry, LuAnne, Amy – and himself! They were nowhere to be seen.

Maybe he'd been wrong about the night! Maybe he'd been wrong about the whole damn weekend! Maybe Jim and Dolly weren't even in town! Maybe it had been last weekend! Or maybe it would be next weekend!

His memory, God help him, was not infallible. The weekend he was attempting to recall – and relive – had happened, after all, forty years before!

As the clock approached 10:30 PM – far later than Parks' memory of the quintet arriving at the lounge – he decided to throw in the towel. His wife most certainly wasn't getting any happier.

"Drink up, Kid," he told her. "I'm sorry Trood. I shouldn't have insisted."

She smiled bravely – the smile of someone about to be freed from the steel jaws of a bear trap.

"Oh, it's all right, Hayworth," she responded. "I guess we probably needed to get out. I'm not as pooped as I was when we came down. Getting caught up in the spirit, I guess."

"You're not a very good fibber, y'know. I should've let us stood in bed. That's one of the many reasons I love you, Goit. You always put up with my little peccadilloes. You humor the hell out of me."

"Not really. I'm … I'm enjoying myself. I am … really. I'm just a little surprised, though. You've simply never wanted to take me to a bar before."

Again, that indescribable edge had returned to her voice.

"Well, I shouldn't have this time either," he answered.

"One thing I _do_ know," she said, her always-soft eyes taking on a slightly frosty dimension – one that he'd seldom seen before. "You always have a good reason for wanting to do whatever it is you want to do, Hayworth. Always. Especially if you're a little insistent about it. Like at breakfast this morning."

"Oh, that. Well, it's just that I … "

Her eyes returned to their soft-brown normal state. She put three fingers over his lips.

"Hush." The velvet had returned to her voice. "It's not that big a thing. I don't indulge you all that much. I always enjoy myself. I'm not humoring you. Not now. I enjoy doing things with you … things that you enjoy … Hayworth. I'm happy that you want to do them with me. Share time with me. Not everybody's husband is willing to do that. You're like a big kid, Hayworth. I guess I've told you that before. I luff you."

"I luff you too, Trood. Tell ya what." He leered at her – and curled an imaginary villain's moustache. "How'd you like to really humor me?"

"Why do I get the feeling," she asked, laughing, "that I'm being propositioned?"

"Maybe it's because that's exactly what's happening."

"Oh good! I thought you'd never ask!"

He called the waiter – and paid the check.

The couple was just rising to leave the overcrowded, noisy, lounge – when Parks saw himself, Jerry, his mother and the two girls enter!

Once again, he began to totally unravel! Despite all his planning – despite his steeling himself – he was completely unprepared to look upon himself! To gaze, for the first time in years, at young Jim

Sidorwitz! He was unable to cope with seeing himself – as a virile young sailor! Slender too.

His mother was still as beautiful as he'd remembered her.

Jerry looked different, for some reason. LuAnne, the girl he'd dated once or twice, looked nothing like the frail young woman – the "China doll" – whose image he'd carried around in his memory all these years. Strangely, Amy looked exactly like the girl he'd recalled. Go figure! Another expression from the future.

As the Hayworths pushed toward the exit, Parks became so engrossed in the five newcomers – that he literally stumbled over a couple at another table; spilling the lady's drink all over her obviously-very-expensive evening gown.

He apologized profusely – offering to pay for cleaning the dress. It was a rambling, disjointed, disoriented, apology.

Trudy managed to get him out to the lobby.

She waited till they were alone in the elevator, before asking, "Parks … what's the matter? Are you all right? You were fine … then, all of a sudden, you seemed to become completely unglued! You can't imagine how pale you got! You're still pale! Not sheet-white … like before. But, you don't look … " She let her voice trail off.

Her concern was evident. Seldom did she call him by his first name anymore.

"I'm … I'm okay," he responded, terribly short of breath. "I … I don't know what happened to me. It certainly couldn't have been those two lousy drinks … although, maybe we should've eaten something first. I haven't the foggiest … what came over me. Not the foggiest. But, hoo boy. Something sure as hell made me dizzy. I'm … I'm feeling better now, though. Just the slightest bit wobbly."

"I'll get you to bed," she soothed. "I'll take a rain check on the proposition. I know you're good for it."

Two days later, the Riviera pulled in to Houston! Parks was totally unprepared for what he saw. The Bayou City was even more "small-townish" than he could ever have imagined.

It seemed impossible that the entire city, for all practical purposes, could've sprung up in 25 short years. The boom of the sixties and seventies had been even more earth-shaking than he would ever have believed possible! Amazing! Totally amazing!

Parks had no way, of course, of knowing the hard days, which would plague Houston in the eighties. In 1979 – at the time of Mr. Horne's visit – the city had seemed "bust proof".

The Hayworths stayed at the *Rice Hotel* downtown. In 1979, the hotel would continue to be a candidate for condemnation and razing – having narrowly escaped the wrecker's ball on more than one occasion. In 1950, it was as opulent a house as any to be found in the southwest.

Trudy appeared unimpressed as they drove around the city. Her husband, though, was astonished at the inevitable changes, which would take place – and the almost-out-of-control building boom which would overtake Houston – in the coming quarter-century.

It took practically no time for them to drive from downtown to the city limits – in any direction. Parks marveled at how stress-free it was – to be able to be tooling a car around a city, which would someday boast a rambling, remarkably-sophisticated, freeway system. A bumper-to-bumper – "parking lot" – freeway system. In the seventies, the new thoroughfares would be clogged with tens-of-thousands of cars, vans and trucks.

Construction had already begun on the Gulf Freeway – the second such roadway in the state. Through the coming years, it would be joined by the Southwest Freeway – not to mention the Katy Freeway, Eastex Freeway, North Freeway, Northwest Freeway and East Freeway.

All would be joined by Loop 610 – which would circle the entire city. Later still – in the nineties – the Loop would be augmented by the Sam Houston Tollway, which also circled the metropolis, just a little further out from downtown.

It was mind-boggling to even attempt to visualize the number – and size – of the immense skyscrapers which would one day arise downtown. One of them – the *Texas Commerce Tower*, 75 stories – would become the tallest building in the country, outside New York or Chicago.

Driving out Westheimer Avenue, Parks looked with almost-disbelief upon the Farmland. The unspoiled landscape. Where, one day, the fabulous *Galleria* – an exceptionally-opulent shopping complex, which contained a skating rink (unheard of in Texas, in those days) – would come into being.

He fervently wished that he could reveal to his wife the vast changes which would affect the city – the entire area – in the not-too-distant future. *The Astrodome, The NASA Space Center*, the incredibly-complex freeway system – and the many and varied buildings, which would run the gamut from the very-beautiful to the horribly-garish. It was almost tragic, he felt, for Trudy not to be able to envision all the wonders which would rise upon the flat, arid, terrain.

Glancing at his spouse, out of the corner of his eye, Parks detected a look of puzzlement. A look which practically shouted, "How can anyone get so excited over a few buildings … and a lot of pasture land?"

They didn't spend as much time in Houston as Parks had intended. There really wasn't much to see. Everything had been located in his mind's eye.

Sadly, there was nothing he could share with Trudy.

By the time they'd returned to Detroit, the Riviera had logged over 70,000 miles.

None of the 1950 models had "struck a nerve" with our hero. He decided to nurse the Buick through the rest of the model year – and wait for the 1951 Mercurys to be introduced. The Mercury line would be basically the same as the 1949 and 1950 models – except for the redesigned rear end. The '51 had always been a favorite of his.

When he dropped in at **Dubin Rent-a-Car's** "World Headquarters", in the *Penobscot Building*, Clark Dubin made it a point to ask if Parks still had "that ratty old Buick". It had always nettled Dubin that our boy had strayed from the **Ford** line.

"That 'ratty old Buick' … as you so indelicately put it, Sir, … is a helluva car. I'm convinced it's going to be a real classic. Probably gonna hang onto it."

"What the hell good is a classic … if the goddam thing won't run?

"What do you mean 'won't run'? It's still cooking like a champion. I thought that maybe I'd wait ... and pick up a fifty-one Mercury. Does that make you happy?"

"Hell, Parks. Get a fifty. There's not gonna be all that much change."

"Well, as I understand it, they've extended the rear fenders ... to where they kind of stick out. I think I'll wait for that one. One of those. Should be a little more classier look than the fifty."

"Now, how the hell could you know that? Parks? Parks, you're really something. I just got pictures of the goddam car last week ... and that's only because **Lincoln-Mercury** is trying to sell me forty-million of the goddam things. I really wonder about you sometimes. I really wonder."

"What's to wonder? It's no big deal. Guy who lives down the block works at the plant, where they build Mercurys. He manufactures the damn things. If anyone should know what one looks like, it'd be him. The way he described it, it sounded really beautiful. If you've got pictures, though, I'd certainly admire to take a look at 'em."

Dubin Rent-a-Car had begun opening offices in Europe and in England. The company was expanding much more rapidly than Parks could've imagined. Of course, Jim Sidorwitz had not come aboard till 1957. He'd never really followed the company's progress before then.

In 1950, the young sailor had been sent from Millington, Tennessee, to the *Naval Air Station* in Norfolk, Virginia. His fear of being sent to Korea had not materialized – much to his relief. He'd wound up at the *Fleet Aviation Accounting Office*, on the sprawling air station. In 1950, he'd known virtually nothing about the car rental field.

Now, in 1950, seated in his rocking chair – in the patio room of his "Dream House" – Parks reflected on the course the company had taken, since he'd first enticed Clark Dubin into the business.

On the Hayworth's brand new, albeit tiny, 45-rpm record player (sitting atop the mighty *Stromberg-Carlson*) Gloria DeHaven was singing *Who's Sorry Now* – from the sound track of the Fred Astaire/Red Skelton/Vera-Ellen flick, *Three Little Words*.

It was easy for our boy to be consumed by almost any variety of reverie, when he heard that recording – one of his all-time favorites.

It had been Clark Dubin's business expertise, he knew, that had so expertly shepherded the operation – from the tiny little company which Parks had founded – to a truly international corporation. A multi-million dollar entity.

Another of the new-fangled "forty-fives" – Eddie Fisher's *Bring Back The Thrill* – dropped, almost silently, onto the turntable and began to play.

Parks was all too aware that he didn't come close to possessing the business acumen to have seen such an expansion come to fruition. It had been just as well that he had turned down the offer to head up the corporation. He'd have been in over his head.

He had always been an "operations man". He'd been able to make **Dubin's** initial Detroit operation profitable – almost from the beginning. He'd built the foundation for the larger national – and now international – enterprise that the corporation had become.

He'd had the foresight to allow the fledgling company to "sandbag" dozens upon dozens of cars, at the beginning of the war – a maneuver which had given Clark Dubin the bountiful "seed money" to launch his firm, on such a grand scale.

Dubin, though, had taken it from there. Without the ebullient Dubin's personal leadership, his expertise – and, yes, his inspiration – the company most certainly would've remained a nonentity in the field.

Doris Day's recording of *My Dream Is Yours* dropped onto the turntable.

There were times when Parks had suffered pangs of conscience – believing that the now-staggering worth of his 20% ownership of the grown-to-be-a-monster corporation was "far too much". Dubin had advised him – on a number of occasions – that he was wrong.

"You started it all, Parks," he would say. "If it hadn't been for you ... you conning me into this goddam business ... I'd still be some half-assed car dealer, trying to schlep out a living. Plus, I lean on your silly ass ... for advice. You are an adviser, y'know. Whether you realize it or not."

"Not really. I haven't even looked at the books ... or the statements ... or gotten involved in any of the management decisions. Not in ages."

"Yeah," responded Dubin, with a curt nod. "But, do you remember someone ... some really brilliant sonofabitch ... telling me that Korea wasn't really gonna affect us all that much? Listen, I was gonna retrench! Retrench, retrench, retrench! Instead, I went ahead and expanded. That gave me a helluva leg up on the competition. Plus, you and I know that you alone saved our ass during World War Two. You got nothin' to be feeling guilty about, Parks. Absolutely nothin'. You started the whole goddam thing. If it hadn't been for you, ain't none of us would be sitting here today. So, enjoy ... ya horse's ass."

Enjoy he did. Parks, Trudy and – during the summer vacation – Charlie always seemed to be traveling.

In August, of 1951, the three of them – plus Amanda Chamberlain – spent almost four weeks touring the East Coast! In the Hayworth's brand new yellow 1951 Mercury four-door sedan. He'd bought them all cameras – and loads of film and flash bulbs – urging all of them to take as many pictures as possible. If they needed more film and bulbs, he'd gladly "spring" for it.

They'd driven to Plymouth, Massachusetts – and toured the replica of *The Mayflower*, as well as the thatched-roofed huts of *The Pilgrims' Village*.

Charlie, especially, seemed impressed to be at the birthplace of the Nation.

They drove out on to Cape Cod. Parks made it a point to single out the Kennedy family compound in Hyannis Port – despite the fact that none of his passengers, he knew, would ever have heard of John Fitzgerald Kennedy. Not at that point in time. He fought an overwhelming urge to take in Chappaquiddick. Finally, he decided against it.

The family spent two days in Massachusetts – then, drove down to New York City. Amanda had never been to "The Big Apple". Charlie, of course, had been a good deal younger, when he'd accompanied his parents on their honeymoon. Parks delighted in giving Amanda – and Charlie – the grand tour of the many world-famous landmarks

His mother-in-law's biggest thrill was to be able to actually walk up into *The Statue Of Liberty*. Trudy's favorite continued to be *The Radio City Music Hall*.

Charlie wanted to go see someone break up another no-hitter at *Ebbets Field* in Brooklyn.

Parks wondered if he dared to bring his son back, for the *National League* playoff game between the Dodgers and New York Giants. He would love to let the boy witness "The Little Miracle of Coogan's Bluff"; Bobby Thompson's three-run homer in the 9th inning of the third – and final – game, to overcome a 4-to-2 Brooklyn lead. The blow would propel the Giants into *The World Series* – against the cross-town Yankees.

The round-tripper – hit off Dodger pitcher Ralph Branca – would go down as one of the most celebrated feats in baseball history. It would rival, for the boy, Lavagetto's hit in the '47 *Series*. Actually, it might eclipse the Floyd Bevans near-miss. The youngster would certainly understand the situation much better than the circumstances surrounding the game at *Ebbets Field*.

If, as Parks' memory told him, a young, unheard of, Willie Mays had been kneeling in the "waiting batter up circle" – when Thompson had unloaded that mighty homer – well, that fact should certainly be brought to the kid's attention.

For Parks to negotiate a trip back to New York for the playoffs would take some doing. Mainly because Charlie would be back in school by the time the pennant races wound up. His mother, of course, would be reluctant to sanction a long absence – just to see a ballgame or two. And, to make a "federal case" out of taking the boy back – all the way to New York City – would certainly raise an eyebrow or two. Especially for such an historic happening! Especially after having set things up for Charlie – when he'd been able to witness the "Lavagetto game"! It would <u>certainly</u> raise an eyebrow! Too many eyebrows.

Our hero would have to "think of something".

On their current trip, the Hayworths and Amanda took in such Broadway musicals as *Guys & Dolls*, "a musical fable", taken from some of the stories authored by Damon Runyon. The words and music were penned by the prolific Frank Loesser. The production starred Robert Alda, as "Sky Masterson".

Alda's son, Alan, would, in the years to come, dwarf his father's stardom.

Irving Berlin's *Call Me Madam* – starring the ever-present Ethel Merman – was a charmer. *Marrying For Love*, from the Berlin score, had long been one of Parks' all-time favorites. He'd come close to singing it to Trudy on numerous occasions – during their courtship. That, of course, would've been a bad move – since the song had not been written yet. It really would've raised an eyebrow! All those potentially-raised eyebrows.

The family also thrilled to Rodgers & Hammerstein's lyrical *The King & I* – featuring a young, up-and-coming, mostly unheard-of, Yul Brenner.

The next stop on the itinerary was Philadelphia. Amanda ate up the historical significance of *Independence Hall*, *The Liberty Bell, Market Square* and the many entities honoring the drafters and signers of *The Declaration of Independence.*

Trudy noticed that a road company was staging Frank Loesser's *Where's Charley* – and, though the spelling of the name was different, she was certain that little Charlie would enjoy the show. The boy did enjoy the production – almost as much as watching the Philadelphia Athletics baseball game, against the St. Louis Browns, at *Shibe Park*. All of which were "not long for this world". The Athletics would move to Kansas City in 1955 – and, after a few years, on to Oakland. The Browns would become the Baltimore Orioles. And *Shibe Park* – later to be named *Connie Mack Stadium* would be razed.

None of that, of course, would be relevant to Charlie's enjoyment of baseball. The kid was becoming quite a fan.

In Baltimore, the group took in historic *Fort McHenry* – where Francis Scott Key had written our National Anthem.

Two of Jim Sidorwitz's dearest friends had lived in Baltimore. Jim had been in the Navy with Don Baldwin. The young sailor had spent a good deal of time in the little apartment that Don and his wife, Doris, had rented in Norfolk. Three or four times in the year-

or-so that he'd known them, Don and Doris had taken Jim home with them – up to Baltimore for a "really nifty" weekend.

He'd loved the city: The row houses, the gaslight-style street lamps, the white marble stoops – which many housewives still washed by hand. All of these things were part of a quaint charm – an enchanting quality – which made the city truly unique.

In 1951, Don would have been discharged – if Parks' memory was accurate. He and Doris would be living in Baltimore – in an apartment that Doris' father had built in the upper floor of Doris' ancestral home. Parks drove past the home five times – but, was never able to catch a glimpse of the couple. Or even see Don's '48 Nash. A pity.

<u>I dunno</u>, he thought to himself. <u>Maybe my memory is wrong. Maybe they're still in Norfolk</u>.

Donald Sidorwitz – Jim and Kathleen's "Number-Four Son" (and the oldest of the three "Dirty Rats") – would be named after Don Baldwin, when the little guy had "showed up" in 1963.

Parks noted a number of inquiring glances from Trudy – the fourth and fifth times he drove past Doris' parent's house. So – no more schleps down Mathews Street.

Our boy caught himself before he made a critical slip: Charlie had wanted to see another baseball game. Parks managed to stop himself – before he advised the boy that it would be another three years before the fabled, loveable, historically-inept, Browns would leave St. Louis for the Maryland city.

"But," he promised the lad, "if the Senators are in town, we'll go see a game or two at *Griffith Stadium*, down in Washington".

None of the group, except for Parks, had ever been to our Nation's Capital. They spent three sight-seeing days there. Early in the morning, of their second day in the city, they were fortunate enough to see President Truman – as he hurried across the *White House* lawn, on one of his famous walks. Charlie got the best picture of the president.

Things were much simpler in 1951.

They attended a Washington Senators baseball game. The team was soundly drubbed by the Boston Red Sox. While, by no means a capacity crowd, the number of people in the stadium was respectable.

Although the fans seemed not to be as caught up in the game as the almost-fanatical supporters of the Dodgers and/or the Giants, the Washingtonians were, most certainly, "in" to the game.

Once again, sadness descended upon Parks.

<u>Enjoy it while you can,</u> folks. <u>You're gonna lose your team too. Both of 'em</u>.

He was aware, of course, that in 1960, Calvin Griffith would transplant the club to the Minneapolis/St. Paul area – to be re-christened the Minnesota Twins. An expansion club – also known as the Washington Senators – would replace the departing team.

In a few short years – Parks couldn't remember exactly when – the new Senators would follow the old Senators out of town; moving to the Dallas/Fort Worth area. They would become the Texas Rangers.

For Charlie, the most fascinating feature of the old *Griffith Stadium* was the words "It's A Hit" – mounted high atop the *Chesterfield* sign on the mammoth right field wall. Each time a player hit safely, the slogan would flash to life! It truly <u>was</u> "a hit"! On those occasions when one of the athletes would boot one, the "E" in *Chesterfield* would light up. The procedure intrigued Charlie – for the entire game.

And just when our hero was certain that the lad was beginning to acquire a bit of sophistication about "our national pastime".

Trudy and Amanda were both thrilled by colonial, picturesque, Williamsburg, Virginia. Once there, the ladies launched a massive shopping expedition. Seemingly, they bought something from every shop in town. <u>Everything</u> from every shop in town?

Parks, along with Charlie, did a little shopping of his own: Picking up three-cornered *Revolutionary War* hats for his wife and mother-in-law – and purchasing Confederate officer's hats for Charlie and himself.

It was a short ride to Jamestown and the replica of Christopher Columbus' ship – *The Nina*. As could be expected, Amanda was thrilled with the wondrous historical museum, adjacent to the pier where the ship was moored. Parks looked aghast at *The Nina* – and wondered how anyone could've crossed the Atlantic, in a ship as small as that vessel. He'd always imagined that all three of

Columbus' ships had been much larger than that. Of course, he'd made the same miscalculation – vis-à-vis *The Mayflower*.

Parks phoned Ben Lozen – Clark Dubin's brother-in-law – from Jamestown, asking the Naval officer if he would be able to show Parks' family through the giant *Naval Operating Base* and the adjoining *Naval Air Station*, in Norfolk.

Lozen, by the summer of 1951, had been promoted to the lofty rank of captain – a bona fide "four-striper". He was commanding officer of a huge warehouse project on the sprawling *Naval Operating Base*.

Parks was anxious to show Trudy, Amanda and Charlie as many aspects of the many and varied Naval installations as would be possible. He was especially eager to see the *Air Station* once again. He'd spent almost three years there. However, one had to be the guest of naval personnel, stationed on the *Operating Base* or the *Air Station* to be able to get inside the gates of either facility. A civilian, with no connection, would not be allowed into either "activity".

Capt. Lozen was a gracious host. With him, they explored almost every foot of the different installations – including the massive array of war ships moored at the far-flung piers. He even drove his guests to the submarine base, a few miles down Hampton Boulevard. The entire tour took well in excess of seven hours.

Parks once again became slightly faint – when, contrary to all odds, he saw himself – as Jim – saunter out of the Post Exchange barber shop, on the *Air Station*.

The appearance caught our boy completely off guard. On a base the size of Norfolk's *Air Station*, the chances of his path crossing with Jim's were infinitesimal. Especially when one considered the fact that the *Fleet Aviation Accounting Office* was housed in a building situated in a remote section of the base – directly across the parking lot from the WAVES barracks. (Every man stationed at *FAAO* owned a pair of powerful binoculars!)

Parks had counted on not having to contend with crossing paths with Jim – fearful that his reaction would be the same as had occurred in the lounge, just off the lobby of the *Hotel Peabody*, in Memphis.

If Trudy had noticed the sudden buckling of her husband's knees – as the group had made its way past the barber shop, at the Post Exchange – she gave no indication.

She did question his obsession for listening to radio station WNOR, however.

While the station would eventually go to "formula radio", its personalities, in the early-fifties were solid gold to Parks. It was great to hear the familiar voices of Bob Storey, Ted Harding, Paul Hennings and Roger Clark – as well as his favorite, Charlie Benz, and the *Date With Charlie* show. The program had used David Rose's whimsical *Serenade To A Lemonade* as its theme. He had to chuckle at the title of Roger Clark's all-night soiree: *Records With Rog*.

When the quartet eventually returned to Detroit, Amanda could not thank Parks enough for having included her in such an extended tour. It seemed almost as though she would never let up in expressing her gratefulness.

It was time, once more, for our hero to experience still more pangs of guilt.

Sometimes, he felt, he couldn't see past his nose. Amanda Chamberlain had led an exceedingly tough life. More harsh, even, than that of Helen. Amanda had come upon very few of the nicer things in the world – although she seemed always to be happy.

When Parks and Trudy had first married, the happy groom had offered to buy Amanda a new house. His mother-in-law had declined with thanks – preferring to remain in the little bungalow, which had been so dear to her for so many years.

Her son-in-law had, though, managed to talk her into letting him pay for a paint job for the exterior of the house – as well as some carpentry work to shore up the sagging front porch.

Eventually, she'd let him put in a new floor – plus a sink, bathtub and commode – in the bathroom, as well as a new sink and Formica counter in the kitchen. Oh – and new eves troughs and drainpipes outside.

It had taken long enough, Parks supposed, but he'd finally come upon the realization that a trip – such as the one just completed – was exceedingly precious to the older woman! Worth more so than a thousand houses. Or a thousand sinks. A thousand tubs. A thousand commodes.

It was the same sort of awakening he'd experienced on the roof of *The Peabody* – when it had occurred to him, at long last, that he'd not taken his wife dancing often enough. It was a situation he'd since corrected.

He certainly could've done more for Amanda Chamberlain. He would work on that state of affairs also.

NINETEEN

Christmas Eve, 1951. Parks had begun to feel twinges he'd not experienced in years. It had been an entire decade – plus a few weeks – since Helen and Jeff had died.

Dear Lord! A whole decade? A whole, entire, ten-full-year, decade?

The impact hadn't hit him until Christmas Eve. December 24th, of course, had been special – ever since 1939. That had been the first time he and Helen had made love.

Each Christmas – since 1941 – he had always experienced, in some dimension, a particularly unique sadness. The pervading sorrow – and the devastating gloom it had invariably produced – had been almost unbearable during those first five bleak years.

Thankfully, since he'd met Trudy – whom he loved dearly – the melancholy had abated. Abated significantly.

But, dear Lord! Ten years! Totally mind-boggling!

In a way it seemed as though it had been eons. In another perspective, it seemed like yesterday that he'd lost Helen. Had lost Helen and Jeff.

It was mid-afternoon, and he was seated at the kitchen table.

The "Dream House" had continued to be just that. The answer to his dreams. He'd never lost his love for it. He felt most fortunate that the fates – or whatever – had allowed him to come back and live in the place which had been so close to his heart, for virtually all his life. A place he had always loved.

Returning

Trudy seemed happy in the house; although he knew, she'd been rather tentative at first. It was gratifying that his wife's apprehension seemed to have vanished after the first month or two.

It was vital – critical – that she also love the place. That she be happy there. That she be more than just happy. He fumbled for the proper word. It wouldn't come. Even little Charlie seemed to love the place. Thank God for that!

Can't keep calling him "little Charlie".

The boy would soon be ten-years-old. His growth, over the past year, had been phenomenal. The kid had probably long-since tired of hearing Parks say, "You're gonna have to get your mother to knit you another sock … you've grown another foot".

Father and son had become practically inseparable. They'd attended so many Tigers, Lions and Red Wings games – that Charlie was becoming a walking sports encyclopedia.

Parks was thankful that they lived in an era when sports personalities were, by and large, looked up to. It would be some 15 or 20 years before they would be referred to as "jocks". It would be almost that long before the word would be used comfortably in mixed company. Jim had never been at ease with using the term in front of a woman. It didn't help that – in far too many cases – those "jocks" had become ego-driven, overpaid, underachievers. The pervasiveness of such an in-your-face, trash-talking, self-centered, attitude had become a cause of abject disgust for Jim – once a bona fide "sports nut".

It was probably just as well that Parks, himself, was blissfully unaware of the many dope scandals, the horrible steroid culture, the strikes, and the "up-yours" attitudes that would permeate virtually all of the major sports organizations – and, in too many cases, entire leagues – in the eighties and nineties. Conceited jocks! And greedy owners! And bellicose, showboating, umps! He'd have wished a pox on all of their houses.

At the beginning of the 21st century, two NFL football players would be charged with murder! An NBA player had been convicted of murdering his pregnant girlfriend. A study revealed that NBA players had sired more children out of wedlock – than there were NBA players.

If Jim Sidorwitz had been upset with the sporting scene in the seventies, he'd have been absolutely sickened at what sports had degenerated to in the nineties.

Christmas Eve, of 1951, found most players – thankfully – still heroes.

Parks could hardly wait till the spring of 1952. The Detroit Red Wings would become the first team in *National Hockey League* history to win *The Stanley Cup* – emblematic of hockey supremacy – in the minimum eight games. The powerful Wings would blow out the Toronto Maple Leafs in four straight contests – and then go on to sweep the richly-talented Montreal Canadiens in the *Cup* finals.

In the life of Jim Sidorwitz – who had taken leave to attend two of the home games – it had been a high-water mark, topping even the 1945 Tigers and their triumph over the Chicago Cubs in the *World Series*.

The Red Wings, of the early- and mid-fifties, were the great teams of Gordie Howe, Ted Lindsay and Sid Abel – who comprised the fabled *Production Line*, one of the most prolific trios in the history of the game. The juggernaut had extended farther than the *Production Line*. Terry Sawchuck – who was to die so tragically in the mid-sixties – was, for the duration of the 1952 playoffs, perhaps the greatest goaltender who ever lived. He'd recorded four shutouts in the eight games – dazzling everyone with spectacular save after spectacular save.

The Montreal players would proclaim – practically to a man – that Sawchuck alone was responsible for the Canadiens not having won one game in the finals.

In addition, Red Kelly was probably the best defenseman to lace on a pair of skates that season. He would play on four *Stanley Cup*-winning teams in Detroit – then, as a centerman, go on to play on four more with the Maple Leafs. Incredible player.

Of course, there was the *"Slobber Line"* of Prystai, Pavelich and Peters.

A very young Alex Delvecchio was just beginning to come into his own.

Parks closed his eyes – and took a sip of his coffee.

Ah, these are the days! The six-team N.H.L.!

The Red Wings dreadnought was virtually unbeatable – especially at the *Olympia*, the storied, tradition-to-the-rafters, building in which they played.

His reverie was interrupted by the jangle of a coin – clanking, noisily, onto the porcelain table in front of him. The coin was a penny. He looked up to see Trudy – a warm smile lighting her pretty face. Her soft brown eyes almost aglow. He picked up the penny from the table.

"What's this for?" he asked.

Then, at last, the light clanked on.

"Oh," he said. "I understand. For my thoughts, hah? You'll have to excuse me ... I'm a little slow today."

She kissed him, warmly, on his right temple. "You're fine today, Hayworth. You're fine every day."

Looking back up at her, his smile, ironically, took on a dimension of sadness.

"Still want to know my thoughts?" he asked.

"I think I already do. Let's just say that I'd be very surprised if you answered, 'Wanna screw?'."

He nodded. "I guess I'm not the best company today."

"You're the best company all the time, Hayworth. You're thinking about Helen, aren't you? I don't mind. I think it's beautiful, as a matter of fact. I know that it's been ten years ... and I know it's been weighing on you. I understand that. How could I not? You wouldn't be you ... if it wasn't weighing on you pretty good. Especially at this time of year."

He patted the hand she'd placed on his shoulder. Once again, she leaned down and kissed him – planting the wet buss smack dab on the tip of his nose.

"Anything I can do?" she asked.

"You're already doing it. You're being you, Trood. That's enough for any man. I luff you."

"I luff you too, Hayworth."

"Even though it's a struggle?"

"Never a struggle," she laughed. "Never a struggle, you fathead."

"You're so romantic, Goit! Wanna screw?"

"No," she answered, shaking her head. "And neither do you. I'll take a cup of coffee … in lieu of it … though."

"A cup of coffee," he shrugged. "A cup of coffee … a piece of ass. Whatever. Easy come … easy go."

"Don't talk dirty, Hayworth. Good try, though. Go back to your memories. I probably shouldn't have butted in. I stood there for … I don't know … for three or four minutes. Right in the doorway. I know your peripheral vision isn't that rotten. You were over Ogden, Utah … as you always say about me. Doesn't take much to figure out why. She must've been a great lady."

"Yeah," he nodded. "She was. But, you've got about the same situation. It's been ten years since Frank died. Don't you get a pang over it … every now and then? Or do you just handle it … handle these things … so much better than I do?"

"No. I think of Frank … from time to time. I've told you before, though, that I don't think I loved him nearly as deeply as you loved Helen. Plus, your son died too. It's not that I handle it any better. My loss just wasn't as great as yours. Like I said … she must've been a great lady."

"Would you believe that I was actually thinking about hockey? The Red Wings?"

"Nope."

He swallowed a lump. His wife was right, of course. The Wings were simply a facade, a distraction – a means of escape from the real burden.

"Yeah," he rasped, at length. "She was, y'know. She was a great lady."

Trudy poured a cup of coffee and sat down in the chair next to him.

"You know," she admonished, "all the stuff you got Charlie was too much. Just like last year. And the one before that. And the one before that. You'll never learn."

"I told you how dumb I am."

"Yeah. Dumb. Like a fox."

She took a long pull on her coffee. Before setting the cup back down, she studied the steaming liquid – her eyes moistening.

"He loves you very much, y'know," she said.

"Charlie?"

"Who else? You're the best thing that ever happened to him. All the games you take him to. All the things you do together. I told you … remember? … that I was worried about marrying you because I didn't feel you'd have the physical dexterity to keep up with him. I sure had that wrong. Now, I worry about something else."

He leaned over – pressing the tip of his nose against the tip of hers.

"Whazzat?" he asked.

"I'm … I'm afraid that you're trying to do too much. He knows that you can't keep up the pace … that, eventually, you won't be able to play catch with him and throw the football with him. He's so proud of you. You're always getting into pickup hockey games … I guess you call 'em … with the kids over at the rink. Or being the referee or something. None of the other fathers get out there … and do the things you do. They sure don't do those things with their kids."

Parks thought of his own sons – the four sons in his "other life". Dave wouldn't be born for another 3½ years. Doug would come along in August, of 1956. Danny wouldn't put in an appearance until May, of 1958. It would be eleven years – and a few months – before Donald, his youngest son (the one named after Don Baldwin, of Baltimore) would make his entrance into the world.

For ten or eleven years after his oldest three sons had been born, Jim Sidorwitz had been able to play ball with them most weekends. However, once "The Dirty Rats" had come along, he'd begun working his many jobs – and the "quality" ball-playing time had been sacrificed, at the altar of economic survival.

Donald had gotten the short end of the stick. It was not until Don had entered the *Little League* program – and his three older brothers had begun to become independent – that Jim had been able to attend his games, and hit fungoes to his "Number-Four Son".

It was entirely possible that Parks Hayworth was trying to make up for Jim Sidorwitz's lack of playing time with Dave, Doug, Dan – and especially Don. Was it too far-fetched to believe that he was trying to compensate for it – through Charlie?

Swallowing with some difficulty once again, he finally answered his wife:

"Well, maybe it's just that the other fathers can't do all of the things they'd like to do. They're all a helluva lot younger nor me, y'know. They're probably so damn busy ... just trying to hack out a damn living. Maybe they just simply don't have the time. By the time they're a few bucks ahead of the game ... and they have a chance to really get involved with the kid ... it's probably too late. Probably always too late. The kid's probably grown. (Heavy sigh.) Simply too damn late."

His voice took on a trace of bitterness – a dimension Trudy had seldom heard.

"The kids are all grown and gone, by then" he continued – muttering more into his coffee cup, than talking to his wife. "The kids are all grown and gone ... trying to hack out a living for their own kids. And not having enough time to spend with them ... until it's too damn late. It's a vicious cycle! And it's not gonna get any better, dammit.'

"Whooooo! Hayworth! How do you know that?"

"Since the war ... since the end of the war ... has it gotten any better?"

"Hey! Hayworth! That's only been five or six years."

"Doesn't matter. It'll never get any better. Only worse."

"You sound awfully sure of that," she replied – letting go a sigh of her own.

"Doesn't take much figuring. It's true that inflation isn't what it was in nineteen forty-six. But, if you stop and think about the baby boom ... "

"Baby boom? Baby boom? I've never heard that expression before."

"I heard someone say something to that effect ... use the term ... on the radio, this morning," he muttered. "Forget who it was."

She smiled, once more – her doe-like eyes glistening, as they did sometime.

"Well," she soothed, "whatever comes, I'm just so happy ... and I feel so lucky ... that, for whatever reason, you're able to spend so much time with Charlie. And ... what's even more important ... you take the time to enjoy him. Genuinely enjoy him."

"It's even more important that he enjoys me."

"He does, Hayworth. He luffs you."

"Well, I luff him. And I luff you. Ain't that luff-ley?"

"Uff course," she responded, with an overdone wince. "But, I'm still a little worried about you. We've gone over this before, Hayworth. You're not an old man ... I'm not saying that. But, I do wish you'd take it a little easy. I really do worry about you, y'know."

"Not to worry," he replied. "I'm in great shape. Strong! Like bool!"

"Yeah. Strong, like bool maybe. But, sometimes, tired like hell. Hayworth ... please ... take it a little easy. You're pushing sixty, y'know. You can't go on being Gordie Howe forever."

"Aw, Goit. You worry too much."

He pulled her up onto his lap. She sat with her arms around his neck – her legs dangling off the left side of his chair. He began to pat her on her bottom – as he always did.

"Don't worry about me, Trood," he said. "I'm fine. Honest."

As they sat so still – the quiet broken only by the steady rhythmic, pat, pat, pat – Parks' thoughts strayed. Not back to Helen, but forward to 1955. He was certain that he would not survive long enough to see Dave born. It was probably just one more reason that he'd never spared himself – while cavorting with Charlie.

He regretted the fact that he and Trudy had no daughters.

His rumination drifted, through the mists – to his own three daughters. His "little girls". No matter how old they'd become, they'd always be his "little girls". He'd always maintained that there is something special between daddies and daughters.

Mike Douglas' recording of *The Men In My Little Girl's Life* had always been a "three-handkerchief job" for him – as was the final portion of Rodgers & Hammerstein's *Soliloquy,* from their remarkable *Carousel* score. In the poignant scene, expectant father, "Billy Bigelow", sings of "My little girl" – and the changes that such a little girl would bring to his self-centered, ne'er-do-well, life.

Jim had given his daughters nicknames – Hogan, Duffy and Clancy. He didn't know why. He'd always called his sons Dave, Doug, Dan and Don. But, he'd always called his daughters Hogan, Duffy and Clancy. Funny, he mused. Awfully funny – when you thought about it.

As the deluge of images whirled through his consciousness – his head resting on Trudy's soft, warm, chest – Parks became aware of a wetness on his left ear. A drop of water. Followed by another. Then, another.

Pulling his head away from the warmth of her bosom, he gazed up at his wife. Tears were trickling down her cheeks.

"I see," he observed, "where you've got tears in your ears."

She sniffed, and nodded. "Yeah," she answered. "My eyes are very far apart."

"Wassa matta you?"

"Nothing," she rasped. "Not a thing. That's why I'm crying. Nothing's wrong. I've never been happier."

"Me too neither, Goit. You're all I could want. You and Charlie. Where is that kid, by the bye?"

"He's over at the church. I'll have you know that *Our Lady Gate of Heaven* is going to have a full-fledged choir for midnight Mass tonight ... a fabulous first. And Charlie's gonna be part and parcel of it."

"Yeah. I knew that. I just didn't think that they'd wind up practicing this late. It's almost four o'clock."

"Those are the sacrifices one has to make for one's art, Dahling."

He laughed – for the first time in hours.

"It's probably just as well," he allowed. "I could sit here for hours ... just patting you on the fanny."

"Wrong! Either your legs would fall asleep ... or my fanny would."

The first days of March, 1952, rolled around. March fifth – the day after his sister's 12th birthday – found Parks buying another rental property! The little house on Penrod! The home to which the Sidorwitz family had moved in 1939 – when they'd "abandoned" the "Dream House". Had "forsaken" it, in little Jim's opinion.

Jim had lived in the little house from '39 till 1947. Probably quite early in 1947. He'd been aware of the fact that the house had changed hands in the early-fifties – as had his grandparents' little "Dog House". Parks had kept his eye on the Penrod home – and, when the <u>For</u> <u>Sale</u> sign had gone up, he'd sprung.

As a child, Jim – as previously stated – had never been especially fond of the place. Any house, of course, would have been a comedown to him – after those happy years on Grandmont.

His sister, Dee, had been born some months after the Sidorwitzes had moved to Penrod. In March of 1940. She had always been fond of the place – especially after the family had moved to the "big barn" on Prairie. Everybody hated that "haunted house" – as his grandmother had always called it. When all had been said and done, young Jim had simply never given the little place on Penrod a chance. He'd make up for that. If given the opportunity, he would buy the joint. And so he did.

Trudy, as she'd strode through the empty bungalow with her husband, seemed to sense something "special" in his manner. She'd confided to Amanda Chamberlain, the next day, that it was somewhat upsetting to her to note the attachment that Parks seemed to experience toward the place.

"This place looks almost the same ... just like the house on ... Rosemont," she told her mother. "The only difference is that the one on Penrod is brick. But, they're laid out exactly the same way. Exactly alike! And yet ... and yet ... he never got all misty-eyed over the house on Rosemont. Not that I know of, anyway. I ... I don't ... I just don't understand it."

"Indulge him," Amanda counseled. "You're just borrowing trouble again."

Parks continued to add to his growing stable of automobiles. He picked up a 1950 Packard convertible – as well as a 1951 Hudson four-door sedan. In addition, he blundered upon a dark-green 1949 DeSoto – the spitting image of Jim's first car. It seemed as though 75% of all DeSotos, in 1949, were that same green. This one had only 6,300 miles on the odometer, and Parks was thrilled with the find.

Trudy, who had accompanied him to **Highland Park Motors** – the DeSoto-Plymouth dealership on Davison and Woodward Avenue, from where Jim had bought his original DeSoto – experienced, once again, that same uneasy feeling. It was almost as though they were walking through the little house on Penrod once more. Especially when he climbed inside the DeSoto – to drive it to his "warehouse" on Telegraph Road.

As before, Amanda Chamberlain advised her that she was "borrowing trouble".

Joining the DeSoto, Packard and Hudson, in the building on Telegraph Road – a few months later – was Parks' yellow 1951 Mercury. He bought a brand new, dark blue bottom/white top, 1952 Lincoln two-door "hardtop" – a car he described as being "half tail light".

The Hayworth stock portfolio continued to increase in value – as did the family's real estate holdings.

Parks spent a minimum of two hours each day with Trudy – embroiled in detailing every aspect of the financial empire he'd built over the years, making a concentrated, subliminal, attempt to apprise her, especially, of the future worth of the many autos in the building on Telegraph.

She showed remarkable acumen in digesting facts and figures – and, in many areas, indicated an insight which began to surpass that of her husband. Their holdings, of course, were listed in both names.

Parks, anticipating his death in a year or two, constantly struggled with the whys and wherefores of his not having helped Jim and Kathleen.

He fought a never-ending battle with himself: Should he or should he not establish a "Help Jim" fund? Surely, if he wanted to, he could find a way to get some sort of princely sum to the young sailor – even in 1952.

Was it procrastination? Inertia? That line of thought had always brought a terrible – a horribly bleak – feeling. He was certain that his inability to avoid procrastinating had cost Helen and Jeff their lives.

Was he to be a slave – for all his life – to such a reprehensible character flaw?

In his brighter moments, he considered that, possibly, he'd not wanted to upset a delicate balance in Jim's and Kathleen's life. He was aware that the Sidorwitzes had, after all, survived all those lean years.

Would a generous largess have taken away from Jim some special badge of courage? Did Parks want to be responsible for such a removal? Especially when no one could be certain how a radically-different lifestyle would affect the kids? Was it not better to simply "let it be"? Would it not be unwise to gamble on the way the children would turn out – were they to grow up in a more-opulent atmosphere? Gambling on an "if come" result to a sudden windfall? And ignoring a sure thing?

Should he not let Jim take what he had earned – and run with it?

The only fact, of which he could be reasonably certain, was the prospect that he'd probably not live to see Dave born in 1955. The prospect, at times, clouded virtually everything else in his life. He developed an almost-macabre obsession with keeping the finances in impeccable order – which would allow Trudy's administration of the program to be accomplished as smoothly as possible.

Until the purchase of the house on Penrod, though, he'd seldom asked her opinion. Beginning with that transaction, however, he began to "run everything by her".

She'd never offered any objections to a single project – despite her reservations concerning his "feeling" toward the little brick house. And the '49 DeSoto.

"Why should I say you nay?" she'd asked, at one point. "You've done beautiful, Hayworth. Almost poifect."

The were sitting in the patio room – listening to a brand new table-model *Webcor* "hi-fi" record player, sitting atop of their old *Stromberg-Carlson* radio/phonograph. The small 45 RPM player had been moved upstairs to their bedroom. The new set played LP's – albums with 8 or 10 or 12 cuts on one disc. Lasted a whole half-hour, in some cases.

Kathryn Grayson and Howard Keel were singing the very beautiful *Make Believe* – from the sound track of **MGM's** new remake of Jerome Kern's glorious *Showboat*.

"I need your input," Parks maintained. He found himself hoping that the word "input" had made no impression. It shouldn't be that big a deal – but, it would be years before the word would enjoy widespread usage. "I may not be around, y'know, to help you administer these things."

"Parks." He knew the conversation was about to take a serious turn – by dint of the fact that she'd used his first name. "You've become almost preoccupied with death," she continued. "Why? Is something wrong? Is there something I should know about?"

"No. Of course not. It's just that … when you get into your sixties … you've got to start thinking about such things. I'd be an absolute fool, if I didn't. And it's important to me … terribly important … that you and Charlie are provided for."

"Charlie and I are fine. In my wildest dreams, could I have ever imagined being so happy? And all the time? I mean, I don't remember one single unhappy day. Do you realize that, Hayworth?"

He was glad to hear her back to calling him by his last name.

"I mean," she went on, "every morning, I wake up and thank God for you. I swear it's true. If there's something wrong with you … something you're not telling me … and it involves you going into the hospital or something, even if it's for a long time … or even if it's some kind of specialist … in Switzerland or something … and you're afraid of tying up our funds … or depleting 'em … don't be. I wouldn't even think about it. I'd give up the whole shebang … in a minute! In less than a minute! You're more important to me … and to Charlie … than a dozen stock portfolios. Or a million rental properties. I love you Hayworth. I don't need some stupid classic car to cuddle up to on a cold winter's night."

"A specialist? In Switzerland? God, Trood, but you're awfully damn dramatic, in your old age. I think you've been seeing too many movies. C'mon, Goit. There's nothing wrong with me. Nothing at all. I just don't want anything to louse up your future … yours and Charlie's."

"I don't know how many times I'm gonna have to tell you this, but, you're our future." Her eyes began to dampen. "Don't you dare louse it up ... by letting something happen to you. It's the little things that mean so much to us. Like your getting those tickets for the hockey playoffs next week. I know they're hard to get ... so maybe I shouldn't be talking about them being little things ... but, you know what I mean. Charlie's climbing the walls ... looking forward to seeing the games. He talks about it all the time."

"Yeah, well he's not any more excited than I am. Should be a helluva series ... both of 'em."

"Don't the Red Wings have to beat whoever they're playing next week? Doesn't it have to be where the winner of the series goes on to the next series? Doesn't the loser ... well, isn't their season over?"

"Yeah. They've gotta beat the Maple Leafs. The Wings'll moider 'em."

"How can you be so sure?"

"The Wings have one hell of a team. Ain't no one gonna take 'em. The Leafs simply don't have the talent to contain 'em. No one has. Not enough to take four games from 'em anyway."

"Parks ... who are you?"

The question caught him completely off guard. Helen had once asked the same question – asked it with those same exact words! He hadn't expected it from Trudy. Especially since she'd just finished telling him how happy she was with him.

"What ... what do you mean by that?" he asked, weakly.

"Just what I asked. I probably shouldn't be getting into something like this. Like I said, I'm happy with you. Ecstatically happy with you. I really am. I should probably keep my big mouth shut. But, Parks, there are ... there are so many things that bother me. I'm sure that I'm being a complete horse's ass ... for rattling cages like this."

Another storm warning – in addition to her liberal use of his first name: He'd seldom heard her use an expression like 'horse's ass" before. Nothing, most usually, more than a "damn" or a "hell". Well, not outside of the bedroom, anyway.

"I wish ... I just wish, Parks," she continued, "I wish I didn't have so many of these ... of these ... of these feelings. I wish they'd all just ... well ... just go away."

"What kind of things? What sort of things about me are such ... are such a bother ... such a worry to you?"

"Maybe 'bother' wasn't the best word I could've thought of. But, Parks, I get these ... such weird ... such really weird feelings ... when you ... when you ... "

"When I what?"

"Well, when some of the things you say don't always fit. Plus, you hardly ever talk about your childhood. You never talk about your days in Houston. As loquacious as you are ... and you just simply never mention anything about your days down in Texas. Clark Dubin told me once ... that he'd tried to check you out, at one time. Back when you first began to work for him, I think. He said that you'd gotten him so enthused about getting into the rent-a-car business, that he was afraid that he'd acted with his heart ... and not his head. So, he tried to check you out ... to remove his worries about you. Anyway, he said that he couldn't find any trace of you in Houston. Said he ran up his phone bill trying to find one scrap of information about you. And ... nothing! He said that the company you told him you'd worked for ... well, that the company you said you worked for ... that it didn't exist."

Parks was visibly shaken.

"Why ... why on earth would Clark tell you something like that?"

"Well, he didn't tell me. Not exactly. It was more like he asked me. It was back when the company ... when **Dubin Rent-a-Car** ... was starting to really take off. This was maybe three or four years ago. Maybe a little longer. I can't really remember. He apparently wanted to make you some kind of offer ... some kind of position. I have the feeling that he was more thinking out loud than anything else. Whatever it was, though ... whatever he had in mind ... I got the impression that he figured that it might make you ... make you ... make you vulnerable. Vulnerable ... if you had some kind of skeleton in your closet. He was just trying to find out from me if I knew anything about you ... from way back in nineteen thirty-seven or thirty-eight. It hit me like a ton of bricks! It finally occurred to me that I didn't know anything ... not a damn thing ... about you. About your life in Texas. Just a few snatches of conversation here and there. But, nothing really concrete. Yet, when we're talking about things that've happened here in Detroit, you're generally very explicit. Expansive as you can be. But, things in the forties ... and now in the fifties? Before that? Nothing."

"And what do you think, Trudy?" His voice had taken on an edge she'd not heard before. A strange, indescribable, tone.

"I ... I don't know. I think that I'm probably talking when I should be listening. I always seem to manage to screw things up. Seem always to zig ... when I should be zagging. But, there are times when ... well, when I just can't ... control my curiosity about you. About your past."

"I ... I had no idea ... no idea at all ... that my past was such a bother to you."

"Like I said, 'bother' may not be such a good word. But, well ... yes. Yes, I guess it is. Having said too much already ... way too much ... I just want you to know that, if you've got a storied ... or even a scarlet ... past, I don't care. I really don't care ... if you can believe that. I love you. I love the Parks Hayworth that I've known all these years. Whatever you may or may not have done in the past ... well, they all contributed to the Parks Hayworth that I know and love. If some of those things ... any of those things ... were what society considers to be wrong, well I'm still grateful ... because they've had a positive effect on you. Someone once said we're all the sum total of our experiences. That's fine by me."

The tension diminished – somewhat.

"Why would you think that I've had a scarlet past?" he asked. "Do you think I'm an escaped convict or something? If so, let me assure you ... let me promise you, let me swear to you, by all that I hold holy ... that I've never ... never in my life ... been in jail. Nor am I running from the law. I'm not ... I promise you ... on the lam. Not running from anything. Any person or any thing. I wouldn't lie to you! You've got to believe that, Trudy. There's absolutely no one ... not a soul ... looking for me."

"I ... I believe you." Her soft brown eyes misted over. "I know you wouldn't lie to me. I never really thought of you as ... well, as ever having been in jail. That never occurred to me. I have to think, though, that there may have been ... may still be ... some things that you may believe that it's better I don't know about. I'd be fibbing ... if I told you that it's not a little unsettling. If it happens that ... somewhere down the line ... if it happens that you feel as though there's something you want to tell me, well, I'd be honored. I <u>will</u> be honored. I really will."

<u>Would that I could, Trudy. There are so many things I'd like to share with you.</u>

"I'd do my very best," she went on. "I <u>will</u> do my very best ... to understand. I love you ... just as you are. I don't need to know more than I already do. I don't even know why in the world I even asked the stupid, silly, damn question in the first place. You're a fine man ... the man I love. The man I always will love. The man Charlie will always love too."

Parks started to respond – but, his wife held up her hand.

"Do you know what Charlie told me the other day?" she asked. "Now that he says his prayers by himself, he told me that he still says the *Angel Of God* prayer. It's your prayer ... and, because of that, it's still so special to him."

"I'm honored," he replied, in a husky whisper. "I really am. He's a heck of a kid. But, let me ask you one other thing: What is it ... besides Clark Dubin telling you that he couldn't track me down in Houston ... that bothers you? Actually, back in thirty-seven and thirty-eight, no one really kept records much. Especially down there. None that were all that accurate, anyway. None that were all that exact. We were all pretty much like pilgrims down there. Prospectors, maybe. Settlers."

He thought of the multitude of computers and data processors which would come along in the seventies – wherein the most minute of details seldom escaped the all-inclusive vacuum cleaner of a world of memory banks.

He couldn't know that, in the nineties, that same world of computers and data processors would become a <u>universe</u> of memory banks – able to dredge up even more than the most minute of details.

In nanoseconds. And that the turn of the century, computers were to become even more sophisticated. He'd have been totally unable to cope with the dot-com "explosion" in the nineties.

"Especially in Texas," he continued. "They all operated pretty much off the seat of their pants down there. Like I said, we were almost like pioneers ... and the same held true for most other ..."

"Seat of their pants? That's a funny expression."

"I thought you'd heard it before."

"Not that one."

"Well, whatever. Clark just got bum dope on me ... and my company not existing. If he'd have bothered asking me, I could've straightened everything out. That wasn't very nice of him to have asked you all those questions like that. I always thought he had more class than that. More class than just about anyone I've ever known."

"He does, Hayworth. Really, he does. He just reeks of class. I wouldn't be upset with him, if I were you. He told me that he was just trying to look out for you ... and I believe him. He just didn't want to expose you to something where you might get hurt. I'm convinced that it was his only thought. He's very fond of you. You talk about operating off the seat of your pants ... that's Clark Dubin. By the time he started hearing back from Houston, he'd decided that ... one way or another ... he was going to stay with you. Stick with the way you were operating ... no matter what. He was that impressed with you."

"I would hope so."

"In answer to your question, though," she said, "there have been a few disquieting things. Other than what Clark Dubin said. What Clark Dubin asked."

"Like what?"

"Well," she responded – sighing deeply, "Loretta called me ... about a week or so ago. We had a long talk."

Parks was certain that he was not going to like what was coming.

"Oh?" he asked, guardedly. "What kind of long talk?"

"Well, she knew the Barrys. Knew them pretty well, I guess."

"The ... the Barrys?"

"Yes. The Barrys. The people you bought our house from. The one on Penrod."

"Oh. Oh, yeah."

"Parks! I can't believe that you didn't recognize the name!"

"I did. I guess I didn't think that you'd remembered it. Thought that there might be, maybe, some other family named Barry ... one that I should be remembering."

"No. Same family. Anyway, when Loretta found out that the Barrys had sold you the house on Penrod, she said she got this really uneasy feeling. She said the same people ... family named Sidorwitz ... who'd bought this house, back when it was built ... they'd also bought the house ... our house ... on Penrod. Moved from here ... over to there. Over to Penrod. Twelve or fifteen years ago."

"Why should the fact that we happened to buy two houses that ... by some far-fetched coincidence ... happened to have been owned by the same family bother you? It was just a coincidence ... like I said. Did they also own the house on Rosemont? Has anyone checked that out? How about the house down the block? The Brogan's house? Are you just taking Loretta's word for all this? All those houses on Penrod ... the ones down at that end of the block anyway ... they all look alike. She could be wrong, you know. I really don't think that Loretta's playing with a full deck, sometimes."

"It's not just that, Parks."

She was still using his first name.

"You love this house," she went on. "You've always wanted to live here. You remember how scared I was when you wanted to move from Rosemont? Obviously, I had absolutely no reason to be scared. But, I was. I wouldn't be again ... but, I was then. Still, I see that ... that look you get ... when you look around this place. Even now ... after all this time. There are times when ... as a woman ... I wish that I could put that glow in your eyes. Parks, I caught almost the same look ... almost the same gleam ... when we were walking through the place on Penrod."

His laugh was contrived – overflowing with nervousness. Did she notice? She probably did.

"Oh," he replied, "I think you're letting your imagination run away with you. I was turned-on by this house ... I told you why."

"Turned-on?"

"Yeah. You've heard that before."

"I guess I have. Maybe. I don't remember. It's cute. Parks, whenever you get nervous, you come up with the damndest expressions. Things like, 'off the seat of my pants' and 'turned-on' and lots of other stuff. And don't tell me that you're not nervous now."

"Of course I'm nervous. Anytime you're upset ... whether it's with me, or anyone else ... I get nervous. I get especially shook up, when you're upset with me."

"Shook up?"

"Yeah. Shook up. Listen, Trood. Despite what you may think, it was just a coincidence that I fell in love with this house ... and then we happened to buy another house that just happened to be owned by the same family. My tastes, apparently, run the same as theirs."

"Loretta told me something else. She said that you ... she's sure it was you ... came down to the office where she was working. This was twelve ... thirteen ... years ago. Some lawyer's office in the *Guardian Building*."

"Entirely possible. I don't remember it, though."

"She told me that when she saw you for the first time ... when you answered the door, that day she and Richard came to see about renting the house ... she said that she was sure she'd seen you somewhere before."

"I don't understand. How could she see me for the first time ... and then tell you that she's seen me before? I still don't think that her elevator goes all the way to the top."

In spite of herself, his wife laughed at the expression – one which Parks wished he had back.

"No," she replied. "No ... what she meant was that, when she and Richard came here the first time ... to rent the house on Rosemont ... she said she felt as though she'd seen you somewhere before. But, she couldn't remember exactly where. Said it took her the longest time. When she was finally able to place you ... she remembered that you'd come into her office. That you'd had some kind of breakdown, or something. Some kind of attack, maybe. The way she described it, it sounded like the way you sometimes get dizzy ... like down in Memphis that time. Anyway, she said she went to get someone to throw you out ... but, I guess, you decided to leave, of your own volition."

"Well, I'll tell you what, Trood. Loretta has some kind of really weird imagination. That wasn't me. Couldn't have been. I don't remember every office I've ever been in, but I've never had a nervous breakdown ... or whatever ... in one. That, I'd have remembered. I'm telling you ... Loretta doesn't have both oars in the water."

"The way she described it, this guy really lost control of himself. Went all to pieces."

"Well," he growled. "it sure as hell wasn't me. I'd have damn well remembered."

"The thing that bothered Loretta," Trudy persisted, "was that this Dolly Sidorwitz ... the lady who used to live in this house and in the one on Penrod ... she worked there at the time. Worked in the same office as Loretta. This guy ... whoever he was ... he was doing his best to try and talk to this Dolly lady. That's when he came unglued. I guess it was pretty upsetting to this Dolly Sidorwitz."

Parks realized he was pulling at his right earlobe – and immediately dropped his hand to his side. No need to telegraph – to emphasize – how nervous he'd actually become.

"Well," he answered at length, "Like I said, it's Loretta's imagination. It's playing tricks on her. She's having some kind of stupid pipe dream. I'll go along with the houses belonging to the same person. It's kind of weird ... but, I can understand it raising a few eyebrows. Even then, all we have to go on is Loretta's word for that. We don't know it for a fact. But, with that cockamamie story she's trying to sell ... about me falling apart in her stupid, damn, office ... I'd tend to doubt that she really knows what the hell she's talking about."

Trudy sighed once more.

"Maybe you're right," she allowed. "Maybe she's just making the whole thing up. I can't imagine why she'd do such a thing, though. It just sounded like too much of a coincidence. I just wondered if ... if ... "

"If what?" His voice betrayed a definite, undeniable, caution.

"Well, this Sidorwitz lady ... she's supposed to be something like twenty years your junior. That also sounded like too much of a coincidence. I ... I ... I just wondered if you had some kind of ... some kind of ... of fixation for younger women. Look at the differences in our ages."

"Then, I wouldn't have gotten serious about Helen. Would I?"

"I ... I guess not. I don't know. I don't know what to think, half the time. It's just that ... with all these coincidences ... I just had to wonder: If this Dolly Sidorwitz is some kind of shirt-tail relation to you, or something. Or if maybe you'd had an affair with her."

The thought of Parks having an affair with his own mother left him aghast!

"What the hell are you talking about?" he roared. "No! Of course not! I've never had an affair with her! What the hell kind of accusation is that? I don't think I've ever met the lady! Don't know who the hell she is!"

"Okay! Okay! I believe you, Parks! Don't get upset!"

"Upset? Upset? I'm not upset! Well, yeah ... I guess I am. I don't want anything to come between us, Trudy. You're the most beautiful thing that ever happened to me. I'm sure as hell not going to stand by ... and let someone bollix it up! Let someone screw it all up!"

She arose – and sat down in his lap. She pulled his head down against her chest.

It was fully two minutes before he began to pat her on her bottom.

The silence had hung heavily in the small patio room.

"Ya scared me there, Hayworth," she rasped.

"Scared ya?"

"Yeah. I was wondering if you ever were gonna pat me on the fanny. In fact, for a minute there, I got really scared. I was afraid that you'd never pat me on my bum ... ever again."

"Hah!" His voice reflected the break in tension. "Fat chance!"

"You mean fat bum."

"Nah! Great bum! Just made for patting."

"Did you really mean that, Hayworth? About how I'm the most beautiful thing that ever happened to you?"

"Of course. Of course I did. You needed to ask?"

"Somehow ... well, somehow ... I always felt that place belonged to Helen. I wasn't unhappy about it. Was never jealous of it. I just, somehow, thought that she'd always rated above me, in that area. I actually understood that ... understood it would be that way. Understood that ... going in. And it was always all right with me. But ... "

"That means that I haven't said it enough to you ... not as often as I should. I love you very much, Goit. You are the most beautiful thing ever to happen to me. Of course, Helen'll always hold a special place in my heart. We were very close ... very happy together. But, we weren't together as long as you and I have been. Helen and I didn't have the opportunity ... the years with one another ... to build the many special memories. We couldn't form the beautiful private things, that you and I have shared. That we do share. Besides, she's not Charlie's mother."

Trudy began to cry. "Hayworth, that's the most beautiful thing anyone's ever said to me. Ever."

She planted a wet kiss on his nose – then, pressed his head back into her breasts.

Tears continued to stream down her cheeks – some of them coming to rest in her husband's hair. Parks, of course, was relieved. She'd begun to call him "Hayworth" again. Another crisis, overcome. He hoped it was overcome, anyway.

He stopped patting – and pinched her derriere, lightly.

"Hey," he whispered. "Wanna screw?"

Charlie was not due home for another two hours.

She leaned back – precariously – and smiled at him.

"I thought you'd never ask!"

Hand in hand, Parks and Trudy made their way upstairs – to the master bedroom, a giant room, which took up probably three-quarters of the front of the house. Not one of "those" master bedrooms. No adjoining bathroom or plethora of built-ins or anything.

She sat him down on the bed, knelt in front of him – and removed his shoes and stockings. Rising, she unbuttoned his shirt – and helped him out of it.

"Such soivice, Goit," he said, flashing a broad grin.

"It's only the beginning, folks," she responded in her best carnival barker's voice. "Only the beginning."

Nudging him gently into a prone position, she unzipped his trousers. With one deft motion, she yanked his slacks – along with his undershorts – down over his hips! In a matter of seconds, they were lying on the floor!

Then, standing over him, hands on hips, she laughed. "Yew shore dew look funny, Stranger," she said. "Bare-assed nekkid, an' all."

He smiled up at her. "You know? Everyone tells me that."

His wife removed her clothing – and laid down beside him. Rolling over onto his stomach, Parks began the foreplay! After he'd brought her to the desired level of passion, he entered her! She gasped, wrapped her legs around his buttocks – then, exhaled deeply! Slowly, he began to stroke into and out of her!

As he pressed down– the fifth time – he suddenly stiffened! Emitting a loud, animal-like groan, he collapsed on top of her – shivering uncontrollably.

She relaxed her legs and began patting him on the bottom – as she always did, when he'd achieved orgasm!

"I love you, Hayworth." Her voice was a husky whisper.

When he didn't respond, she bit lightly on his earlobe and rasped, "Hey! When a naked lady … one you've just finished screwing … says she loves you, that usually calls for some kind of brilliant reply. Like, maybe, 'Oh? Yeah?'."

Still, he didn't move!

"Hayworth?" Then, a little louder. "Hayworth? Parks? Parks? Oh, my God!"

His eyes were half-opened! His breathing was exceptionally labored!

"Parks! Parks! Honey … are you all right? Parks? Parks? Parks … speak to me. Say something, Sweetheart!"

She rolled him off of her! Lying on his back, Parks' body seemed to be taking on an eerie, almost-clammy, feeling! His temperature seemed to be plummeting!

Terrified, Trudy leaped from the bed, bolted down the hall to the stairs and – taking the steps two-at-a-time – raced to the small desk, at the foot of the staircase her husband so loved!

Snatching up the phone, she dialed the operator! When the woman came on the line, Trudy screamed that she needed an ambulance – then, blurted the address into the instrument!

Slamming the receiver into its cradle, she dashed back upstairs and – still nude – raced to her stricken spouse!

He hadn't moved! Well, he was beginning to writhe – ever so slightly. He remained, though, in a limp-eyed stupor!

"You ... you're going to be all right, Darling!" Her voice seemed octaves higher than normal. "You're going to be fine! They're ... they're sending an ambulance! It's on its way! Oh, Parks! Parks ... I love you! Dear God ... please! Please, dear God! Please! Please let him be all right! Please don't let anything be bad-wrong! Please! Please ... let him be all right! Please, please, please!" Then, she screamed, "Please!"

She sprinted down the hall to the bathroom – and returned with a wash cloth!

After cleaning him up, she snared his bathrobe from the closet – and attempted to put it on him! It was impossible! His limp weight was simply too much for her to lift! To cope with! Even his arms weighed a ton! She simply couldn't negotiate them into the arms of the white terrycloth garment.

The panic-filled silence was shattered by the wail of a siren – as the ambulance careened onto Grandmont, roaring up the block from West Chicago!

Trudy hastily threw the robe over Parks' body! The attendants would just simply have to understand!

It wasn't until she heard the ambulance screech to a halt in front – that she'd become aware of her own nakedness! Grabbing her white terrycloth robe, she flung it on – as she raced down the hall! She finished tying the sash – as she reached the bottom of the stairs!

The two white-coated attendants burst through the doorway and followed Trudy – as she frantically barreled back up the stairs!

Despite having to wrestle with the cumbersome stretcher, the two men managed to keep up! True professionals.

Taking one look at Parks – who was beginning to double up, beneath his robe – one of the attendants shook his head slowly, sadly, and muttered, "It don't look good, Missus."!

Frenzied, Trudy screamed: "Well, get him to the hospital ... damn you! Get him to the hospital!"

The two men, matter-of-factly, placed Parks on the stretcher – causing his robe to fall to the floor! Trudy re-covered him – once the attendants picked the stretcher up!

The men carried their patient down the stairs!

Their passenger's position was very precarious – especially when they reached the landing! Tilting their patient around the corner had caused the robe to fall once more!

The situation further traumatized Trudy!

She waited till they were ready to burst out the front door – before covering her husband, once more!

It was a long, tortuous trip for the bathrobe-clad Trudy – to *New Grace Hospital*!

TWENTY

For four days, Parks Hayworth hung between life and death!

At one point, he was actually "clinically dead" – as medical authorities would define the condition in the seventies.

However, as became obvious, "clinical death" can sometimes be far removed from the real thing. It was entirely possible that the team of doctors – working so feverishly over the stricken Parks – did not <u>know</u> that their patient was "clinically dead". Lacking, as they were, the "sophistication" of the late 20th century. So they went right on with the task at hand – trying to save the victim's life!

When Parks' heart had, in fact, stopped, the medical team had – immediately – applied a massage technique – and restarted the vital muscle!

What was ultimately diagnosed as a heart attack would keep our hero in a coma – until the fifth day! It was then that he began to stir!

It was a shocking revelation, for him, to realize that he was still alive. He had been certain – as he'd lain, writhing about on his and Trudy's bed – that he was on the verge of death! That the Grim Reaper had actually come for him!

His wife – haggard and drawn from the strain of the crisis (and from her five-day vigil) – was half-seated, in a straight-back chair and half-slumped over Parks' knees.

During those critical five days, she had never left his side. Her mother, of course, had jumped in, immediately, to take charge of Charlie – and was bringing her daughter periodic changes of clothes.

That had been especially vital at first – since Trudy had been clad in only her bathrobe.

The nursing staff – obviously moved by Trudy's unwavering devotion – made certain that she had more than enough food, fruit juices and coffee. The staff was, by then, headed by Elizabeth – the lady who'd informed Parks of Helen's and Jeff's deaths.

When she felt her husband's legs move – ever-so-slightly – beneath her breasts, Trudy's doe-like eyes snapped open! Tears began to trickle down her cheeks – as she beheld the patient, who had blinked once or twice. The spasmodic opening and closing of his eyes appeared almost to emit a sound – a veritable thunderclap – which seemed to fill the room!

He was attempting to focus those eyes! His breathing was even – although it became a good deal more rapid, once he was able to determine the identity of the person in the blur! Slowly – with excruciating sluggishness – his vision began to clear. The figure of his wife began to take shape – as the heavy shroud of mistiness fell slowly away!

He tried to smile! He didn't quite make it!

He attempted to lift his arm toward her. He didn't quite make that either!

His leg movement had been a reflex action – as consciousness had begun to return. Outside of that one stirring, our hero seemed unable to move anything!

He wondered if he was paralyzed!

It was, of course, a panic situation! Yet, the fright seemed to envelop him – in slow motion! A film clip, of what total paralysis would mean to him, to his wife, and to his son, began to flicker through the movie projector of his mind – at about one-quarter speed! The entire situation seemed totally out of sync!

Most of the torment centered around his inability to demonstrate any emotion toward his spouse! Any emotion toward anything! Obviously, it mattered not to Trudy. She was standing, bent over – the top of her body pressing down over the top of his own.

She was kissing him – all over his face! Kissing every inch of his face – which was becoming moist with her tears! He was heartened by the fact that he could, at least, feel the kisses – and the wetness!

He wondered – again, in slow motion – if he was losing his mind! His wife – his beautiful wife – was all over him! Planting kiss upon kiss – upon the entire surface of his face! She was paying, it seemed, special attention to the tip of his nose!

And there he was: All wrapped up in the sensation of wetness!

The "film" began to increase in speed! What if he was completely paralyzed?

The image of his father – half-paralyzed, after his stroke – flashed onto the screen! Had he, Parks Hayworth, suffered a stroke? A stroke even more debilitating than the one which had so horribly incapacitated Bernard Sidorwitz? The old man had never recovered! Not really! He'd never been able to use his right arm again – and had lost his right leg, from the knee down. Dear Lord!

A bitter pill! A horrible thought! He would've shuddered, he was certain, had he been able!

The therapy techniques of the seventies – where Pop had been – were certain to have been far more advanced than those in the fifties – where Parks was!

Was this it? Was he to become the next thing to a vegetable?

His father had been able to speak – after a fashion. The words, though, had come through – completely garbled! No one could understand what Pop was saying!

Obviously, though, it was all making sense to the old man, as he was saying it!

Bernard had been able, however, to understand what people said to him. He seemed to have been alert enough. He appeared to be "in" to baseball, football and hockey games on television. He was just unable to speak – except for the jabberwockey.

Was that to be Parks' fate?

At first flush, it appeared to him that he would be unable to use even half his body! Nothing seemed to move! Not one part of his frame reacted to his commands!

The "film clip" was racing madly at that point! His thought processes – thankfully – seemed not to be retarded! That was encouraging! On the other hand, his father had probably thought the same thing – and had wound up talking in jabberwocky!

As if having been struck by a bolt of lightning, it suddenly occurred to him that he was actually utilizing part of his body. He'd begun to pat Trudy on her shoulder. He'd been occupied in that little endeavor – for the better part of a minute. Maybe even longer – it was hard to tell! Hard to fashion any conception of time.

The movement, though, was very, very encouraging!

It was – let's see now – his right hand! He ordered the patting stopped! The hand obeyed! Thank God! He bade it resume! The patting began once more! Remarkable!

Now, his left hand: He ordered it to pat her on her bottom! Trudy was leaning over the bed from that side. Miraculously, that hand obeyed!

It was, however, an ordeal! He managed two passes at his wife's derriere! Then, the arm dropped over the side of the bed – weighing, he was certain, about 400 pounds!

Now to smile! Was he ready for the big time?

He could feel his chapped lips crack! Even that felt good! So welcomed!

He was certain that he'd managed a smile – probably from ear-to-ear! It was, in actuality, little more than a fleeting – albeit heart-felt – smirk. It had lasted, maybe, a half-second!

Trudy had completely missed it!

She was continuing to rain wet kiss after wet kiss on his forehead – while massaging his temples lightly! Her husband was able to feel the coolness – the actual sensation of coolness – of her hands, as they worked their magic, upon his fevered flesh!

Sensations were coming slowly! But, they were coming! He was able to feel her body – her breasts, actually – as she pressed down against him.

"Oh, Parks! Parks, Parks, Parks, Parks!"

The voice was coming from far away. Maybe two flights up!

He wasn't certain whether she'd just begun to speak to him! Or had he been so caught up in his own plight – that, only then, had he begun to hear her fatigued voice?

"You ... got ... a ... great ... butt," he managed to rasp. The sound of his own voice seemed to fill his head – almost like an explosion! He wondered if Trudy had heard! He wondered if he'd been even halfway coherent! Please Lord! Please let it not be unfathomable jabberwockey – like that which had poured forth from his poor father.

"And," she sobbed, "you're a ... a fathead!"

He smiled again! For a full second or two! His wife caught that one!

Why was he so tired? So damnably tired?

The blackness of sleep – it was sleep, was it not? – began to envelop him!

Through the darkness, he was able to discern Trudy's voice. Once again, it was coming from someplace far away. *Venus*, maybe? It barely pierced the gloom.

"Rest Hayworth, Darling! The doctor says you'll need lots of rest. Go to sleep, Baby. I'll be here when you wake up! I promise! I promise you, my dearest Parks!"

Parks' sleep came in fits and starts – mostly fits. He had absolutely no conception of time. Had not the foggiest idea how many times he may have opened his eyes, kept them open for a few seconds – or, on a good day, maybe even a minute or two – then, drifted back into the nether world of darkness once more.

Eventually, he began to become aware of the fact that there were times when he would "come to" and find the room in semi-darkness – illuminated only by a small night light, on the wall to the left of his bed. Other times, the brilliance of the sunlight would drench the room – practically blinding him. From time to time, it appeared as though dusk had settled over the room.

Each time he opened his eyes, though, Trudy was there! Sometimes she was asleep. Sometimes, his beautiful wife was looking at him – looking lovingly at him – with that special warm glow that she'd seemed to have invented. One time, he believed he remembered seeing her sipping a cup of coffee or tea.

As the days went by, Parks spent more and more time awake. After three days of veering into and out of consciousness, he was able to remain awake for periods as long as 30 or 35 minutes. In addition, he was able to speak to his wife!

More importantly, she was able to understand him – an answer to a fervent, oft-repeated prayer! Seldom was he able to remember what they'd spoken about. And he was certain that he'd lapsed back into a deep sleep – while smack dab in the middle of a sentence. Had pooped out – on more than one occasion.

He was well into his second week, in the hospital, before he was able to remain awake for any significant period of time: An hour or so, at first – lengthening into five-, six-, seven-, and even eight-hour stretches, as the third week ended.

He was gratified to discover that, not only did he have full use of his mental faculties – but, full use of his body as well! He seemed good as new – except for the fact that he was exceptionally weak! He tired so easily – so quickly!

His heart had been permanently damaged.

It would be months – possibly years – before he'd be able to resume anything remotely resembling a normal life. They didn't refer to it as a "lifestyle" in 1952.

Trudy had never left the hospital. Seldom had she left the room. Her mother had continued to bring her changes of clothes – then, assume the vigil at Parks' side, while the younger woman took a shower and changed.

The nurses had continued to bring Trudy food and drink – most of which went unconsumed. She'd lost 17 pounds during the ordeal.

Charlie remained under his grandmother's care. Amanda had moved into the "Dream House" – a wise, strategic move, inasmuch as it was a block away from Charlie's school.

Once Parks had established himself on the way to recovery, Trudy began to, reluctantly, leave the hospital at night – usually around 10:00 PM. She would return – without fail – no later than 7:00 AM the following morning.

After our hero had spent a month-and-four-days in the hospital, he was able to walk to the window – and look out at the parking lot.

Amanda Chamberlain would bring Charlie – who, because of his age, was not allowed up to Parks' room. The boy would stand down on the slim stretch of lawn, between the parking lot and the sidewalk – and wave to his father! Parks was able to see – even from his third-floor window – the tears glistening in the afternoon sun, as they trickled down the youngster's face.

Finally, after the seventh week, Parks would be allowed to go home!

In 1952, patients were, of course, kept in the hospital for much longer periods of time. Look, Ma! No HMOs!

In addition, Trudy wound up contriving to keep her husband hospitalized three days longer than the doctor had deemed necessary.

Her purpose was two-pronged:
1. First of all, as she'd confided to her mother, she was afraid she'd be unable to keep her husband down. "Each day he stays there," she explained, "is one more day of undiluted recovery ... and one more day of added strength."
2. The second reason – the most significant one – amounted to facing the fact that Parks was forbidden to climb stairs. The prohibition would be in effect for months – maybe years.

In the "Dream House", the master bedroom – as well as Parks' office, and the only bathroom – were on the second floor. Up that staircase that the patient had always loved.

The doctor suggested having the house remodeled:

"You could turn the patio room into a bedroom," he'd theorized. "You might even think of turning the dining room into a bedroom. The kitchen is certainly big enough to accommodate a dining area. If you ripped out that one wall in the kitchen, you could install a bathroom right under the stairway. You could put a closet, right there in the dining room and ... "

Trudy had cut him short. "You don't know what that house means to him," she explained. "If I laid one glove on that place, it'd destroy him. No, I'll think of something."

She'd approached Loretta and Richard. Trudy offered to trade the use of the "Dream House" – for the little place on Rosemont for a year or two. The Hayworths would pay moving expenses, of course – both ways. Richard was willing! However, Loretta declined! Trudy – who was certain that she and Loretta had become fast friends – was furious! Worse, she felt betrayed!

To make matters worse, the tenants on Penrod were equally reluctant to swap – leaving Trudy at a dead end. They'd signed a year's lease – which had seven months to run.

Trudy's hands were tied. A similar offer to the Brogans would, of course, be futile. The house in which they lived was laid out virtually the same as the "Dream House". Only the living room didn't run front-to-rear. And no patio.

The only logical solution was to buy another house! An executive decision – a rather strange term, one that she'd heard her husband utter from time to time. She hoped that Parks would be proud of her business acumen: She would buy a one-story home – ideal for her spouse's convalescence.

She managed to keep Parks in the hospital – and "out of circulation" – until she was able to complete the hurried transaction, and to resolve the attendant details. Till she could "get all her ducks in a row", another rather odd expression her spouse had used occasionally.

In addition, she took it upon herself to lease the "Dream House" to, by all considerations, a responsible couple.

By the time Parks was "liberated" from the hospital, he claimed that he'd gone "stir crazy".

The magic day did come, though!

They wheeled him down to the "loading dock" – quoth Trudy – and assisted him into the car. Trudy then eased the Lincoln out onto Meyers Road, turned left – and headed toward West Chicago. When she finally reached that intersection, she made another left, toward Wyoming Street – rather than to the right – in the direction of Grandmont!

"Hey!" bellowed Parks. "What's the big idea?"

She patted him on the knee.

"Don't worry about a thing, My Little Chickadee," she responded. "You're in the very best of hands."

"Yeah," he agreed. "The hands have always been great. Fanny's not bad either. It's the head ... the ol' gourd ... that I'm worried about. They haven't changed the City of Detroit … while my back was turned … did they?"

She grinned.

"You'd be surprised," she answered. "Can't trust those little rascals. Not for one second. Actually, I've got a bit of a surprise for you, Hayworth."

"A surprise? What kind of surprise, Trood?"

"A house kind of surprise. You know the doc won't let you walk up and down the stairs. And there are more stairs in the house on Grandmont, than you can shake a stick at … if you're inclined to that sort of thing."

A look of utter dismay crossed Parks' face.

"You … you didn't sell it," he rasped. "You wouldn't have sold the … "

"Of course not," she replied, with a broad grin. "I rented it … leased it, actually. To a perfectly lovely couple. He's a lawyer. Has a practice downtown … in the *Majestic Building*. She's a schoolteacher. Teaches right up the street … at *Coolidge* … so, it's perfect for her. In fact, she knows Charlie a little bit. He knows her a lot. Told me that every kid in school does his best to stay away from her. Outside of being mean and cruel … and torturing little kids … though, she seems awfully nice. They've leased the house for a year. Got money up the you-know-where."

"My compliments to the financier," he responded. "But, what about us? Where do we wind up living? Did you kick Loretta and Richard out? You've always liked that house … loved that house … on Rosemont." He looked around. Looked ahead, looked back over both shoulders. "Naw," he continued. "Naw. You couldn't have. We're heading the wrong way. Did you, maybe, go ahead and rent us a house?"

"Actually, it's more like I bought us a house."

"Bought one?" His eyes lit up. "Really? That's wonderful, Goit! Where?"

"Shutta you mouth. I gone show ya."

She drove east on West Chicago, past Wyoming, past Oakman Boulevard – and across the railroad tracks, which ran along side the **Ditzler** and the **Exide** plants.

Parks glanced, nervously, over his left shoulder – then, over his right one.

"Where ... where is this house?" he asked – in what he'd hoped was a casual tone. He didn't quite bring it off.

"Shaddapa you face. You'll see it soon enough."

"How much did you ... did you pay for it?"

She shook her head – emphatically.

"Oh no you don't," she admonished. "You know what the good doctor said. You're not to get your head-bone involved in the ol' finances. Any of 'em. We're awash in black ink ... that's all you have to know. I've been able to handle things pretty well ... or I think I have, anyway. If I have a problem, I can always go to Mister Dubin ... or to Elliot. But, so far anyway, there haven't been any problems ... denks God. You, yourself, said that you thought I had a pretty good head for business."

His smile was not as robust as he'd intended.

"The rest of you ain't bad either," he observed. "Nice butt!" He took a deep breath and continued. "Wanna screw?"

She laughed out loud.

"No," she answered firmly. "And that's another thing. Doctor says that we're to be as chaste as little cherubs. For a while, anyway." Then, she muttered under her breath, "dammit".

"Aren't cherubs people who run around naked? Besides, maybe the good doctor doesn't know what the hell he's talking about."

"He knows. Remember what happened last time?"

"Yeah. But, what a way to go! Beats hell out of cancer!"

"Parks! Oh, Parks! Please, Honey! Please ... don't say things like that! Don't _ever_ say things like that! Please!" She turned to face him, for a second; her soft-brown eyes beginning to overflow. "Not even kidding," she admonished. "It's not funny."

"I'm sorry, Trood. I didn't mean anything."

"I know." She blinked back the tears. "But, I came so ... so ... so close to losing you! Please don't joke about it anymore. Okay?"

"Okay, oh mistress of mine."

"And don't go and talk sexy ... about mistresses and stuff. Ain't gonna do ya no good ... dammit."

"Aye aye, Ma'am."

Trudy slowed the car, as they reached the corner of Burnette and West Chicago – negotiating a right turn onto Burnette. Halfway down the block, she braked to a slow roll. Then, she eased the Lincoln up over the curb, across the sidewalk and onto the long front lawn! The big car coasted to a stop – under the huge maple tree, in front of the little house, situated at the back of the lot!

His grandparents' "Dog House"!

Parks looked at his wife. "I ... I don't understand."

"The lady ... the one I bought the house from ... she told me that her husband used to park his car up here ... and it didn't hurt anything. He'd done it for years, I guess. Nice old lady ... named Swenson, she was. A widow."

Parks' head began to spin. In his weakened condition, he was completely unprepared for such a surprise. He could visualize himself suffering another heart attack!

Already pale, he'd begun to turn completely white!

"Parks! Parks! What's the matter, Darling? Are you all right? Say something, Parks! For God's sakes ... say something! Anything!"

He swallowed hard. Slowly, he felt his equilibrium begin to return!

He nodded, slightly – still wan and shaken!

"Yeah," he was able to mutter. "I'm ... I'm all right. I'm ... fine."

He laid his head back against the top of the luxurious leather seat, behind him – and closed his eyes. Visions of his childhood – and his grandmother – flooded through his memory! Even the spill he'd taken – on his first day in 1939 – flashed onto and off of the monitor of his recollection!

He'd been aware of the fact that his grandmother had sold the "Dog House" – during the time that Jim Sidorwitz had been in the Navy. Obviously, the sale had been consummated in 1952. As Jim, he'd had absolutely no idea to whom it had been sold.

Even though Parks, as Jim, had come to despise the neighborhood, the "Dog House" had always held a sort of glowing mystique for him. He would drive past it – and never fail to feel a warm, satisfying, glow, as the wonderfully pleasant memories of his grandparents would wash over him.

He felt an uncontrollable shudder – at the thought of having spent the unhappiest years of his adolescence in the big "barn", just a block-and-a-half away. He'd had to dodge thugs like the despicable Art Sarnes. He'd had to learn to cope with his father's one, singular, all-purpose, reply to anything Jim would have the temerity to say: The ever-popular "Horseshit!"

"Hayworth? Hayworth? Are you all right, Parks? Are you upset with me? Did I do wrong? Did I botch the whole thing?"

A labored smile crossed his lips.

"No," he rasped. "No, ya done good, Kid. Ya done good. What made you … uh … why'd you buy this house … this particular house … though?"

She fought – unsuccessfully – to hide the hurt.

"You don't like it, do you?"

"I love it, Trood! I can't thank you enough! It's perfect! I just wondered how you happened to pick out this particular house."

"Well, it's got that ridiculously large front porch … for one thing. The lady threw in the two rockers and a glider … and, oh yes, a studio couch. With the porch screened in like it is, I figured that … on hot nights … we could sleep out there on the porch. Mrs. Swenson said that's what they used to do. Her husband and her. The place didn't have a tub or a shower. Can you believe that? So, I had a stall shower installed. Looks kinda funny … but, it's there."

Parks closed his eyes. In his wildest imaginings, he'd never thought he'd ever live in the "Dog House". Neighborhood to the side, it held so many pleasant memories.

"It's great, Goit," he responded. "I just don't know how you happened on to this house."

"Oh, Hayworth. Sure you do. You've driven by here … any number of times. I just sort of figured that you were intrigued with this house. And, God knows, I'm aware of how you are … when it comes to houses."

The last line sent a slight, inexplicable, shiver through him!

He reached over and began to rub her shoulder.

"Yeah," he allowed. "I guess you sure enough do."

"I tried, actually, to get Loretta and Richard to trade places with us. Loretta put the kibosh on it. I think you're right, Hayworth. I think she's a real flake. People on Penrod … they weren't too thrilled either. They didn't want to trade houses, dammit. So, I simply decided to just go ahead and buy us a house … one that I thought would be ideal for your recuperation, or whatever. I remembered this little house with the big porch … and how fascinated you always seemed to be with it. I made the lady an offer … a very generous one … and she accepted. Are you proud of me?"

He leaned over and kissed her.

"Of course I'm proud of you," he exclaimed. "I've always been proud of you. How could I not be? You've always been a source of pride and joy for me … and now you're abusing the privilege. I luff you."

"I wondered if I'd ever hear you say that again … just like that. You … you're really not upset with me? For buying this house? I sort of paid cash for it. It wasn't very expensive."

"No. Of course not. Of course I'm not upset with you. How could I be? I think it's neat. I certainly won't worry about you handling the finances. You're gonna make me look like a rank amateur."

"Not really. But, I try like hell."

"Scootch up," he said.

"What?"

"Scootch up. Lift your fanny up … up off the seat."

She looked at him in utter dismay – but, complied.

He reached under her – and patted her on her bottom.

"As you were," he barked – removing his hand. "I really do, y'know," he continued, as she sat back down.

"Really do? Really do what, Hayworth?"

"Really do luff you."

The couple settled in to the little "Dog House". Parks spent most of his time in his grandfather's high-backed wicker rocker – on the huge front porch. As previously mentioned, the porch ran the entire front of the place. Inasmuch as it was the only home on the block, which was situated at the back of the lot, there were few obstacles to block out the welcome breezes.

Once summer had descended upon them, the Hayworth's slept virtually every night on the front porch. Air conditioning was unheard of for a private dwelling – at least in "The Motor City" – in 1952.

Parks had reached a point where he seldom thought of the seventies – when virtually everything was air-conditioned. Trudy, of course, had never been exposed to the massive shopping centers, the sprawling apartment complexes, or the ever-constant "cold button" in virtually all the cars assembled from the mid-sixties on. She could hardly be expected to miss that which she'd never experienced.

After two days, Charlie moved in with his mother and father.

The first thing the boy did – upon seeing his father for the first time in almost two months – was to run up and kiss him! He almost knocked Parks off his feet!

The first thing Parks did was to apologize to the lad for not having taken him to the hockey playoffs.

Parks, of course, had bought the *Stanley Cup* playoffs tickets before he'd become incapacitated. It had fallen to Amanda Chamberlain to take the boy to the games. She'd never attended a hockey match in her life – before the spring of 1952.

At first, she'd considered taking her grandson to the games a chore. She was happy to oblige, naturally – but, it was a chore. That attitude lasted till the referee dropped the puck – for the opening face-off, in the very first game. From that point on, she was hooked! She became even more fanatical a fan than Charlie – no mean accomplishment.

In the four games played at *Olympia*, she'd become so involved that she could easily recognize – and identify – each and every Red Wing player; in addition to a surprising number of Maple Leafs and Canadiens athletes.

Parks – as a gesture of thanks – would buy Amanda and Charlie seasons tickets for the 1952-53 campaign. He really wanted to purchase four sets – so that he and Trudy could be included. However, the doctor vetoed the idea – after his wife had "snitched".

Once Charlie had returned to live with his parents, he inherited the one bedroom, in the three-room house. Trudy bought a hide-a-bed sofa for the living room – which, like the porch, sprawled across the entire front of the house. She and her husband would sleep there – when it was too inclement to "flop" on the front porch.

The remainder of 1952 was one of recuperation and convalescence for Parks.

Trudy was never more devoted to him than during that time. She drove Charlie out to *Calvin Coolidge School*, each day – until the semester ended, in late June.

In September, the youngster would be transferred to *Ruthruff Elementary* between Stoepel and Livernois, on West Chicago – the school his sister had, at one time, attended – three blocks from the "Dog House".

As fall rolled around – and Charlie began the semester at his new school – Parks and Trudy would walk the mile-or-so to Grand River and Joy Road, two or three times a week. Those sojourns – on foot – made the doctor extremely happy.

After a tour of "mild shopping", they usually took in a movie at *The Riviera* or *The Annex* or *The Rainbow*. The three theaters were within a block of each other. *The Rainbow*, was right across the street, actually, from the much larger – and more ornate – *Riviera*. Parks enjoyed the tiny theater because it featured old two-reelers from the late-twenties and early-thirties: Laurel & Hardy, Charlie Chase, Zazu Pitts, Thelma Todd & Patsy Kelly, The Taxicab Boys, et. al. The flicks were unbelievably hokey – but a hoot!

On occasion, the couple would walk up to Oakman and Grand River, to *The Beverly Theater* – across from the **White Tower**, of which Parks was so fond.

Although it was obvious that our hero had come a long way, he and his wife didn't walk everywhere. From time to time, they would drive out to **The Blue Ribbon** – the enchanted setting, where Parks had asked Trudy to marry him.

On especially nice days, they would drive out into the country – and stroll through *Kensington Park* or *Walled Lake Park*.

In late September, Clark Dubin sold **Dubin Rent-a-Car Corporation** to **Barth-Knowlton Corporation** – a giant conglomerate, although the term was seldom used in the fifties.

Dubin, himself, retained the wildly-prosperous **Ford** dealership – but, never fully inserted himself into the day-to-day operation.

Returning

Over the previous five or six years, he'd paid scant attention to what went on there, on a daily basis – except for a thorough reading of the weekly Profit & Loss Statement. Nothing on that sheet got past him. Ever!

The sale of the car rental operation left him free to devote himself, virtually full-time, to his hotel empire! Dubin had become enthralled with his hotel – across from *Midway Airport*, in Chicago. He'd bought the place as a last resort. It was the only way he'd have a shot at the traffic through what, in those days, was the world's busiest airport!

But, he'd gotten caught up in the business – and wound up buying three other large houses, in and around "The Windy City". Then, he built a brand spanking new one on the island of Bimini. He would add a dozen more, before the end of the decade.

Jim Sidorwitz had gone to work for **Dubin Rent-a-Car** in 1957. The company had been in the throes of a cash-flow crisis. It would continue till 1962. There had been broad speculation, among many analysts during the late-fifties, that **Barth-Knowlton** would "flush" its car rental subsidiary. However, Parks knew that the parent corporation would succeed in "toughing it out".

By the end of 1962, **Dubin** would be, once again, a thriving concern. Many observers had blamed the car rental division's money problems on the fact that its parent conglomerate had paid Clark Dubin "way too much" for the entity.

In 1952 – after the **Dubin** sale – Parks decided it would be best not to ride out the slump. The **Barth-Knowlton** stock would go way down, he knew, immediately after the purchase. It would continue a downward spiral for another year-or-two.

Then, in 1958 or 1959 (he couldn't remember the exact time period) **Barth-Knowlton** stock would <u>really</u> take a nosedive. If he were not alive at that time, Trudy might panic – or be persuaded to panic – and sell the stock. Sell it far too short.

He suggested to his wife that she contact their broker – and order him to sell! The broker complied – and the sale brought the Hayworths an immense profit – Clark Dubin's bountiful legacy. Clark Dubin's wonderful gift.

On the day before Christmas, 1952, Parks insisted upon an appointment with his doctor. The convalescent had rebounded well, he believed – and was feeling more sprightly every day. Much stronger than he'd have believed possible – even a month or two before.

He'd had a number of questions to put to the good doctor. He was reasonably happy in the "Dog House" – despite the fact that he was less than enchanted with the neighborhood. He was extremely anxious, of course, to return to his glorious "Dream House" – when the tenants' lease would expire in May. The doctor, tantalizingly noncommittal, advised him that it was entirely possible.

"We'll have to see," he finally decreed.

Happily, the most important question was answered in the affirmative!

On the way home, Parks prevailed upon his wife to stop at the **Cunningham's Drugs** store at Oakman and Grand River. She parked the Lincoln in the lot behind the store – and remained in the car, while Parks went inside and bought a Christmas card.

The selection was rather sparse, at that late date. However, he managed to spot a nondescript card – one which would serve his purpose. He was without a pen – and had to buy a cheap ballpoint. Seated at the soda fountain, he scribbled a short note under the verse, stuffed the card into the envelope, tucked the flap inside – and hurried back to the parking lot.

As he climbed back into the car, he handed the card to Trudy. She opened it and read it to herself – then, broke into hysterical laughter! The verse was eminently tender.

But underneath, Parks had scrawled two words: "Wanna screw?"

TWENTY ONE

With an enjoyable Christmas (heh heh) behind them, the Hayworth family launched a count-down: The couple to whom Trudy had leased the "Dream House" would be vacating the premises – in May, when their lease would expire.

Parks was hell bent upon securing the doctor's okay to move back at that time.

He'd set upon a program of therapy. He would, by God, be able to cope with the stairs on that magnificent staircase in that glorious place on Grandmont – come hell or high water! Even if it meant moving the hide-a-bed sofa to the "Dream House" – and using the patio room as a bedroom, he was going to return to the wondrous venue "where I was meant to be". He <u>would</u> return to the "Dream House."

Our boy would probably even go along with Trudy's prodding – to install a bathroom, immediately off the kitchen. Hopefully, it wouldn't be necessary. He really didn't want to do one single thing to "louse up" the "virginity" – the "sanctity" – of the place.

Part of being "antsy" – yearning to move back into his wondrous house – was attributable to Parks' trepidation about the neighborhood, in which the "Dog House" was located. It most certainly would not prove to be a better place in 1953, than it had been when Jim had lived/survived in the "haunted house", on Prairie – in 1947.

He'd never felt more "liberated", in his life, than when Dolly had succeeded in moving them from that "barn" to the small, one-bedroom, apartment in Highland Park.

He would be as anxious to leave the area in 1953 – as he'd been on pins-and-needles to flee the neighborhood in 1947.

Because of his uneasiness, Parks kept a wary eye on Charlie's comings and goings. He was certain that the neighborhood would've remained a spawning ground for young gangsters – such as Art Sarnes had been in the mid- and late-forties.

Our hero had no idea whether Sarnes still lived in the big yellow house over on American Street – two blocks away. He'd never driven down that block. Had given it a wide berth.

"Hopefully," Parks had muttered to himself, on more than one occasion, "the son of a bitch'll be dead! That'd be nice."

As a teenager, Jim had run afoul of both gangs which had operated in the neighborhood. He'd managed to avoid them, thankfully, in their normal, nightly, rounds of breaking-and-entering. As a result, he'd found himself to be virtually the only youth in the area – without a Juvenile Court record.

Truancy, yes. But, no breaking-and-entering – or any of the other dandy little enterprises in which the neighborhood cut-throats had indulged, on a daily/nightly basis.

Jim had been branded a "Goody Two-Shoes" – a sissy – by the hoods. On numerous occasions, he'd wound up flat on his back – "just on general principles". Twice, he'd been admonished that, "You're lucky to be walking … you chickenshit sissy". It was, of course, because of the neighborhood ruffians and his "horseshit" problems with his father – until his parents had separated – that the area had become a living hell for him.

Since moving in to the "Dog House", our hero had kept an uneasy eye peeled – for any of his old antagonists. He'd not seen one of them. He attributed that fact to the probability that most of the schmucks should already have outgrown the "gang scene".

Possibly, they were all in jail! Or dead – an even more-satisfying scenario.

On the other hand, the punks which would've taken the place of Sarnes and his cohorts were probably equally as ruthless. Over the years, it had become the character of the neighborhood.

In his frail condition, Parks knew that he'd not stand a chance against those young thugs. It was a frightening prospect: He would be hard-pressed to protect young Charlie – and/or Trudy – against bodily harm, in a physical skirmish.

His wife, of course, could not have known the extent of hoodlumism in the area – when she'd bought the little house from his grandmother. On the surface, the neighborhood seemed placid enough. Peaceful enough. However, Parks was certain that, on more than one occasion, Trudy had experienced a few second thoughts of her own.

As March became April, Parks was delighted to find himself feeling much, much stronger. Although the doctor had advised him that he would never "be as good as new", he was given "official clearance" to move back into his cherished "Dream House".

He'd begun driving once more. However, Trudy insisted that she accompany him on literally every trip – no matter how short or insignificant. That being the case, he was unable to indulge himself in his loner-style nostalgic excursions around the city. It was probably just as well. At that point, such trips were not a big priority. Young Jim Sidorwitz would still be in the Navy – another week or two from receiving his Honorable Discharge.

In mid-April, Jim would hitchhike from Norfolk to Brownsville, Texas – where Kathleen lived. He'd spend a little more than three weeks, "freeloading" with his bride-to-be and her parents – and, of course, propose marriage.

Kathleen would, of course, accept.

However, as mentioned before, she'd promised her parents that she would finish her high school education. She would not graduate till June, of 1954.

After those three "freeloading" weeks in Texas, Jim would hitchhike up to Detroit, get a job, buy a car – and prepare to return, in triumph, (in his glorious 1949 DeSoto) to Brownsville, in September, of 1954, and marry Kathleen. The couple would journey back up to Detroit – and "live happily ever after". *The Donna Reed Show*!

The spring of 1953 would hold no allure for Parks Hayworth – nostalgic trip-wise.

As April neared its middle, the Hayworth family encountered its first skirmish with the local hoodlum gentry. As fate would have it, Parks was not present:

Trudy and Charlie had driven up to **Stanley's Meat Market**, on West Chicago – next door to **Freddie's Bar** – when two young thugs, ambling past, began to make snide remarks about what they'd perceived to be the youth's image, as a "Mama's Boy". Not much different than what young Jim Sidorwitz had been forced to endure, during his fearful tenure on Prairie Street.

Charlie had just finished setting the two large bags of meat upon the front seat of the Lincoln – as his mother climbed behind the wheel.

"Hey!" nasaled one young hood – a six-footer, easily head-and-shoulders taller than Charlie. "Look … if it ain't little *Dennis The Fucking Menace* and his mommy."

The boy paid them no heed – and began to climb into the car, next to his mother.

The taller of the two pulled him back out!

"Listen, you little shit," he snarled. "When I talk to you … you fuckin' well stop an' you fuckin' well listen! You hear me, you little Asshole?" Turning to his smart alec companion, he sneered, "This kid ain't got no couth, Herb."

"Well," responded the other youth, "Suppose we teach him some couth."

The first hood shoved Charlie back into the side of the car! The boy bounced off the vehicle – and brought up as vicious an uppercut as he could muster! It landed flush on the chin of the tallest thug – sending him reeling backward!

The young creep was more surprised than hurt!

"You little motherfucker!" he screamed. "Get him, Herb!"

Before Charlie was able to jump into the car, Herb pulled him straight up!

"Here he is, Lou! Kick the shit out of him!"

Lou, approaching the boy, reared his massive fist back – aiming a potential hay-maker at the youngster!

However, unnoticed by the two young "toughs", Trudy had reached beneath the front seat – where she'd seen fit to hide a tire iron! Before Lou could land his devastating blow, Trudy had come up behind him! She smashed him in the head – with her steel weapon! The force of the vicious blow sent Lou sprawling to the cement! He bounced from the sidewalk into the rear wheel well of the Lincoln – then back down to the unyielding concrete of the curb!

Herb let go of Charlie! His hand snaked down into his pants pocket! In a flash, he'd produced a menacing, switchblade knife! The chilling sound of the blade snapping into view seemed to resound throughout the entire neighborhood!

The youth stalked toward Trudy, who was standing her ground – waving her tire iron as though it was a baseball bat! The weapon showed minute bits of Lou's scalp and hair – imbedded into the lug nut end!

Charlie sprang back toward Herb! He clasped his hands together – and brought his coupled hands down, with every ounce of strength he could muster!

He connected – full on – with the back of Herb's neck! The knife fell one way – and Herb staggered another.

As the thug fought to retain his footing, Trudy swung her weapon, once again, in a ruthless arc! The heavy instrument landed full-force on the back of Herb's head – rocketing him back downward, his face smashing into the pockmarked cement!

Both young hoods laid there – writhing in terrible agony! Two men burst out of the bar! One of them was Freddie – the owner! At the same time, Sophie, the buxom, corpulent, wife of Stanley – the butcher – huffed to Trudy's side!

"I called the police," wheezed the 250 pound-plus Sophie!

Trudy remained hovering over Herb – tire iron at the ready!

"Holy Christ," exclaimed Freddie. "I called the cops too! I ain't never seen nothin' like that! Never … in my whole life! And in broad daylight, yet!"

Trudy seemed oblivious to their presence! Trembling, she kept her eyes riveted on the writhing form of Herb! Charlie stood over the semiconscious Lou!

The second man from the tavern joined the boy!

In less than five minutes, two police cars roared up to the scene!

Once the police had arrived, Charlie began attending to his mother! Trudy, shivering uncontrollably, leaned backward – against the Lincoln – retaining her white-knuckled, death grip on the bloodied steel implement!

Sophie and Freddie were able to describe the entire sequence to the officers.

One of the policemen had radioed for an ambulance! It would be impossible to get a statement from Trudy – until the two thugs were removed!

As the ambulance was about to pull away, one of the four officers climbed inside with the still-writhing Herb and the as-yet-out-of-it Lou! His partner followed in their squad car!

Trudy, at length, was able to converse – albeit haltingly – with the two officers who'd remained. She was unable to furnish much more information than had been provided by Sophie and Freddie.

Once she'd finished, one of the officers pried the tire iron from her vise-like grip! He placed it on the floor of the passenger's side of the Lincoln.

"Here," he soothed – offering her his card, "Try and keep this card ... to where you can find it easily. I'm Officer Gelding. This is my partner ... Officer Cornelius. I've written the name of the headman at the Juvenile Division ... over at our Petosky Precinct. He's 'Hips' Kolloway. If any of these punks ... or any of their friends ... give you or your boy any problems ... any problems at all ... give me a call. Or call Officer Kolloway. Officer Kolloway has a special interest in this crowd. He'll be glad to do anything he can ... anything! Uh ... you're sure you're all right? Are you okay, Ma'am?"

Trudy nodded – shakily.

Officer Cornelius drove Trudy and Charlie the half-block to the "Dog House", in the Lincoln – while Officer Gelding followed in the patrol car.

Parks – visibly shaken at the recount of the brutal, ruthless attack – was unable to hide the chest-swelling pride he felt toward his wife and son.

"We're gonna have to really watch it," he warned, once the officers had departed.

Trudy and Charlie seemed to have gotten over the trauma – but, just barely!

"They're a bunch of cut-throat bastards," Parks continued. "Fortunately, we'll be moving back to Grandmont before long. But, while we're still here, we're going to have to be careful … awfully damn careful."

"You … you don't have to sell me on that," agreed Trudy, half her voice still among the missing.

"I don't want to frighten you guys," said her husband, "but, I'm going to buy a gun. I know how to use one … so don't worry about it. With that crowd, you can't afford to get caught short."

He looked at his wife – deep into her doe-like eyes. "I'm sure glad you didn't get caught short today," he muttered. "It's easy for the police to say that we should call 'em, if we've got a problem … and they mean it. They do the best they can … God bless 'em. All of 'em. But, you guys know and I know that you can't always get ahold of 'em quick enough! It's a physical impossibility for them to protect us … or anyone else … twenty-four hours a day, seven days a week. Can't be done."

"What kind of gun you gonna get, Dad?" asked Charlie, suddenly enthused.

"I dunno. Probably a .38 Police Special. I'm sure I can get one from Elliot. Well, through Elliot. I hope I'll never have to use the damn thing … but, I will, by God! Another thing: Charlie? I'm sorry, Kid. But, I'm gonna start driving you to and from school. Hate to do it … but it's for your own protection."

"And for your mother's peace of mind," added Trudy.

Within three hours, Elliot Voorhees had delivered a *Smith & Wesson* .38 revolver – and a box of fifty rounds of ammunition! Bullets – with hollowed-out tips!

Later in the evening, Officer Cornelius phoned with the names of the two young thugs: Herbert Sarnes and Louis Duncan.

Both with extensive records at Petosky Precinct's Juvenile Division.

Herbert Sarnes was the younger brother of ruthless Art Sarnes – Jim Sidorwitz's principle tormentor.

Apparently, Herb was following in his brother's fingerprints!

Two days later, while Parks and Trudy were sitting in the Lincoln – waiting to pick up Charlie, from school – they got their first taste of retribution.

Their car was parked – idling – in front of the firehouse, directly across West Chicago from the school building – sitting halfway between Stoepel Street and busy Livernois.

At 3:15 PM, the dismissal bell rang and – within five minutes – the entire school seemed to have emptied. However, Charlie was not among the horde of youngsters who had abandoned the building in such haste – and with such relish.

Trudy, in the passenger's seat, put her hands on her husband's right forearm.

"Oh, Parks! I don't see him! Dear Lord, Parks! Do you ... do you suppose that he could be ... ?"

At that moment, the boy sauntered out of the main door. He'd been detained – he would advise his parents later (much later) – by two sixth-graders who'd asked a seemingly unending series of questions about the confrontation he and his mother had endured with Herb and Lou.

The youngster turned left and headed for Stoepel – where he would cross West Chicago in front of the waiting Lincoln.

Said Lincoln had been filled with Trudy's "Whooosh!" It was a sigh of sheer relief! Parks, at the same time, uttered a silent prayer of thanks!

As Charlie stepped into the street, a light-green 1949 Plymouth roared to life! The automobile – barreling north on Stoepel – ran the stop sign at West Chicago and careened around the corner! The speeding machine was headed directly at Charlie!

Trudy saw the Plymouth before Parks – and screamed!

"Charlie!" shouted Parks! "Charlie! Look out!"

The youngster dove back up onto the curb – without a fraction-of-a-second to spare!

The Plymouth bounced off the curb – then sped along West Chicago, for a block!

Running the red light at Livernois, the driver whipped off a screeching right turn – onto Livernois, heading south!

Parks gunned the Lincoln – snapping off a squealing U-turn, in front of the school! Charlie was picking himself up – when his father hollered for the boy to jump into the car! The lad responded instantly! Quickly, he scrambled into the back seat of the still-rolling automobile – as his mother pushed open, and then slammed closed, the passenger's door!

Parks jammed his foot down on the gas pedal! Leaving a copious amount of rubber, he caused the Lincoln to effect an almost-two-wheeled right turn onto Livernois!

By the time the Lincoln passed Westfield – one block south – Parks was doing 75 miles-per-hour!

Trudy – one hand braced against the dashboard and the other on the door, in those pre-seatbelt days – was able to ask, "Do you see the car, Parks?"

He nodded.

"Green four-door! In the center lane, up there," he muttered.

As the Hayworths sped through the second intersection – Dover Street – Parks had pushed his car up to 87 or 88 mph! It was one block to the busy intersection of Livernois and Joy Road! At that point, Parks was no more than 350 feet behind the fleeing Plymouth – which was in the process of zooming through the green light! Parks made it on the yellow-almost-red!

Our hero, at that point, had a definite advantage: The next traffic light was at Tireman Road – almost a mile away. In a straight-away chase, the newer Lincoln would prove a much more powerful machine – than the older, much smaller, Plymouth.

Three blocks south of Joy Road – about halfway to Tireman – Livernois curves slightly to the left. By the time the Plymouth began to make the swing, the Lincoln was right behind it! Both cars were barreling along in excess of 95 miles-per-hour – as Tireman loomed ever nearer!

The Plymouth was cutting in and out of traffic – in a desperate, frantic, attempt to shake Parks' tenacious pursuit!

As the Plymouth veered sharply to the right – speeding along the rows of parked cars – Parks saw his chance!

Tires squealing in protest, he swerved the Lincoln sharply to the left – into the on-coming, center-most, lane of traffic! Then, quickly, he roared the powerful automobile back onto his own side of the street – cutting off two other cars!

He barreled up along side the Plymouth! It was at that moment that he discovered who was behind the wheel of the renegade car! It was Art Sarnes! His old tormentor! Parks would know him anywhere! Even though Sarnes was locked in a life-or-death situation, he still wore that ever-present sneer that Jim Sidorwitz had come to know – and hate!

Something inside Parks snapped!

Pulling six- or eight-feet ahead of Sarnes' car, he swerved the Lincoln to the right – invading the path of the speeding Plymouth!

Trudy screamed! Charlie froze!

Art Sarnes tried – frantically – to avoid the Lincoln! He succeeded!

In so doing, he lost control of his own vehicle – sending the Plymouth crashing into the rear of a parked car! The huge, immobile, Packard was not barricade enough to halt the hell-for-leather momentum of the lurching, out-of-control, Plymouth!

Ricocheting off the Packard, Sarnes' car flipped onto its roof – collapsing the top of the unit! The metal slammed down upon the front seat – as both sides of the two-piece windshield popped free, and all four doors blew open!

The automobile skidded across the sidewalk – and plastered into the front of a brand new, glass-brick, building! The Plymouth hit the structure with such force – that it exploded! On impact! If the crash hadn't killed Sarnes, the raging inferno that, instantly, consumed his car would have done the trick!

Parks fought the Lincoln to a screeching halt – narrowly missing another parked car! Once he'd brought his vehicle to a stop, he semi-collapsed! His throbbing head rested on his arms! His hands still clung – with a vise grip – to the top of the steering wheel. He was oblivious of the tumultuous scene taking place – mere feet from his car!

Said scene was sheer pandemonium! Dozens of people were running, shouting, screaming! In the background, the sound of police and fire engine sirens, filled the afternoon air!

Trudy – shocked at her husband's seeming-collapse, at the wheel – expected the worst! Had Parks' heart finally given out? Was he alive?

"Parks! Parks! My darling Parks!"

She managed to pull him away from the wheel and lay him back against the seat.

Only then, was she able to establish that he was breathing!

"Mom!" screamed Charlie, from the back seat. "Is he all right? Oh, God! Dad!"

Parks managed a smile. A faint smile. He labored to raise a hand. Then, he spoke: "Yeah." His voice was barely audible. "I'm okay. I'm fine. Don't worry. Just not used to … to this … this sort of thing." Then, his smile broadened. "I got the son of a bitch!" He said it – more to himself than anyone else. A satisfied – and satisfying – smile crossed his lips. "I got the son of a bitch!"

Trudy, completely oblivious of the crush of people gathering around the car, buried her head in Parks' chest – and began to cry softly.

In a matter of minutes, fire trucks, ambulances and police cars swarmed all over the scene.

Trudy gave the first patrolman to approach the Lincoln the card that Officer Gelding had given her. She did her best to explain what had happened – beginning with the confrontation with Herbert Sarnes and Louis Duncan.

Then, engaged in a monumental effort to remain calm, she asked if they could get her husband to the hospital.

"I don't need to go to no damn hospital," protested Parks. "I'm all right! I'm fine! Honest! Nothing wrong! Nothing at all! Just a little winded … that's all."

The police, once they'd established that there was no medical emergency, asked that the Hayworths accompany them to the Petoskey Precinct station. One of the officers drove the Lincoln. Parks moved over into the passenger's seat. Trudy had climbed into the back with Charlie.

"It's nice of you to drive, Officer" commented Trudy.

"My pleasure, Ma'am. Not ever' day I get to drive a Lincoln."

It was not until they'd arrived at the police station that Parks was able to determine that there had been absolutely no damage done to his car. He'd not actually rammed the Plymouth. Close, though. Once again, he uttered a silent prayer of thanks.

It was entirely possible, he thought, that Mister Horne and "the boys" might have been looking out for him. Who knew, though?

Inside the station, the reports were filled out, signed and filed.

Trudy insisted upon knowing whether anyone – other than Sarnes – had been seriously hurt in the fiery crash. The Plymouth had sent thousands of shards of glass brick – flying in every direction inside the building. The machines – the ones in the front part of the metal-casing-heat-treatment plant – had already been shut down for the day.

No injuries!

It was almost 7:00 PM when the Hayworth family walked out of the precinct house. Parks was obviously exhausted.

Trudy slid behind the wheel. She negotiated the Lincoln the short way to Joy Road and turned right. However, when she reached Grand River, she wheeled the car to the left – toward downtown. She was heading in the opposite direction from the "Dog House".

Her husband had begun to doze. When he felt the car make the "wrong turn", his eyes snapped open. He'd "caught that act" before – on his way home from the hospital.

"Where ya headed, Goit?"

"Policeman's orders," she replied. "We're going to spend the night in a hotel."

"Wuffo we gonna do a thing like that?"

"You remember that big, heavy-set, policeman I was talking to … while you were filling out the report, or whatever it was?"

"Yeah?"

"Well, that was Officer Kolloway. He's head of Juvenile at Petosky. Officer Gelding … one of the cops who came when Charlie and I had the problem with those kids … "

"Kids," sneered Parks. "Hah! Some goddam kids!"

"Well, when we had that trouble," Trudy resumed, "Officer Gelding told me about Officer Kolloway. When Mister Kolloway found out who was involved in this thing, he came down to talk to us ... talk to me. You were tied up at the time. But, he told me that they'd been able to determine that the guy who tried to run Charlie down was the older brother ... older brother of one of those bastards who attacked Charlie and me. The one known as Herb. Uh ... you don't seem surprised at that, Hayworth."

"I'm not."

"You expected it?"

He sat straight up – and patted his wife on her knee.

"Yes and no," he replied. "I can't say that I was really expecting it ... but, it sure as hell doesn't surprise me. With a bunch like that, you never know what you're in for. Nothing they'd do would surprise me. Little shits."

"Well," she replied, with a deep sigh, "it caught me by surprise. Anyway, you remember what you said about them being sons of bitches?"

Parks nodded. "I meant it too."

"Well, it was an accurate description ... according to 'Hips'."

"'Hips'?"

Trudy laughed, and nodded. "Officer Kolloway's nickname. Anyway, he told me that there's yet another brother. Another Sarnes kid."

Parks closed his eyes. He hadn't remembered a third brother.

"Just a youngster," his wife continued. "Only about eleven or twelve. But, he's, I guess, just as vicious as the other ones are ... even at that tender age."

"Were."

"Beg pardon?"

"Not are," he emphasized. "Were. At least in one case. That pissant in the Plymouth is deader'n a freaking doornail. Past tense."

"Yeah, I know. That's why the police don't want us going back home tonight ... or even for the next few nights. That Lou punk has a couple of brothers too. I guess Lou's due out of the hospital tonight or tomorrow. Cops are gonna keep an eye on that ... and send him to the detention home. I guess Herb's going to be in the hospital for a few more days."

"Pity," snarled Parks, cryptically. "I was hoping it'd be nothing trivial."

Charlie broke in: "If you could've seen 'em, Dad, you'd know that they got banged up pretty good."

Parks smiled. "Couldn't happen to a nice pair."

"If you guys'll let a lady finish … " interjected Trudy, in mock anger.

"So finish," encouraged Parks – patting her, once again, on her knee.

"Well," she huffed, "that's better. Now, where was I? Oh, yeah. The officers think that this crowd is so bad … so damn rotten … that they'll probably try something. Something really bad. At the house. They don't think it's safe. Safe for us to be there. At least, not for awhile."

Parks sighed. "Well," he muttered, "we can't stay away forever."

"Oh, a few days won't hurt." Trudy tried to make her voice light and airy. "Besides, I gave 'em permission to enter the premises. Officer Kolloway said they'd probably have a policeman … and maybe a policewoman … out there. For a while, anyway."

"Sounds obscene," observed Parks with the most obscene leer in his arsenal.

"Oh poo! They figure that, if they stake out the house … I think they call it … they might catch the little darlings. Without us being in any danger."

"Sounds good to me, Trood."

So saying, he slouched back down into the seat once more.

"Take me where you will, Madam," he declared – overdramatically. "Do with me what you must. My entire body is herewith in your most capable hands. I ask but one thing: Be gentle."

"Now," asked his wife, "who's being obscene?'

For four days, the Hayworths lodged in adjoining rooms at the *Statler Hotel*, downtown. Trudy used the time for what Parks called "massive shopping expeditions". Charlie, for the most part, accompanied his mother on her jaunts. Parks remained in the room that he and Trudy shared – and slept a goodly portion of the time.

On the fourth day, Trudy insisted that her recalcitrant husband join her – on one of her celebrated shopping tours – and buy some clothes.

"I'm gonna chip those ratty ol' rags off you," she insisted. "And have the hotel burn 'em. If I have to look at you … in that outfit … for one more day, I'll go positively nuts."

He went quietly.

On the evening of the fourth day, Trudy phoned "Hips" Kolloway. The officer advised her that the police had occupied the "Dog House" since the evening of the encounter which had taken the life of Art Sarnes. So far, he reported, nothing had happened.

Kolloway still felt it would be unsafe for the Hayworths to return home. He asked that the police be allowed to remain in the house for a few more days. He told Trudy that he'd taken Sarnes' attempt upon Charlie's life personally. He had made it a sacred quest of his – to see that the entire crowd wound up doing time. "Lots of time."

"Kids tend to be a little impatient," he explained. "It's not like a bunch of adults … a ring or something. These are not professionals. Ones who know you'll have to come home eventually. Those folks … the pros … will just go ahead and outwait you. Not kids. Not these young S.O.B.'s. It's not often we have a really good chance to catch these little honeys … in the act of trying something rotten. If we're able to play this thing right, we can maybe send the whole kit-and-caboodle … the whole batch of 'em … right up the river! Maybe, never to be seen again. <u>Hopefully</u> never to be seen again. I've had a … a thing … a vendetta about these little you-know-whats! For a long time! So, I'd like to ask you … as a personal favor to me … like to ask you if we could occupy the house for a little bit longer. It would <u>really</u> give me a feeling of satisfaction to send these little … you should excuse the expression … these little turds up the river. Like forever."

"That'd be nice," answered Trudy.

Then, turning to Parks, she related, "Officer Kolloway wants to continue having officers out at the house. Indefinitely. Whatcha think, Hayworth?"

Parks took the phone.

"Officer Kolloway?" he began. "Listen. I'll go you one better. We're climbing the walls down here. I've been thinking. This might be a good time for us to take a nice long trip. I can't let my son go back to school, anyway. Not right now, in any case."

Charlie let out a whoop and jumped onto – then back off of – the bed!

Trudy hugged onto her husband.

"Oh, Hayworth! Will it be all right? Will you be all right? I don't know if … "

He patted her on the bottom.

"Yeah," he answered. "I'm fine. I'll probably have to press you into service as chauffeur … from time to time … but, I'm game if you are."

Kolloway, still on the other end of the line, waited till the happy scene played out – before asking, "What do you mean you'll go us one better, Mister Hayworth?"

"Well, if we're going on a trip, I don't feel like I ought to take the Lincoln. It's like me … getting a little tired. Tomorrow, I'll buy another car. Neither of us … Mrs. Hayworth nor I … are all that picky. So, we should be able to blunder onto something we can drive. Take immediate delivery. I think that … if someone parked the Lincoln in front of the house … that may shake some of the snakes out of the grass. I usually park it up on the front lawn, y'know. Up under the maple tree. That'd be the place to leave it."

"Great! That sounds swell, Mister Hayworth. I like that. I can probably send someone down to pick up the car tonight."

"Well, it's getting late. Besides, I'll need the Lincoln to get out and about tomorrow. Till I can get another car. Tell you what: I'll drive the Lincoln out to the precinct … sometime tomorrow afternoon. Early evening, maybe. Mrs. Hayworth can follow me out … in whatever means of conveyance I manage to beg, borrow or steal. Then, we'll be out of your hair … gone for maybe a couple or three weeks. A month, maybe. I really don't have the foggiest idea where we'll wind up going … but, I'm sure we'll think of something. So, the house … and the car … are yours for the duration. For how-ever-long you'll need 'em."

"That's great, Sir. I'd have to think that it won't be long before those little gems make some kind of move. Especially with your car out in front. Those arrangements are ideal. I'm sure the captain'll be glad to have the car there ... to lend some authenticity. I'll let you go. I know you have things to discuss with Mrs. Hayworth and the boy. He's a fine boy, Mister Hayworth. Fine boy. We'll see you tomorrow, then."

Parks couldn't decide the kind of car he wanted to buy. He loved his Lincoln. But, the 1953 model looked almost exactly like his '52. He wanted something a little different.

He finally settled on a Cadillac Coupe deVille.

The following morning, the Hayworths tooled the Lincoln out to the **Griffith Oldsmobile/Cadillac** dealership, at Grand River and Prairie. The dealership had a number of pretty, brand spanking new, Cadillacs from which to choose. Trudy's gaze fell on a beautiful powder-blue model. A Coupe D'Ville – with a dark-blue roof. Their new car!

Charlie was thrilled! "Wow! A Cadillac!"

His mother, on the other hand, seemed to become more and more apprehensive as the negotiations proceeded, inside the salesman's cubbyhole office. Claustrophobia?

Once they were out of the dealership – walking up to the confectionery, a block away, on Burnette and Grand River – Parks patted his wife on the derriere and asked, "What's the matter, Goit? Are you upset?"

The trio entered the confectionery – and seated themselves at the counter. They would have a cup of coffee or two – while waiting for **Griffith's** to finish servicing their new car.

"I don't know," Trudy answered, at length. "I guess that it's just that we ... we just wrote one helluva big check. I guess that it ... well ... it just threw me, just a little bitty. I mean ... to pay out that much money! All at one time! For just ... just a car! It's not like we were buying a house or something! I just couldn't ... "

"Aw," soothed Parks, "I think we got a really good deal on the Caddy. It was pretty much what we wanted. We were lucky, I think ... that they had such a gorgeous one. Had it right in stock. Had it available."

"It's not just the Cadillac, Hayworth. I guess I know that the check for the car was ... well, it was just the beginning. We're going to have to withdraw a lot of money out of the bank ... get some travelers checques, I guess ... if we're going to be gone as long as you say. I guess I'm just a little uneasy about spending all that money, is all."

"Well, you're the *Chancellor of the Exchecquer.* If you say we can't afford it, well then ... "

She patted his backside.

"We can afford it! We can afford it! I guess, just this once, I wanted to play *Ebenezer Scrooge*."

They dropped the Lincoln at the Petosky Precinct – and headed back downtown.

Once they'd returned to *The Statler*, Parks caught a nap – while his wife and son set out, once more, on a shopping foray; for luggage and a few last-minute items. The booty included numerous pairs of slacks, a half-dozen shirts and an assortment of socks and underwear for our hero.

At 6:00 PM, they checked out and headed out Michigan Avenue – with Trudy at the wheel. They spent the night in a quaint little tourist home in Ann Arbor – home of **The University of Michigan**. Once again, Parks realized how thankful he was for the absence of the big motel chains. The little inn had a unique charm. It was delightful.

After they'd eaten at a picturesque little tea room, down the street – and had seen Charlie safely ensconced in his room, next to theirs – Parks and Trudy showered together and dried each other with huge, soft, fluffy, powder-blue towels (not unlike the color of their new car, noted Trudy). Then, still unclothed, they climbed into the soft, luxurious, downy-mattressed, bed.

He was beginning to doze – as she snuggled up to him.

"Know what I like about you, Hayworth?" she asked – kissing him on the nose.

"Whazzat?"

"Everything. That's what I like about you. Just everything. This unexpected trip. The way you treat Charlie. The way you treat me. Everything."

"Trood?"

"Yes, Love?"

"Trudy ... I don't know how many years I have left."

"Oh poo! Stop that! You'll outlast me and probably Char ... Parks? Parks ... are you all right? You are ... aren't you? I mean ... if you feel this trip is too much ... why, we'll just turn around and go ... "

"Hey! No! I feel fine! Next thing I know, you'll have me back in that damn Swiss hospital again. It's just that I'm sixty-one-years-old. And that ain't young. I just want you to know that everything I do ... whatever pissy-assed little accomplishments I may have attained ... I owe to you. To you and Charlie. Whatever I might do to make you proud of me, I owe to you. To the both of you. I love you both very much. You've made me so very happy. I'm a little retarded, though. I should've thought of this trip a long time ago."

She laughed softly – tears gleaming in her soft-brown eyes.

"It would've been too much for you this past year," she rasped.

"Yeah ... maybe. But we still should've done something like this trip, longer ago than that."

"Poo! You've always taken us places. Lots of places. That trip to the East Coast ... that wasn't chopped liver, y'know. Mother'll never get over that one."

"This time, though, I haven't the slightest idea where the hell we're going. None whatever."

"Don't worry about it, Hayworth," she whispered, nestling her cheek into his shoulder – still fresh from the shower and brisk toweling. "You always think of something," she rasped – as she let her hand wander down the front of his body. "You'll think of something this time too."

George D. Schultz

TWENTYTWO

The trip would last almost two months. It would cover the Midwest, the far-west and the Southwest. When Parks decided to "do something", he really "did something".

The Hayworths spent a week in Chicago. It was May, of 1953 – and the baseball White Sox were still the "Go-Go Sox" – one of Parks' all-time favorite teams. With the likes of "Nellie" Fox, "Minnie" Minoso, Luis Aparicio, Jim Landis and Billy Pierce, the club brought a generous amount of excitement to the fans on the Windy City's South Side.

Parks and Charlie took in two games at *Comisky Park* – just before the Sox left town. Father did his best to describe the nature and character of the team to son. Mother joined "the boys" on their first jaunt to the venerable ballpark. One wonders if our hero would've been as thrilled with the new *Comisky Park* – as he was with the old one.

Equally as venerable, of course, was "Beautiful *Wrigley Field*" on the city's North Side. There, the Cubs cavorted during the day – never at night. No lights! "The Friendly Confines" had been the last holdout against night baseball – and Parks had been positive that the storied old ball yard would never be fitted for nighttime illumination.

How could he know that, in August of 1988, the fabled, storied, reeking-of-tradition, old ballpark would finally capitulate. Truly, the end of an era.

As soon as the White Sox had left town, the Cubs had returned from a long road trip. Parks and Charlie didn't miss a single day of "the grand old game".

The "Cubbies" were truly one of the "National Pastime's" most futile franchises.

The club's one bright spot – in a sea of ineptness – had been the 1945 *National League* pennant. They went on to lose the series to Jim's beloved Tigers.

Parks was, of course, unaware of the team's near-miss in 1984 – to say nothing of the manner in which the club would blow the *National League Championship* in 2003, when a fan intercepted a foul fly close to the stands, before the Cubs leftfielder could catch the ball. The following year, the team would have a playoff spot all but mathematically assured – with a week or two remaining in the season – only to go into a total nosedive. Would miss out altogether.

In the '45 *World Series* – the final year of the wartime ballplayer – one pundit had described that "Fall Classic" as one which, "I don't think either one of 'em can win".

Parks had intended to take in all seven games of the '45 Series. He had, of course, attended none.

Having enjoyed the Windy City, the trio drove north to Milwaukee – stopping on the way to look in on the sprawling *Great Lakes Naval Training Command*, where Jim Sidorwitz had gone through Boot Camp, in the fall of 1949. Located just south of Waukegan, Illinois, the massive base had stood for decades as a major naval training facility.

Jim had driven through the area in 1978 – and had been dismayed to find the base totally different from the place where he'd taken basic training. It had been simply one more thing, which had "bummed him out" – another contribution to his longing to return to the past. In 1953, with his wife and son, our hero was gratified to see that Camp Barry remained, on one side of the **Chicago & Northern** railroad tracks – along next to "Main Side". Across the tracks, sat the familiar Camps Dewey, Downes and Porter.

The immense installation was more-or-less as he'd remembered it. Ahhhhh!

Trudy – apparently caught up in Parks' preoccupation with the base – asked, "Hayworth? Were you ever in the service?" The question caught him completely off guard! He'd never anticipated it!

Frantically, his mind raced – trying desperately to fathom the mathematics: If he'd have been in the Navy, when would it have been? What years? How old would he have been? Would the Country have been at war?

Seeing his perplexed state, his wife soothed, "Never mind, Hayworth. I was just curious. I knew it was a big thing for you to see the base down in Norfolk. I just … "

"No," Parks interrupted – then, wished he'd not been so abrupt. "I always wished that I'd joined the Navy," he continued. "But, I just never did."

He'd managed to compute that – at age 63 – he'd have been 23, in 1913.

"I tried to volunteer for World War One," he went on, surprising himself that he was able to tell such off-the-wall fibs. Well, actually, tell lies – as far-fetched as what he'd just told his wife. "But, I was almost twenty-five at the time … and I don't believe they were interested. At least the Navy wasn't. The Infantry might've given me a shot … but, not the Navy. Things were a helluva lot different in those days. I did come to Chicago … took the train up here to *Great Lakes*."

He fervently hoped that there had been a **Chicago & Northern** train – which would've run between Chicago and Milwaukee during the first World War. If the line hadn't existed, he prayed that his wife would find no reason to research that fact.

"I … I haven't been here in all those many years," he continued. "It's amazing … the way it's changed."

His wife appeared to accept his explanation. Key word: Appeared. He wished he could be certain, though. For the remainder of the trip to Milwaukee, he would catch her – from time to time – looking at him, with a disturbing, unrelenting, intensity.

Our hero did his best to fill the miles between *Great Lakes* and Milwaukee with light banter. Mostly pertaining to the Boston Braves and their relocation – earlier in the year – to Milwaukee.

The team would, subsequently, abandon the Wisconsin city for greener pastures in Atlanta. However, in 1953 – the team's first year in Wisconsin – the club had the area wildly caught up with baseball fever.

The Hayworths spent three days in Milwaukee – taking in two Braves games – then, pushed on to the Twin Cities area; Minneapolis and St. Paul. Parks took care to drive through Winona, Minnesota – taking in the town where his mother had been born.

Once again, he found himself the target of Trudy's intense gazes. He knew that he'd spent too much time in – shown too much interest in – the small town. Especially, when it had taken him 15 or 20 minutes to find High Street – where his grandmother's sister and brother-in-law lived.

From the Twin Cities, the family set their course westward.

May 25th found them pulling into Salt Lake City, Utah. The city, surrounded by those majestic mountains, was the "squeaky-clean" place Parks had remembered. He had long maintained that, "The city looks as though they slosh the town out every night … with *Listerine*."

In 1970, when Jim and Kathleen had brought their children to Salt Lake City, *The Great Salt Lake* had been in danger of "drying up". The tour guide had explained to the Sidorwitzes, at that time, that the huge body of water was not spring-fed. He'd likened it to a gargantuan puddle of salt water – left over from the age when the Pacific Ocean had covered that part of the country. *The Bonneville Salt Flats*, of course, were another legacy of that period.

Since there had been little precipitation in the area over the years, the water in the gigantic lake had not been replenished. Year by year, the lake was growing smaller, due to evaporation. While the water would evaporate, the salt, of course, would not. That being the case, the water had become saltier and saltier, as time had passed. It had been impossible for Jim – in 1970 – to have pictured how greatly the massive body of water would have shrunk in the seventeen years, from 1953.

The guide had indicated that the lake – over the coming decades – would continue to grow smaller and smaller; and, he'd said, after another six or eight centuries, it was very possible that the lake would dry up altogether. "Another Salt Flat."

That, quite obviously, had been before the heavy rains of the eighties had inundated the area – and replenished the gargantuan lake.

Parks and Trudy, especially, enjoyed touring the huge Mormon complex.

In 1970, Jim and Kathleen had been unable to devote the time they would've liked to the complex. The children had grown restless. Especially the "Dirty Rats".

In this 1953 pilgrimage, Charlie – while not terribly enthralled – was interested enough in the various lecturers and displays, that he didn't hamper his parents.

It was from Salt Lake City that Parks phoned Elliot Voorhees for the first time.

The latter advised our hero that the tenants had vacated the house on Grandmont – and that he was having a new gas furnace installed, replacing the old coal-burner. In addition, the roof was being renovated – and a "john" being installed off the kitchen.

"Trudy got to you, hah?" laughed Parks. "I wasn't going to say anything."

"I haff my orders," Elliot replied, in his best Gestapo voice.

The Hayworth's finances, Elliot reassured him, were in great shape – a not-unexpected bulletin. But, one which would allow him to be better able to enjoy the long trip.

The only real fly in the ointment had been the gnawing residue of Trudy's questioning, outside *Great Lakes Naval Training Command* and her quizzical stares, during their time in Winona. Possibly, his imagination could be running away with him. His wife had given no hang-your-hat-on indication that anything was amiss. Was <u>he</u> "borrowing trouble"?

If his wife's conduct in Salt Lake City was any yardstick, Parks, most certainly, had been "borrowing trouble". (Why did Amanda Chamberlain's expression keep ricocheting through his brain?) Trudy seemed especially euphoric. Never before, she advised her husband, had she ever beheld such natural beauty. Nothing as stupendous – as those majestic, purple-hued mountains, which virtually surrounded the city..

"Maybe we could retire here, huh Hayworth?"

"Retire? Ya getting' old, Ma?"

"There's times, Pa, when I think I done caught up with ya. In fact, there's times, when I think I done passed ya by."

Parks winced. Thoughts of "Miss Honey" – "Mister John's" wife, who'd died after a long, apparently painful, illness – kept invading his thoughts!

They drove on to Las Vegas. While "Lost Wages, Nevada" was booming, even then, it was nothing – compared to the Las Vegas Jim and Kathleen had visited in 1970.

Of course, the 1970 city would be dwarfed by the mega-hotel/casinos, which would dominate the city's skyline as the millennium was coming to an end.

The town had never been child-oriented. Charlie, though, managed to content himself with basking in the hot desert sun – and spending so much time in the hotel's swimming pool – that Parks told the boy that he should be "growing gills".

"It was nice of you to let Charlie pick the hotel, Hayworth," Trudy observed. "He's in love with that long, winding, slide, into the pool."

"Well, he's not gonna have much to do, but eat and swim, while we're here. It's important that he has a neat pool to swim in. The kid's gonna look like a prune, though, before we blow town."

With the boy spending virtually all his time at the hotel, Parks and Trudy made the rounds of the casinos' floor shows, which included magnificent performances by such as Dean Martin and Jerry Lewis, Louie Prima and Keeley Smith, Vic Damone, Al Martino, Peggy Lee, Patti Page, and Dick Haymes. And, of course, they occupied themselves – from time to time – by throwing the occasional quarter into the odd slot machine. Mostly, though, it was the stage shows. Trudy had been especially dazzled by the Martin & Lewis gallop.

Then, they pressed on to California.

In Los Angeles, Parks learned, from Elliot Voorhees, that – two nights earlier – the police stakeout at the "Dog House" had borne fruit, if one could call it that!

The officers, he'd advised, had spent an inordinate amount of time at the little house. The operation was proving to be futile. Officer Kolloway was close to issuing the order to abandon the project. Fortunately – or, more probably, unfortunately – he'd held off. Held out. The cops had "hung in there". Kolloway had been able to withstand incredible pressure from the chief of police, himself. The chief had wanted him to pull out. Had "Hips" not been so unrelenting in his crusade to put that particular crowd "out of commission", he'd never have pushed the issue as he had, in this particular situation.

Four youths had broken in – bent on revenge for the injuries, sustained by Herb Sarnes and Lou Duncan – and, most especially, the death of Herb's older brother (and Jim Sidorwitz's old nemesis) Art Sarnes!

It had led to quite a battle!

Two of the interlopers had been Herb Sarnes – and his younger brother. <u>Both</u> had been slain! Lou Duncan had not been involved! Nor had any of his siblings!

One of the hoodlums had been a sixteen-year-old girl! She'd suffered a broken nose – and had lost two teeth – in the melee! The fourth thug – a seventeen-year-old male – had come out of the encounter uninjured! He and the tooth-challenged female were in custody.

Three officers had been stationed inside the tiny house – down from the four, originally assigned. One of the policemen, Officer Cornelius, had been shot twice – apparently by the Sarnes brothers! He was not expected to live! Dear Lord! The evidence indicated that the Sarnes brothers had used zip-guns – at close range – before the doomed officer had ever had a chance to react! Both bullets had lodged in Cornelius' head!

Another of the officers – a woman – had taken a severe slashing! Part of her right breast had been severed! She was the one who had shot Herb Sarnes dead! According to Elliot, she'd emptied her .38 into Herb – then reloaded and poured six more bullets into the young man's lifeless body!

The third officer – who'd come out of the battle unscathed – had killed the younger Sarnes, with one well-placed bullet! The lad was eleven-years-old!

"My God, Elliot," gasped Parks. "Eleven-years-old? Eleven-damn-years-old? I ... I can't believe it! I've never heard of anything like that."

"Yeah. Vicious bastards! All of 'em! The younger Sarnes boy ... Richard or Rickie, or something ... was even more of a cut-throat than his two older brothers. Hard to believe as that might be."

Parks sighed. "Yeah," he mumbled. "I guess they must've taught him well."

"You're right. They did teach him well. So well ... that they're all dead. All three of 'em ... deader than hell."

Once more Parks sighed. "Couldn't happen to a more deserving crew ... although I'd have to say that I'd hate to be their parents. Be those kids' parents ... and feel all the things that they must be feeling."

His thoughts rambled to his seven kids – in his "other life"! God! What would he do – if he'd have lost three of his sons? Any three of his kids? *Any* kid! Any *one* of them! Dear Lord! He shuddered – violently! He was glad his major domo couldn't see.

"Well," advised Voorhees, "I guess it's safe for you guys to come on home now. You weren't planning on living on Burnette anyway, were you? I mean, the house on Grandmont should be ready, by the time you'd ever get back ... even if you left today."

"Tell your nefarious wrecking crew to take their time on Grandmont, Elliot. I have a feeling that we won't be back for awhile. We're having a helluva time. Ol' Charlie's in orbit."

"Orbit? You sure know how to turn a phrase, Parks. Never heard that one before."

Our boy winced. In four years, the Russians would launch *Sputnik*! The phrase would become overused. Would become hackneyed. Not the case in 1953.

"I'll bet that kid thinks he died and went to heaven," Elliot continued. "He's missed out, you know, on a few weeks of school-housin'."

"Aaaaah. It won't hurt him. He's a smart little son-a-ma-gun."

Elliot laughed. "Takes after his mother."

"Of course. Look who she married."

"Ouch! Walked right into that one, didn't I? What do you want to do with the joint on Burnette?"

"Sell it," snarled Parks, again wincing – when he heard his grandparents' beloved "Dog House" referred to as a "joint". "Get what you can for it. Don't give it away. I've enjoyed living there. All except the final few days. But," he sighed deeply, "I guess I'll be just as glad to be rid of it."

"Where you guys headed?"

"I dunno. Probably we'll take a run at *The Grand Canyon*. None of us have ever been there. Something I've always wanted to see. Trudy too. I don't think Charlie's all that thrilled … but, you never can tell. We'll be out probably another month or so. Can we still afford it?"

"Yeah. You're doin' fine. By the bye, ol' Clark Dubin said to give you his regards … and to tell you that you're really a traitorous son of a bitch. For buying that Cadillac, don'tcha know."

Parks laughed. "You'd think I'd have softened him up with the Buick. Outside of nominating me for The Benedict Arnold Award, what else did the dear boy have to say?"

"Nothin' much. The **Barth-Knowlton** deal was finalized. Finally. Took all this time … to dot all the damn I's and to cross the stupid T's. And to get the final check to whoever was supposed to get it. I've never seen such a complicated set-up in my life. The little diddling around that I do is strictly minor-league … compared to the size and the out-and-out magnitude of that deal. Clark did say, though, that he was a little surprised … shook him up a little … that you'd dumped your stock."

"Well, it was just a hunch, Elliot. Let's just say that … without Clark's steady hand at the wheel … I didn't have as much faith as I probably ought to have."

"Some hunch. Have you seen what's happening to the stock?"

"Oh, I've kept my eye on it, a little."

"I'll bet you have. It's taken a hell of a dive! Do you think it'll go any lower?"

"I'd bet on it."

"Good. In that case, I won't buy any. I thought that it might've bottomed out. Thought maybe I'd pick up a few shares for a song."

Parks laughed. "I've heard you sing, Elliot. A song from you … ain't gonna get you nothin'."

The family spent three days at *The Grand Canyon*. The beauty and grandeur of the *Canyon* was even more overwhelming than either Parks or Trudy could've imagined.

Even Charlie got caught up in the splendor of the amazing "hole in the ground".

"Thanks, Dad," he'd said. "I wasn't 'specially looking forward to coming here. Sounded awfully educational to me. But, it's something that I'll never forget."

From the *Canyon*, the Hayworths headed east – with no particular destination in mind.

The second day out – as the Cadillac's radio picked up a rather strained signal from the Dallas/Forth Worth area – it occurred to Parks that, by June, of 1953, Jim Sidorwitz would have already hitchhiked from Norfolk to Brownsville. He would've asked Kathleen to marry him – and would've subsequently hitchhiked up to Detroit.

Parks memory was that he would've gotten home to "The Motor City", by then. Quite possibly even would've bought his beloved – his cherished – 1949 DeSoto. Certainly, he would've been doing his best to establish himself in preparation for the September, 1954, nuptials.

Parks decided to veer southward – and head toward Brownsville!

The best he could hope for, he knew – would be to catch a glimpse of Kathleen, as a teenager. Something deep inside him unleashed a yearning to see his former wife – as a radiant young woman – once more.

It would, at best, take the better part of three days to reach the southern tip of Texas. Perhaps longer. Probably longer. He really shouldn't make such a trip, a major portion of Parks' psyche warned. He was, after all, happily married to Trudy. In addition, his wife had become more and more questioning of some of his reasoning, of late.

Still, he did yearn to see Brownsville – and maybe young Kathleen – once more.

Brownsville! The city that everyone had called "The armpit of the universe" – or even worse. Hot, dusty, sweaty, poverty-stricken Brownsville.

He'd last seen the city, of course, in 1979 – during one of his many trips to see the "Dirty Rats". Brownsville, by the late-seventies – like most cities in The Lone Star State – had come a long way. Everything – well, practically everything – had been thoroughly modernized, depriving Kathleen's hometown of a certain charm.

But, was that not true of almost any city?

Part of the charm of the thirties and forties – to Parks' way of thinking – had been the absence of the look-alike fast-food franchises. Each one looked like every other of the outlets, of those huge corporations.

In the forties and early-fifties, there were no **K-Marts**, no **Holiday Inns** no **Cinema I, Cinema II, Cinema III**, etc. etc. etc. No standardized automobile dealership signs. No massive shopping malls.

In the seventies, all cities seemed to look alike. In 1953, each city seemed to have a personality all its own. In 1953, Brownsville, Texas, was unique! In spades!

Parks sighed. His memory was flooded – with such things as walks down the town's main drag, Elizabeth Street, during, the day, when Kathleen was still attending high school. There had been an Oldsmobile dealership, which had always parked its brand new cars heading the wrong way – Elizabeth Street being a one-way thoroughfare, at that point.

The **Sears** store, in downtown Brownsville, would still be fairly new – having been built in 1948. In 1953, it had been one of the few modern buildings in the entire city. By 1979, the gigantic retail chain would've closed the store – and moved their highly-sophisticated, and highly-expanded, operation to a brand new, ultra-modern, monster of a shopping mall on U.S. Highway 77.

In 1979, Kathleen would work at the **Montgomery Ward** store in another mall: *Amigoland*, close by the Mexican border. In 1953, that site was an unkempt, weed-laden field.

Parks glanced at Trudy out of the corner of his eye. It would be a long way, he reasoned, to travel – purely for nostalgia's sake. Especially when one has nobody with whom to share memories. On the other hand, if he didn't make the trip then – at his age – when <u>would</u> he?

He was fighting a million battles within.

Trudy began to rub the back of his neck – then, the tops of his shoulders. It broke – it shattered – his reverie.

"What're you hatching in that evil little brain of yours, Hayworth?" she asked. "I can smell the wood burning from here."

He laughed. "Who writes your material?"

"Some fathead. Can't think of his name. Quite a comer, too. Has a lot to offer. What was his name? Oh, yeah. Hayworth, it is. P. Hayworth. Ever hear of him?"

"Hmmmm. P. Hayworth. Could his first name be Parks? Who hasn't heard of him? Why, he's … "

"Don't let it go to your head, Hayworth. Hayworth? I can hear the cannons firing … up there inside-a yore haid. Why? What's the battle, oh husband-of-mine?"

"Oh, I don't know. I was just thinking ... "

"A bitter pill," she responded, with a laugh.

"Very funny. Ho ho! That's rich!" That had been a line that Jerry Lewis had used a couple of times during the performance, in Las Vegas. "Now," he continued, "before I was so rudely interrupted, I was gonna tell you that I was thinking about maybe taking you guys down to the Rio Grande Valley."

"What's down there?" asked his spouse.

"The Rio Grande."

"Thanks a lot. My turn to say, Ho ho! That's rich."

"Educational too. We could go on across to Mexico."

Charlie broke in: "What're you guys talking about?"

"I'm sure Dad'll let us know," responded his mother with a laugh, "if he ever figures it out."

"No," persisted Parks. "I haven't been down to the Valley in years and years. Kind of meant to go … when we drove down to Houston. But, it didn't work out. I used to have some good times in the Valley … when I lived in Houston."

Trudy grew serious. "Why did you travel so far ... to go to the Rio Grande Valley?"

"Do you know how far the Valley is from Houston?"

She nodded. "About three-hundred-and-fifty ... maybe three-hundred-and-seventy-five ... miles." Her answer, of course, surprised him.

"You knew that?" he responded. "How'd you know that?"

"I can read a map."

"I know you can. But, what I meant was how did it happen that you were gauging the distance from Houston to the Valley?"

"Why are you making such a big deal out of it? When we were in Houston, I thought it might be nice to go to Mexico. So, I clocked it on the map. Finally decided against asking you. Thought it was probably too far. Didn't want you to poop out on me."

"Ahhhhh. I'm unpoopable."

"It is to laugh," she answered with a smile. "If you don't know anything else, I'm sure you know that you are ... most assuredly ... certifiably poopable. But, we digress, oh exalted Hayworth. Wuffo you used to go to the Rio Grande Valley?"

"Oh, the company I was with would ... now and then ... rent a car that would turn up in Brownsville or Harlingen or somewhere down there."

"Must've been a good-sized company."

That was a warning! Her remark put our boy on the defensive once more. He thought back to when Trudy had advised him that Clark Dubin had, at one time, tried to check out his rent-a-car tie in Houston – and had been unsuccessful. Parks, of course, had assured his wife that the reason Dubin could not affirm the connection was that the company, for which he worked, was very small. Had, in fact, gone out of business.

"Not really that big," he replied, as casually as possible.

"That sounds odd," persisted Trudy. "I know that Mister Dubin didn't start renting cars ... renting 'em one-way ... till the company got to where it was quite large. Getting large, anyway."

"Oh. Well, you have to remember that it's kind of a whole different thing ... down in Texas. Much different than in the North. You really can't compare the two. All the cars down there, for one thing, wound up with a helluva lot more mileage on 'em ... because everything is all so spread out. Made the cars worth less ... on resale ... with all that mileage on the clock. Other side of the coin, though, was the car market. It was much better ... cars brought a much higher price ... than in Detroit. Otherwise, the rental business wouldn't have been worthwhile. As it was, a lot of companies didn't make it ... mine included."

She sighed deeply – and discovered that she'd been making patterns on his right shoulder, with her fingernails.

"Well," she responded, at length, "I always wondered why it was that Mister Dubin could never find the company you said you worked for down there. I thought sure that ... when we were in Houston ... that you'd have shown me where you used to work. Where you used to live. Now that I think about it, though, you never really showed me hardly anything in Houston at all. Where you lived, where you worked, where you hung out! Nothing. I thought that ... someone as nostalgic as you are ... I thought that you'd have shown me all your old haunts. All your stomping grounds. In fact, the more I think of it, the more ... the more ... the more ... "

"The more what?"

Her fingernails had ceased their exercise on his shoulder.

"Well," she began, "well ... the more I think about it, the more hard to fathom it is. You get all choked up, y'know, over the house on Grandmont ... where you've never lived before. And ... to a lesser degree ... the one on Penrod, where you've also never lived. Even our little house on Burnette. It's just awfully difficult to accept that you could've lived in Houston ... for all those many years, anyway ... and not wind up getting all dewy-eyed, over one single place. Not a one!"

Parks could feel the perspiration, exuding from his body – especially in his hands.

"Well," he muttered, "for openers, Miss Smarty Pants, I didn't live in a house in Houston. It was just a room ... a small room. A very small room."

"Like the one on Mansfield and Grand River?"

Parks had always admired the bulldog-like tenacity Trudy had so consistently displayed, through the years. But, he just wished that she'd back off – this one time.

He shook his head emphatically.

"No," he said. "More like that shabby hole I lived in ... after Helen died. It was a very depressing place. You've never seen me get dewy-eyed ... as you put it ... over that crappy hovel near the dealership, have you?"

"No. That's true enough. But, you were in mourning ... when you lived in that 'crappy hovel'. Were you also trying to escape from something in Houston? Is that why you were living in a depressing little room? Houston seemed ... to me, anyway ... like a bright and cheery little town.

Little town. He wished he could tell his wife and son that Houston would replace Detroit as the nation's fifth-largest city in the late-seventies. He sighed heavily.

"No," he murmured. "I've told you ... that I wasn't trying to escape. From anyone ... or anything. I just wasn't the wealthiest person in the world. Houston didn't have a great many apartments, in those days. Still doesn't ... as far as I know. Rooms were hard to find. A real seller's market. An apartment was out of the question. For the likes of me, anyway."

He closed his eyes, for a brief instant – visualizing the endless number of huge, sprawling, apartment complexes that would spring up in southwest Houston, in the sixties and seventies. Well, they'd pop up all over "The Bayou City" – but, most especially, it had always seemed, in the southwest quadrant.

"I wasn't trying to escape anything," he continued, "when I moved into that building on Grand River and Mansfield. That place wasn't all that posh. And it certainly wouldn't have meant all that much to me ... if I hadn't met Helen there."

Trudy slapped her hand off her forehead!

"And," she said, "Helen, most assuredly, wouldn't have put her husband through some kind of inquisition. Oh, Hayworth! I'm sorry! I didn't mean to be so ... so bitchy! It's just that ... just that sometimes I get so curious ... so damn curious ... that I ... that I just can't seem to ... "

He smiled slightly.

"You're not bitchy." His voice was barely audible.

"Yes, I am. I know I am. And the hell of it is … I can't seem to help myself. Well, I guess I can … most of the time. But, sometimes, I just go nuts trying to answer all the questions that keep ricocheting around in my alleged mind. I'm sorry … really sorry … Hayworth. I got off on a whole tangent there … and, really, I didn't mean to. If you want to go to the Rio Grande Valley … then, dammit, I'm all for it."

Parks felt as though he'd just survived a massive crisis! The passing of the cloud seemed, almost, to make him slightly lightheaded.

"I think," he observed, "you guys'll like Matamoros … which is right across the border from Brownsville. It's very interesting. It's not quite like going across into Canada … like we do in Detroit. We're talking about a whole different culture … with an entirely different language. A different race. Altogether different than we are."

Trudy had begun tracing patterns on her husband's shoulder once more.

"Do people in … uh … Brownsville just simply run across the border, into Mexico? Like we run across into Windsor?" she asked.

"Yes and no. When I lived in Texas, you couldn't get liquor by the drink in the state. As far as I know, it's still the same today. Well, in Mexico, they've got a whole district … set aside for bars. And it's a thriving district. And they've got a lot of pretty good restaurants. So, many people go across … and make an evening of it. The rate of exchange … dollars into pesos … is vastly different from exchanging United States dollars into Canadian dollars. I haven't the foggiest idea what the Mexican exchange is these days. Probably something like thirty-five or forty pesos to the American dollar. It's not like the few cents difference between our dollar and Canada's."

He was, of course, unaware that the value of the peso would plummet – right into the toilet – in the eighties. The Canadian dollar would also fall in value – vis-à-vis our currency – but nothing like the peso. In 1953, the United States/Canadian dollar exchange was only a few pennies. At one time, the exchange favored Canada.

"Like I said," he continued, "it's a whole 'nother thing. I believe you'll enjoy it."

"I'm sure we will," answered his wife. "I'm sorry now that I didn't ask you to go down there, when we were in Texas before."

"I'm sorry that you didn't too. I'm sorrier yet that I didn't think of it. Hey! I just thought of something else, guys! Tell ya what I'm gonna dew! I'm gonna take ya to San Antonio too. Maybe Dallas and Fort Worth. Austin. Hell, you've never been there, Goit. Not to any of them. That's another thing: I don't know why I didn't think of any of this. It'll be educational for the anthropoid in the back seat, too."

Sneaking a quick look at the boy, in the back seat, Parks laughed and said, "But, I'm sure you'll enjoy it anyway, Charlie."

While, in a way, Parks missed the burgeoning Interstate Highway System, the absence of the super highways allowed him and his family to visit more small towns and villages – and to observe the unique character of each.

Though it took almost two days to reach Dallas, Parks did his best to make stopping in the area – which would come to be known as "The Metroplex" – as interesting as possible, for his wife and son.

He took them past the *Cotton Bowl* stadium – and through **Southern Methodist University's** campus. The grounds seemed so serene – so scholarly. Who would ever guess that these placid, academic, surroundings would be abuzz with the football scandals in the eighties? Scandals which would reach into the governor's office? Scandals which would result in the *National Collegiate Athletic Association* decreeing the University suffer "the death penalty" for the school's football program?

"They say that the definition of an atheist," said Parks, as they drove away from the serenity of the scenic campus, "is someone who goes to see the **Southern Methodist/Notre Dame** game ... and doesn't cheer for either side."

Our hero was having a difficult time: Now that he'd brought his wife and son to the Dallas/Fort Worth area, what was there to show them? The area was just beginning to boom. But, you certainly couldn't tell it from a quick tour through either of the cities.

He showed them the vaunted Fort Worth Stock Yards – and that was about it!

Until he drove back to Dallas! Once in the downtown area, he pointed the Cadillac west – toward *Dealey Plaza,* at the western edge. He believed that it should be incumbent upon him to assure that Charlie and his wife see the *Texas Schoolbook Depository Building.* In little more than ten years, President John Fitzgerald Kennedy would be assassinated – by bullets, evidentially fired from the nondescript – sort of ugly – red building!

In the summer of 1953, very few people were aware that John Kennedy was alive. Would it be so soon – that virtually everybody on the planet would be aware of his death?

The following day, they drove down to Austin, picturesque Capital of The Lone Star State. Like Houston and Dallas, Austin was a mere speck of the city it would become in the seventies and eighties.

The skyline was still uncluttered. The dome of the *State Capitol Building* could be seen from virtually anyplace in town! It was especially beautiful at night. The same was true of the tall, slender **University of Texas** tower – located in the northwestern part of town. Beautifully illuminated at night, it shared the Austin night sky with the *Capitol.*

Parks took care to point out the tower to his wife and son. In 1965, a sniper would climb to the top of the tower and – spraying bullets in every direction – would wound dozens of people, as they filed into and out of the stores and restaurants on busy Guadalupe Street below.

From Austin, they motored west. Drove the short distance to Johnson City – ancestral home of Lyndon Baines Johnson. Effecting a purely educational posture, our hero pointed out the fact that they were in the place-of-birth of a fast-rising young senator – one who was finishing his freshman term. LBJ had been elected in 1948.

Then, on to the *LBJ Ranch*, on the Pedernales River. In 1953, the ranch was but a whisper of what it would become in the sixties

– when "Landslide Lyndon" would ascend to the presidency, upon the tragic death of President Kennedy!

"Why are you taking us all this far out of the way?" asked Trudy. "Just to show us where an ordinary senator comes from? Or lives? What's the big deal?"

"I don't mean to bore you," replied Parks. "Actually, he's really not just an ordinary senator. He's quite a guy. Only been in the senate for about five years … but, he's already made a name for himself. I really believe he's destined for great things. I figured that … as long as we're this close … we ought to take a look at some of these things. Besides, this is beautiful country. Gorgeous country. I thought that these hills out here would … well, I thought that they'd do something for you. At my age, I may not be able to bring you back. Someday, you might be glad that you came to these places and saw these things."

"That's what bothers me," Trudy answered. "Here I go again. I'm sorry, Parks. God … it seems like I'm always saying I'm sorry. But, at times like these, I get … well, I get the damndest feeling. Just the damndest feeling! Like you know something about this place … know something that nobody else knows. It's … it's spooky, is what it is. Just like the day before yesterday … in Dallas. You went out of your way to point out that big, ugly, red building. What was the name of it?"

"*The Texas Schoolbook Depository.*" Parks wished he hadn't been so quick to answer.

"Yes," responded his wife. "That one. What's so special about that one … that particular … building? That single building? What's so special about it? That's about the only building … the only anything, really … that you pointed out. That was the only thing … in the whole, entire, city. There were taller … more imposing … buildings. But that was the one … that was the one you called our attention to. Why is that, Parks? Why? Why that exact … that particular … building?"

She was calling him Parks – an ominous note!

Charlie interrupted: "Aw, c'mon Mom. Dad's only trying to teach his dumb son a few things. Go easy on him."

Our hero grinned – thankful for the boy's diversion.

"Yeah," he echoed. "Go easy on me. I'm old. I'm gonna die soon."

Trudy paled.

"Oh, Parks! Oh, Hayworth! Oh, Hayworth ... please don't say things like that! Don't even think 'em!"

"Then, leave him alone." It was Charlie, once more. The statement staggered Trudy. Rattled her – from head to toe.

Parks had never heard the boy speak to his mother that way. He reached around, into the back seat, and ran his hand through his son's blond hair – which always seemed to have a mind of its own.

"Thanks, Kid," he said with a smile. Then, to his wife, "Our little boy is growing up."

"Yes," agreed Trudy, with a nod. "Maybe his mother should grow up too. I'm sorry, Parks. I apologize. I apologize to you too, Charles."

She was still calling our hero by his first name. In addition, she never called her son "Charles" anymore. How imposing a red flag was that?

"Believe me," she went on, "I'm not looking a gift horse in the mouth ... although it must seem as though I am. It's ... it's just that I ... I get such an uneasy feeling. I wish I could describe it. That ... that ugly red building ... that was the only one you pointed out ... in the entire city of Dallas. And ... "

"Aw, Mom," injected Charlie. "He showed us *The Cotton Bowl* too. I thought it was great. I even enjoyed that college campus ... whatever it was. It was great."

Trudy sighed – then, smiled. "It was," she agreed, at length – her voice retaining a certain edginess. "It was," she sighed, closing her fawn eyes.

They opened again! They almost seemed to crackle! Almost as though lightning bolts were sparking within them! She seemed to be caught up in a raging inner conflict!

"Don't ask me why," she said, her voice sounding terribly fatigued, "but I've had the feeling that ... the damndest feeling that ... that the red schoolbook building ... or whatever they call it ... is going to be very important in the future. Sooner or later, it's gonna be significant. I can't explain why I feel that way ... but, I do. And now, I get this same feeling about this senator. I can't put my finger on it. Do you know what it reminds me of, Parks?"

"No," he answered, curtly. "What does it remind you of, Trudy?"

"You'll think this is stupid." Her manner lightened somewhat. "But, do you remember when you took … when we took … Charlie on our honeymoon? To New York? You just about moved heaven and earth … to see that he went with us. And you just about moved heaven and earth … to see that he got to see that one *World Series* game. The one that turned out to be the most famous game in history. One of 'em, anyway. I don't remember why, now. But, it was … "

Charlie broke in! "It was because Floyd Bevans had a no-hitter going until … until … who was it, Dad?"

"Cookie Lavagetto," furnished his father.

"Yeah. Cookie Lavagetto. He hit a double … I think … and broke it up! Broke up the no-hitter … and won the game for the Dodgers!"

Parks grinned – broadly. "Ya done good, Kid. I'm proud-a ya."

Trudy, though, remained in one of her more tenacious moods. "That's beside the point," she persisted. "I had the damndest feeling then … when you were so insistent that we go to that game. To that particular game. And you kept pointing out to us, exactly what the situation was."

"Aw, C'mon Trudy. Anyone who's ever seen a no-hitter, they know that it beats all of … "

"You led us," she persisted. "Led us so brilliantly … now that I look back on it … right up to the point where that Cookie guy got that hit. When he hit that ball, Charlie … as young as he was … knew exactly what had happened. I even almost did. But, Charlie actually did … he knew! He understood the full significance of it. And he was just a snot-nosed little kid."

"Ah-HAH!" Parks struggled, mightily, to appear casual. "But, a smart, snot-nosed little kid. There's a difference, ya know."

"So be it," she sighed heavily, once again. "All I know, is that … no matter what you say, or how you try to explain it … I had this uneasy feeling in my tummy then. And I've got it now. And it's disturbing as hell. I had it in Dallas! Especially in Dallas! I've had it many times ... and it's something I wish I could deal with a little better. That Saturday night, in Memphis ... that was another example. Or that place ... that big compound ... in Massachusetts. On Cape Cod. I don't know what causes it. I wish I did. All I know is that it's there, dammit. It's there ... and big as can be."

Parks attempted to mask the panic he was feeling inside. He was certain that he'd gone too far! Much too far! He probably would not be there to see it – but, in 10½ years, Trudy's words would take on mind-boggling importance.

He was certain that – should he persist in pointing out additional future sites of earth-shaking importance – Mr. Horne and "the boys" just might put him into another coma! Not unlike the one which preceded the deaths of Helen and Jeff!

<u>They're certainly capable, God knows, of laying me out</u>!

He could never afford a repeat of such a situation!

George D. Schultz

TWENTY THREE

The Cadillac was headed toward San Antonio – also a picturesque city, about which our hero knew a great deal. He'd been there a number of times – and had developed a particular fondness for "The Alamo City".

In 1977, when Alice – his "Veteran Fiancée" – had traveled down from Detroit to visit Jim, he had taken her on virtually the same tour. The biggest difference was the fact that Jim and Alice had begun their trip in Houston – and had ended up in Nueva Laredo, Mexico, across the border from Laredo, Texas.

When the Hayworths arrived in San Antonio, Parks subjected his wife and son to a rather drawn-out "Cooks Tour". He'd apparently been successful in masking his surprise at the smallness – of what would become, in the seventies, the nation's 10th largest city.

They toured *The Alamo*. Charlie liked it – but, Trudy seemed unimpressed.

"What's the matter, Goit?" Parks inquired.

"I … I don't know. It … it just seems so small. I thought that it'd be about the size of the *Olympia* or something." She was referring, of course, to the sports arena, where the NHL's Detroit Red Wings played. It would be another four years before Fred Zollner would move his NBA franchise – the Fort Wayne Pistons – to Detroit, to become co-tenants with hockey's Wings.

The Hayworths sauntered along the beautiful, charmingly-unspoiled, *River Walk*, which wound its way through downtown San

Antonio. The Indians had referred to it as "The drunken old man walking home" – because of the river's meandering route.

Parks would never have been able to visualize the vast number of luxury hotels, which would arise along the gorgeous walk – beginning in the late-seventies and continuing through the millennium. The high-rise hostelries and the trendy restaurants and the rich variety of boutiques were all in the future.

The Convention Center had not been a gleam in anyone's eye, in 1953 – nor had the sprawling *Hemis-Fair* complex or the "Space Needle"-type revolving restaurant.

Trudy was enraptured with the unspoiled, not-very-commercialized (yet), *River Walk* – with its colony of quaint curio shoppes, cantinas, and not-at-all-upscale outside restaurants! There was, of course, the unique outdoor theater – which featured the stage on one side of the narrow river and audience seating on the other.

His wife was completely enthralled as they'd walked along the picturesque route – as had been many other women, through the years. Including Alice.

Our hero endeavored to maintain the educational posture he felt was necessary. Such a pose would be, in his mind, <u>critical</u> – to bury his previous emphasis on *The Schoolbook Depository Building*, Johnson City and the sprawling *LBJ Ranch*. He literally swamped his wife and son with an avalanche of facts, figures, stories, and legends, concerning Texas in general – and San Antonio in particular. He would close his eyes for minutes at a time – attempting to dredge up every single fact he'd ever heard about the charming city.

He even expounded upon his tongue-in-cheek theory that Santa Anna must have attacked *The Alamo* from the roof of the **Joske's** department store, adjacent to "The Cradle of Texas Liberty".

He took his wife and son to *St. Ferdinand's Cathedral* – under which the remains of the heroes of *The Alamo* were buried.

On their second day, he drove them – an extensive tour – to the many old Spanish missions. He explained that the *Mission San Juan Capistrano* was not the fabled mission in California – to which the celebrated swallows always "came back" every year.

They toured *La Villita* – the picturesque (that word again) old Mexican village – and continued through the ornate *Spanish Governor's Palace*.

Even in the fifties, San Antonio was the site of the largest Mexican population center – outside of Mexico itself. Both Trudy and Charlie seemed to be enchanted by the unique culture. And why not? The people seemed much more basic – much less sophisticated – in 1953. Parks supposed – emitting a monumental sigh – that the same thing probably held true for just about everyone else.

Up and down the streets of the city, he tooled the Cadillac – in a relentless effort to spot some landmark, turn up one additional fact. Any bit of information which he might've neglected to inform his family. He never missed a chance to point out the quaint Spanish street names – and unique signs.

"Oh, Hayworth," Trudy enthused. "You should've brought me here the first time."

"Yeah," he murmured. "I know."

On their third day, the family journeyed to *Mission Stadium*, to take in a San Antonio Missions, *Texas League* baseball game. The Missions lost to Beaumont – which, at one time, had been the primary farm club of the Detroit Tigers. It was utterly incredible to Parks – familiar with the immense San Antonio of the seventies – that anyone would mention the city in the same breath as the much-smaller Beaumont. Of course, the latter city – part of Texas' "Golden Triangle" – would, like virtually every other Texas city or town, grow much, much larger in the seventies, eighties and nineties. It was awfully difficult for Parks to put a yardstick to <u>any</u> of the Texas cities.

The 350-mile trip to Brownsville was the longest leg of the Texas tour.

It hadn't occurred to Parks that there would be precious few restaurants – and rest rooms – along the route. They stopped for a long lunch break in Corpus Christi. The city, at that time, was well off U.S. Highway 77 – and Trudy seemed to be becoming more and more impatient.

As they got back on the route to Brownsville, a flood of memories overtook our hero: They drove through Kingsville – on what was then the US-77 bypass. The highway took them past the tiny motel where Jim and Kathleen would spend their wedding night – in about 15 months.

The famous *King's Ranch* loomed just south of Kingsville – a long, arid, narrow, stretch of road, bereft of gasoline stations (and much of anything else) for 54 miles.

"My greatest fear," expounded Parks, as he'd headed into the primitive stretch, "was to get exactly twenty-seven miles into the damn ranch … and then break down."

Fortunately, the sun was beginning to set, as they came out of the potentially treacherous territory – and into the tiny town of Raymondville. The heat, by then, wasn't quite as intense.

They arrived in Brownsville shortly after seven o'clock.

In 1953, the nicest hotel in the city was *The El Jardin*. They took two rooms for the night. Trudy had never seen a hotel quite like it.

"Looks … looks like something out of an old Turhan Bey movie … or maybe *Casablanca* … or something," she observed, nervously. Exceedingly nervously.

Charlie was also uneasy. He asked if the door, which connected the two rooms, could be left open.

They awoke early the next morning. Both Trudy and Charlie were anxious to leave their rooms. To leave the hotel. Parks had rather enjoyed the place. After having spent the sixties and seventies in Formica-laden motel room after Formica-laden motel room – all of which looked the same – he appreciated the uniqueness of *The El Jardin*.

Given the tremulous state of his wife and kid, our boy decided that it would be best not to venture into the hotel's coffee shop. He did his best to try and remember a truly fine restaurant in town. Nothing came to mind.

They had breakfast, finally, at **Fisher's** – a nice little coffee shop, "catty-wumpus" across Elizabeth Street, from the Post Office. It was a place where Jim and Kathleen had sometimes eaten lunch – during much of the three weeks Jim had spent in Brownsville. His famed "freeloading" tenure in the Rio Grande Valley.

After they'd devoured plates-full of bacon-and-eggs – everybody had seemed especially hungry – Parks took his wife and son on a tour of Brownsville. As they drove through the narrow, unpaved, streets, he sensed that Trudy was experiencing the same ill-at-ease condition she'd spoken about in Dallas and Johnson City.

For her husband, though, it was somewhat satisfying to once again drive up and down – through the neighborhoods of 1953 Brownsville.

It was also a bit of a jolt! He'd not remembered the squalor as having been quite so pervasive. Perhaps, for the fifties, in South Texas, it wasn't all that pronounced. It was sure a far cry, though, from the vast, modern, sprawling, city of 1979. It would, of course, become even more cosmopolitan as the turn of the century had come and gone.

He drove past Kathleen's high school. At that time, it was the only one in the entire city. *Brownsville High*, on Palm Boulevard. In the seventies, there would be three high schools. The building which housed Kathleen's alma mater would, when expansion came, be converted to an intermediate school.

Parks negotiated a left turn off Palm Boulevard – onto Elizabeth Street – and headed back toward downtown. It was at that intersection that Elizabeth became a one-way street – heading east. Sure enough – there were the Oldsmobiles, heading in the wrong direction. The dealership was much smaller than Parks had remembered.

As Jim, he'd stopped there a few times – to use their restroom. – on his daily walk in from *Brownsville High* to **Fisher's** café or to the lunch counter at **Kresge's** or **Woolworth's** or **Walgreen's,** after leaving Kathleen at the school entrance.

He felt an especially harsh tug on his heartstrings – as he passed *Sacred Heart Catholic Church*. On September 12, 1954, Jim and Kathleen would be wed in that church. The building was exactly as he'd remembered it. Every nook! Every crevice!

Once back downtown, he snuck a look at Trudy, out of the corner of his eye. She seemed impassive.

He doubled back out Washington Street – to the point at which it dead-ended, at *Brownsville High School*. He turned left, once again, onto Palm Boulevard. At Elizabeth Street, this time, he turned right

– heading away from downtown. He drove the two blocks west – to the laundry where Kathleen's mother worked, as office manager.

He parked in front of the big white building – and watched an elderly Mexican man, as he dickered with a salesman, in front of the Studebaker dealership next door. The old geezer must've taken umbrage at something the salesguy said. He roared away from the dumbfounded man – smothering him in a cloud of dust.

Parks thought that was quite humorous. Trudy didn't appear to be impressed. He had no idea what Charlie might be thinking – alone in the back seat.

How long would he be able to sit there? Especially since he had no idea whether Kathleen was anywhere in the area! Maybe, if he drove by her house, he could –

At that moment, the door to the laundry's office opened! Out stepped Kathleen! An 18-year-old woman!

He'd forgotten that – during her summer vacation – she sometimes worked for her mother. She was – her beauty was – absolutely breathtaking! Remarkable! Parks couldn't remember Kathleen as having been that beautiful. Incredible!

As she made her way toward the sidewalk – and toward the Cadillac – she seemed to wear that special look! That look that Parks had forgotten, as the years had gone by.

How had she ever lost that "Gee Whiz" look?

Well, seven kids would do it, he supposed. With the mix-and-stir formulas! And the *Birdseye* diapers – ones that had required a minimum of three rinses! And, of course, the measles! And the chicken pox! And the mumps! And the cut hands! And the skinned knees! And the snotty noses! That'd do it! For sure!

That – and having to scrape and scrounge and grope and grapple for every damn, lousy, stupid, nickel that she and Jim could lay their hands on!

Parks wondered if Jim had, at that time, also possessed some kind of special "look" – one which would've attracted Kathleen. If there had been such an – such an aura about Jim – it would've faded, he was certain. Probably would've faded fast. Just as Kathleen's ambience had gone AWOL.

His train of thought rather startled him! The fact that he was inching the Caddy along side the young woman – as she walked up Elizabeth Street – was also quite shocking!

He slowly accelerated – rolling past the vibrant young woman. He was certain that she was walking the block-and-a-half to the **Den-Rus Drug Store** – where, during the "freeloading" time, she and Jim used to sip cherry phosphates, at the end of her school day.

It was his recollection that Kathleen and Jim had drunk from the same glass – using two straws to draw out the bright-red, effervescent drink. How about that – for a romantic image? His memory was probably playing tricks on him. They'd each probably had their own glass. For a nickel, he would've been a sport. Back then, anyway.

His reverie had caused him to take his foot off the gas. Kathleen caught up with the Cadillac! She looked directly into the car! Her gaze shot past Trudy – and focused on Parks! He did his best to avert his eyes – but his wife-in-another-life held them! Locked them in! Welded them onto her own! For fully ten seconds! An eternity!

Could she have known who he was? Impossible! How could she know? But, that look! Dear Lord, that look!

Was he getting paranoid? He'd experienced the same feeling outside the "barn" on Prairie Street – when Pop had stared at him! Neurotic? Probably.

"Well," Parks could barely recognize the high-pitched, fluttering, falsetto, voice as his own. "enough of Brownsville. Let's … uh … let's head on over to Mexico."

Matamoros was pretty much as Parks had remembered it.

The three Hayworths sauntered through the market place – dickering with the merchants there. They were traipsing through the "old" market place. The "new" market place – air conditioned, and sporting sophisticated computer-type cash registers – would not come upon the scene till the seventies.

Our hero was still shaken by his encounter with Kathleen. His wife and son, though, seemed wrapped up in shopping. They certainly appeared to be enjoying themselves.

Parks managed to pull himself out of his torpor – long enough to buy Charlie a huge, black-velvet, Charro hat – the most ornate he could lay his hands on. It was hand made. The workmanship, of course, was of the highest quality. Even the Mexican people appeared to have more pride in their craftsmanship in 1953.

Trudy was enthralled with all the jewelry. The amount and the variety! The thousands of baubles! She stocked up – liberally – with necklaces, earrings and bracelets.

She also picked up a bountiful supply of leather goods – purses, belts and shoes.

The memory of Parks' encounter with Kathleen seemed to fade as the afternoon wore on. He reached a point where he delighted in "hondeling" with the merchants – on virtually every purchase.

His manner of bargaining quite upset his wife at first. Anyone could see that the shop people and craftsmen and craftswomen were poor, "peddler-type" people.

"And they certainly aren't asking an-arm-and-a-leg for their goods," admonished Trudy.

The people, in most cases, were not as impoverished as they appeared, explained Parks.

"Dickering is part of the game," he continued. "The merchants are ... well ... they actually expect it. In fact, the measure of whatever respect they may have for the customer is pretty well pegged to the price. The amount ... within reason, of course ... the customer can chop off the asking price. It's really a game ... a big game ... to them."

Jim Sidorwitz had felt the same revulsion the first time he'd "gone across" – with Kathleen and her parents. Kathleen's father – born in Venezuela – had spoken a higher, more pure, form of Spanish, than most people in the area. Rather intimidating. He was most adept at getting around the merchants. "Eating their lunch," as Jim had called it.

On this sojourn, in 1953, once he'd succeeded in getting the merchant to drop his or her price 25% or 30%, Parks would purchase the item – at the full asking price. Once the "game" became apparent to Trudy and Charlie, they delighted in employing the same tactics. Charlie turned out to be much the better of the two.

"You lack the killer instinct, Goit" Parks chided his wife.

Running his hand through the boy's hair, (which, as always, looked as though he'd combed it with an eggbeater) he expounded – in a terrible Scottish brogue – "Aye, noo there's a foine lad".

After six or seven hours in Matamoros, the Hayworths returned to Brownsville – and another night at *The El Jardin*.

Before they turned in, they had dinner at **Fisher's**, then, took in a movie – *Kiss Me Kate*, with Kathryn Grayson & Howard Keel – at the *Majestic Theater*, directly across Elizabeth Street from the post office.

The following morning, they headed north once more.

Parks made it a point to plan an extended stay in Houston. He pointed out landmark after landmark – most of which he'd had to invent. Such as the room, in which he was supposed to have lived – and the site of the company for which he'd purported to have worked.

They drove out to the *San Jacinto Monument* – located at the site of the battlefield where Sam Houston's troops had put Santa Anna's army to route, securing Texas' independence. Donning his educator's hat, once more, he connected the story of *The Battle of San Jacinto* – with the significance of the heroes of *The Alamo*.

"If those cats at *The Alamo* hadn't given ol' Santa Anna all he could handle," he explained, "Sammy Houston wouldn't have been able to regroup his forces … and kick the crap out of the Mexican army, over here, a couple weeks later."

Trudy laughed. "My. You sure do have a flair for teaching history, Hayworth."

Her husband smiled broadly.

"That's because I've lived through so much of it," he responded. "One of these days … when a certain snot-nosed kid isn't around … I'll tell you of the legend of The Yellow Rose of Texas. She was supposed to have been a former slave, who … uh … dallied with Santa Anna, himself. The boy really should've been preparing to do battle with Sam Houston. The story goes that he got caught … literally … with his pants down."

"Oh, poo," said Trudy, pinching his cheek. "You're making that up."

"Not really. Well, maybe someone else may have dreamed it up ... but, not me. Whatever ... it plays well in this part of the country."

"I'll tell you something else, Mom," offered Charlie. "I've learned a lot on this trip ... in spite of myself. I guess it's like you said, Dad. You can resist like ... "

"Charlie?" admonished his mother.

" ... heck ... " smiled Charlie.

"Good save, Kid," said Parks, grinning.

"Anyway," continued Charlie, "you can resist like all-get-out. But, some of the school-housin' ... like Dad calls it ... is gonna stick. I really did learn a lot."

"Yes," agreed Trudy – a strange, almost eerie, quality in her voice. "I've learned a lot too."

While her statement seemed to have no effect on Charlie, Parks felt as though he'd just been run down by an out-of-control steamroller!

"Well," Charlie advised his mother, "it was a heck of a lot more educational ... and much more interesting ... than sitting in that hot old classroom."

Parks didn't hear the boy. What had Trudy meant by her remark?

They spent the night in Houston. It was there that Trudy expressed her wish to return home.

"I hope you don't mind, Hayworth. But, all of a sudden, I'm all traveled out. I want to go home. I appreciate your taking us on such a nice long trip. So does Charlie. But, I just think that we'd all be better off now ... if we just went on home."

They took off early the following morning – driving all the way to Memphis.

Once again, they stayed at *The Peabody*. As before, Parks took Trudy dancing – at the club on the roof. This time, all three thrilled to the music of Sammy Kaye and his Orchestra. Trudy especially enjoyed "Swinging and Swaying" – Kaye's advertised motto. This time, though – no "remote". The woman was quite disappointed. She'd thought the radio broadcast went hand-in-hand with the dance band. Part of the package.

The next morning, they pushed on to Indianapolis. Trudy drove most of the way. The dancing had been much more taxing than Parks had anticipated.

They arrived in Indianapolis, as dark was descending upon the city and checked in to the first motel they came upon. After a quick meal, they bedded down for the night.

The next day, Parks drove Trudy and Charlie to the famed *Indianapolis 500* race oval. Trudy was spectacularly unimpressed. Not so, young Charlie.

Once again, Parks felt as though he might've gone too far. The only race he'd ever attended at the fabled "brick yard" had been the one which would be the next race – about 11 months away. Memorial Day – 1954! That would be the contest in which the 1953 winner, Bill Vukovich, would be killed!

Parks remembered that he'd been looking directly at Vukovich – the moment his car had flipped and gone over the wall. One of Jim Sidorwitz's best friends, from work, had been working the lap cards for Vukovich – and Jim had traveled with him, down from Detroit, for the race.

The spectacular crash had soured Parks on the competition ever since!

Gazing back at the exuberant Charlie, he was afraid that the boy would ask to be taken to the '54 race. Parks would never allow the lad to witness such gory history in the making.

Cookie Lavagetto was one thing. Bill Vukovich was quite another.

Off they went to Detroit! The trio took lunch in Fort Wayne, Indiana – and supper in "The Motor City".

They'd wound up at the **Marcus** hamburger joint on Livernois, between West Chicago and Joy Road. The last time the Hayworths had ventured out on Livernois, Parks had chased down Art Sarnes – to the latter's death!

Our hero had been lusting for a **Marcus** hamburger for months. They were truly unique – rectangular in shape and slightly longer than a hot dog. **Marcus** served them in hot dog buns. The meat was deep-fried – in what Parks had always referred to as "a sort of greasy gravy". Although the process may sound atrocious to the reader, the burgers, themselves, were absolutely delicious. Parks loved them. So did Charlie.

Trudy had always maintained that she wasn't that fond of them. However, since "the boys were so hell-bent on them" she'd not had the heart to say them nay. The sacrifice proved to be not that immense. She'd wolfed down two of the substantial, juicy, sandwiches.

It was great to see the wondrous, glorious, "Dream House" once more! The place never looked better to Parks. Or to his wife and son.

Once inside, our hero climbed his glorious staircase to the second floor. It wasn't as taxing as he'd feared.

After showering, he was content to fall into bed – and off into a deep sleep. He would not awaken for 18 hours.

It would not be until the following evening that he would check out – and bestow his blessing upon – the "john off the kitchen".

TWENTY FOUR

Once the Hayworths had settled back into the house on Grandmont, Parks nestled into a more-or-less routine. After a rather lengthy briefing session with Elliot Voorhees – a meeting which, naturally, included Trudy – our hero took control, once again, of the family's finances. It was understood, of course, that Trudy would share in every decision – every venture.

Elliot, as usual, had done an exemplary job of guiding the finances. The Hayworths had returned to Detroit a good deal more solvent than when they'd left. The nation's economy was still experiencing a decided upswing. Parks' investments were, as you might imagine, reflecting those advances.

With the coming of fall, Charlie was again enrolled at *Calvin Coolidge* school. It would, obviously, be a much better situation than returning to *Ruthruff*. How could he ever forget – how could he ever put from his mind – his final day at the latter school?

They bought Trudy a 1953 Studebaker coupe. The car had undergone a radical styling change – and was much more European-looking than any other American car.

Trudy had fallen in love with it.

"It looks like it's going thirty-miles-an-hour ... even when it's standing still," she enthused. "Besides, while I love the Caddy, it's just too big. This little car ... I can see everything so much better in it."

Parks, once again, offered to buy Amanda a new house. As before, she declined with thanks.

"This old house holds too many memories for me," she reflected. "Maybe when I'm old and senile … in another forty or fifty years … you can maybe put me up in a small apartment or something. But, for now, I'm perfectly happy … right where I'm at."

Trudy never went shopping without picking up a blouse, sweater, coat, dress, bottle of cologne – or some attractive piece of jewelry – for her mother.

Parks and Trudy made it a point to take Charlie and Amanda "out steppin'", at least one night each week – many times to the free concerts presented by *The Detroit Symphony Orchestra* on Belle Isle or at the State Fairgrounds, on Woodward Avenue and Eight Mile Road.

In 1953, it was still safe to visit either – or both. Even at night.

On other occasions, the quartet would attend a live stage show – or simply go to the movies.

Parks – with doctor's approval – purchased four season-tickets to the Red Wings' home games for the entire 1953-54 hockey season.

Once Charlie was back in school, his parents found themselves with a good deal of private time. For the most part, they utilized the "together moments" at home – listening to records or smooching.

Occasionally, they'd wind up upstairs – in the master bedroom.

During many of their lovemaking sessions, Parks was certain that he could discern a noticeable "freezing" on his wife's part – probably, he determined, brought on by her recollection of his heart attack in that same room. Under the same circumstances.

He began to be a little more "creative". Very often, they would make love in the patio room. From time to time, they would journey downtown, indulge in a lavish meal at lunchtime, take in a first-run movie – and then check in at *The Statler*.

It was at such times that our hero would reflect upon the changes in his wife:

On their extended trip, she'd seemed to question a significant number of his actions – even some of his statements. At home, she was an entirely different woman:

Devoted, affectionate – seldom questioning.

On those days, when Parks would indulge in one of his "Sentimental Journeys", Trudy most often used those occasions to take Amanda to lunch and a movie – and, perhaps, a shopping expedition. During his cruises upon the sea of nostalgia, our boy would usually drive around Highland Park. By the fall of 1953, Parks was certain that Jim would, most certainly, have bought his beloved 1949 DeSoto.

Jim would be living – with his mother and sister – in an apartment house on Tyler Street, just behind the Highland Park post office building.

He'd returned from the Navy – by way of Brownsville – in the late spring of that year. He would remain in the apartment on Tyler until his marriage to Kathleen, in September of 1954. Grappling, all the while, with Dolly's reservations about the logic of the upcoming nuptials.

Jim had taken a job at **Midland Container Corporation**, in Hamtramck, as an order-entry clerk, on the branch's sales desk.

Midland was an Indianapolis-based corporation. Most of the executives were natives of the Indiana city – and, indeed, had graduated from **Indiana University**. One of them, Bill Fischer, had taken a liking to Jim – and had invited him to the *Indianapolis 500* race in 1954. It was Bill who'd been working Vukovich's lap cards at the time of his fatal crash!

Parks Hayworth had become intrigued – obsessed, maybe – with watching Jim Sidorwitz. Spying on himself as a young man. An uncomplicated, idealistic, youth – possessed with the hopes, dreams and aspirations of an incredibly-optimistic, less-than-sophisticated, future. A mere lad – beginning a long journey into the great unknown.

It certainly took no exceptional memory to keep track of Jim's schedule: Because of his betrothal to Kathleen, Jim didn't date. Consequently, he was at his mother's apartment – virtually every night. Well, there was the occasional night baseball game and numerous hockey matches. The young man always drove to work each morning at eight-thirty – and returned to the Tyler Street apartment every evening at five-thirty.

What could be simpler than that?

Saturday morning usually found him in the alley – behind the apartment – washing and *Simonizing* this cherished DeSoto.

He attended church at *St. Benedict's* on Sunday morning – and, most often, spent the balance of the day at Dolly's apartment. There was the occasional Sunday foray to *Briggs Stadium* to take in a double header. You could get into the bleachers, in those days, for fifty-cents. There was no way Jim could have a bad day – for a "half-a-buck".

Bernard Sidorwitz, most often, spent his Sundays at Dolly's apartment. For the most part, it was a matter of Jim's father – engaged in a futile attempt to convince the woman that she should take him back.

Jim and his father had begun to get along – somewhat, anyway – during those days. The relationship gradually improved over the years. Till Bernie's death.

The easiest time and place for Parks to look in on young Jim was at noon – during the week. It was lunch time. The young man virtually always ate – either by himself or with a couple other **Midland** employees – at a small bar and grill on the corner of Mt. Elliot and Domine streets. On the days that Parks and Trudy would go their separate ways, Parks was certain to be at the little restaurant – two blocks from the **Midland** plant and offices.

It was troubling to Parks – that he'd become so hung-up in watching Jim. Could it be that the end was drawing near?

He found himself viewing "the end" much more philosophically than before. He even imagined that he might be around for a number of years.

Who knew? Maybe he <u>would</u> turn out to be "Mister John". Immediately, he'd dismiss that thought! That would make Trudy "Miss Honey"! He couldn't <u>bear</u> to entertain such a scenario. NO! Most assuredly, he was <u>not</u> "Mister John".

He was preoccupied with the thought of seeing his children once again! The time was drawing nigh! Dave would be born in June, of 1955! That was less than two years away! He could hardly wait!

During the first half of 1954, Parks found himself becoming particularly "antsy".

While he certainly enjoyed the many things he was able to do with Trudy, Charlie and Amanda, he found himself using almost any excuse to break away around noontime.

More and more, he reveled in looking in on himself as a groom-in-waiting. Jim was so obviously looking forward to his new life with Kathleen – to begin *The Donna Reed Show*. Parks was at a loss to explain – even to himself – why he should be so fascinated on one hand. And so disturbed on the other hand – by Jim's demeanor.

<u>Why don't you just cut loose and let the kid alone</u>? <u>Let him go ahead and live his life</u>? <u>What the hell can you do to contribute</u>?

His midday sojourns were beginning to have an effect upon Trudy. While our hero always seemed to come up with a plausible reason to leave, he was certain that his absences were becoming – more and more – a cause of concern for his wife. And yet? And yet, he couldn't help himself! At least, he <u>wouldn't</u> help himself!

Did she believe that he was seeing someone else? Another woman? He desperately hoped that she did not. Still, he couldn't control the overwhelming urge to look in on young Jim – and the upsetting, terribly-mixed, emotions that the exercise invariably brought about.

"Jim, if you only knew," he would mutter, under his breath.

How long would the same "Gee Whiz" look remain in the lad's eyes? When would it fade? When would it flicker out altogether? Sooner, he was certain, than the same light he'd seen in Kathleen's eyes.

Eventually the stars would disappear – from both pairs of eyes. How sad.

Later in the spring, the Red Wings captured the *Stanley Cup* once again – defeating the mighty Montreal Canadiens, in the seventh game of the thrill-packed series.

It was in the second period of "sudden death" overtime – when Tony (Mighty Mouse) Leswick potted the winning goal!

Parks recalled that Jim had been at that game – the only contest the young man had attended during the entire playoffs. By contrast, Trudy, Charlie, Amanda and Parks had taken in each home game – in both playoff series.

The final game had been overshadowed, to a point, by a reported death threat to Red Wings stars, Ted Lindsay and Gordie Howe. Both players had been threatened that – should they compete in the seventh (and deciding) game – they would, at some point during the contest, be shot!

Both stars played – and played well – but it would be the defense-minded Leswick who would return the fabled *Stanley Cup* to "The Motor City", after a one-year absence.

With the scoring of the "sudden death" – the winning – goal, the crowd at the *Olympia*, of course, had gone absolutely bonkers! Lindsay skated the length of the rink, pointing his hockey stick – as one would aim a rifle – at various sections in the balcony. The capacity crowd went wild at every "aim"!

It would be weeks before the euphoria would wear off for Charlie and Amanda – especially the latter. She had become – hands down – the family "Hockey Nut". Trudy hadn't gotten quite so "high" as the other three. Therefore, she didn't have quite so far to return to Earth.

Parks' descent was far more pronounced. Everything seemed to go flat for him.

In late June, Trudy, Charlie, Amanda and Parks boarded the steamer *Put-In-Bay* – at the foot of Woodward Avenue – for the beautiful cruise down the Detroit River and across Lake Erie to the island of *Cedar Point*, in Ohio, for a two-week hiatus.

Parks was having an even more difficult time trying to stay "in" to his family's vacation – another element which disturbed Trudy. The pressure on her was building every day. She was, of course, aware that it <u>was</u> pressure – a mysterious, unidentified pressure. Even if she'd been able to understand it, how would she cope with it?

On the evening of their tenth day, the couple was seated in a little outdoor tavern, at the *Breakers Hotel*. They looked to be enjoying themselves.

Trudy was determined to get to the bottom of her husband's lethargy.

"Okay, Hayworth," she said with a sigh, "I give up. What's bothering you?"

"Huh? Bothering me? Nothing. Nothing at all. I'm ... I'm having a great time."

"In a pig's fanny you are."

"What's the matter, Goit? I'm, maybe, not dancing enough for you?"

"You're dancing fine for me. It's not that. You've been about as flat ... as that chesty barmaid over there is not."

"I hadn't noticed the chesty barmaid."

"My point exactly. That's just exactly what I'm getting at. Hayworth, you seem all caught up in ... in nothing. Well, nothing ... but the blahs. Ordinarily, you'd have been staring at the cocktail waitress' fanny. I don't even think that you're aware that half of it is hanging out. And that, for sure, is not my fanny-man husband. C'mon, Hayworth. What's wrong? Tell ol' Mamma Goit."

"Nothing, Mamma Goit. Honest. I just can't seem to get into much of anything these days. Maybe that comes from having too much. Too much time. Too much leisure. Too much money."

"Too much Trudy?"

"No! No ... of course not! There could never be too much Trudy."

"Well, there's going to be ... unless I go on a diet."

Her doe-eyes took on an extra dimension of softness. Tears began to well up. She managed to blink them back.

"Seriously, Hayworth," she rasped. "What's bothering you? It can't be money. Not unless you know something that I don't."

He managed a weak smile.

"That'll be the day," he responded. "No ... it's not money. Like I said, maybe it's just that I've got too much time on my hands. When I had to work and sweat for a living ... it really kept my competitive juices flowing. Now, there's really not a hell of a lot of battles left to fight."

"I thought that's what everybody strove for. To be able to enjoy themselves ... without a life-and-death battle every day."

Parks thought of *Tevye's* classic explanation of the philosophy behind *The Fiddler On The Roof*: "Trying to scratch out a simple tune ... without breaking his neck."

"I ... yeah. I guess we all do strive for that," he answered, with a deep sigh. "That's supposed to be the goal. The panacea. But, I think it must be human nature to always want just a little bit more... no matter how much you've already got. I think we're probably programmed to think that, if we can accomplish just a smattering more ... no matter how many battles we may have already won ... we could, then, be totally happy. I don't know as anyone can be totally happy. Completely happy. Not all the time, anyway."

"Programmed? I've never heard that word before. That's pretty deep, Hayworth. You've never waxed philosophical like that in the past. Unless I haven't been listening."

"You listen fine, Trood. Couldn't ask for a better listener. Couldn't ask for a better anything. From that first night ... in Frankenmuth ... you always listened to me. Listened while I just rattled off at the mouth. It just seems like, lately, I can't seem to get out of this stupid damn rut. I keep thinking, y'know, all these deep thoughts. Didn't used to do that. Maybe it's old age a-creepin' up on me."

"Parks?"

Danger! Warning! First name being used!

"Whatcha want?"

"Parks ... if there was someone else ... if you were tired of me ... you'd tell me. Wouldn't you?"

"Someone ... ? Trudy! There's no one else! Nobody! Zero! Zilch! Nada!"

"But ... you would tell me?"

"Yes. Yes, of course. But, there's no one! What's bringing all this on?"

"Well ... well, you've acted so ... so strange these past few months. Almost since we got back from our trip. You seem so ... so, I don't know ... so preoccupied. I don't know. I just don't know. It seems like ... half the time ... like you're somewhere. Somewhere else. Almost like you're ... like you're not with me. Even though I can reach out and touch you."

A tear trickled down her cheek.

Parks was at a loss! How to respond to something – something like that? Something which had just pelted him? Hit him – like some kind of lightning bolt?

The silence weighed tons!

"Was it because I was so ... so bitchy?" she pressed. "On the trip, I mean. God knows, I didn't mean to be. I can see where you'd be tired ... tired of all the putting up with all the bitching at you all the time! The bitchiness! God! That's all I did ... was bitch! Bitch, bitch, bitch! That's all I did! Bitch about that stupid red building in Dallas! And Senator Johnson's ranch! All that kind of ... kind of ... "

"You weren't bitching at me."

"Yes I was. And ... and I really ... I just don't ... I don't know what comes over me sometimes. I try not to let things bother me. But, it's ... "

"Well, if they bother you ... if something's bothering you ... then you ought to bring it out. That's definitely not bitching."

"Well, something's wrong! Parks? Where do you go so often? During the day? Right about noon? Oh, dammit! Here I go again! I'm ... I'm sorry, Parks. I'm just being bitchy again. Where you go is ... well ... it's your business. It's just that ... it's just ... just that ... "

"Just what, Trudy?"

"Is ... is it that there's another woman? Is that where you go so often? To see her? Maybe she doesn't question you like I do! Maybe she's content to ... "

"Trudy! Listen to me! I <u>swear</u>! I <u>swear</u> to you! There's no other woman! <u>None</u>! There couldn't be! How could there be? It's you I love ... not someone else!"

"Well," she sniffled, "I guess I couldn't blame you ... if there was someone else."

"You wouldn't have to. I'd blame myself."

"Well, you see ... " she began – and then stopped.

"'You see' what? What, Trudy? Tell me."

She dabbed at her eyes with a cocktail napkin.

"I ... I ... I ... oh, Parks!"

Tears flowed in earnest!

"I ... I'm so scared," she wailed. "So ... so frightened."

He reached across – and took one of her hands in both of his.

"Trudy! What is it? Why? Why are you scared? What could possibly be upsetting you like this?"

"I ... I just ... I just worry. You're gone so often, y'know. Always about the same time. I try not to let it affect me. But, sometimes, I come up with the damndest ... the most God-awful ... visions. I can see you in bed ... with another woman. Doing the same things we do! Telling her the same things you tell me! I don't know if ... "

"Trudy! Please! You've got to believe me! I've never even looked at another woman! I swear that to you! By all I hold holy! I swear that to you. On my mother's eyes!"

"Well, then ... where do you go?"

Her voice was much too loud. She immediately cupped her free hand over her mouth – as six or eight people, at adjoining tables, turned to stare.

"This really isn't the place to discuss something like this," he admonished. His voice was soft, but, the words were tightly clipped.

Her eyes – having blazed for the briefest of seconds – softened.

"I know," she rasped. "I'm sorry. I should know better than to get so ... so upset."

"Well," he replied, sighing deeply, "it would behoove me not to cause you to <u>be</u> upset." His voice had lost its edge. "I had no idea, Trudy. Honestly. I didn't. I would imagine that it would be hard for you to fathom ... but, all I do is to drive around. Stop for a hamburger or something ... when the mood strikes me. There are so many changes going on in the city. The expressways ... for one thing. There, for the longest time, I had a helluva time trying to figure out what they had in mind with that interchange."

"Interchange?"

"Yeah. It's amazing. When they get it completed, you'll be able to get off the Ford Expressway ... and go either way onto the Lodge. No matter which way you're headed on the Ford. And, if you're on the Lodge ... going in either direction ... you can switch on to the Ford. That's ... why ... it's amazing! I could never have imagined such a thing."

"You ... you mean you ... you spend that time ... staring at an expressway interchange?"

"Well, not entirely. The things that they're starting to do on the waterfront. And, where the expressways are going. It's remarkable. The Lodge'll eventually hook up with Northwestern. Schoolcraft'll probably wind up being a damn expressway ... "

He had to put the brakes on the direction in which the conversation was headed. He couldn't tell her, of course, that – in not-too-many-years – she'd be unable to drive the short block on Burnette, from Grand River to West Chicago. There would be a freeway – as they would come to be known – in the middle. And Schoolcraft, absolutely would become a freeway.

"Well, if expressways are so invigorating," she responded, "why are you always feeling so ... so ... so blah? Is it a thing where it's difficult? So absolutely difficult to leave a stupid expressway ... and come home to me? Why ... why, Parks ... why don't you take me with you?"

"It's not a come-down to come home to you. You're being too dramatic. I just figured that ... well, that you wouldn't be all that interested. Besides, I never really know where I'm going, when I head out."

"You ... need to be alone? Away from me? Is that it? Away from me?"

"Trudy, this is really not the place to ... Of course it's not a thing ... where I'm trying to get away from you. How could you even think that?"

She shook her head slowly.

"I don't know, Parks." Her voice was a strange mixture of sadness and almost-outrage. He'd never heard her speak in that tone before. "I don't know anything ... not one thing ... anymore," she continued. "I just never thought I'd ever hear you say that it was important for you to be by yourself. Obviously, that's what makes you happy ... if what you say about there not being another woman is true. It's also obvious that you're not that thrilled about being around me! Or Charlie! Or Mother ... for that matter. And here you are ... stranded on an island! <u>Stranded</u>! With the three of us!"

"Trudy! You're building this whole thing out of proportion ... way out of proportion!"

"Well," she answered with a deep sigh of her own, "it's apparent that ... that there's trouble in Paradise."

"Well, there shouldn't be," he muttered. The entire conversation was sapping him – more than he'd realized. "I had no idea that my little sojourns were causing you so much distress. I'll stop them.

It's not that big a deal. But ... you're going to have to believe me ... there's no other woman. If you had a problem with my going off ... why, you should've told me. Should've told me ... rather than letting it build up. Instead of letting it fester ... into such a great big production."

Her eyes blazed now!

"Well, it seems to upset you ... if I ever have the temerity to question you," she responded, sharply. Then, she softened once more. "There I go again ... being bitchy."

Parks, by then, was completely drained.

"No," he managed to say. "You're not being bitchy. Let's go back up to the room, okay? I'm ... suddenly, I'm very tired."

They left the little bar. As they made their way back to their room on the third floor of the rotunda, Parks wondered if his wife believed he was using his very-real fatigue – as a cover, to terminate the conversation. He wished he had the answer to that one, himself. Did Trudy really believe that he was being unfaithful?

If that was the case, he, obviously, didn't know the woman to whom he'd been married for seven years. Not as well as he'd thought.

Apparently, he didn't know himself as well as he'd thought either. What was it that seemed so disrupting? That <u>was</u> so disrupting? That was disrupting a story book lifestyle? A veritable paradise? With the woman – and the boy – that he loved? With the woman and the boy that he loved so deeply? What could possibly be upsetting the proverbial apple cart?

Could it possibly be the impending marriage of Jim and Kathleen? Possibly!

The big day would take place in less than three months. September 12th. But, why should the coming of those nuptials affect him? Why should the situation so influence him? To the extent that it obviously was causing him so much distress?

Was there something – some overwhelming something – inside him which might be causing him to yearn to attend the wedding? Jim's and Kathleen's nuptials? On that stifling Sunday, in the Rio Grande Valley?

In 1954, in South Texas, virtually everyone worked a six-day week. Sunday was the universal day off. Therefore, it wasn't the least bit unusual for a marriage to take place on a Sunday. Jim and Kathleen were wed at *Sacred Heart Church*, on Elizabeth Street – at the regular 10:30 AM Mass.

Could our hero get Trudy to Brownsville? Could he weedle her into attending 10:30 AM Mass?

Probably not. He guessed that his wife would be far from enamored of still another trip. Especially to Brownsville. He could picture her asking, "Why Brownsville?"

Another consideration would be Charlie. They would not be able to take the boy with them. September 12th would be a week or ten days into the new school term. Trudy would be convinced – Parks was certain – that the kid had missed more than enough school the previous year. Truth to tell, she'd be right. Positively correct.

It had taken some negotiation to convince the powers that be, at *Ruthruff*, to promote Charlie – after his having missed so many school days. Parks always had the feeling that the school's acquiescence had amounted to nothing more than a "sympathy promotion".

In either case – promotion or failure – the school would not have to deal with Charlie. Let the people at *Calvin Coolidge* jack with the situation.

So, the chances that his wife would consent to pulling his son out of school – for a purely impulsive trip to an obscure city in a remote part of the country – were slim and none. What else would there be for them to see, down there? The ten-thirty Mass?

No, the project would raise too many eyebrows! Bring forth too many unanswerable questions. Especially if Trudy were to recognize Kathleen! Determine that the glowing bride was the young woman who'd gazed so intently into their car!

Or, if she'd recognize the groom as the young sailor who'd entered the bar in Memphis – just before Parks had gone to pieces!

TWENTY FIVE

September, 1954, came to Detroit wearing a sullen, rainy gown. Labor Day found Parks sitting in the patio room – listening to Van Patrick describe the Tigers' double-header, on the radio – while Trudy busied herself making last-minute preparations for Charlie's school year, which would begin in just three days.

As each day of that interminable week passed, our hero had become more and more restless. He hated the fact that he seemed unable to control the torpor which had consumed him! That had held him in its life-strangling grasp for so many months!

The fact that, in deference to Trudy, he'd given up his almost-daily sojourns to the café on Mount Elliot – to look in on Jim – hadn't really helped. Hadn't changed much of anything. However, it was the least, obviously, that he could do. He'd regretted – to the n'th degree – the fact that the trips had been such a worry to the woman he loved so deeply. However, staying away from Jim had probably only contributed to the continual, never-ending, blahs. Who knew why? Who knew any-damn-thing?

In addition, his continual listlessness was a situation which was becoming more and more worrisome to his wife.

Finally, on Friday – two days before Jim and Kathleen were to be married, in Brownsville, Texas – she attempted, once again, to bring the predicament to a head.

Parks, seated at the kitchen table, was playing solitaire – a diversion in which he'd seldom indulged. Seldom before September first. Trudy seated herself across from him.

"Hayworth," she began, "we simply can't go on like this. I ... I don't know what I'm doing wrong. I wish ... oh God, how I wish ... I did. How I wish I knew! Please ... please ... please tell me, Parks. Please! I beg of you! Please ... tell me!"

Her soft, brown, eyes were unable to hide the hurt. The terrible pain! A tear trickled down her cheek.

"Please, Honey," she continued. "Please let me know what's bothering you. Even Charlie's noticed it. Whatever it is, Parks ... please believe me ... I'll correct it! I will! I promise! I'll work ... oh, I'll work so hard on it! I will! But ... you've got to tell me. You've got to tell me, Parks! I've ... I've run out of guesses!"

The tears came faster! Then, they poured out! The dam had burst!

"You've simply got to," she managed to say – between sobs.

He took both her hands in his – and half-led, half-pulled her around the table and onto his lap. Once seated, she put her head on his shoulder – and continued to cry, softly.

He began to pat her on the bottom. She'd never experienced a reaction that was more welcomed.

"You haven't done anything wrong, Trood," he rasped. "Honest. Not one thing. Not one. It's me! Honest ... it's me. I could never have asked for a better wife than you. A better friend. A better lover. In a million years, I couldn't ask for more. I don't say it often enough ... but, it's true. I love you, Goit. I love you deeply ... very deeply. I really don't know how you've put up with me ... with me being such an old poop ... over these past few months."

"Oh, Hayworth," she sniffed – planting a wet kiss on his nose. "You're not an old poop. I just ... "

"I mean it," he interrupted. "I just don't know ... I really don't know ... what's the matter with me. I really and truly don't. I just can't seem to ... well ... shake myself out of these stupid damn doldrums. I didn't mean for it to be this way. Don't mean for it to be this way. I honestly don't. Not to you. Not to Charlie. Not to anybody. I'm just as sorry as I can be. Sorry that I really have been such an old poop. I can't tell you what you've done wrong. Because you haven't done anything wrong! Neither has Charlie."

"Then, what is it?" she asked, hugging him tightly. "How can I help? How can Charlie help? Do you want him to go over … stay at my mother's for awhile? Do you want the two of us to go over there for awhile? Would that help?"

The suggestion sent a shudder up Parks' spine! The blackest of feelings overtook him. He shook his head – emphatically.

"No! No, of course not! That'd … why, it'd only make things worse. I love you. I love Charlie. The last thing … the last thing in the world that I'd want … would be for you to go away. You or Charlie." He sighed deeply. "I really can't tell you," he muttered, "why I'm acting like such a jerk." His voice was a shade above a whisper.

Then, the thought hit him!

"Maybe," he posed, "it's me who should go away for awhile."

She pulled back – and looked down at him! Her fawn eyes penetrated – deep within his own!

As soon as he saw the look of bewilderment – the out-and-out heartbreak – which crossed (and remained upon) her face, Parks wished he'd never said it. Her expression screamed disappointment! She did her best to shake it off – to recover!

"Well … uh … yes," she managed to reply. "Yes, Parks. Uh … if you think … if you think that you should … uh … get away, I would … ah … that would be … it'll be fine. I mean, we all need to get … to get away somewhere … uh … from time to time."

He attempted to kiss her – but she jerked back, averting his lips!

"I didn't mean it like that, Trudy. I honestly didn't. I'm not tired of you … or need a change from you. I love you very much … despite my stupid remarks. My stupid remarks … and even stupider suggestions. I was just … I was simply … talking before I was thinking. One of my great talents, nowadays."

"No … uh … it's … it's okay. I mean, fine. Uh … you know that, whatever you want is … is … ah … is fine with me, Parks."

"Good try, Goit. But, not even close. I just meant that I … I was thinking. Elliot was saying … just the other day, he was saying … saying that he'd been talking to some guy from Houston. And this guy … he's got a parcel of land down there. A track that he's trying to sell. Elliot says that … what he's asking for it … Elliot says that it's dirt cheap. He wanted to know what I thought about it … and if I'd be, maybe, interested. If it's where I think it is … and my memory isn't as good as it used to be … "

"That'll be the day," she replied, overcoming – at least, partially – some of the hurt.

"It's not, Trood. Really. But … if that land is where I think it is … it'll be worth a helluva lot of money, someday."

"How do you know that, Parks?" Her voice was, suddenly, dripping with ice cubes.

"Just from … from what I know about Houston."

"Parks … you haven't been there. Not in years. Not for any length of time, anyway. And you're going to clean this guy's clock? Take him to the cleaners? Oh, Parks! That's such a feeble excuse. Look! If you want to go somewhere, then … dammit … go! But, don't … don't grope for some half-assed excuse. It's not … necessary. You're a big boy now. If you want to get away from us, for awhile, then … goddam it … then, go!"

More evidence of how badly he'd hurt her: She never – ever – said "goddam"!

"Oh, Trudy … I was just … just thinking out loud. I'm not … I'm really not … trying to find an excuse to … as you say … to get away. You're right. I am a big boy now. As incredible as that may seem to you, I've been aware of that fact for a good while now. What I haven't learned is that I should stop thinking out loud. It was just a thought, Trudy. Just a thought. Pure and simple … more simple than anything else. Something that just popped into what is laughingly referred to as my brain. Better it shouldn't have."

She leaned down and kissed him.

"I'm sorry too, Hayworth. I didn't mean to blow my cork like that. I'm just … I'm just at my wit's end, that's all. I feel so … so … so damn inadequate. I've always been able to meet just about any challenge. Until now! Whatever I do … whatever I do, these days … it just seems like it's just not enough. Never enough. It's so … so … damn futile!" She began to cry again. "So damn futile," she repeated. "It just seems like there's nothing I can do."

"You're doing fine, Goit. You always ... always, always, always ... do fine."

"Yeah," she sniffed. "Sure." She pulled a handkerchief from her apron pocket and dabbed at her eyes – eyes which were still spilling over. "Sure I am," she said, bitterly. "I'm a damn wonder!"

"You are, Trood. You are a wonder, y'know. Honest! Like I said, it's me! It's my fault. No one else's. Mine. Me. I'm he one who's ... who's inadequate. I've got everything I've ever wanted. Everything I've ever longed for. Everything I've dreamed of ... my whole life through. And I still can't shake the stupid dumps. I'm as sorry as I can be, Trudy. I'm the one to be apologizing ... and I do. I do apologize. I apologize for being ... for being ... for being a complete and utter horse's ass."

She laughed lightly – despite her tears.

"You're not a horse's ass. You're not an old poop. And you've no cause to apologize. Instead of making a federal case out of everything, I should've tried a little harder to help you shake yourself out of the blahs. Instead, here I am ... creating more and more problems. Being a pain-in-the-fanny."

She sat straight up in his lap.

"Know what, Hayworth?" she asked – groping for a cheerfulness which wasn't there. Could never be there! It was a valiant effort, though.

"No," he answered, sullenly. "What?"

"Maybe it would be a good idea for to fly down there to Houston. Maybe you should check that property out. If this guy wants to give away his property ... then, why shouldn't we get the benefit? Who better than us?"

"Nah. It was just a thought. You were probably right the first time. I haven't been down there enough times ... not in the past fifteen years ... to know what the hell's going on. He's probably one of those world-famous Texas wheeler-dealers ... looking to line his pockets with Yankee dollars. Some of those guys are pretty good, y'know. They'll stick their toe into the ground ... and scratch their butt. Then, they'll tell you a story about their great-granddaddy ... and let you talk yourself into buying whatever goofy thing it is that they want to sell. When it's all over, you can't even remember bringing it up. All you can do is to look in the mirror and say to yourself, 'What the hell did I just do?'."

His wife shook her head emphatically.

"Well, I don't think you should dismiss it, Hayworth," she said. "Not out of hand. I really don't. If your first inkling was that the stuff is going to be valuable ... then, maybe you'd better go on down. Have a look. As long as I've known you, you've never been wrong about that sort of thing. Ever! You amaze me! If you don't, at least, take a look ... you'll probably blame yourself for blowing a chance of a lifetime. I think ... I really think ... that you ought to fly down there. Check it out."

For a full minute, the silence hung heavily in the kitchen. Parks became aware of the fact that he'd begun to pat her on the bottom, once again. He sighed heavily.

"Would you like to come with me?" he asked.

"Huh-uh," she answered with an emphatic shake-of-the-head. "No. I'm kind of all traveled out. Besides, Charlie's just starting back to school ... and I've got a million-and-one things to do around here. I think that ... that taking a trip alone ... will probably do you a world of good, Hayworth. You'll come back all refreshed ... and we'll make mad, passionate, love."

He laughed.

"Yeah," he said. "And they'll never let us back into that airport again."

The DC-7 settled into a smooth landing pattern at *Houston International Airport*.

In the sixties, the installation would be renamed *William Hobby Airport*. In the eighties, it would be greatly expanded. It hadn't occurred to Parks – until the plane set down at the older facility – that the massive, sprawling, *Houston Intercontinental Airport* (later to be re-Christened *George Bush International*), up north of town, wouldn't even be a gleam in anyone's eye, in 1954.

Hurrying into the terminal, he inquired as to where he might buy a ticket to Brownsville. When he'd booked passage, in Detroit, Trudy, of course, had been at his side. He dared not purchase a ticket for any other destination than Houston.

Returning

Once on the ground, our hero was faced with the possibility – the very real possibility – of being unable to connect with a flight to Brownsville!

He was directed to the **Trans-Texas Airlines** ticket booth. To his dismay, he learned that he'd be unable to get a flight to any point in the Rio Grande Valley – before late Sunday afternoon. There was not an overwhelming flow of traffic into or out of the area in 1954 – something of which he should've been aware.

Parks looked at his watch. 5:00 PM! Saturday – five o'clock in the afternoon!

The wedding would take place at 10:30 AM the following morning!

More fuel for the funk: He had lied to Trudy – for the first time in his life!

Was being stranded in Houston – kept from reaching his destination in time – was that to be his punishment for such perfidy? If so, it was certainly well-deserved.

What to do?

He wished – fervently – that Trudy had come with him. He could've simply booked passage to Brownsville – and eliminated the deceit. Eliminated the grappling to get out of Houston. He'd never – ever – pull such a stunt again! Without his beautiful wife beside him, everything seemed so – so hollow! So damn empty!

He had the choice of renting a car – or chartering a plane. The thought of going downtown – to the bus station – had never occurred to him.

The bewildered traveler didn't feel up to driving the seven or eight hours – especially at that time of day. It would be dark – before he even reached Victoria, 120 miles to the south. His eyes were not what they used to be. He'd gotten to where he detested driving at night. He'd be asking for trouble.

He inquired about charters. The aviation charter services did not exist at anywhere near the scale of the seventies.

Finally, he was able to locate the owner of a private plane – a single-engine *Cessna*. He advised Parks that he would fly him to Brownsville for $150.00 – cash! A hundred-and-fifty 1954 dollars. More than most people made in a week. It was highway robbery

– but, the weary customer didn't have much choice. Truly a seller's market.

Parks was so overcome by the chilling, bleak, feeling of foreboding – as the small, light, plane taxied out to the runway – that he was on the verge of canceling the flight.

"Trudy," he muttered to himself, tears cascading down his cheeks. "Trudy … I'm so sorry. I'm so damn sorry."

At 6:35 PM, the tiny plane took off for the Rio Grande Valley!

It never made it!

As the little aircraft made its landing approach to the Brownsville airport, a sudden, brutal, gust of wind literally picked the plane out of the air, flipped it onto one side – then, slammed it into the hard, parched, ground! With devastating force! It happened too quickly for the pilot – or his passenger – to react!

The plane crashed – and burned to a cinder!

On Sunday – September 12, 1954 – as Jim and Kathleen Sidorwitz were exchanging vows in Brownsville, Texas, the phone was ringing at the Hayworth residence, in Detroit, Michigan.

Trudy answered. She listened for a moment – then, gasped! She half-fell into the chair by the desk at the foot of the stairway that Parks had so loved! And began to sob!

"I … I can't believe that," she managed to say, into the instrument. "I don't believe that! You … you must be mistaken!"

Charlie rushed to his mother's side! Kneeling beside her, he wrapped his arms around her waist!

Obviously, it was bad news!

"My … my husband?" Trudy rasped. "My husband was … was flying to … flying to Houston. Not … not Brownsville. What? Not a commercial flight? A charter? Small plane … from Houston? He … he chartered a plane? From Houston? I'm sure that you're mistaken! You <u>have</u> to be! You <u>must</u> be! You simply <u>have</u> to be!"

TWENTY SIX

In November, of 1979, a woman in her late-fifties climbed the wrought-iron stairs to a condominium in southwest Houston. She paused at the top of the steps and gazed out over the fancy railing – and down into the well-manicured courtyard below.

Two young men tossed a Frisbee back-and-forth, in the fading late-afternoon glow of the chilly fall day.

Heaving a massive sigh, the woman moved to the door – onto which the numerals 268 had been nailed. Using the huge, ornate, brass knocker, she rapped – loudly.

Two or three minutes passed. As she reached for the knocker once more, the door opened – and an attractive, 20-year-old woman stood facing her.

"Yes?" asked the younger woman, with a warm smile. "Can I help you?"

"Is your name Cynthia?"

"Yes."

"I'm aware that your last name is Norman. But, was your maiden name Sidorwitz?"

The smile vanished! It was replaced by a look of concern. She nodded in the affirmative.

"Is ... is there something wrong? Is it my father?"

The older woman smiled – and nodded gently.

"I have some news for you ... about him," she advised. "May I come in?"

"Oh! Of course. Yes. Please do."

Once they were both seated, the younger lady asked, "It's … it's something about my father, isn't it? I talked with him a couple nights ago. I talked with him a couple nights ago and he seemed so … I don't know … so strange."

"What did he tell you? Did he say something about a trip? A journey?"

"Yes. Yes … how did you know?"

"Allow me to introduce myself, Cynthia. My name is Trudy Hayworth. I'm not sure you're going to believe what I have to tell you. There are times, when I don't know whether I believe it myself … even after all these years."

"After … after all these years? I don't understand, Miss Hayworth."

"I'm not really certain that I do myself. Understand it, I mean."

"Please, Miss Hayworth. I'm … I'm so worried about my father. Please don't beat around the bush. He's … he's dead, isn't he?"

Trudy nodded.

Cynthia burst into tears!

"I knew!" she bellowed. "I knew! I could tell! We were so … so much alike. I just knew! I just … knew!"

"I knew your father very well, Cynthia. That will be difficult, I'm sure, for you to believe. In point of fact, I know quite a bit about you. Your father … he called you his 'saint', didn't he?"

Cynthia, weeping quietly, nodded.

"Somehow," continued Trudy, "I knew you wouldn't go all to pieces. Somehow, I know that what I'm telling you … I know that you'll … you'll eventually believe it. If not now … then, eventually."

"What … what do you mean?"

"Well," Trudy sighed, "it's a long story. One that's awfully cockamamie … as your father would say. You see, Cynthia, I knew him as someone else. I was … I was married to him."

The younger woman – already shaken – paled! The older woman reached over and placed her hand on her hostess' shoulder.

"Try and imagine," Trudy soothed, "try and believe that your father found some kind of way of ... of ... of going back in time. Back through time."

Cynthia bristled! Her color quickly returned!

"Look, Miss Hayworth! I don't know who you are ... or what you want ... but, I don't appreciate your playing with my head like this. I'm worried enough about Dad ... without all this. We were ... he and I were ... very close. If he'd have been married to you ... believe me ... I'd have known. If he'd even had an affair with you, I'd have known. He hasn't really gone with anyone. Not since he broke up with a lady named Alice ... up in Detroit ... and came down here, a couple years ago."

Trudy reached into her purse – and withdrew some snapshots.

"Here, My Dear," she said, proffering the photos to the young woman. "Look at these. Are these pictures of your father?"

Cynthia took the photos. Leafing through the 15 snaps, her eyes grew wider – as she saw a man who looked exactly like her father, gazing out at her! The man was dressed in the fashions of another day. Some of them showed the man leaning against automobiles of a bygone era.

Many of the snapshots showed the man – who so closely resembled her father – standing beside the lady sitting next to her. The woman appeared to be much younger.

The man looked older, in some photos. A good deal older than her father.

Other photographs showed the man, along with Trudy – and a young boy. As Cynthia leafed through the pictures, the boy was shown growing into his prepubescent years.

Running through the photos once more, Cynthia half-nodded at one snap after another.

"It ... it certainly does look like Dad," she admitted, at length. "But ... but ... but, how ... ? I mean ... I don't understand."

"As I said, I'm not positive I do either, Cynthia. But, just for the sake of argument, try and accept ... for the moment ... that I may not be quite as bonkers as I appear. Please try and believe what I'm saying. Your father ... he did! He found a way to go back in time! He really did!"

Cynthia began to reply – but, Trudy stopped her with a raised hand.

"Please! Hear me out," Trudy continued. "There was absolutely no record of him … before nineteen thirty-nine. None! Believe me! I checked! Very extensively! Hired detectives! The whole nine yards! No record, whatsoever! Parks Hayworth did not exist … not before nineteen thirty-nine!"

"Parks Hayworth?"

Trudy nodded – emphatically.

"Parks Hayworth," she affirmed. "That's the name he took … or was given."

"But … but, how?"

"I don't know. I really don't. I doubt that I ever will. I just know that it did happen! The significance of the name didn't strike me until one night … in nineteen sixty-two, it was … when I was watching a schmaltzy old movie on tee vee."

"Schmaltzy?"

"Another of your father's words," Trudy replied, with a smile. "This movie was called *Down To Earth*. It came out in the mid-forties."

"I'm not sure … but, I think I remember Dad speaking of that one. What was it about? He had so many of those old musicals that he always wanted me to watch with him. I guess one of his biggest disappointments was that we never got to watch *Going My Way* together. It was his favorite. He loved all of Bing Crosby's movies."

"Yes. He told me … a number of times … that *Going My Way* was his favorite. But, we never got to watch it together either. This movie, though … the one I'm talking about, *Down To Earth* … it didn't have Bing in it. It was about the goddess of the dance … who was Rita Hayworth … coming down from heaven. She fell in love with some hoofer … who was producing a play about her. She thought it was a terrible show … that this guy had her all wrong. The guy was played by Larry Parks. It wasn't till I saw that picture … on that night … that the name hit me!"

"The name? The name … hit you?"

Returning

"Yes! Don't you see? Your father's name was Parks Hayworth! The two stars of the movie were Larry Parks and Rita Hayworth."

"Oh, Miss Hayworth! That was probably just a coincidence. I mean, to assume that … "

"No! No … it wasn't a coincidence! It wasn't! Cynthia … you've got to believe that it wasn't! I know that it wasn't! When I first started to get serious about your father, I'd mentioned the movie to him. Even described it a little. He asked the darndest questions about it … and I wound up with the darndest feeling. I can't tell you! His reaction … to my telling him about that movie … just gave me … well, it gave me … it gave me the spookiest feeling. The willies. The thing with his name being a combination of the names of the two stars … well, it didn't occur to me. Not at the time."

"I still think you're reading too much into something that … "

"The picture had a character … named Mister Jordan," Trudy pressed on. "He was kind of a go-between … between heaven and Rita Hayworth. Sort of God's emissary to her. Your father became … became, well … became rather rattled, when I mentioned the Mister Jordan character."

"Yes?" asked Cynthia. Her forehead was knitted. She was trying to fathom what this interloper was telling her. "Why would this Mister Jordon … why would it … ?"

"I'd told your dad that I wished that someone like Mister Jordan would make him … could make him … twenty years younger. If you stop and tally up the mathematics involved, there was a good deal of difference between your father's age and my age. It bothered me … more than just a little bit … at the time. Really bothered me. Parks … your father … may have gotten back to nineteen thirty-nine … through someone like Mister Jordan. Of course, that's only a wild, shot-in-the-dark, theory. One that I've come up with … over just the past few years. I do know, though, that it more-or-less floored him … when I'd mentioned the Mister Jordan character."

"I can't … I simply can't understand … why you'd believe something like that, Miss Hayworth."

"I'm sure that I'd be saying the same thing," responded Trudy, with another sigh, "if I were in your place. But … Mister Jordan to the side … your father knew everything … simply everything … that was going to happen. It was incredible! He saw to it that Charlie ... that's our son ... got to see things that were to become world-famous. There was a *World Series* game ... back in nineteen forty-seven ... that he insisted we go to. It was on our honeymoon."

"In nineteen forty-seven?"

"Yes. That's what I'm getting at. Please! Bear with me, Cynthia. Your father had to know that this game was going to go down in history. Something to do with some pitcher ... for the Yankees ... pitching a no-hitter. I still don't understand it all that well. Charlie ... he could fill you in on every detail. But, that's my point! Parks ... your father ... insisted we take Charlie along on our honeymoon! I'm convinced that it was so that he could take Charlie to that game! Charlie's never forgotten it."

"Now, I'm really confused," confessed Cynthia. "If Charlie was your son ... how could you have taken him on your honeymoon? Miss Hayworth, I hate to say it, but, I ... I really think that maybe you've ... you've ... "

"That I've flipped? Flying with my flaps down? That I don't have both oars in the water? Another one of your dad's pet expressions. Actually, I'd had Charlie ... before I ever met your father. My first husband ... Charlie's father ... was killed. At Pearl Harbor."

Cynthia lowered her eyes. "I'm sorry," she answered softly.

"Charlie was about five, when I met your father. The two of them got along famously. He really was your father's son. There were times, when I swore that he was more your father's son ... than he was mine. Your dad loved kids ... as you know. He was always mugging at them ... when we'd run across them, at a restaurant or a store or someplace. I always felt that he should've had a large family. Never could understand why he didn't have a zillion kids. As it turned out, he did have a zillion kids."

"I don't ... I can't believe ... that this is happening," said Cynthia.

"I wouldn't either. All I ask, Cynthia, is that you hear me out. Then ... go ahead and make your own decisions."

"I'll ... I'll try. But, I've never heard such an off-the-wall story."

"I can believe that."

Trudy reached over and took the young woman's hand in her own. Bushels of love seemed to pour out of her soft brown eyes – as she gazed at the beautiful young woman that her husband had sired.

"Your father appeared in nineteen thirty-nine," Trudy began. "In Detroit. There simply was no Parks Hayworth before then. None! He married a woman named Helen Shaddon ... before me."

"Wait a minute! He had yet another wife? Oh, Miss Hayworth! This is just too far-fetched! Really! Just too much to ... "

"Well, it's a fact. Helen died. She had a son stationed on a Navy ship ... one which operated out of Pearl Harbor. Looking back, I believe that Parks ... your father ... knew what was going to happen. He apparently tried his damndest to get that poor boy out of there. I don't know what ... or how many things ... he may have tried. Apparently, he tried to pull any number of strings. But, he wasn't able to get Jeff out of there. Not before the Japanese attacked."

Cynthia squeezed Trudy's hand.

"That's ... that's tragic, Miss Hayworth," she said. "I knew about Pearl Harbor. Dad talked about it lots. But, of course, to me it was just ... well, just ... just history. I never knew anyone who was directly affected by it. I feel so ... so insensitive."

Trudy returned the hand embrace.

"When the boy was killed, by the Japs," she rasped, "it was too much for Helen ... your father's wife. She collapsed and died ... a day or two later."

Cynthia winced.

"Oh, how sad," she whispered. "How very sad. How absolutely awful."

"I'm sure that your father never stopped blaming himself ... for both deaths. He threw himself into his work ... like you wouldn't believe. I've never seen anyone ... ever, in my whole life ... work like that. He had to be punishing himself. It's the only answer."

"Well, Dad always worked hard."

"I'm sure he did. I know he did. But, you've never seen anyone push himself like your father did then. Like he did ... when Helen and Jeff died. I'm sure he was trying to kill himself ... as horrible as that must sound. If you know your dad ... know him as well as I think you do ... then, I'm sure you can visualize him reacting in just that way. In just that manner."

"Yes," admitted Cynthia – lowering her eyes. "Yes, I guess ... I can. What ... what kind of work was he ... did he do?"

"Guess."

"Rent-a-car?"

"You win the cigar! He founded **Dubin Rent-a-Car**!"

"Oh, Miss Hayworth. Come on! This is simply too much. **Dubin** is a huge company. Our main competitor. I work for **Hertz** ... out at the airport."

"I know. And you're exactly right about **Dubin** being such a huge company. But, you can check ... it started in Detroit. And stop and think! How big could **Dubin** have been in thirty-nine? Your father sold Clark Dubin ... on the idea of branching out his **Ford** dealership. Going into the car rental business. Your father, of course, had a lot of expertise in the field. He made **Dubin** a success ... right from the go. Apparently, he was able to sandbag a lot of cars ... to sell during the war. I'm convinced that he knew that the factories would stop producing cars ... and that **Dubin's** rental cars would be exceptionally valuable. They were what kept the company ... the rent-a-car company ... afloat, as I understand it. Can you believe any of this? I mean, conceding the fact that your father did, indeed, find some way to go back in time?"

"I ... I guess so. I don't know. I ... I guess so."

"It's true, Cynthia. I worked for the dealership. That's where I met him ... met your dad. I loved him! I loved your father! Loved him ... very deeply! I really did!"

Tears began to trickle down Trudy's cheeks. She gulped three or four times – in a vain attempt to choke off the crying.

"I'm sorry, Cynthia," she said, as she wept. "I thought that ... that after all these years ... I thought that I could really ... "

"Can I get you something, Miss Hayworth? A cup of tea? Cup of coffee?"

"That would be nice," Trudy sniffed – patting her young hostess' hand. "Maybe in a few minutes."

She made a Herculean effort to compose herself. For several minutes, the room was filled to the brim – with silence! The heaviest silence imaginable.

"As I said," Trudy began once more, "your father took Charlie and me practically everywhere. He practically rebuilt my mother's house ... rest in peace. He made a good deal of money ... a lot of money, in fact. He always knew exactly which stock to buy, which hockey game ... or baseball game, or whatever ... to bet on. He bought a whole fleet of cars ... ones which, over the years, became positive classics. Worth a lot of money ... a heck of a lot of money. All of them. Every blessed one of them."

Cynthia nodded. Her eyes were beginning to overflow once more.

"Dad always was a nut for old cars," she said.

"Well, of course, they weren't old cars ... not when I knew your dad. But, you're right ... he was a nut about them. I've sold most of the cars, through the years. All offers that I couldn't refuse. Made an enormous amount of money on each and every one. I still have his first car, though. Thirty-seven Ford. He loved that car. Couldn't bring myself to sell it ... even though I've been offered heaven-and-earth for it. I'm really glad that I didn't."

"Dad used to talk about a car that his father had ... when Dad was a kid. It was an old Ford. I think it might've been a thirty-seven ... but, I'm not sure."

Trudy's eyes regained most of their sparkle. The tears dried – slowly!

"Cynthia," she prodded, "I want you to think, for me. Think hard. I want you to think really, really, hard about this. It's very important. Did your father ever talk about a house? A house in Detroit? One that he was really hung-up on?"

"Oh yes! He talked about that quite often. I can't remember the exact street it was on ... but, he used to drive us kids by it, every now and then. Point it out. He dreamed, one night ... dreamed that there was a heaven upstairs. Up in the attic of that house. He said something about having to crawl through a hole in the ceiling of a closet ... something like that ... to get up there."

"Was the house on a street called Grandmont? Does that ring a bell?"

"Uh … yes. I think so, anyway. I'm not quite sure. My brothers could tell you better than I can. We went by it a number of times, when we lived up there. I suppose I should be better at remembering things like that. I really believe, though, that it could've been on Grandmont. It was down the street from some school. A grade school. I do remember that."

Trudy reached into her purse, once again – and produced another photograph.

"Is this the house?" she asked – her voice filled with emotion.

Cynthia took the snapshot – and studied it carefully.

"Yes," she answered. "At least, I'm pretty sure it is. It looked a little different, when I saw it. A little run-down. Of course, that was just four or five years ago. It was a pretty old house."

She handed the photo back to her guest.

"Did your father ever mention a … a "Dog House"? A little house on Burnette? One with a huge front porch?"

"Oh yes! He talked about that one all the time too. It was his grandma's house. She was his … he used to say … his best buddy, when he was a kid. He loved that house. I don't remember what street it was on. Again, maybe my brothers could help you out on that. The house, though … it was torn down. Quite a few years ago, I guess."

"You see? You see? It all fits!" said Trudy, triumphantly.

"Fits?"

"Yes! Your father simply <u>had</u> to have that house on Grandmont. The one down the block from the school. The one that he dreamed had a heaven in the attic. Simply had to have it! I've never seen anything like it. He practically worshipped that house. Never got tired of it … anything about it. I've never seen anyone feel for a house … not like your father felt for that one."

"When … how … did my father die?"

"I was coming to that. You see, my life with your father was as happy as anyone's life could've been. I loved him so much. I really did. You've got to believe that, Cynthia. And he loved me just as deeply. I know he did."

Trudy's eyes began to brim with tears once more. Cynthia's gaze was riveted to a spot on the beige carpeting in front of them.

"I'm ... sure that must be true," the younger woman rasped.

"Well, before he died ... just before ... your father became quite restless. Almost like a man I'd never known before. I couldn't understand it. I'd never seen him like that. Anyway, he told me that he wanted to fly down to Houston ... to check out some property that he was thinking of buying."

"Wait a minute, Miss Hayworth. This ... all this ... was taking place up in Detroit?"

"Yes. He turned up in Detroit ... in nineteen thirty-nine. Now, in nineteen and fifty-four, he was going to fly down to Houston ... like I said. Going to fly down here and look at some property. Except that he wound up chartering a plane ... from Houston to Brownsville. Tiny plane! Dinky little plane! And ... God help me ... that's where he died! The plane crashed!"

She began to cry once more.

"Brownsville?" asked Cynthia. "Brownsville? That's where my mother lives."

"I know. Cynthia ... your father died on September the eleventh ... in nineteen fifty-four. Does that date have any special significance for you?"

The younger woman closed her eyes – sending a tear trickling out of each one.

"I know that their wedding anniversary was on September the twelfth. I think ... I think they got married in nineteen fifty-four. Why ... why that would've ... that would've been the day before ... before my mother and dad got married!"

"Exactly," agreed Trudy, with an emphatic nod. "Exactly. When they called me from Brownsville ... to tell me that your father's plane had crashed ... I can't tell you how ... how ... how betrayed ... I felt. He'd told me he was going to Houston ... period. He didn't say anything about Brownsville. Never mentioned Brownsville."

Her hand shaking slightly, Trudy reached into her purse, once more, and extracted a frail, yellowed, newspaper clipping and photograph. She handed them to Cynthia.

"Why ... why that's ... that's my mother and father."

It was indeed. *The Brownsville Herald* had sent a photographer to the reception of Jim and Kathleen Sidorwitz. In small-town Brownsville, of 1954, a local girl marrying a man from Detroit was more-or-less news. The paper had printed a picture of the happy couple – as well as a roster of relatives and friends who had made the trip from Michigan.

In the seventies, such a wedding would never have caused a ripple.

"At the time," explained Trudy, "I didn't realize the significance of that article ... or the picture. The only reason I clipped it was because of the name. I recognized the name."

"Recognized the name?"

"Yes. I happen to have known that the house your father and I were living in ... the one he dreamed about, the one on Grandmont ... I happened to know that the house had been owned, at one time, by Bernard and Dolores Sidorwitz. Your grandparents. Not only that, but they'd also owned another house ... a little house ... your father insisted we buy. On a street called Penrod. That's where your Aunt Dee was born. Anyway, I saw your grandmother's name in the article ... as being in town for the wedding. That's what made me take notice. Plus the fact that the couple in the photograph ... your mother and your father ... they looked really familiar."

"Familiar? You knew Dad? You knew my father then? As a young man? From ... from ... from in nineteen fifty-four?"

"No. I didn't know that young man then. It took me a long while to figure out who he was. Where I'd seen him. Or where I'd seen your mother. I'd seen the guy in the picture once before! In Memphis."

"Memphis, Tennessee?"

"Yes," Trudy nodded. "It was back in nineteen fifty. When the man ... in that picture ... walked into the bar where your father and I were sitting, your father almost fainted. It took me years and years and years ... to finally figure out that your father was seeing <u>himself</u>! Seeing himself ... as a young man. As a young sailor. That'd be enough to shake up anyone! A few years later, we saw the same man ... your father ... down at the Naval base in Norfolk."

Cynthia heaved another massive sigh.

"Dad was in the Navy. I know he was stationed in Norfolk. Again, my brothers would know this better than me ... but, I think he went to a special school in Memphis. I think he was there for only a short time. But, I'm pretty sure that he's spoken of Memphis. Of being stationed for awhile in Memphis."

"In the summer of fifty-three," Trudy continued, "we saw your mother. She was walking along a street in Brownsville. She was still a teenager ... and very beautiful. She looked into our car ... directly into our car! Looked right at your father. I had the spookiest feeling at the time ... but, I didn't know why. In any case, the couple in the picture looked familiar ... and the name rang this bell. So, I clipped the article and the photo."

"You ... you clipped the article and picture? Was it in the Detroit papers?"

"No. I came down ... flew down ... on Monday, the thirteenth. To claim the body. Your father's body." She shivered. "What was left of it. Dear Lord!" Another head-to-toe spasm! "The article ... the article and the picture ... they were in Monday's paper. Monday's paper ... in Brownsville."

"Wait a minute, Miss Hayworth!" Cynthia's eyes suddenly lit up. "Just a minute! If you truly loved my father ... as you say you did ... and if you knew who he was and that he'd come back through time ... and if you had all this money ... how could you just sit around? Just sit around ... and let him and my mother work their fannies off? Trying to keep their heads above water? Surely, you must know how much it takes to try and raise seven kids! I mean, if you'd ... "

"I didn't, Cynthia. Please believe me ... I didn't know! Not until a few months ago, anyway. Not for sure, anyway."

"Why should I believe that?"

"Why should you believe any of this? I don't know that I would. I feel as though you probably have much more faith than I do. And that you're probably much more mature and understanding ... as young as you are."

"I don't know about that." The younger woman's manner softened.

"Well, I do. Or, at least, I think I do. Anyway, as I said, I felt betrayed ... terribly betrayed. Your father had told me that he'd been put wise to this property in Houston ... by our business agent. But, Elliot ... the agent ... said he'd never heard of the property. He'd never met the prospective seller ... and he'd never talked to your father about anything even remotely resembling property in Houston. When he told me that, I almost hated your father. You have to remember, Cynthia, that there's an awfully fine line between love and hate. It wasn't until later ... literally years later ... that things sort of began to piece themselves together."

"Things? What things? What do you mean, 'piece themselves together'?"

"Well, when John Kennedy took Lyndon Johnson as his vice presidential candidate ... in nineteen sixty ... I got this same spooky feeling I'd gotten so many times before. Your father had taken us ... Charlie, my mother and I ... on a trip, in the early-fifties. To the Eastern Seaboard. Your dad went to great lengths to point out the Kennedy complex, on Cape Cod. I'd never heard of John Kennedy ... or Bobby or Ted either. Then, a couple years later, Parks ... your dad ... took Charlie and me to the boyhood home of L.B.J. ... and then up to his ranch on the Pedernales River. Again, I'd never heard of Lyndon Johnson. Not too many people had, at that time. But, your father said he thought that L.B.J. would be someone special someday. He wanted us to see those things. Also ... on that same trip ... your dad pointed out that *Texas Schoolbook Depository Building*, in Dallas. Remember, now ... this was fully ten years before President Kennedy was assassinated ... by shots fired from that very building. It was about the only landmark that your father ever pointed out ... in the entire city of Dallas. Only, it wasn't a landmark then. I couldn't understand it, at the time."

"That's ... why, that's amazing."

"Yes. Amazing. Anyway, once the president was shot ... and I'd seen where Oswald had shot from ... I started to sort of put two-and-two together. It was a year ... maybe a year-and-a-half ... after I'd seen that movie with Larry Parks and Rita Hayworth. You can imagine ... if the thing with the name shook me, the assassination really rattled my cage!"

Returning

Trudy stopped for a minute – trying to ascertain Cynthia's reaction. The young woman's face seemed to run the entire gamut of emotion.

"There were other things, of course," Trudy continued, at length. "A lady, who had worked with your grandmother ... lady named Loretta Zandrynski ... had rented a house from your father and me. She's the one who told me that the house on Grandmont ... and the one on Penrod ... had been owned by the Sidorwitzes."

Cynthia nodded, absently. She seemed numbed by her visitor's narrative.

"Then," advised Trudy, "your father had his heart attack!"

"A heart attack? Dear Lord! What else?"

"Yes," nodded Trudy. "A heart attack. I've always felt a little guilty. It was after a rather spirited discussion between your father and me ... about some of the things that Loretta'd had to say about your dad. This was in nineteen fifty-two. Your dad was sixty-years-old."

"Miss Hayworth," Cynthia responded – putting up her hand. "This ... this is so hard to fathom. The last time I saw my father, he was forty-something. Forty-seven I think."

Trudy put her hand on Cynthia's knee.

"I know, Baby," she said. "I know."

Once again, tears spilled from the younger woman's eyes.

"That's," she sniffed, "that's what my dad used to call me. 'Baby'. Me and my sisters. He always called us 'Baby'. All of us."

"I didn't know that ... but, somehow, it fits. Anyway, after your dad got out of the hospital, we needed a house ... where everything was on one floor. Well, I knew that your father had been attached to this little house on Burnette. He'd driven me by it a number of times. So, while he was in the hospital, I went and bought it from the lady who owned it. Turned out that the lady was your great grandmother. Your dad's 'best buddy'."

"That's incredible."

"You bet it is."

Cynthia slumped back on the couch. Trudy patted her on the knee.

"It really wasn't until about four years ago that I began to think seriously in terms of Parks actually … really … having come from the future," advised Trudy. "The whole thing still sounded totally stupid … completely ridiculous … even though the names and the events and everything else suggested it. They were all falling into place. It was just one of those things that … well, you still think it's totally impossible. You simply can't bring yourself to accept it … no matter what. But, finally, I got off my fanny … and hired a detective agency."

"To track down Dad's past?"

"Yes. They determined that Parks Hayworth simply didn't exist before thirty-nine. Not in Houston. Not in Detroit. Not anywhere. So … on a whim … I turned 'em loose on Jim Sidorwitz. That was about three years ago … maybe a little less. Tracking him down took a little doing, believe it or not. I didn't know if he lived in Houston or whether he lived in Detroit. Or even Brownsville. By the time the detectives got a handle on him, for me, he'd already moved down here to Houston … and was working for **Valu Rent-a-Car**. But, you see? That took till June or July of this year … before I was certain of who he was! And what he was! And where he was! When they sent me a picture of him, I could see that it was Parks Hayworth. The Parks Hayworth that I'd known and loved … the Parks Hayworth that I was married to. He hadn't changed hardly at all. Well, not that much."

"I … I can't imagine … can't imagine the … the … the shock that … "

"When I came down here … a few months ago … I didn't confront him. Didn't confront your dad! Not personally! Jim Sidorwitz never met me. He wouldn't have known me, anyway! Wouldn't have known what I was talking about … had I'd told him that I'd been his wife! But, don't you see? He would've recognized me when he met me in thirty-nine! I'm sure that he would've. It's all so terribly complicated."

She allowed herself an ironic laugh.

"He was married to me," she half-whispered, "in forty-seven … but he wouldn't have known me in seventy-nine. Can you imagine?"

"No, Miss Hayworth. I can't imagine. Dear Lord, it must've been horrible for you. How could you cope with such a ... such a ... such a ... ?"

"Well, I figured that it wouldn't be that much longer ... before he came back to join me. Came back to love me. So, I just kind of kept my eye on him ... and tried to learn everything I could about him. About him ... and everyone close to him."

"That's why you know so much about me?"

"And the rest of the children ... your brothers and sisters. Even your mother."

"Now I'm the one who's spooked!"

"Don't be," replied Trudy. "Anyway, yesterday your dad didn't show up at work. Today, I went to his apartment. Sure enough, he wasn't there. He's not there. His car's in front ... but, he's gone! He has to have left ... on his trip back to thirty-nine. Can you believe any of this?"

Cynthia nodded – hesitantly.

"I ... I guess I ... I guess I can," she stammered. "I guess I do. The only reason is that ... the night before last ... Dad called me. He talked about ... about this trip he could take. It was a really strange trip. He didn't say that. Not in so many words. But, I could tell. He said he couldn't tell me about it ... and that bugged him. He's always leveled with me. Always. That's why I told you that you couldn't possibly have had an affair with him ... not without my knowing about it. It must've been a very difficult choice for him ... choosing to go back, like that. Leaving us and all."

"I'm sure it was," agreed Trudy. "He'd always leveled ... as you say ... with me too. Until that trip to Brownsville. I'm sure, now, that he'd wanted to go down there ... see himself marry your mother. It was so like Parks ... so like your father. I know that I'd never have been able to understand it back then. As to your reference about my not taking care of your father and mother ... or you kids ... even though I'd wound up with a few bucks, you have to remember that I really found him just a few short months ago. Of course, I found him struggling to make ends meet."

"He always struggled to make ends meet," advised Cynthia. "He and my mother both. Always. They <u>always</u> had a God-awful time trying to get by … financially."

"I'm sure he did. I'm sure <u>they</u> did. It costs a buck or two … to provide for seven kids. I really don't know how he did it. How he and your mother could've done it."

"He always said," responded Cynthia, "that he did it rather badly."

Trudy nodded.

"That sounds like him," she said. "Anyway, I finally wound up buying the company that your dad worked for. It took some doing. The guy who owned the company was a … he was a real … was a really a … "

"Bad guy?" furnished Cynthia.

"Right! Well, actually, he was complete bastard. A sonofabitch … you'll pardon the language."

"That was Dad's opinion too."

"I'm sure. The guy really held me up. He knew that I wanted to buy the company in the worst way. And that's what I did. I bought it in the worst way. He really socked it to me. I had no choice. What could I do? I had to pay his price. I only gained control of the company about a month ago. Well, a little less than a month ago. It was a very complicated transaction. Took a good deal of time … more than it should have. For all that time, my hands were tied. I really couldn't help your father. So, you see, I actually haven't had all that much time to try and give him a boost. By the way, did he ever tell you who his new boss was?"

"Yes. His name is … is Charlie. It's Charlie something."

"It was our son! Charlie! Your dad was introduced to him … when my son became his boss … as Charlie Lawrence. It wouldn't do to have him work for someone named Charlie Hayworth. Not have him work for a Charlie Hayworth. Then have him find out … when he was going to marry me … that his kid would wind up being named Charlie Hayworth. Not good."

"So … Dad's new boss? He was really his son? Dad's son? His and yours?"

Trudy nodded – and smiled, broadly.

"I was sure he'd never recognize him! Charlie has changed a lot since fifty-four."

"I ... yes. I can imagine."

"As I'm sure you can realize, Charlie has always looked upon Parks ... your father ... as his own father. He is Charlie's father ... which, in a way, makes my son your brother. It may sound as off-the-wall as anything else I've said, but ... in a fashion ... you're as much my kids as Charlie is your father's kid. I'm not trying to come off as an 'Instant Mother', or anything. Give you the bum's rush. But, just think about it."

"Oh, Miss Hayworth! This is almost too much to handle."

Trudy reached over and patted the younger woman's knee once more.

"I know," she soothed. "I know. It'll take awhile."

She pulled a handkerchief from her purse – and dabbed at her eyes.

"Can you imagine," she asked, at length, "how this has affected Charlie? He loves your father. Was as close to him as any son can possibly be. Closer than most. And Jim Sidorwitz had absolutely no idea who Charlie Lawrence was. Charlie's thirty-seven-years-old now. He was four or five, when your dad first saw him ... and twelve, at the time of your father's death."

"I ... I never thought of that. It must have been ... must be ... very difficult for your son."

Trudy nodded – and blinked back another tear.

"Yes," she rasped. "Terribly difficult. Charlie wasn't capable, of course, of being completely formal with your dad. He couldn't operate on a true boss/employee basis. For one thing, it's not his nature. He kept saying to me, 'Mom, I wish there was some way I just could go up to Dad and put my arms around his neck and hug him ... and tell him how much I love him'. He told me that he's almost called him 'Dad' ... a couple or three times. Managed to catch himself. But," she sighed heavily, "it's really and truly been exceptionally tough on my son. It really has."

"I ... I'm certain it has."

"You're father must've mentioned the raise he got."

Cynthia smiled once more.

"Yes," she affirmed. "Biggest raise he'd ever gotten ... in his whole life. That was one of the reasons, he told me, that he was wondering if he should go ahead and take the trip. I guess that it's kind of ironic, isn't it? I mean ... if he hadn't taken the trip, he'd never have gotten the raise. Even if it was just for a really short time."

Her smile was filled with irony.

"He was going to buy some new furniture," the younger woman explained. "He was even talking about moving to a different apartment ... but, I don't think he'd ever really want to move from the one he's in. The one he was in. He loved that apartment."

"I'm sure he did. I looked in through the windows ... when I was over there a few minutes ago. It was your father all over."

She took Cynthia's hand into her own once more.

"Yesterday was the first day he didn't show up for work," she said, with a faint smile. "I figure that it was his first day back in thirty-nine. But, I wanted to be sure ... absolutely certain. So, I waited till today ... to run by his place. He didn't come in today either, of course. He never missed work, y'know. So, it was obvious that something had happened. Like I said, his car's still over there."

Trudy let go of the younger woman's hand – and arose. Cynthia also stood – and hugged her visitor.

"I ... I wanted you to know where your dad went." Trudy's voice was a husky whisper. "I promise you ... he was a happy man. At least he was happy when he was with me ... once he was able to get over Helen and her son dying."

"I know that what you ... what you say ... I know it's true."

"He once told me that he thought he was in heaven ... with Charlie and me. That ... that meant so much ... so very much ... to me. It still does."

"I'm sure it did, Miss Hayworth ... Mrs. Hayworth."

"Trudy."

"Trudy." Cynthia's voice was hoarse with emotion.

She hugged Trudy once more – and kissed her on the cheek.

"You seem schmaltzy enough," the younger woman rasped. "Schmaltzy enough to have been good for Dad. I'm convinced that you were the woman that he'd been looking for all his life."

"Some of it, maybe."

"No," Cynthia replied, emphatically. "He despaired of ever finding anyone in this day and age ... the way things are today. It's probably the only way he could've found someone. Had to go and find her in the past. He was terribly nostalgic, you know."

"I know."

"He always said that he wanted someone to be Judy Garland to his Gene Kelly. Jeanette McDonald to his Nelson Eddy. He often told me that he suffered from terminal schmaltz. You seem to be the same way. Very hokey. I mean that as a compliment."

"I know you do ... and I take it as such. Yes, I guess I'm probably as hokey as they come. Or so I thought ... till I met your dad."

"I ... I don't know quite what I'm going to tell my brothers and sisters ... or my mother, for that matter."

"I think I'd tell 'em just exactly what I've told you. Somehow, coming from your father's saint ... I think they'll all believe you. If not now ... well, then eventually. They may not be as full of faith..."

"Or as gullible."

"Do you really think you're being gullible, Cynthia? Do you really think that? What reason would I have for coming here and telling you these things? Don't you somehow ... in your heart ... know that, if anyone could've found his way back into the past, it would've been your father?"

"I ... I guess so. Yes, I suppose I do."

"I'm sure your brothers and sisters ... and your mother ... will wind up feeling the same way. If not now ... well, in time. After all, they were all aware of how hokey and nostalgic your father was too. I'll leave this stuff with you ... pictures and all that. Oh yes," she reached into her purse, once more, "do you know what this is?"

"It ... it looks like a rental agreement ... a rather primitive one."

"Bingo," Trudy smiled. "Look at the date."

"April fourth? Nineteen forty?"

Trudy nodded.

"You recognize, of course, your dad's writing. Or, rather, his printing."

"Yes. He always printed. It sure looks like his. Where … where did you get this?"

"Actually, I had a terrible time latching onto it. Fortunately, Mister Clark Dubin was kind enough to indulge me. He's retired now, but he got the people who manage his old **Ford** dealership to scavenge around in their rusty-dusty archives. Up on the second floor. They've moved since then. Out to Birmingham. But, they managed to come up with three or four of these. This is the oldest one I could lay my grubby little hands on."

Once again, Cynthia sighed deeply.

"I appreciate," she said, "what you've done … what you've told me … Trudy. I don't know if my brothers and sisters are going to buy the story. Not as readily as I did … as I do. As I am. Somehow, though, I don't think I'll have any trouble convincing my mother."

"I can understand that. Show your brothers and sisters the pictures … and the rental contract." She dug further into her purse. "Here! Here are a few notes that he wrote me over the years. Your dad always put the date and time on all his notes."

"That's right. He always did."

Cynthia began to read one of the very-private notes. Tears welled up in her eyes, once again – and began to overflow. She broke down completely – and wept.

Trudy took the younger woman in her arms – and pressed Cynthia's head down on her shoulder. She patted Cynthia's back – and simply let her cry it out.

After some three or four minutes, the younger woman raised her head.

"Thank you," she sniffed. "I'm all right now. It's just … it's just … hard to imagine that my father'll never be back. That I'll never see him again."

Once again, she began to weep.

After another minute or two, she took Trudy's hand into her own, and rasped, "I'm terribly saddened … that I'll never see Dad again. But, I'm happy that he got to spend all those years with you. All those happy years."

It was Trudy's turn to grow misty once more.

Returning

"You're the one your father always called Hogan. Is that right?"

"Yes. I'm Hogan. My sisters are Duffy and Clancy. Dad never called us girls by any other names."

"Well, you're a fine young lady ... a fine young woman. I know how very proud of you your father was. I had to kind of relate to your father ... during these past few months ... vicariously. Through Charlie. To hear Charlie talk, your dad was proud ... intensely proud ... of all you children. Every one of you. Charlie said he seldom spoke of anything ... or anyone ... else. He told me that your father had a pet saying ... one that went something like, 'When I'm called to the big rent-a-car counter in the sky, I will have left the world a hell of a lot better place than I found it ...by dint of the fact that I've sired those seven wonderful kids.'."

"I know. He used to say that to us all the time. I'm honored that he'd also say it to other people."

Trudy's hand made one last plunge into her purse.

"Here," she said – handing Cynthia a long, narrow, piece of light-blue paper.

"Give this to your mother. It's a cashier's check ... for five-hundred thousand dollars. I'd appreciate it if I could impose upon you to take it down to her, personally. I would, of course ... but, she doesn't know me. And, if I were to mail it, it'd take a letter the size of an encyclopedia for me to explain the check ... and all of what happened to your dad."

Cynthia stared at the check.

"Five-hundred thousand dollars? Dear Lord! Trudy! I've never seen that much money in my life! In my whole life! But ... why?"

"You said it yourself. Your mother and your father worked their fannies off ... trying to stay one step ahead of the wolf. I'd like to think that your father received his reward ... his financial reward. But, I know your mother is slaving away ... twelve hours a day. For people who don't appreciate it. Who don't appreciate her. She's still looking after your kid brother and your sisters. This should, maybe, help ease things a little for her. In a way, it's her money, anyway."

Cynthia hugged Trudy once again.

"I … I can't thank you enough," she said, "for coming here and telling me about … about Dad. And what happened to him."

"I couldn't do any less," Trudy replied. "Of course I'd come."

"Well, you were able to turn a very … a very sorrowful … experience into a not-so-sorrowful one. If that makes any sense."

"Yes, Cynthia. Yes it does. I'm the one who's honored."

"I'll miss my father … we all will. But, the fact that I knew he was so happy will help. Make it easier to take. You must be a very special lady … one that was good to him. And good for him. I'd like to be friends with you … get to know you better. Charlie too. He may have lost a father … but, maybe my brothers and sisters and I might have gained another mother. And another brother."

Trudy burst into tears! It was totally spontaneous – and highly unexpected!

"I really didn't dare hope you'd say anything like that," she said, between sobs. "Well, actually, I guess that I'd hoped for it … but, I knew that I couldn't expect it."

"I mean it sincerely, Trudy. I'd like to meet Charlie. I'm sure my brothers and sisters would too. Meet … and be close to … both of you. Is that possible, do you think?"

"Another of your father's famous lines," sniffed Mrs. Parks Hayworth. "I thought you'd never ask!"

THE END

About The Author

George D. Schultz was born in Detroit, Michigan on December 22, 1931. He has sired seven children – all of whom have, according to our George, "turned out magnificently".

He has lived in Detroit; in San Marcos and San Antonio, Texas; in Deans and Metuchen, New Jersey; in Buffalo, New York; in Houston, Texas – and now, in his retirement *Shangri La*, in Northeast Texas.

In his life, he has worked in the rent-a-car field, in the consumer finance business, in the (hiss – boo) collection agency business. He's "carried a book" handling a "debit route" in the life insurance game. He's also gone a couple rounds as a bartender. This in addition to four years in the U.S. Navy.

Printed in the United States
57068LVS00003B/22-30